CAGE OF PRIVILEGE

BY

Lane Lee Lansing

REGENCY MEDIA LLC

©2012

Barclay & Katrina,

Cheers to the sordid tales of the West Hills and beyond!

Lane

First edition
December 2012

ISBN: 978-0-9884178-2-3
Book and cover design by Sherry Wachter
Cover image © Regency Media LLC

www.cageofprivilege.com

Printed in the United States of America

To supportive parents,
the Comitianto Consortium,
& CJBB

Chapter 1
LIFE CHANGES
2010

Strolling down Fifth Avenue on her daily walk through Central Park and past the Metropolitan Museum of Art, she glanced up at the cooperative building and eyed the apartment that she had just sold. Jane Chambers Torrance wanted a departure from New York City's lifestyle, especially after the brutal murder of her son the year before which had remained unsolved. While everyone in the city revered her, the abrupt decision for an exodus from the cultural capital of the world puzzled her peers.

"What has this life really meant?" she asked herself, reminiscing about the nearly sixty years she had spent in the city.

Thinking of the years spent of building her own company, museum board service, luncheons, society events, and philanthropic grant making, an answer escaped her. Since she had arrived in the city at the age of eighteen, she had always lived life on her terms. Her controlled existence was about to take on a journey to where she could possibly find independence and peace. Over thirty years had passed since the sudden death of her husband Clay when his personal airplane crashed into the ocean. Having been married to the founder of the largest energy exploration company in the United States, Torero Resources, she was still burdened by obligations with the company where she still held of the title of chairwoman of the executive committee as its largest individual stockholder. Over the years, she had little opportunity to liquidate any stock as the well-known wife of the founder who had been considered a partner in building the vast business empire. Even a minor sale of a portion of her significant stock holdings equaling nearly $2 billion could make the tectonic plates of the market move, destabilizing the delicate dance of share price and market cap.

She had traveled the world, had more influence than most, and was ironically considered one of the first ladies of the city she had decided to abandon. Her last days in New York had been peppered by a constantly-moving motorcade between the Hamptons and the city, attending parties thrown by numerous friends and the charities that were of course saddened to learn of her pending exit – along with her $5.9 billion personal net worth and $950 million philanthropic foundation.

It was an end to a dynastic foothold that had lasted more than fifty years, one that certainly some of her almost-former neighbors in the cooperative she reigned over during most of that time were happy to see end, including members of the society strata who could afford the stringent requirements and lifestyle necessities but were never invited to even apply. To even be considered able to place an application for review with the cooperative's board at The Grand on Fifth, a personal connection was needed with someone on the inside – meaning an owner of one of the 25 units which each occupied a full floor of New York City's finest monument to wealth and privilege had to offer sponsorship before a potential buyer's real estate agent was even involved. Background, family, source of wealth, and other considerations like religion and tawdry gossip about the possible shortcomings of each applicant were all topics of inquiry by the Draconian trio of board members whom Jane personally championed each year at the cooperative's annual shareholders meeting and election which took place in her unit.

Her opulent penthouse apartment had the top two full floors and a sizable terrace that was designed as another room to accommodate large functions during the social season. In addition to the usual laundry list of necessities, applicants were assessed for what kind of staff they would bring to live with them– the minimum expectation being a chauffeur, cook, butler, maid, and social secretary. Art collections were audited, interviews with former neighbors conducted, and by the time approval may have occurred, the entire building knew all the substantive elements of the new resident's life – and that's the way they liked it. As long as fortune continued to shine, a newly christened unit owner was ushered into the closest circle of friendship, a cocoon of golden fleece.

Being rejected by the board was a sure way to enter blacklists for candidacy on the city's leading boards, clubs, and even restaurant reservation lists – even though most of the top echelon in society would never be seen dining in a public place. Instant rejection for residency included politicians, both current and former, individuals who made their money too quickly or were related to those where unscrupulous methods like gaming had made fortunes, members of the entertainment industry, and a historic disdain for people of the Jewish faith and blacks.

The amenities at The Grand were unmatched, and with a minimum of $50,000 in monthly resident fees for each unit, the building was neatly stocked with an ample security force, fully functional private spa and athletic facility, ballrooms and other entertainment spaces that were the envy of anyone who had the privilege of being invited inside. At The Grand, an entry directly on Fifth Avenue existed for foot traffic, but the residents almost always used a gated motor court directly beneath the building's large grand ballroom that was accessed through a long driveway. An island of cascading fountains danced amongst magnificent Chihuly glass sculpture alluring curious onlookers to attempt entry only to be led away by plainclothes security agents, most who were former members of the United States Secret Service.

Valets catered to a constant stream of high-end autos that almost made the building look like a chic hotel. Courtesy parking was also available for guests in the underground lot, which had capacity for 200 vehicles. Any resident who drove a noisy sports car even near the private entry porte cochere on the way to the building's lower parking lots was issued a citation and a healthy fine by the Board. With a collective net worth of nearly $40 billion dollars living within its walls, the residents certainly deserved to commune in peace and with privacy.

Jane used the proceeds of the $47 million sale of her apartment to fortify her self-imposed need for security by building a residence in the little-known Portland in the Pacific Northwest to be closer to her younger brother United States Senator Malcolm Chambers of Oregon and his family as he neared the retirement at the end of his term. She also purchased a home in Washington D.C. located on Whitehaven Street near Observatory Circle, just behind her dear friend the wife of the British Ambassador, Princess Marina. Marina's husband, HRH The Prince George, Duke of Sussex was the youngest cousin of Her Majesty the Queen and the first member of the Royal Family to act as a diplomatic representative on behalf of the British government in almost fifty years. The Queen had granted Marina special authority to be styled as a princess in her own right, as she was royalty of minor significance by German ancestry, and a distant cousin.

"It's easy to spot someone who wasn't brought up with money and privilege," Jane often thought during her contemplative walks as she witnessed the annual parades of new figures at all the charitable balls in New York trying to buy favor with the establishment. She'd then reflect, "the only reason you know this is because you're one generation removed from poverty!" While the media often covered her public appearances and initiatives she championed, she was part of a class of citizens who shunned attention. She was, however, rarely scrutinized due to her good works in numerous diverse communities through the Torrance Charitable Foundation.

The influence she carried in politics by virtue of her brother's powerful Washington sphere was also notable. They had, as a brother and sister collaborative, placed the children of key supporters in numerous positions of power in New York and Oregon as well as in nation's capital throughout the years, thereby concealing or suppressing any criticism that could have even possibly been pondered by any opposition. The Senator's political machine was nearly impenetrable, even with a deeply concealed yet ferocious wandering eye to which scores of pages, interns, and attractive young staff members had succumbed – all male and selected for both intellect and looks by seasoned stateside staff who instinctively knew the exact type of individual that would appeal to him.

The death of Jane's only child affected her deeply, particularly for how he was murdered. According to the police forensic analysis, it happened in very different stages – partly overdose, partly struggle, and partly execution – and oddly enough in a short chronological timeframe in one night. New York law enforcement had nicknamed it the 'Salome Murder' – primarily because Joey's head had been severed from his body and hung from a hook inside his posh Dakota Apartment on the corner of West 72nd and Central Park West. Forensic experts were puzzled how the body could have been 'killed' three times over during the course of several hours, but it was obvious that three very different perpetrators had somehow been involved. No conclusive evidence existed to adequately assist them in making a determination if he died at the first, second, or ultimately with the third and final act or who might have been involved in any of the attacks. While much smaller than Jane's, Joey's apartment was still one of the most sought-after units in his building, with 10,000 square feet and ample public rooms for entertaining. After he barely graduated from Jefferson Lewis Academy in 1985 with the help of a host of personality-regulating drugs and a guardian who had tried to keep him on task, Jane had purchased the residence for him prior to the strengthening of the building's cooperative board that despised all the usual suspects including individuals who did not conform to the building's stringent admission standards. Hoping that independence would help fortify his character, she was consumed with fear that her sole heir would be unable to run the company after her eventual death.

A refreshing change for Jane would be the relaxed lifestyle that the Pacific Northwest offered while still being able to have the vibrant social life that she had grown to love with friends and family in Washington, D.C. She exited the apartment to depart on her first research mission for how she planned to live the next chapter of her life. Her Bentley left the building for the airport to be transported to Oregon aboard her personal jet, a stunning Bombardier Global Express.

Chapter 2
THE NEW RESIDENCES
SAME YEAR

As she sipped champagne, the jet passed Mt. Hood, Oregon's highest peak, signaling her final descent into the Metropolitan Portland area. Jane was ready to scour property options on her own as a familiar to the area but still an outsider who hadn't really set foot onto Oregon's soil in decades, having preferred the comforts of the East Coast and Europe to her hometown.

She felt that the new environment afforded her additional security through the ability to cloak herself under a veil of anonymity on her maiden sojourn to freedom. She would eat alone, shop alone, and drive alone – always listening to everything that was said in her immediate vicinity as she honed the nearly-lost sleuthing skills from her youth which had propelled her success in marrying Clay and thus becoming one of the most prominent women in the world.

A fiend for details, Jane privately scouted every imaginable location for the Portland compound she had personally envisioned to be built. While not unreasonable acreage for the Middleburg Hunt Country or The Hamptons, finding a five-acre plot of land directly within the urban landscape of Portland's seemingly-tony West Hills was a difficult proposition.

After a month of analysis and driving on every inch of roadway to review possible locations, she determined "the one" on Greenleaf Drive, which was perfectly pitched atop of one of Portland's seven hills and commanded views of both the city and the valley. On a surprisingly spontaneous shopping trip through the downtown Portland retail district, she found her answer to land acquisition. When a boutique did not host her individually after hours, it was her custom to don a tasteful jogging suit and large sunglasses so as to not be recognized – and shelved most of her good jewelry on such expeditions except the 10-carat engagement ring that her beloved Clay had given to her, the one symbol of power that told any clerk, "treat me well."

She found the retail environment of Portland to be relatively forward, but obviously nowhere in a class close to New York City. But, for a lady of 75 returning to family roots in the City of Roses, it would do just fine for a bit of therapeutic shopping. The clerk, a young man who immediately spotted the quality of the ring - had lined up boxes of the best shoes for her to try on. The excitement of shopping amongst people was exhilarating as she pranced up and down the aisle, remarked to herself how dead-on he was for almost predicting her exact taste.

Sitting next to her was a woman who was having a similar joyous experience, also trying on a number of different shoes. The woman was impeccably dressed, and the clerk was showering her with the same gracious attention. Jane admired how well he toggled back and forth between them in their individual quests to find shoes they both obviously didn't need.

"Oh, I must have this Chanel pair!" her neighbor exclaimed. "And, I want them in both the black and the navy!"

"Well, it appears that it's your day for shopping," Jane interjected in an uncharacteristic bid for conversation. "It's so hard to find something that makes us utterly happy."

"I'm celebrating," the woman confessed. "It's my first really significant commission in real estate – so I'm gearing up to play with the big girls!"

Fondly remembering her first commission check and that she did the exact same thing in New York City at Saks Fifth Avenue, Jane had met a friend. "I used to work in real estate many years ago," Jane noted.

"Why aren't you still in it?" quizzed the woman, completely unaware of whom she was speaking with. She barely could contain her excitement. "I just closed a huge deal where I represented the buyer for a property that I picked up from an open house. Big luck, you know how it goes."

"Yes I do," Jane admitted. "I sat for one solid year selling condominiums in one building in New York. It was hell, but the experience changed my life. But, that was years ago – and, I married well," showing the woman her enormous yellow diamond ring.

"New York City! What a difficult market! I'm Kate," the woman announced, extending her hand toward Jane.

8

The friendliness and honesty of the young creature impressed Jane. "Jane," she replied.

"Nice to meet you – amongst the shoes," Kate giddily observed, making a gesture at all the boxes on the plush carpet in the store surrounding them.

The clerk came back, wading through the copious amount of boxes in front of Jane, finally reaching Kate. "Your receipt, ma'am," he said with a defining lisp. Handing her a bag and his hand to grasp hers, "I'm Adam if I can be of any assistance; Here's my card."

"Speaking of cards – where are my real estate manners?" Kate wondered. "Here you go," handing her own embossed card with polished individual logo.

"Beautiful," Jane admired. "It's too bad I don't have my own card. I'm in the process of moving."

"Well, give me a call and we can have a coffee or lunch sometime. It's always nice to meet people new to the city," Kate suggested. With that, she was off! "A pleasure to meet you!" She departed the store with her new confidence-in-a-bag.

"Now that's driven - someone who will go somewhere," Jane noted to herself. "And . . . I just might help her do it."

"How are you ma'am?" checked Adam, approaching after Kate's spirited departure.

"Fine, bag them all up," Jane ordered and handed him her credit card.

"All twenty pairs?" Adam asked excitedly.

"Yes, one can never have enough shoes," Jane remarked with a smile, pondering for a second the $22,000 she had just decided to spend.

He rushed off to bag all the boxes. "How will you manage this? Would you like to pull your car around and I can place them in the back for you?"

"No, I'll send for them tomorrow," she said, eyeing one pair from Christian Louboutin. "Except for these. I'll take them with me."

"Thank you Mrs. Torrance," Adam said, remembering her name from her credit card.

"That commission should give him a night to remember out on the town" Jane thought to herself as she left, hoping the young man wouldn't speed somewhere on break to buy cocaine. She had enough thinking about the drugs, something her son had been particularly susceptible to with a ferocious playboy lifestyle prior to his murder. She had enjoyed her foray into the retail jungle, but it was time to get back to the hotel and get prepared before she went to the opera's opening night with her sister-in-law, Barbara Chambers, who was chairing the evening's festive opening night ball immediately after the performance.

———◆———

"I've had the entire park tented for this," announced Barbara, as Jane and her new Louboutin shoes settled into the backseat of the Lexus that contained her sister-in-law. "I can't wait for you to see the design."

"What are you talking about?" asked Jane, looking confused.

"The party, darling!" Barbara offered. "Certainly not the opera, at least not here in Portland!" Living half the time in the nation's capital had spoiled her with both the Washington National Opera and The Met.

Both ladies laughed as they were whisked away to the party that would unofficially announce Jane's new residency in the city. Jane's brother Malcolm had left for the District earlier that day to participate in another attempt at peace talks for the Middle East.

"Where on earth did you get this car?" Jane wondered.

"This is Oregon, Jane! It's about the only thing that's halfway decent that a politician's wife can get away with having without the media spouting off about it," Barbara said.

Jane, who was used to the plush comfort of her Bentley Arnage sedan, shrugged it off as another oddity of the city. Soon, they arrived in front of the Carlson Auditorium and Barbara shrieked, "They haven't turned on the lights yet," referring to the elaborate set decorated for the party she had planned directly across the street at the large full city block park that was tiered in fountains. Busily, she pulled out her mobile phone and made a quick call. "The lights are not on and it's 30 minutes before the opera begins!" she plainly stated. "We'll go around the block and when we return, the lights ought to be on."

Jane looked up at the auditorium, which recently had received its new name. "When did this become the 'Carlson'?" she asked Barbara.

"All an insider thing, that's for sure," Barbara advised, still frustrated by the light incident. "Another bureaucrat trying to look good as a swan song – got the family to slap its name on the auditorium for one and a half million – which was absolutely ridiculous in this day and age." Naming rights for an auditorium - even in Portland - started much higher, for at least $5

10

million. "Almost as bad as the cheap marble they used to put the name on the building," she sneered, privately thinking Chambers would have been a much better name for the auditorium.

Barbara, who was known for her habitual rants and raves to both her sister-in-law and her husband the Senator on a great variety of topics, had devoted her life to service of the state she loved. She and Senator Chambers lived a comfortable yet modest existence in Portland and Washington, D.C. Therefore, Jane did not reveal the afternoon's extravagant retail tour to purchase shoes.

"By the way, when are you going to find a home," Barbara asked Jane.

"I think I may have found a person to help me get the land I'm looking for, and I'm going to build it," Jane revealed.

"What business do you have in building anything? Just buy. Sarah Codman's place is perfect and for sale right now on Humphreys," Barbara suggested. "You don't have any experience building anything and I'm sure it would become a ten-year project like your apartment was after Clay died."

"Nonsense! I know exactly what I want – I can import nearly everyone from New York to make it happen and just go on an extended trip – leave someone in charge – and when I come back, it'll be done! Less than a year." professed Jane.

The car door opened, and both ladies emerged in their Valentino gowns. In an unusual departure for the city's understated wealth, Jane had brought with her several jewelry ensembles for Barbara to consider wearing from her latest raid on Fred Leighton – a shop that Jane loved because of the sheer volume of beautiful pieces to select from. One rarely saw such a display in Portland as while those who could afford such jewelry did indeed own it, but saved wearing it for vacations to Europe and winters in the desert. "Fred Leighton always looks like a junk store with everything piled on top of everything else," Jane had repeatedly said. "But, you can't argue with the selection."

"Stick close to me, honey," Barbara slyly whispered. "It's your first night out in the city and I don't want you to fuck it up."

"If there's a fuck-up, my dear, it'll be you or your party," Jane retorted, with which they both smiled and moved inside the auditorium through the stage door in order to greet the cast after admiring the lights at Barbara's party scene across the street that had been turned on for her arrival.

"Not funny," Barbara responded. "Tonight's about magic – so let's make some happen. You're not royalty, but a few billion dollars helps."

The party was a reason why everyone who was part of Portland's imaginary social establishment showed up that evening. "Nose-bleed" seats for the ball, as Barbara called them, started at $1,000 per person while patron tables sold for as much as $25,000 apiece. A scale model of the party set had been commissioned by Barbara to be placed in the lobby to show the 3,000 members of each night's audience something they would most probably miss, as the party's tickets had been apportioned to the major patrons of the opera who attended different performance nights – meaning 300 of the gala's 700 guests would arrive after the opera at ten o'clock in the evening to join the patrons coming from opening night after the final curtain.

Navigating to the box level of the auditorium was a task – as Barbara had to greet and introduce Jane to numerous guests.

"Darling, may I present my sister-in-law, Jane Torrance of New York City," she said, bringing Jane closer to meet one of the city's leading real estate brokers. "Jane, meet Bobbie Jo Atwood – someone who can help you with your task of finding property here."

"A pleasure," uttered Jane, as she was pulled by Barbara to the next group, nearing the center box, reserved that night for members of the Opera Ball committee.

"Ursula! How are you?" Barbara exclaimed, reaching over to the next box to hug Ursula Carter, a serpent-like French national who had married one of the leading specialists in plastic surgery in the city.

"Fine, darling," Ursula hissed in a thick dramatic French accent that she had never lost after over 40 years in the United States. "Just back from Paris this morning. I'm exhausted but I had to attend. Look over there, it's Betsy Parker – John's latest face!" The cadence of speech was unbearably predictable as she reviewed her husband's work on many of the room's faces, breasts, stomachs, and buttocks. The accent was alluring to any number of weak souls that Ursula coaxed into working for her charitable causes. She scanned the crowd with eyes that honed in on influence and wealth like a sixth sense.

"I have a surprise for you," Barbara suggested. "My sister-in-law Jane just moved to Portland and she's my date this evening."

"The one with all the money?" Ursula whispered in her signature 'hush-hush' voice that was always loud enough for anyone around her to hear.

"She's the one," shared Barbara, bringing Jane over to meet Ursula and knowing that the 'Little Napoleonette' would be scheming on how to contrive a donation for one of her projects.

"Jane," Barbara said, signaling her over. "Ursula Carter."

"Pleasure," Jane acknowledged, distracted from conversation with two of her brother's Congressional colleagues. Right as they were introduced, the lights dimmed signaling the start of the performance. The audience fell silent as the curtain opened for Mozart's The Magic Flute.

One of the tangible benefits that Jane knew she would miss about New York City was her association with The Metropolitan Opera as a board member. During the performance, she recoiled several times, especially in listening to the haunting refrains from The Queen of the Night's aria, 'Der Hölle Rache kocht in meinem Herzen.'

"That singer is on par with Florence Foster Jenkins," Jane whispered to Barbara. Both quietly chuckled in reference to the wealthy but talentless early twentieth-century singer whose comic appeal had garnered significant popularity in New York society. Due to their experience with opera companies in Europe and the East Coast, their ears had adapted over the years to appreciate musical quality and voices that were just not available in what was considered a 'tier two' city in the hierarchy of the opera world. Dutifully, they applauded enthusiastically at the end of the aria with the rest of the cheering audience.

The opera ended with a standing ovation as Barbara and Jane ducked out a side door of the box level to escape the scene and go immediately across the street where the guests had begun to arrive. In the staircase, Barbara reminded Jane of some ground rules for the evening.

"Now, please do not be critical of the opera," Barbara pleaded as they nearly busted a gut laughing in the stairwell. "Not only are these people supporters of the arts, but more importantly they also give to election campaigns – and our retirement is on the line with any future contributions."

"I didn't just fall off the back of a truck, Barbara," replied Jane, knowing that the campaign funds of a member of Congress were typically converted to personal assets upon retirement. Hence, the robust campaign office action during what would be his last year in office was significant. "How many times do I bite my tongue even in New York?"

"I know, but a reminder is always helpful," advised Barbara.

"The last time I went with you to the opera here, it was Aida. Do you remember that particular performance?" asked Jane.

"No need to mention it yet again," Barbara cautioned.

"As you'll remember, The King of Egypt's vocal tremolo was so severe it was reminiscent of an old theatre organ." Jane mimicked the singer and forged ahead with the conversation despite Barbara's level of discomfort.

"Yes, I think that's the last time they let someone in their apprentice program do a key role," Barbara explained. "Now, let's focus on this party."

—◦◦◦—

As they crossed the street, the spectacle of pageantry unfolded in grandiose scale and was a testament to the committee's year-long pursuit to create a perfect scene to rival the finest season opening galas anywhere. Large magnificent lucite stalagmites had been constructed for the tunnel that guests would enter as they were transported into the depths of a fantasy world. A serenade of the operatic voices poured faintly down the tunnel. Supernumeraries clad in loin-cloths glowed with fluorescent paint that covered their bodies as they hovered over acoustic drums to create a melodic tempo that was starkly opposed to the music that signaled guests might be entering another world. Beverly Hills' famed event planner Martino Quimby had been commissioned to design a set for the event that would enchant and surprise. He and his team had labored for a month constructing the elaborate set – the first time a public park had been transformed in such a way in the city, and the results were already the talk of the town.

The thunderous falls from the two-story high park fountain were a backdrop for the basin where the guests would dine and dance. Submerged lights in the water moved in graceful patterns to cast beautiful shadows against the trees and aquatic ballet. A series of cables had been deployed high above the park so that at the appropriate time, cast members from the opera would fly in and land on the stage to sing. A special orchestra from New York City had been flown in for the occasion to entertain while chefs from the city's best restaurants had the task of delighting everyone with a five-course Epicurean experience.

Through several lobbyists, the Senator had secured premier sponsors so his wife looked as if she herself had produced the most notable soiree of the century. The best imported Champagne and wines, party gifts from Tiffany, and enormous towers of orchid centerpieces graced each table, with the most honored patrons receiving the best seats that filtered out all the way to those who could afford to buy a ticket and not much else.

"I wish Malcolm were here to see the finished product," Barbara lamented as they moved through the tunnel toward the party.

"Well I have no reason to ever be impressed," Jane said softly. "But you've outdone even a New York party with this!"

⤛⋯⋯⋯⤜

The two statuesque ladies observed as the park filled with guests. As promised, the rip cords installed high above the scene carried trapeze artists clad in costumes with huge wings to signify that guests had truly been transported to a mythical realm.

"I love this," Jane admitted, wondering if they were so unapproachable that no one came up to visit with them. "Are we toxic? No one seems to be interested in talking with us?"

"Darling, right now all eyes are on us," Barbara offered with a permanent political smile she had learned to wear over 40 years.

"For what reason?" Jane asked, not really noticing any overt glances or stares.

"Speculation," Barbara mused. "This next year is going to bring a lot of change to the political landscape in Oregon, and everyone wants a part of it."

"Who are they all?" Jane wondered, looking into the sea of guests.

"Over there at that table – those are the Jews who are in charge of the Jews. At the club there might be a membership committee, but they run the Jewish subcommittee that decides if you're an acceptable Jew first. Of course the committee isn't actually a recognized group, but more of an informal thing," Barbara conjectured.

"We have a bit of that in New York as well," informed Jane.

"They're regionally segmented as well," Barbara suggested as she spied a gaggle of jeweled white haired ladies who had each been chauffeured to the occasion by dutiful friends. "Those old ladies – all in their 90's - live on huge estates in Dunthorpe just south of town. Not one of their families will want the work after they die. It's an end of a generation of formal perfection."

"Just like poor dear Brooke," Jane understood, thinking of her old friend in New York who was forced to abandon her manicured gardens and estate and relegated to a lonely imprisonment without friends by her family as they systematically sucked the cash from her significant reserves.

"It definitely is interesting to watch. We represent all of them," Barbara noted of the different constituencies that both she and her husband theoretically answered to. "You're actually very brave. If someone attended tonight's event that they knew was a billionaire several times over, they'd be hit up for everything from speaking engagements to donations. You can't go anywhere without having to endure some plebeian request from any number of jackasses who want their ear."

"Do you think I would have considered moving if Clay were still alive?" Jane asked with curiosity.

"Maybe, but you two were unstoppable, and now you're unstoppable on your own," Barbara counseled with pride.

"Everyone in this room is in an obvious clique," Barbara advised, pointing out a variety of people. "The banks run with the power companies – see there. There's Ursula Carter with the wealth management set. And, look at how those young attorneys are cavorting on the dance floor! Shameless!"

"It takes all kinds," Jane said, scanning the crowd. "Who's your favorite?"

"My favorites won't come until later. They'll put in a brief appearance before darting out the door," Barbara said of several key campaign donors who all had large privately-held companies in the state. "After the acknowledgments let's get in the car and go up to Liza's for a drink."

"In these ball gowns?" Jane asked.

"Sure, why not?" Barbara laughed. "It's Portland, anything goes!"

Mixing with the crowd, Barbara had the pleasure of introducing her sister-in-law to numerous other faces that Jane would soon just forget. She now had a single focus for transition, and was excited at the possibility of executing her strategy as soon as possible.

Chapter 3
THE EARLY YEARS
1954

Jane Torrance had not received anything more than a high school education prior to her arrival in New York, but in the post Korean War environment, it was easy to get started in real estate as a way to make ends meet. After being entranced first by the glitz and then the opportunity of a big city as a young girl from the Pacific Northwest, she set out to educate herself in the style of a seasoned European Royal. Her photographic memory captured key elements from books she poured over at the library where she read on how to appropriately function within society each day, consuming nearly 5,000 volumes of information on topics from art appreciation and real estate to investing and history.

She interviewed extremely well and joined a respected residential real estate firm as an associate and was assigned the role of assistant for a major new development that was to be the new crown jewel of the city's Upper West Side on Riverside Drive, a converted apartment cooperative that had previously been a hotel. Jane was paired with one of the city's most powerful and seasoned brokers, a robust British woman named Annie Johnson who was an unlikely candidate for success in real estate. Annie had worked throughout World War II as a supervisor for women working in factories producing ammunition for the war effort – and was considered a female bulldozer that bucked the trends in what was still a male-dominated profession at the time. Her large signature dark rimmed glasses accentuated powerful brown eyes and sharp masculine features. In a few short post-war years, she had built what was considered one of the most successful real estate practices in the city – drawing on the power of the feminine equation of any couple.

"Never sell it to a 'him,'" Annie said. "It's his money but it's her home."

Jane absorbed everything she could from her new mentor. Annie's advice on any myriad of topics was appreciated as Jane was just a speck of dust with relation to the types of individuals she would work with at the cooperative sales office.

The two agents played off each other beautifully – Annie's power of negotiation was coupled with Jane's looks and seemingly-abundant worldview to sell like a team of wrestlers as they completed the daily grind toward the goal of 100% occupancy. In fact, the two ladies became good friends, as Jane had no one else in the city and Annie acknowledged it was a lonely existence as one of the only women to be successful in real estate at the time.

About six months into Jane's job, Annie developed pancreatic cancer and the much younger real estate agent found herself as the sole representative for the 37 units that remained for sale. The owners of the real estate firm didn't feel that additional personnel were needed on site since Jane had adapted so well to the profession, so she was then asked to manage the office on her own. The only thing out of the entire job that worried her is how she would sell the penthouse unit that took up half the top floor.

She kept up her routine of hitting the library and museums daily in a thirst for knowledge and decided to take some weekend jaunts to Boston and Washington to get a flavor for the East Coast. Enjoying Long Island, she loved walking on the beach and became a New York convert with little interest in returning to her home state.

As she was locking up the office one evening, the bell rang signaling a prospective buyer. Never to be one who would refuse a potential sale, she went out to the lobby to see how she could be of assistance.

Waiting outside in the rain, huddled closely to the door, stood a man wearing a hat and long coat.

"May I help you?" Jane asked as she opened the lobby door.

"I was sent here to look at some apartments for sale," the figure explained, removing his hat.

The young eighteen-year-old girl who had pretended to be twenty-one in order to secure her position was transfixed by what she saw. An exceedingly attractive blond gentleman with sharp jaw line who was an even six feet tall, he responded to her deep gaze and lack of words with a hand shake.

"Are you in charge of sales?" he asked Jane, extending his hand. "Clay Torrance here."

"Oh, yes – absolutely," Jane responded. "Jane Chambers. I'm sorry, it was a long day today. Please come in the office."

The suited gentleman followed her with a kick in his step, eagerly wanting to see what units might be available.

"What are you looking for," Jane nervously queried from behind her desk as her potential client looked through some of the floor plans.

"An apartment," Clay joked. "Actually, something for my fiancé and I when we get married next month."

"Oh, something to start a family in?" Jane suggested. "Let me get the keys and show you."

Jane's attraction to Clay had been momentarily displaced by her desire to move inventory and expedite the possible sale due to a commission.

"We'll start with the best, and move down from there," Jane suggested as they reached the elevator. "So, what line of work are you in?"

"Energy exploration," Clay explained.

"Energy exploration," Jane pondered. "Sounds rather involved."

"Not so much," Clay said. "Basically, it's equipment for how you find oil, gas, coal – and transport it. Nobody's ever done them all together."

"Manufacturing is certainly big," Jane said as they exited the elevator at the Penthouse floor. "Where do you do it?"

"I grew up here in the city," Clay noted. "Our headquarters is here, and we have foundries in Texas, South Carolina, and California."

Jane unlocked the door of the penthouse unit and they walked in to immediately see the lush view of the Hudson River from the enormous windows.

"Four bedrooms, all the amenities – a nice terrace – your fiancé will love it, as well as the security if you're away on business," Jane touted the selling points with adept skill, luring her client to become a buyer in 'one of the finest buildings in the city.'

"Price?" Clay questioned.

"Reasonable - $610,000," Jane said.

"Let me bring my fiancé here in the morning to see what she thinks. I'm not much for looking at a lot of different things," Clay admitted.

"Excellent, any particular time?" Jane asked.

"I think ten will be fine. That'll give you enough time to open," Clay laughed.

As they walked through the lobby, Jane paused and said, "Thank you again, Mr. Torrance. And, your fiancé's name?"

"Her full name is Her Royal Highness, The Princess Elena of Romania. However, you may call her Ella," he replied.

"A Princess in our building. That would be a wonderful addition!" exclaimed Jane as she walked him to the door. "See you tomorrow."

———✦———

Promptly at 10 a.m. the next day, the door ringer buzzed noting the arrival of the building's hopeful royal resident and her soon-to-be husband.

"May I present my fiancé, Ella," Clay introduced.

"Your Royal Highness," Jane made a deep curtsy to the woman.

"No, you don't have to do that," Ella counseled with a rich European accent. "I'm an American now."

"Well, we are pleased nonetheless," Jane said. "I think you'll absolutely love the penthouse. Mr. Torrance, would you mind if Ella and I looked at the penthouse together? It's something we women like to do."

Clay was left alone for what seemed to be over an hour in the lobby, thinking of all the things he could have been doing at his fledgling company, Torero Resources, rather than waiting on his fiancé and real estate agent to approve the home. Finally the elevator door opened and the smiling ladies hopped out to join Clay.

"Well?" he asked.

"She's a negotiator – but she saved you $20,000," Jane wryly advised Clay. "$590,000."

The dollar amount was of little consequence to Clay, whose family had homes in Newport and Long Island in addition to the magnificent townhouse between 5th and Park Avenues. As a rebel explorer who was gifted intellectually, he had graduated from M.I.T. with degrees in Materials Science and Mechanical Engineering and went to Texas to work on an uncle's oil field. With a special knack for understanding complex issues, he used his background in Metallurgy to successfully solve many of the production problems of the oil field's equipment and started his own company, naming it Torero as an homage to bullish instincts to persevere until a task was complete. The concept had taken off beautifully, and within a short few years Torero was well on its way to capturing the position as the largest company of its kind in the nation.

"Fine!" Clay said, kissing his princess and shaking Jane's hand. "We'll take it."

"I'll send the paperwork to your office then," Jane indicated, knowing they had kept him waiting far too long in the lobby. "You both have a phenomenal rest of the day."

Jane had done exactly as she had planned, selling to the woman but also knowing that this man wasn't about to put up too much of a fight. She also knew that she would personally deliver the paperwork to his office, and she had carefully orchestrated the visit to signal her continued interest in him, despite the princess.

"Since Ella is such a good negotiator, we're taking a trip to Tiffany to spend the balance!" Clay announced on their way out the door.

With a smile on her face as she waved goodbye to them; however, she seethed with jealousy as Clay and Ella departed. The next several nights – despite the coup of selling the Penthouse unit – proved sleepless for Jane as she thought constantly about Clay and a possible future together. Her youthful spirit gave her resolve as she fantasized how to capture Clay's affection, and she didn't have much time before the wedding to cast a spell that would drive a wedge between the princess and her prize.

Princess Elena had one singular goal in her race to find a husband, it was well-known that royalty - without a country to rule - were popular accoutrements of wealthy Americans. Clay's family was no exception to this rule. While the roles had been reversed in the case when Alva Vanderbilt engineered the wedding of her daughter Consuelo to the 9th Duke of Marlborough bringing considerable needed resources to the land-rich cash-poor nobleman, having a princess in the family would be a definite enhancement to their station within their stateside peer circles.

The upper class embraced the intoxicating presence of royalty in the New World, while anyone in Old World society privately denounced the unions as poor taste. While she had nowhere near the net worth of her distant British cousins, the princess's $400,000 inheritance did allow her some flexibility to position herself to make a connection with a potential suitor. Her work in maneuvering through society had landed her with a world-class family in the Torrances, whose collective net worth hovered around $20 million at the time.

Determined to impress her male obsession, Jane had promptly closed the sales office the day that the deal had been negotiated to start a research project into the world of energy exploration and its challenges. With the New York City library being a rich depository on even the most obscure subjects, she went to work so she could fluently discuss his business and passion at their next meeting in a few days.

--⊷--

Perfectly coifed to destroy Clay's princess love, Jane strode into the Torero offices on Park Avenue with her signature walk. Armed with her newly-acquired knowledge of his business, she felt her fifteen minute meeting could be successful to at least lower the glimmering fly into the water to catch her prize.

"Jane Chambers for Mr. Torrance," she announced to the receptionist.

She sat down and waited to be called into Clay's office, bringing forth the paperwork from her briefcase so she could be immediately ready with the unpleasant task of signing paperwork so she could then spend the balance of time in conversation, slowly luring him away from Ella with both her stunning beauty, sophisticated air and a unique trench-level understanding of business and how to survive.

"Ms. Chambers," Clay greeted his guest, emerging from his office. "Have you come here to take money from me?"

"Only a deposit," Jane replied with her best smile. "And of course the paperwork to sign."

"A beautiful view," Jane commented of Clay's office. "Since it's a cash deal, we only have three places for signatures."

"You've made the entire transaction go so smoothly," he complimented on her client service.

"So, energy exploration must be a fascinating line of work," Jane strategically suggested. "How many companies do you work with?"

"All of them," Clay noted. "Amoco, Texas Oil, Getty. Each project is different based on what they're doing as well as the geological formations we're up against."

"So it's beyond just rigs and pumpjacks?" Jane innocently asked.

"Very good, Ms. Chambers," Clay commented. "Are you a student of the oil business?"

"Not particularly. But, I do read a lot and I'm a quick study," Jane replied.

"Well, we've perfected the blowout preventer, blended metals to make our drill bits last up to nearly 10,000 feet, and have virtually eliminated any downtime associated with rig equipment."

"Impressive," Jane smiled. "Any business outside the country?"

"Iran is now in play – and several of our clients just formed a consortium to sign an agreement with the Shah," Clay disclosed. "I sometimes wish Ella had an interest in the business."

"I was going to talk to you about that. The Princess is going to need someone to show her the city," Jane offered, feigning concern for the welfare of the Princess as a new resident. "To show what to do and where not to go – things like that. I wouldn't mind doing that."

"She'd be so appreciative," Clay said. "How much do you charge for that?"

"Not a thing – it's part of the service I offer my clients," Jane replied.

"Nothing goes unrewarded, I can assure you that," Clay informed as he got up. "I just hope that she can make friends."

"She is a little aloof," Jane noted. "But, that's royalty – after all, she is the daughter of a king."

"Yes, but even in society a title can carry you only so far," Clay explained. "She has a very fragile personality and is especially anxious about how she'll be perceived here."

"I'll call her this afternoon to see if I can take her to lunch," Jane suggested, getting up from her chair in front of the desk to exit the office. "Thank you again for everything."

"Thank you for making the connection with the apartment," Clay said, smiling. "She'll move in at closing, and I'll move in after the wedding."

As she left the office, pure coincidence brought Ella walking in the door.

"Ms. Chambers?" Ella asked. "Is that you?"

"Your Royal Highness," a shocked Jane responded with a coy look about her, knowing that the princess might be by to have lunch with Clay at the time she was visiting him. "Yes, I was having Mr. Torrance sign some of the paperwork for your penthouse. In fact, he suggested that we go to lunch so you can learn a little more about the city."

"That would be delightful," the Princess indicated. "What's your week like?"

"Nothing like the present," Jane remarked. "How about tomorrow?"

"Wonderful, I'll have reservations made for noon at the Colony Club," Ella noted.

"A perfect place to begin an introduction to the city," the younger-but-wiser tutor said of the private women-only social headquarters that the Princess's mother Her Majesty The Queen had belonged to prior to her death, even though the Atlantic separated her from the establishment that she only had visited twice in thirty years of membership that was perhaps given to her as a courtesy. As the family's princess of seniority, the membership had been transferred to Ella after the Queen's death.

⚬

Jane was ready to do battle with the aristocrat, but she assured herself it would be a mental war that was waged to rid Clay of his princess bride. She put on her most striking suit that she'd saved for months to buy from Saks Fifth Avenue and made her approach to the Colony Club. Other agents in her main office were members and Annie Johnson her mentor had been one as well, but Jane was far too young to afford the initiation fee and monthly dues. The princess was the only one who knew that she herself was banking on the wedding, as her inheritance and the luxuries and station it provided her would only last three years. Jane rationalized her intense hatred of Ella with the usual mix of jealously and the fact that she didn't view her as an acceptable mate for Clay.

Walking down Park Avenue to the club to meet Ella, her confidence increased by the minute as she schemed ways to unseat the princess who was obviously no better than a cheap whore in her quest for money and prestige. She thought Clay's family was just as bad by initiating what seemed to be a 'request for proposal' from eligible royals. Word on the street was that nothing less than a princess would be fitting as Clay's mother pulled the marionette strings from her palatial Park Avenue apartment in orchestrating the union. Jane knew the battle would be tough, as the old bitch would most probably deem her unworthy of her beloved son after she disposed of the slut masquerading as royalty.

"Your Royal Highness," Jane whispered with a smile as she entered the club's main entrance.

24

"Ms. Chambers – how do you do?" the Princess responded. "Shall we go upstairs to the ladies lounge?"

"It would be delightful," Jane replied.

"I'm so pleased we're able to meet. I'm hoping that it becomes a regular occurrence," the eager Princess said with sincerity.

"It undoubtedly will," Jane hoped.

The ladies talked for what seemed to be hours. Glasses of champagne were consumed while Jane recounted her experiences in real estate for the European princess as stories went back and forth about the rich and powerful they had both dealt with. Jane was building trust with a woman whom she secretly compared to a greedy spoiled bitch.

"You'll definitely make a splash," Jane suggested. "But, have you met his mother yet?"

"I am having her to tea at my hotel next week. Should I know something?" the Princess asked.

"You better wear your best tiara – she's behind it all," Jane indicated.

"Behind all what?" the curious Princess followed.

"The marriage. Do you think he'd get married otherwise?" Jane asserted.

"Well, he loves me – so I hope he would," Ella said with uncertainty.

"My dear – I guess that's why I'm here today – to tell you the real story so you don't get hurt," Jane joyously announced with a serious undertone.

"I'm a bit confused," the Princess responded. "What exactly are you trying to say?"

"He's 28," Jane put forth.

"And what is wrong with that?" the Princess asked.

"A confirmed bachelor – to be sure," Jane explained, thinking the princess would immediately understand. "And, if he does meet up with a woman, he prefers the company of negroes – big fat ones, either servants or prostitutes."

With Jane's plot unfolding, the princess's level of discomfort increased by the minute. Her hopes of money with love were an added bonus, but a woman of her stature would be scorned by her royal peers and New York society if she dared to initiate a sexual liaison to satisfy herself in the absence of her husband.

"It's not that bad," Jane counseled. "Surely there are many marriages like that in the city. Everyone ultimately knows and has a understanding that you're simply there as a breeding machine and fur coat rack."

"What mistake have I made?" the Princess asked herself aloud.

"Your Royal Highness," Jane reassured. "What you're doing is very 'royal.' Maintain the relationship for the money, and have a liaison in Beverly Hills or Palm Beach when you have the need. Many of the bisexuals in Hollywood are considered some of the most prolific lovers of the day – you'd be a definite catch to have an affair with. Where are you staying here in the city, anyway?"

"The Lowell," the Princess answered, devastated by the revelation that her true intentions for financial stability were plainly evident. The thought of her fiancé in bed with another man or a devilish black strumpet made her sick to her stomach. "Excuse me for a moment, please."

As the Princess rushed to purge the lunch into the toilet, Jane smugly sat observing the other ladies in the dining room, knowing that she herself would one day be welcomed into the membership as Mrs. Clay Torrance. Not realizing that the inbreeding of European royal families typically caused a host of genetic imperfections including severe mood swings and depression provoked in the most minute fashion, Jane had not fully understood that she had lit the fuse to deconstruct the wedding which was indeed a legitimate proposition. Nothing Jane had revealed about Clay was true – but the fragile Ella fervently believed that her new friend would certainly not deceive her. What could have possibly been gained from the lowly real estate agent providing information that the Princess felt would ultimately save her honor and that of her family's?

The Princess finally returned after popping several pills to relax and the pair left the dining room and kissed prior to departing from the club.

"Thank you for your honesty," Ella confided, having absorbed Jane's truth. "I think I need to lie down."

"I'll walk with you," Jane said, putting on her strong 'ally persona' to comfort the Princess as she escorted her the few steps it would take to reach the Lowell. They walked in silence, arm in arm, as Jane watched Ella keep tears from streaming down her face. "It's OK – it will all be OK."

"Thank you, again," the Princess offered her new friend upon reaching the hotel's entrance. "I'll call you tomorrow in the morning."

Jane felt invigorated as she strolled down to Fifth Avenue, feeling alive and ready for her challenge to wed Clay. In her estimation, she had succeeded in putting the princess on notice that the whole city was watching her and knew exactly the type of person she was marrying. Her Royal pride would of course prevent her from ever confronting Clay about what she had been told.

⟶◆⟵

The princess stepped into the lobby, and then quickly changed her mind and peeked through the window to see Jane strutting down the street more than a block away. Smiling, she slinked out the door and took a brisk walk to Bergdorf Goodman. Upon arriving she was warmly greeted by the doorman, and the counter ladies rushed to call the personal concierge. While only a minor royal figure, having a princess in the store was particularly exciting for everyone.

"Your Royal Highness," exclaimed Gwen, the senior stateswoman of the sales force who was dedicated to working with clients of note. "Why didn't you call? We could have made special arrangements."

"It was a whim," the young Princess flippantly said. "What I want is a Russian Sable coat."

"This way, Your Royal Highness," Gwen directed. "They are particularly expensive, however."

Couldn't the Princess get the respect she deserved even at Bergdorf's? With that comment, Ella went into overdrive and decided it was her objective to spend at least one quarter of her inheritance – not only to needlessly show the inconsequential saleswoman her financial wherewithal, but also to appease her inner desire for happiness through something that provided instant gratification and not much more. Material goods had always been a most certain antidote to depression for the rich-but-shallow members of her extended family tree, and the Princess reassured herself that her appearance back out on the street in her new coat could be nothing less than a media event. She thrived on the stares – curious onlookers wondering who might be blessing them with a rare public appearance – and fed off the attention that was as addictive as a good line of cocaine – but as short in duration.

"Price is not an issue," Ella snapped back.

"Yes, I heard your marriage has been announced," Gwen said, referring to her pending nuptials with Clay and slipping the coat on Ella. "Absolutely seductive."

27

"Is it beautiful?" Ella asked.

"Most assuredly, Your Royal Highness," Gwen declared, hoping to lure the princess to other sections within the massive retailer. "You know, there might be something to go with that. Have you ever purchased a Don Loper dress?"

"I don't think I have," reported the Princess.

"Very popular with celebrities," Gwen revealed. "Perfect for a trip to Beverly Hills."

The Princess's brain, overanalyzing every word or expression since her lunch with Jane, wondered why Gwen would mention California or Beverly Hills after Jane had mentioned it at lunch. Did she know about Clay's proclivities as well? The secret must not have been as closely guarded as Jane had implied.

"What about jewelry?" asked the Princess.

"Certainly – we have a particularly lovely selection of estate tiaras from the collections from Palm Beach and Newport," Gwen advised. "You must have many, however."

Ella looked incredulous, as if Gwen was taunting her and had perhaps known that her father the King had liquidated most all of the crown jewels as a matter of survival.

"I'd love to see them," Ella prodded.

As she was taken into a private room walled with royal blue velvet that was behind a thick glass door, Ella was amazed to see twenty five of the most beautiful diamond tiaras, tastefully displayed on tiers in the same blue velvet. The lighting danced with the diamonds as if each orphan were competing to be taken home with the Princess. Frowning on several of the tiaras that she recognized as imports from European cousins that the Americans had purchased during war time, she focused on several of the easily-identifiable pieces from Garrard and Cartier. After trying on several of the jewels in a relatively rapid timeframe, Ella chose an intricate Edwardian version with pear-shaped diamond droplets.

"Shall we have it delivered to you, Your Royal Highness?" Gwen asked.

"No, I'll take it with me," the Princess said, apparently disregarding the cost of the tiara at $50,000.

Laden with several bags including one that held the tiara and its case, the princess emerged from Bergdorf's victorious. After spending nearly

$125,000 between several items, she gingerly strolled back toward the Lowell, taking in the city and all the people. Most certainly her bags and coat had caught the attention of the masses, and she was content with the subtle praise from passersby that often would only mean a turn of the head to inspect her ensemble a second time.

She arrived at the hotel and was greeted by the doorman who swung the door open as she headed toward the elevator. Settling into her room, she began to undress and unpack her purchases. From her closet, she removed a long ball gown that had typically been reserved for ceremonial court occasions when the family would meet in a variety of international cities since many cousins had been exiled from their countries of origin. Pretending they were still indeed ruling families, they carried on as if they were truly in power as heads of state.

Lacking servants to respond to her commands, Ella poured herself a Scotch from the decanter, popped a few more tranquilizers, and closely examined the tiara, reviewing every stone and its placement in the intricate design. Turning on the radio and finding a station playing a symphony, she put on the court attire one piece at a time. The sash symbolizing her rank, various jeweled honors, necklace, and long white gloves followed by rings. Atop her perfectly coifed hair she positioned the tiara. It was a dazzling look for the young princess and worthy to be immortalized on the currency in her native country.

Reminiscent of the formal balls from her youth, she waltzed herself around the room, pretending to be in the company of Clay. However, her mind produced a very different crowd that had assembled to surround them. The Hollywood set had materialized during their dance – men wearing not much more than hot pants, sailors, witty publicists smiling, and a contingent of Negro musicians and whores began to interrupt the sweet symphonic melody as Ella seemed to get lost in the imagined world she had momentarily created.

"Honey, you better wear that tiara," shouted a hefty colored woman in servant garb, dancing up to Ella with an enormous smile while she simulated a thrusting action with her ample mid-section. "When you aren't home, I'm gonna get your 'bent' husband in bed!"

She turned to locate Clay, who by that time had been convinced by the party-goers to disrobe to his underwear – a near-full erection was cradled in the pouch as a dizzying flurry of men rubbed against him, cheered on by the jazz musicians and the variety of street-class vixens. His body was perfect, yet there was nothing the Princess could do to rectify the situation at hand. The closer she got to the group to prove her own sexual worth to him, the further they danced away in another direction, taunting her like a fish in a race to seize the baited hook.

The only option was to leave the party. Ella located her new sable coat and jettisoned herself to the bathroom – fleeing to the only safe house available to rid herself of the apparitions of her future. Laughing loudly, she propped herself up against the sink, looking dismally into the mirror at the second-rate princess who had been consigned to whore her own title out to the aristocracy of America.

"Fuck this," she angrily hissed, putting on more lipstick as she attempted to look as seductive as she could for her waiting court in the main salon of her suite.

The Negro servant woman materialized behind her, offering her sage wisdom with a comforting, motherly touch. "You know he's a priss, don't you?" she asked.

"I know," Ella sobbed, acknowledging the apparition. "What would you do?"

"Honey, I'd just die. I couldn't handle a homosexual for a husband. I know some women can do it, but it's about self-worth!" the servant proclaimed with the truest expression of concern.

"What should I do then?" asked the Princess.

"End it," encouraged the black spirit as she planted the idea.

"It's ok to do it, then?" Ella wondered, almost as if she were asking permission from herself.

"Hell, yes, it is," the servant woman endorsed with a comforting coo, smiling like it was a non-issue. "You look so radiant right now, it would be a shame to waste it on him. Get into that bathtub. You know what to do."

"I'm so embarrassed," the Princess explained, perpetually concerned for how she'd be viewed in the newspaper. "Will it come out that I have nothing?"

"If you're going to go, this is the way to do it – clean and simple," the spirit beaconed her to the bathtub, playing specifically to Ella's motivations. "You're a princess! If you did it after you got married, they'd know exactly why it happened. This will get headlines – and will show the world how strong you are."

"Thank you. Thank you so much," Ella said, reaching toward the spirit who was no longer present in the empty bathroom. The intoxicating desire to experience death consumed the Princess as she reached for the razor blade she used to slough off any excess body hair. Getting into the bathtub fully garbed in her tiara, court dress, and fur coat, she settled in for a magnificent final sleep. The sable cushioned her as she removed her rings and gloves and proceeded to slash her wrists, letting the blood flow toward the drain. Magically ending her life was perhaps the most dignified thing she'd ever done, fading away into a fantastic dream where she and Clay could perpetually be together without the nagging torments of her imagined realities.

The night went by and Clay had called and called to the Lowell, trying to reach the Princess. He finally talked to the manager early the next morning, trying desperately to see if anyone on staff had seen Ella as he'd seen her every day for the past month. Deciding to walk over to the hotel to press the issue, he arrived at the front desk and located the manager, who reluctantly called for housekeeping to join them as they opened the door to investigate the disappearance of the Princess.

"Ella," Clay called throughout the suite, without success.

"Your Royal Highness," the manager called, entering the bedroom – also having failed to locate the Princess.

"Check everywhere," Clay ordered – seeing that several doors were closed and that each one could be an option to where she might be hiding.

"Sir, please come quick," the manager frantically yelled, having opened the bathroom door.

The fur coat concealed most of the caked blood that had discolored to nearly a black tone. Ella's body looked at peace, eyes open, motionless – a porcelain doll whose perfect painted picture for her future had been shattered by Jane just the day before.

"My God," Clay screamed as he entered the bathroom. "Hurry, help get her out of there."

The two men and the woman housekeeper struggled to move the Princess, but the coat and dried blood had stuck to the bathtub creating a tug of war between them and Ella's final resting place. Finally tearing the coat out of the bathtub, the housekeeper rushed to call an ambulance.

"What on earth could have happened here?" Clay asked in disbelief.

"She had reported to the desk clerk that she had been shopping at Berg-dorf's, sir," the manager noted.

"That explains the coat," Clay said, holding back tears and secretly pondering removing her clothes as he never had seen the Princess's nude body and wanted a final fantasy to stoke in his memory for what had become a morning ritual of self-gratification. "My real estate agent had lunch with her yesterday, too."

"She did come in the hotel alone," the manager recounted from his daily update on the guests from his staff.

———

As the ambulance and police arrived, the suite quickly filled with a number of official personnel in addition to Clay and the manager.

"Sir, do you have any idea about her state of mind," the police sergeant in charge asked Clay.

"Certainly not anything that would cause this," Clay responded in a measured cadence. "I do know for a fact that she had a small inheritance, but she was going to marry me and that wouldn't have been a problem."

"Please write your contact information for both work and home down here," the sergeant said. "We have some things we need to investigate. Are you aware of any others that may have seen her yesterday?"

"My real estate agent Jane Chambers," reported Clay. "She's selling that new development over on Riverside Drive where we were going to buy a place together."

"I'll need her information as well," the sergeant said, handing the piece of paper back to Clay. "Sir, I suggest you leave the hotel – we have a lot of work to conduct here. And, I'm very sorry."

Clay stopped in the hotel's lobby to pull Jane's card out of his wallet and called her office.

"Riverside Circle," Jane answered.

"Hello Ms. Chambers – this is Clay Torrance," he said.

"Well, how are you doing? I had the most wonderful lunch with Ella yesterday," Jane acknowledged.

"That's what I'm calling about," Clay confided with some trepidation.

"Is everything all right?" Jane asked with concern in her voice.

"How did she seem yesterday?" Clay queried.

"Just bright and hopeful for the future," Jane suggested, lying with superb talent.

"She's dead," Clay somberly indicated.

"What? I just saw her!" Jane screamed.

"The police agree it was a suicide. She was wearing a tiara, fur coat, and her court dress with full royal regalia and jewels, and slit her wrists in the bathtub of the hotel," Clay explained.

"I'm in shock," Jane said in disbelief. "How utterly bizarre. I am so terribly sorry, Mr. Torrance."

Jane was absolutely elated by the news, as she had expected that the story she'd planted would result in the princess merely searching for greener – meaning wealthier – pastures, and had to hold back an enormous smile and giggle as Clay reported the suicide and the circumstances surrounding it. Jane simply listened to Clay carrying on about their love, and how it was completely devastating. Dancing around the office with glee during the phone exchange, she could only think that a royal bitch would check out in such a dramatic fashion.

After she had finished her job in consoling Clay, her next phone call was from the police sergeant.

"Riverside Circle," Jane answered.

"Ms. Chambers?" the man asked.

"Speaking," Jane replied.

"I'm an investigator with the New York Police Department collecting information about what appears to be a suicide of Princess Elena of Romania at the Lowell Hotel," he said.

"Absolute tragedy," Jane said. "Mr. Torrance just called to inform me. You know I had lunch with her yesterday at the Colony Club."

"Did she seem agitated or upset?" the sergeant asked.

"Not in the slightest," Jane quipped. "It was a celebratory luncheon to welcome her to New York.

"Anything unusual about her?" the sergeant continued.

"Not especially, other than her repeated comments about being nearly out of money," Jane lied to set the stage for the mental conundrum of why a relatively wealthy Princess would choose to end her life especially having just purchased a noted penthouse and a fiancé who in his own right was well on the way to becoming one of the nation's great industrialists.

"We're beginning to see a common thread with that," the sergeant disclosed. "We'll call you if we need additional information."

"I'm terribly sorry," Jane consoled, smiling into the handset and making a distorted face. "Good day."

Jane decided to ease into her approach to win Clay's affection. She merely would write a letter of condolence to him and wait a week to further discuss the penthouse purchase or how he was doing in the wake of the Princess's abrupt departure. Then she decided to take a break and visit the penthouse – what she envisioned would become her future residence. As she arrived at the top floor and opened the apartment door, her mind went to work on the type of furnishings she would buy. Dancing through each room, she sung the praises of the Princess's wisdom to commit suicide and leave her to pick up the broken pieces of Clay's existence. Someone would be needed to sustain him as he grew the business, and Jane knew she was the ideal partner to position him for greatness beyond his own aspirations.

Having read of the funeral that was attended by many of the minor European royal families in addition to Clay and the New York set, Jane was delighted that the chapter of the Princess had finally come to an end. Dialing Torero, she reached Clay.

"Mr. Torrance, Jane Chambers calling," she said.

"Ms. Chambers, I've been meaning to call you to thank you for your kind note. I know Ella appreciated your kindness as well," he indicated.

"She will be missed," Jane echoed. "I'm unsure if you're interested in talking business quite yet."

"I am, actually," Clay revealed, several weeks having passed since the death itself. "I intend to keep the apartment."

"I was hoping you'd still be interested – it's an amazing place," Jane noted.

"When is closing?" Clay asked.

"I extended it several weeks out to give you time to think," Jane replied.

"Very considerate," Clay said. "Make it this Friday, and I'll have the bank wire the money over."

"Consider it done," Jane beamed, hoping that the balance of the apartments didn't sell too quickly to allow her the opportunity for many chance meetings with Mr. Torrance.

With men being powerless to the allure of the female, it wasn't long before Jane's comely presentation effectively sealed her own fate as the future Mrs. Clay Torrance. He could hardly avoid noticing Jane as she flounced around the building in her finery, showing off the balance of the apartments to any number of buyers. He had invited her for lunch, and was impressed by Jane's remarkable esprit – a quality the princess most certainly lacked. As a down-to-earth man of wealth with incredible intellect, he told his friends of the young lady jousting with him in conversation, and was completely smitten by her. Jane's only hurdle was the other Mrs. Torrance, Clay's mother, who had personally championed the royal union. Surprisingly, however, the old broad with all of her snobbishness seemed to embrace the young Jane as well. As Jane programmed herself to overcome any personality conflict, she simply evolved with knowledge from each meeting to effectively counter any objection anyone had – a skill that had served her budding career in real estate.

Jane didn't know it was the night that would change her life when Clay suggested they dine at 21, an old tradition of many men in the city for the night they chose to propose. The Maitre' d sat them at Clay's favorite table and handed Jane a special menu.

'Love,' was the word set in calligraphy at the top of the menu.

"Where's the normal menu," Jane wondered, looking around at other tables.

"A special night this evening," Clay suggested, seemingly absorbed in the prix fixe offering.

"It's not Valentine's Day," she retorted.

"No, it isn't," he responded, engrossed in the menu and rather distracted.

Without much warning, a waiter brought a dome-covered platter and placed it before Jane. Puzzled, she looked to Clay for advice.

"Open it," he said.

She lifted the cover from the platter to see a lovely calla lily. Disguised near the bloom itself was an exquisite 10-carat ring. Jane was nearly speechless as Clay got up from his seat and knelt before her.

"For a year you've been a rock to me," Clay explained, holding Jane's hand. "I only wish I could have met you earlier just for the sheer pleasure of spending more time with you. Will you do me the honor of becoming my wife?"

By this time, everyone around the couple was staring, awaiting Jane's response.

"Absolutely!" she glowed as they kissed and embraced. "I have loved you from the moment we first met."

The small crowd applauded the young couple as Jane slipped the ring on her finger.

"To the future Mrs. Torrance," Clay announced to the restaurant. Everyone raised a glass to toast them.

⤖

Determined to stay virtuous until their wedding, Jane's plan involved withholding herself from Clay until after the festivities. By organizing a very small ceremony followed by a lavish honeymoon, she avoided the task of inviting her family to New York for the occasion.

Her life changed substantially over the month leading up to the wedding day. She herself moved into the penthouse that she had labored so heartily for the Princess to endorse and began working with a designer so that Clay could literally 'move home' before departing on their honeymoon to Hawaii, the little-discovered beach paradise of Waikiki where they both could only tolerate a maximum five-day stay. The workaholic mentality was contagious between them as they bounced ideas off each other for real estate and Torero's ever-expanding product lines to ease the burden of sourcing for the burgeoning need for natural resources and oil. In fact, the two loved planning so much that they hardly left the hotel, other than a quick jaunt around the island one day.

The sex was particularly fiery as Jane had predicted, but she guarded herself with care to be sure to cement herself into the company culture of Torero by refusing to have a child until the ideal opportunity as she was far more ravenous for success than her already-wealthy husband. The Torrances did not immediately engage themselves in the social fabric of New York as there was simply not enough time. As Clay would go out on major sales trips across the country, Jane was firmly in charge of the office at home.

For the next four years, the couple was more of a business partnership than a marriage as they forged ahead with their master plan for growth. The employees of Torero's headquarters, a number that had grown from 35 to over 100, had learned to respect Jane out of her sheer dedication to Clay and the business. She worked amazing hours for being so young and learned the business from the ground up, having participated as a backup for nearly every position in the office. By 1958, the unusual business couple team had transformed the small company into one with sales of nearly $150 million.

"Darling, I'd like us to go home early today," Clay said.

"Why's that? We're not done for the day," Jane replied.

"Yes, we are!" Clay argued as he dragged her to what was now a chauffeur-driven car.

The vehicle turned up Park Avenue on its usual path through Central Park to their Riverside Drive residence, but stopped and parked in front of what was considered the newest rival of the renowned architect Rosario Candela's opulent apartment buildings that had popped up around the city throughout the 1920's.

"Are we going to the museum?" Jane asked, pointing at the Met a block down the street.

"No, we're going in this building," Clay explained, pointing toward a recently-constructed tower perched on the corner of Fifth and East 78th. "It won't take long."

As they got in the elevator, Jane would have never guessed that she would be moving into the building, would proceed to live there 50 years, and have the distinction of being one of 25 owners of New York's grandest cooperatives.

The elevator door opened to the gallery of the penthouse, of which behind it was window after window looking onto Central Park.

"What is this place?" Jane asked.

"It's yours – if you want it," Clay responded with a smile.

"You're joking!" Jane laughed.

"Would I have pulled you away from your desk at the office if I weren't serious?" Clay suggested.

"Honey, it's just amazing," Jane said, looking throughout the top-floor unit – not even having reached the main salon that held a special surprise for her. As she entered the room, the only thing hanging on the wall was a Picasso painting, a distorted contemporary work for the time painted just three years prior.

"It's a gift from Uncle Victor and Aunt Sally to celebrate our new home," Clay explained as he officially launched their other vice to what would propel them to become some of the most prolific collectors of art in the 20th century.

"Can we afford all this?" Jane asked, sensing the purchases may have been beyond even their means.

"Honey, we've been saving for four years and we cleared $10 million last year alone," Clay replied. "We can afford almost anything now. You have two floors, a roof terrace, and 19,000 square feet to work with here."

"It's a lot to take in – and a lot of work as well," Jane admitted.

"But it's Fifth Avenue – you've always said you'd eventually land here," Clay reminded her.

"And, here we are!" Jane yelled, giving her husband a hug and dancing around him in a rare burst of excitement for the usually-reserved business-woman.

——◈——

The next decade would find the couple with the finest New York apartment, near-unlimited resources, and a sheer dedication to make their business prosper. She maintained a strict policy against children, something that everyone thought was particularly odd for a woman of means with an attractive husband to choose work over a family and a life of relative comfort. What the ladies of society didn't understand is that she was in many respects the force behind the company but still made time to effortlessly socialize with her peers. Her ability to assimilate information quickly allowed her to easily predict trends and outmaneuver any competitor while Clay focused on the technical aspects of the business by building a world-class research lab on Long Island that was fed by the talent from M.I.T., his alma mater.

The 1960's were a true Renaissance period for the Torrances, but a total distraction was about to occur as Clay relentlessly lobbied for a baby and won the battle in 1968. Jane was disgusted at the thought of expanding in size and having a literal parasite swim inside her for the term of pregnancy.

She prayed that her two previous and secretly-executed abortions would assist in cancelling out Clay's potent seed, but he was able to impregnate her in only a few attempts. At the same time, the family was in a particularly fortunate position to bankroll her brother Malcolm's political career as he and his new wife Barbara embarked on their own ambitious journey toward the Senate in Washington.

Joseph Chambers Torrance was born on June 3, 1968 and even Jane was excited with the prospect of a new cadet to mold in her battle for success. She spent the few days she decided to stay with the baby at home after the birth plotting out a life of the best schools, learning a second and third language, and fantasies of training their son to further the dynasty into the next generation elevated with even more prestige and power.

It was painfully obvious by age five that Joey, as he had become known, was a psychological cripple and a particular embarrassment to Clay and Jane that their near-perfect genes produced such an unfortunate anomaly of flesh. At one point, they had considered placing him in a special residential unit of a psychiatric hospital in upstate New York as numerous tests had come back inconclusive but would have since revealed the commonly diagnosed but extremely severe version of attention deficit disorder. With the additional debilitation of dyslexia, Jane rendered her son a useless commodity who of course would always be well-cared for, but had become of little relevance after proving unable to walk in the ambitious path she had designed for him after birth. Coming to terms with her genetic failure to produce a suitable heir to the Torero Empire made her even more resolute in the iron grip she extended throughout the company. With the energy sector being heavily dominated by males, she was fast becoming a legend in the industry – something that even impressed Clay's ruthlessly judgmental mother.

After taking the company public in 1975, the couple fortified their position as two of the youngest members of the wealthiest class in the city and nation. Purchasing more and more art with a special emphasis on the Impressionist and Contemporary categories, the Torrances thrived in their chosen lifestyle of co-executives that was considered by many to be one of the most unconventional unions that the city's storied past had seen. While he was still in charge, she definitely ran the show and Clay consulted with her on nearly every major decision affecting the company. They both sat on the newly-created board and controlled a 35% voting block, having sold the balance of their shares to eager investors looking to profit from the nearly recession-proof corporate engine.

Rarely entertaining in their magnificent penthouse, the Torrances as a couple preferred to weekend with friends in the Hamptons or visit her brother who was in his first term as a senator in Washington, D.C. Joey was relegated to a life with nannies, as Jane never felt it was appropriate to bring a contingent with them that always included several servants to care for their needy son on week-end jaunts.

"Mrs. Torrance," her assistant Nancy called as Jane picked up the phone in her bedroom one summer morning while readying herself for a day at the office without Clay, who routinely would leave on business travel. "Are you seated?"

"Why yes, I'll be in the office shortly," Jane replied. "Is something urgent?"

"There's been an accident," Nancy sniffled, holding back tears at her desk.

"Why kind of an accident?" Jane inquired.

"Air traffic control reports Mr. Torrance's plane as missing," Nancy explained.

With her stomach turning, Jane reassured herself, "with his instrument rating? I seriously doubt that."

"They'll keep you personally briefed on your arrival," Nancy indicated.

"Thank you," Jane shuddered, hanging up the phone with her heart pounding, burying her head in her hands and letting out an enormous cry that resonated throughout the vast penthouse.

"Mom, is everything all right," asked Joey in a muffled voice, standing at the door to her suite.

Picking up her Chanel bag and regaining her composure as she felt she was the only rock to hold the entire family together, Jane walked toward the door.

"It's nothing, honey," Jane said to her son, knowing that any disruption to his fragile thoughts might cause as a serious outburst. "Run along now and go find Nanny."

As the boy rushed down the hall and then down the grand staircase to locate his surrogate parent, Jane called for the driver to take her to the Torero office.

———

"Any news?" Jane asked upon entering her office suite.

"Nothing yet," reported Nancy. "Do you think we should involve your brother?"

"Give it thirty minutes, then I'll make the call," replied Jane.

The women sat in Jane's office, cloistered and not saying a word. Nancy had been with them since Jane formally joined the company after her marriage, and was nearly as concerned for Clay's safety. With little to do during the short time frame, they both played solitaire in a rare moment of downtime which Jane would ordinarily have never allowed herself or her staff.

Like clockwork, Jane spoke immediately upon reaching the appointed time.

"Nancy, please make the call," Jane requested.

As Nancy got up to go to her desk, Jane collected herself and rehearsed what to say to her brother.

"Senator Chambers," the intercom announced to Jane, who automatically picked up the telephone.

"Malcolm," Jane said somberly.

"Janey!" the Senator responded. "How are you?"

"I need your help. Something's happened to Clay's plane," Jane explained.

"Something?" Malcolm asked.

"It's missing. I need some help. No one's giving any information up here and I need him found," Jane pleaded.

"I'll make some calls. Where was he going?" the Senator asked.

"He'd fly all over the place by himself," Jane noted. "The flight plan was to Bermuda, which isn't that unusual."

"So, Coast Guard for sure," Malcolm suggested, trying to calm his sister.

"Thank you so much," Jane said, hanging up the phone and contemplating what to tell their employees if the plane had crashed.

———

Within minutes, the Senator's call prompted the Coast Guard to launch several cutters out in the Atlantic while instant satellite photos were analyzed to spot any wreckage in the vast ocean along the flight path. It didn't take long for intelligence to locate the wing of an airplane that was ripped from the fuselage upon crashing into the ocean. A special diving unit was

41

summoned to bring the submerged plane along with its sole occupant to the surface. Clay's skull had been literally split open by hitting the instrument panel during the speedy descent and impact with the water. The deformed head was not fit to be identified by even the strongest stomach.

⤚⬥⬦⬥⤛

On the Senator's instructions, no information was to be communicated to Jane. Anything that was uncovered would be his duty to report to his sister.

Wrought with anxiety, Jane paced in her office while Nancy stood guard in the executive lobby area.

"Senator Chambers," Nancy announced over the intercom.

"Anything?" a desperate Jane said into the handset.

"Janey," the Senator said in a saddened tone. "It's not good. They found him."

Jane burst into tears and began to hyperventilate. Nancy rushed to her side as she wept while still trying to talk to her brother as he attempted to console her.

"What happened? Why would he do this to me?" she wailed.

"Honey, it was an accident," the twenty-year veteran secretary comforted her now-sole employer. The much older Nancy cradled Jane has she continued to cry while still holding the phone.

"Barbara and I will be with you as soon as possible," Malcolm announced. "May I talk with Nancy for a moment?"

Jane handed the phone to her secretary without objection.

"Senator Chambers?" Nancy said in a quiet voice as she continued to hold Jane.

"Don't leave her side, and don't say a thing until I get there," Malcolm ordered. "The news will be out before we arrive, and my press secretary will make a statement on behalf of the family. Put Jane in the car and take her home immediately."

"Certainly," Nancy agreed. "I'll stay with her."

"Here's your purse," Nancy said, handing the bag to a disoriented Jane. "Walk with me."

The two ladies regained composure to appropriately walk through the Torero offices and to the elevator without emotion. Feeling like two hunted creatures venturing into a wolf pack of suspicion, neither of the ladies felt comfortable to even look at the staff for fear someone would somehow understand their angst, thereby stirring up gossip and unrest amongst the entire company upon learning their founder had perished unexpectedly. Even with over twenty years as an equal partner, Jane always had Clay to back up her decisions – and that privilege had just been permanently eliminated from her life. The most important thing to Jane at the moment was maintaining the stock price and the company's public image as the finest innovator of its kind in the world in the wake of the sudden death of its founder.

Upon arriving at her apartment building, Jane and Nancy immediately went upstairs. Jane located Joey who was playing with his nanny and began to explain the situation.

"Honey, something's happened to Dad," Jane explained to her son. "He's been called to Heaven early."

Knowing Joey was capable of near-instant hysterics, Jane tried to soften the blow to the mentally fragile young man.

"Where's Dad?" Joey innocently asked.

"He's gone, honey. And, he won't be back," Jane hesitated.

Joey erupted in tears, clung to his mother and was surrounded by both the nanny and Nancy. Nancy herself could not hold back and began to cry and embraced the others including the boy who was in the middle of the three women as they instinctively had formed a circle to protect Joey whose emotional difficulties would continue to haunt him for years to come.

A hardened Jane ordered no funeral or memorial service, preferring to grieve privately over the next month and not even allowing Clay's family access to her or her son. She would communicate with her senior-most vice presidents at Torero as well as having daily visits from Nancy who would deliver paperwork to review. Frustrated with Joey's inability to cope with the loss of his father, she evaluated boarding schools so perhaps a fresh and different approach to discipline would rehabilitate the wayward youth. She banned discussions of Clay among her family, servants, and at the office. While Barbara had stayed an extra week, Malcolm returned to Washington right before the August recess and took Joey with him as they collectively decided that the boy approaching his teens would benefit from being with his cousins for a month to alleviate the already-present emotions from losing a father at such a young age.

With the resolve of a champion, Jane returned to work with even more drive than before. Bypassing her Board and appointing herself Chairman and CEO as the largest individual shareholder of the now-public company, she intended to usher in the next decade as what the *New York City* magazine had called the "most powerful woman in the city".

Chapter 4
A DEAL
2010

"**H**ello Kate, this is Jane. We met buying shoes a few weeks back," Jane announced over the phone.

"How are you," Kate shrieked, as if speaking to a long-lost friend.

"Fine," Jane acknowledged, not revealing that she was indeed moving to the city. "Do you have some time today to look over some maps of some property with me, I think I'm in the market for Portland and I thought of you first since you were so personable when we met."

"Certainly, and thank you," Kate sparkled with genuine appreciation. "Where in town are you?"

"In a claustrophobic suite at The Parkway, it would be nice to get out of this hotel," Jane confessed.

"So you don't have to walk far, let's meet at the Regent Club at 3 p.m. One block away on Salmon Street. Look for the green awning and doorman and you're there. Also, skirts for us ladies," Kate explained.

"I understand. See you this afternoon," Jane said.

Membership in the Regent was limited, and sponsorship by a member and four additional member references were essential to qualify for consideration. While other clubs had been subjugated to take mere commoners from the business class and lower ranks of society into their doors during hard economic times which had forever changed the pristine landscape of their membership rosters, this small club diligently used its full investigatory powers signed over to it by an applicant nominee to scour credit history, criminal background, and any other factors needed to appropriately vet potential members. The place had an air about it, much like Jane's New York co-op building, which signaled that any amenity that could be available to its members was indeed present.

The Regent sat at the foot of Portland's beautiful park blocks, a gorgeous brick building that had been designed a century ago to meet even the most modern demands of hosting events for its carefully-selected members. It had been expanded over the decades by wise Boards of Directors to fully cater to each member's social spectrum. With downtown parking at a premium, the club had added a parking structure next to it after the Korean War. A lavish spa and salon replete with swimming pool and exercise facilities graced the lower level of the structure and the rooftop ballroom and spacious terrace served to help celebrate special events like the weddings orchestrated to solidify power bases amongst the city's leading families. A sizable endowment fund allowed the club carte blanche for constant improvement, other than sporadic haggles with Portland's extremely liberal City Council, which would have delighted in seeing the Regent turned into a shelter for the homeless.

Kate, admittedly not an insider to Portland's wealthy elite, received sponsorship from two of her closest college friends, Sue Helen Chastwick and Brent Chandler. Her nomination was seconded by several other acquaintances whom she had met over the years as a native of the city. Cloaked under the radar screen of the watchful membership committee as a relative unknown - and therefore a non-controversial nominee – she was elected to the club's membership without issue. She selected the Regent because it exemplified the best of everything. Tradition would never die there, a place where members and their families would continue to enjoy untold privileges for years to come.

Jane walked into The Regent Club wearing a chic pink and orange Chanel suit augmented with select jewelry designed by Karl Lagerfeld himself, stunning Kate in the lobby because she remembered a woman in her sunglasses and casual jogging attire, and not a creature who defined the essence of style.

"You look simply beautiful," said Kate, who was wearing a plain black business suit, tasteful pearls, and the shoes she had purchased when she met Jane.

"Thank you. And, thank you for being available," said Jane, seeing that Kate had worn her special purchase in Jane's honor. "Nice shoes!" They both laughed as Jane followed Kate.

"I've arranged for us to use the Ladies' Drawing Room upstairs," Kate motioned to the staircase. "It's private and there's a big table where we can look at your maps," she said, gesturing to Jane's briefcase.

As they walked up the grand staircase, Jane couldn't help but be impressed with how the club looked. It even rivaled some of the finest clubs in New York - the types that didn't need reciprocity or gimmicks as selling points to be at maximum capacity with wait list at all times. The ornate silk wallpaper with flocked designs almost shimmered and seemed to encase the beautiful artwork that hung on the walls including sketches by Dali and avant-garde paintings from the likes of Mark Kostabi.

Most of the pieces were donated from the private collections of Regent members to the club's art foundation as a tax loophole for the mid-tier wealthy who weren't in a position to finance and organize their own. They were guarded with premium security that was not noticeable to the common eye. At one point, a busboy had attempted to remove a small painting from a banquet room only to be arrested moments later upon exiting the building, having been caught on camera making the actual heist. Cameras had been deployed throughout the club specifically trained on any object of value while still offering total discretion for member activity and conversation.

They arrived at the Ladies' Drawing Room, secluded away from everyone. Service staff would not intrude on them without being summoned by bell. As they sat in the room that was beautifully appointed in the French Empire tradition, Jane confessed to Kate, "Prior to us building a business relationship," Jane said, "I want to disclose something to you."

Kate wondered what on earth Jane was about to reveal.

"Does my last name mean anything to you?" Jane queried.

"I don't think I even knew your last name, everything happened so quickly at the store," Kate said.

"Torrance. Jane Torrance," Jane explained slowly.

"Jane Torrance. Let me think." Kate wracked her memory to figure out any possible connection. Finally it clicked. "The New York City Jane Torrance? Why are you here in Portland?" Kate exclaimed.

"I'm looking for a different existence than what I had in New York," said Jane. "I am relocating to both Portland and to Washington, D.C. I already found the perfect place in D.C., but I'm going to build here in Oregon."

"Why Portland?" Kate quizzed in disbelief.

"I was born here, and you perhaps know my brother Malcolm Chambers," explained Jane.

"Senator Chambers?" questioned Kate.

"Yes," Jane paused. "That, and my son was murdered last year in New York. This is a needed change of scenery. Security is an ongoing concern as the case was never solved."

"I'm very sorry," Kate said.

"It's all right. Well, it's not 'all right', and it nearly sent me over the edge. To lose a child is the most difficult experience that I don't wish on anyone. It made me re-evaluate priorities and these tired old bones," explained Jane, motioning to her limbs.

Kate, who was 35, hoped that she looked as fabulous when she reached Jane's age, which was 75. The polished elder seemed so matter-of-fact in her disposition, and at ease considering the tremendous upheaval in her life during the past year.

"Let's get to these maps?" Jane suggested, bringing up the beautiful crocodile Lagerfeld briefcase to pull out some maps her assistant had printed for her in the general vicinity of where she was looking. "I have driven all over these hills looking for something ideal, land that feels secure and works for the plan I have in my head."

She motioned to a select neighborhood, very familiar to Kate who was as much of a researcher as Jane, and had coveted working the potential territory of all seven of the prized West Hills in the city – from Dunthorpe to Forest Park.

"Greenleaf Drive," Kate beamed. "Absolutely stunning, very private."

"My assistant did a little research on the actual land, and I need all thirteen parcels of land along the ridge to do what I want to do," Jane noted as she pointed out the boundaries for the land acquisition. The wide parcels would lend dynamic views from a shear cliff at one end while also providing ample space to build.

"A challenge . . . well, I'm glad you decided against 'The Grid'," Kate counseled, referencing a fine neighborhood down the hill several miles and closer to the downtown core. "The fault line goes directly up Clifton," Kate noted, trying to share some not-often-publicized information about one of the streets in what was considered the best real estate in the city. "If a big earthquake comes, those homes will all be dust."

"Ah yes, well, this piece of property isn't going anywhere, I had one of the company geologists run some reports on the area and now all that needs to happen is the purchase," said Jane.

"Not that easy," Kate countered. "In Portland, news travels faster than any other city and you have to be as quiet as possible to get things done expeditiously."

"Understood. My sister-in-law wanted me to work with Bobbie Jo Atwood – a real bitch from what I saw. You're the girl, and I like being quiet. What do we do?" inquired Jane, allowing the new agent an opportunity to earn her commission.

"Here's the strategy I'd propose. Let's check with an attorney to see what we can do to make sure this goes unnoticed. I have someone in mind, a local old boy – someone with superb discretion," Kate advised.

"I hope its not that complicated," Jane said.

"That's the price for remaining anonymous. The minute word hits the street about interest from a buyer – especially a wealthy one - the price can skyrocket. It doesn't look like any of the properties we're after is on the market. What's your budget?" Kate asked as she looked up the neighborhood on her iPad.

"Twenty million." Jane had drawn the line in the sand for Kate to work with. It represented a $500,000 commission at a minimum, but Kate would have to work the neighborhood in a systematic way as to not draw attention to the multiple transactions. In fact, the deals would ultimately propel Kate toward local fame in coordinating the largest set of simultaneous urban residential transactions the state had ever seen.

"So what will you build?" Kate wondered.

"You'll be the first to know," Jane replied.

"Can you meet sometime tomorrow with the attorney I have in mind?" Kate asked.

"Yes, any time after noon – there's a conference call with the Board tomorrow that begins at nine our time," Jane noted.

"Outstanding. I'll call you with a time, and I'll pick you up at the hotel," Kate said.

As they left the room, the two ladies laughed and began to conspire on how to outwit the numerous personalities that would be involved in the transactions.

Chapter 5
THE HUNT
SAME YEAR

"**W**hy are we going across the river?" Jane asked in reference to Kate's car travelling away from the downtown core.

"This will be a real experience for you," Kate chuckled. "Have faith!"

The car parked in front of an unassuming single-story building. A makeshift fountain constructed of manufactured cement blocks greeted the ladies, around it a menagerie of old pots held a variety of floral accents in various stages of decay.

"Have faith?" Jane implored.

"Yes! Daniel has helped my family with legal issues for years. Despite the appearance, he's quite the attorney," Kate explained.

"Faith," Jane reassured herself.

As they entered the lobby of the building's sole occupant that was cluttered with decades of papers and books, they walked down a tiny hallway and arrived at Daniel's office. The 'one-man show' had built the building in the 1950's, and not much updating had occurred since then.

Daniel was characteristically on the phone when they arrived, and he motioned them to come sit in front of the enormous desk piled high with paper. His appearance defied conventional wisdom about his legal expertise. Frayed cuffs on his shirt and a little stain on his blue sport coat made Jane wonder what kind of office they had entered. His thick gray hair desperately needed a comb, but he was trim and looked healthy.

"Then, we have no choice but to sue," Daniel said into the mobile phone, motioning for them to sit down. After a pause, he hung up without saying good-bye.

"That bitch just said 'I'll make note that you threatened the National Bank,'" a puzzled Daniel told both Jane and Kate. "What else is a litigator going to do?"

"Daniel, thank you for seeing us on such short notice," Kate said. "This is Jane Torrance, my client."

"Daniel Sempler. Good to meet you, any client of Kate's can be a client of mine," Daniel joked. "What's going on?"

"Jane would like to buy a significant portion of residential land up off of Greenleaf," Kate explained. "We need to make sure it goes undetected."

"How come?" Daniel asked.

"Two words," Kate offered. "Jane Torrance."

"Jane Torrance," Daniel couldn't place the name.

"I had to do the same thing with her," Jane said in reference to her meeting with Kate at the Regent Club. "My husband Clay was far more public than I have ever been, he founded the energy company Torero Resources."

"Now do you understand?" Kate asked. "Her brother is Senator Chambers."

"Ahhh, high profile buyer, pricing, privacy," Daniel acknowledged. "I've never had a billionaire in this building in all these years. I do know your brother, though. Welcome!" Jane smiled as Kate continued.

"Here is a list of addresses – 13 total parcels," Kate said. "What should we do?"

"When in doubt, do what Walt did in Florida," Daniel explained.

The two women clearly did not understand the reference.

"Walt Disney?" Jane asked.

"Yes, imagine if Walt Disney came up to you and wanted to buy your land? The price would double or more! He set up companies with different names to buy the land for Disneyworld to control pricing and publicity," Daniel offered. "Are the owner's names on this list?"

"Everything, including property profiles," Kate said, referencing the field signifying ownership.

"There are a lot of smart people on here. It's like a small family up there and they all talk," Daniel explained, examining the list of owners. "Here's what we do – we'll set up six different LLC entities originating from Nevada where ownership can be concealed to cloak the identity of the purchaser. The only problem is that the manager of the LLC must be public record. If there's the same manager for each one, then that could raise suspicion."

"I'll take care of that," Kate said. "How long to set them up."

"A week or so," Daniel said. "Are you ready to be a Portlander, Mrs. Torrance?"

"If this works, it will be an honor," Jane replied as she and Kate got up to leave.

"And, tell your brother he still owes me a dollar from a pitch game back in 1968," Daniel said.

Jane opened her purse and placed a dollar bill on Daniel's desk. "Debt paid."

"Thank you! Wait until you get your bill," Daniel called out as the two left his office.

"Now that was a character," Jane noted. "Are you sure he's a better choice than some higher profile attorney?"

"Yes, for they are the worst for talking," Kate explained. "Daniel's good but refuses to run in those circles. A few drinks in the bar and those senior partners from the big firms start breaking their bar oaths spouting off about their clients."

They got in the car and proceeded back to the Parkway. "Care to have lunch?" Kate asked.

"You know, I haven't even left the hotel since I attended the opera ball with my sister-in-law this weekend," Jane divulged. "I'd be delighted."

"We can go to Bayanihan which overlooks the new park," Kate said.

They ascended the stairs of the gorgeous new restaurant that had just moved in. Kate had reluctantly proposed the location because she knew the owner of the former restaurant which had been located in the same space who had abruptly decided to not renew his lease the year before. The owner of the office tower had dined there each day for lunch, had a favorite corner table, and had grown close to the restaurateur. During a short stay in the hospital, the daughter of the building owner assumed control of her father's company and the restaurant owner had asked for some lease concessions due to the economy. While knowing her father loved the restaurant, she flatly refused any concessions and by the end of the week, he had closed the doors to focus on his other restaurants. Kate didn't want to indirectly support the daughter, but was also very curious about the new space and wanted to impress Jane.

"Beautiful," noted Jane, looking at the stunning waterfall near the stair.

"They've tried to capture the essence of the South Pacific," Kate commented. "I am interested to see how the food is."

The ladies were seated at the exact table where the building owner had previously enjoyed sitting, but Kate resisted telling the story to Jane, electing instead to concentrate on the menu options and strategy for acquiring the properties.

"September 30th," Jane announced unexpectedly.

"What's that?" Kate asked.

"My brother will turn 70 and will celebrate retirement after 40 years in Washington," Jane explained. "I want to throw a big party at the new house for him."

"We only have a year?" Kate questioned.

"Let's get to work then!" Jane exclaimed, as they decided on their entrée choices when the server arrived to take their order.

Since several of the property owners were considered some of Portland's quirkiest and most unusual residents – something that was even more acutely evident when those individuals also had high net worth – Kate decided she would do what it took to make the deals happen, perhaps even compromising some of her personal ethics in the process in order to impress Jane.

"Absolutely excellent," Jane noted, with reference to the Ahi salad she had ordered. "Just perfect."

"I'm relieved to hear you say that," Kate hinted. "I love mine as well, but testing a new restaurant is sometimes iffy."

"Well, since it's only two blocks from the hotel, I can endorse it," Jane assured. "What will you do with the property purchase?"

As they discussed some of the intricacies of the transactions and personalities involved, the restaurant was about to close for preparations for its dinner.

"We better go, it's almost three," Kate said as she got up to put on her jacket. "As I said, I have a few tricks up my sleeve that will help the process along."

On the street, the two ladies waved good-bye and Kate went to work.

❦

One of the few major acquisition challenges Kate faced to Jane's coveted thirteen parcels of land on Greenleaf Drive was how to convince the 105-year-old Tess Parker to sell. A shape-shifting personality, she was beloved by Portland's establishment as one of the last great pillars of the city's golden age. However, she secretly delighted in demonizing her family and staff with what could be considered extreme mental abuse. She had been married at sixteen to a man who would go on to found the region's largest bank. At that time, Tess was extremely naïve to the realities of the new life she would lead with her much older new husband George Parker.

Despite having grown up in one of the city's most elegant and iconic mansions, Tess was hardly ever permitted to leave the estate. She was literally transferred from one form of bondage to another at the time of her arranged marriage that had been brokered between families in the city, and Tess was exceedingly bitter for having wasted 70 years first in her family's absolute protection and then under her husband's oppression.

One of her most humiliating moments was when George moved a young male prostitute into the estate's pool house under the guise of hiring him as a gardener and then hired the boy's near-homeless father to work at the bank. No one could say anything, as the Parkers controlled society by contributing generously to its collective charitable causes, and Tess' brother was the publisher of the state's daily newspaper that their father had founded. The prostitute's tenure did not last long, as a drug overdose and subsequent drowning in the estate's pool one early morning came only one month into his stay. Shortly thereafter, the father disappeared and was presumed dead. No doubt, both deaths were orchestrated by the seemingly innocent Tess and flawlessly executed through family connections. George was too much of a commodity to die so early on in their relationship, despite Tess' own family wealth.

A wretch of an alcoholic, each afternoon signaled the start of Tess' daily descent into an abyss of cocktails. Oftentimes her family would join her at her palatial hilltop estate for an early supper only to have a sea of profanities and insults hurled at them by the old woman throughout the evening. They had to tolerate the behavior for fear of the crusty old woman disinheriting disobedient family members. She took great pains with detailed explanations to each guest about their failures in life for the rest to hear. And the material was plentiful, as each child and their offspring had been so unfortunately coddled and spoiled to a point where the symbiotic familial bond had been blurred to create a festering lesion of absolute dependence between the generations.

Men were especially easy target practice, as one son-in-law had attempted to commit suicide due to the consistent caustic exchanges about his bad choices in business, bringing even more material to Tess' relentless repertoire. Had they attempted to poison her or hasten her death in any way, her trusts included a hidden labyrinth of special clauses that would disinherit the entire family if blame were even remotely laid at any of their feet.

She still had all her faculties, and could drink most people including her children and their families under the table, leaving her frazzled caregivers to put her to bed and then drive the dinner guests to their homes in tandem two cars at a time, a standard practice used by busboys at the Westmont Country Club where several of the drunks needed to be shuttled home almost nightly. The advantage the country club scenario presented was that many a divorced lonely member of either gender would often slip a $100 bill to one or both busboys for something more than a ride home.

The one thing that Kate had in her strategic court is that if Tess did die, none of her children could individually afford the upkeep and staff it took to run the compound, including a team of gardeners, cooks, butlers, maids, chauffeur, and housekeepers. If the fortune were split six ways, each branch of the family would receive only $15 million, barely enough to supply any family of note with a sustainable future.

"Mail call," said Betty, Tess' senior caregiver and house manager.

"Let's see what good news has come to us today," Tess said as she extended her boney hand and grabbed away the pile of mail from Betty.

"Bitch," Betty said under her breath in a near-whisper as she walked away. She was 40 years younger than Tess and yet been her personal maid for 45 years.

"What did you say?" clamored the old woman indignantly as she sharply turned around to face Betty.

"Nothing at all, don't be so paranoid," Betty retorted.

"Well watch it, now there's the door," Tess ordered as she threw up her pointed finger and commanded Betty to exit the massive drawing room so she could begin her inspection of the mail.

A polished hand-addressed letter caught her eye with a metallic embossed return address and wax seal. "I haven't seen a wax seal in years," she thought to herself, remembering back to the most pleasant times of her childhood when she was seven, before she had any desire to explore outside the large family estate which had since been occupied by other relatives. The letter contained a hand written note addressed to Tess:

Dear Mrs. Parker,

It is indeed an honor to write to you as someone who has such rich history in our beautiful city. As you can imagine, the acclaim for livability that Portland has received has drawn attention of individuals across the globe. In particular, your property has received interest as the ideal location for a client of mine to purchase. If you would entertain an audience, the individual would like me to explore with you the possibility of purchasing your estate. If you have an interest in discussing an offer, please contact me at your earliest convenience.

Cordially,

Kate Carerra

"Tess Parker here," Tess' phone call immediately upon reading the letter was to the closest association she had to a real estate power broker in the city.

"Mrs. Parker," said Bobbie Jo Atwood, wondering to herself why Tess Parker would be calling her. "To what do I owe this distinct pleasure?"

"Who is Kate Carerra?" queried Tess in a crackling voice.

"Kate Carerra? I'm not sure. Should I know her?" asked Bobbie Jo. Bobbie Jo's legendary ego prevented her from knowing Kate, even if she knew exactly who she was.

"I just received a letter from her, a real estate agent at your office that apparently has a buyer who is interested in my home," Tess explained.

"I see. Will you allow me some time to get some additional information?" asked Bobbie Jo.

"Quickly. Thank you." Tess hung up the phone not waiting for Bobbie Jo to say goodbye. Annoyed, she got up and exited the room and directed Betty to call a full staff meeting.

"How would all of you like to lose your jobs?" said the old woman to her staff that had assembled on the terrace.

"Oh no," Betty thought. "The general has come out for her monthly lecture."

The small crowd of servants eyed the petite Tess as she walked back and forth in front of them on the terrace wearing a mint and gold St. John knit suit with her white hair piled into a perfect coif, and collectively gasped at the prospect of losing work that was for some of them the only job they'd ever known. The majority of her staff were older and seasoned, most nearing retirement within the decade.

"I received a letter from a real estate agent today. She contends she has a buyer for this place and it looks like absolute shit," Tess said indignantly as she talked in an increasingly loud voice as the servants looked confused. "How am I supposed to sell this house if it looks like a fucking shithole, and more importantly, why would I want to live in a shithole?"

By this time, Tess' voice was bellowing at the top of her limited range, tears streaming from her face at the prospect of her unfortunate circumstance. She looked at the white geraniums that were in full bloom and went to where her head gardener was standing.

"Shears, please," she smugly said as she walked up to her senior gardener. The servant who had spent the day trimming the estate's exquisite greenery quickly produced long shears he had carried with him to the impromptu meeting and handed them to Tess.

"I'm going to have this real estate bitch over here tomorrow, and your future is now in your hands." With that statement, she cut the heads off of all the geraniums in two of the terra cotta pots on the terrace.

"You have a choice to make. First off, I don't spend millions each year to make this place look like shit!" she yelled, cutting the heads off of all the geraniums in the next two pots.

"Today and throughout the night, think of yourselves as in some beauty pageant, trying to transform a hideous whore into an acceptable candidate. And, if you're lucky just maybe we can still all live here happily." After cutting the heads off the geraniums in the last two pots, she threw the shears and they sailed through drawing room's window, breaking it. Tess stormed off to go down to Stroh's, her nickname for the grocery store which was conveniently located down the street nestled into the hillside – a rare location in Oregon which had both a liquor outlet and the high-end items she demanded as she personally shopped daily. Motioning for Betty and her chauffeur to accompany her, she departed the scene of mutilated flowers, shattered glass, and broken spirits.

Without waiting for Bobbie Jo Atwood to return her call, Tess dialed the phone number on Kate's card in the backseat on her short commute to the grocery.

"Hello," Kate said as she illegally answered her phone while driving.

"Is that how you answer a business call?" Tess questioned. "This is Tess Parker, you sent me an inquiry about my property."

"Oh, Mrs. Parker," said Kate. "Apologies – I'm driving."

"Come to the house tomorrow at 4 p.m. I'd like to hear what you have to say," Tess said.

"Certainly," Kate eagerly said.

"Don't be late," Tess said as she hung up the phone.

Kate quickly dialed Jane.

"Jane, I have an appointment with Tess Parker, the largest parcel" Kate said, bubbling with excitement over the prospect of potentially crossing a major hurdle.

"Outstanding, when is it?" Jane questioned.

"Tomorrow at 4 p.m.," Kate explained. "Wish me luck."

"Done. Talk to you after your meeting," Jane said.

Walking the tightrope with a living icon like Tess Parker was a lesson in nerves. Kate returned to the office to prepare for her meeting.

As Tess rolled her cart throughout Stroh's, her mobile phone rang in her purse that she handed to Betty to search for and answer.

"Parker Residence," Betty announced.

"Bobbie Jo Atwood for Mrs. Parker," Bobbie Jo Atwood said.

"Bobbie Jo Atwood," Betty motioned to Tess and whispering 'yes' or 'no.'

"Yes," said Tess as she grabbed the phone from Betty's hands.

"Mrs. Parker," Bobbie Jo said. "If anything, this Kate Carerra must be a relative unknown – certainly not someone who has the experience to represent a West Hills property. My son and I would enjoy the opportunity to discuss representation with you."

"I'll be the judge when I meet with her tomorrow," Tess responded. "If I'm not satisfied, I'll call you."

Tess hung up the phone and made Betty play catch with the phone while still holding the giant Chanel bag.

"That bitch is trying to pawn her son off on me," Tess said to Betty. "How long has she been trying to get business from us," referring to her coveted rank as the doyenne of society where she professed that 'us' was a collective of family and friends whom she thought she ruled.

"Oh, I'd say thirty years since she first entered the business," Betty responded. "But you've never been interested."

"And, I'm not interested – I want to see what this other agent has to say," Tess noted. "When we get back to the residence, I'll write the name down for you and you already know Bobbie Jo. Get on your computer and see if you can get some information for me."

"Surely," Betty agreed. "Not that you'll get any more than a self-aggrandized biography and some photo that's probably a decade or more old."

"No need to be a bitch," Tess chided as they glided through the check out. "That's my job," she smiled, turning toward the clerk who knew her all too well.

Kate was in the middle of profiling Tess' property and refining her presentation that would undoubtedly be just a carefully-planned discussion sans any props.

"Why are you trying to work with my clients?" Bobbie Jo demanded as she perched herself on Kate's desk at The Sylvia Siskel Agency's uptown office, a building that both of the real estate agents called home.

"Which clients would those be, Bobbie Jo?" Kate smugly replied.

"You know those are my hills. Everyone in this office does," Bobbie Jo haughtily explained, pointing up toward the West Hills.

"They don't have your name on them, Bobbie Jo. What's this about?" pushed Kate, indignant that Bobbie Jo would even question her practice. She hadn't violated any ethics rules and Bobbie Jo knew it.

"It's about the Parkers. I've been helping my son work with clients that aren't around the lake," an annoyed Bobbie Jo said with a whisper.

"If you have a problem with me or my practice, Bobbie Jo, go talk to Sylvia. But I don't need to take any of your supposed 'clients' to build my business," said Kate with a measured and appropriate response to the self-proclaimed queen of high-end real estate. "Why not go back to Lake Oswego and cool off in your algae cesspool?"

"Look at this card, Kate – do you see the 'A' in Atwood? 'A' is first – not 'C.' And, in this case, 'C' stands for 'cunt,'" ranted Bobbie Jo before storming off, knowing that Kate was completely in the right and there was nothing she could do to technically stop her from marketing to unclaimed clients that didn't have some sort of agreement for representation already in place.

After she left, Kate called her friend Brent Chandler to vent about the exchange she had just had with the queen of Portland's high-end real estate.

"How are you doing Brent," asked Kate.

"Katie!" Brent answered. "All is well, how about with you?"

"I just had a fight with the queen bitch," Kate explained, her nerves on end. "Bobbie Jo Atwood confronted me about honing in on what she thinks is her territory."

"Well you don't sound good – let's meet at the R.C. in 30," Brent suggested.

"OK," Kate hesitated on the verge of tears. While she was a strong force in front of Bobbie Jo which was the most important thing, she was shaking from having the confrontation – even if she were absolutely correct.

"She called me a cunt," a still-stunned Kate disclosed as she took off her coat and sat down in the magnificently-decorated upstairs lounge at the Regent that was typically a quiet place even during the cocktail hour. The corner room had a commanding view up the entire park blocks and all club's activity inside and out could be monitored from their table.

"Who?" Brent asked.

"Bobbie Jo," Kate revealed with a shudder. "I can't believe she confronted me about my client's project."

"Back up. What's involved?" Brent inquired.

"It's a literal domino – and I can't be too specific about it to anyone. But, it does have to do with Tess Parker with Bobbie Jo claiming Tess is her client merely because she's known her for years," Kate said as they ordered their cocktails. She favored the club's heavy RegenTini – which was always considered a most generous pour at about seven ounces. After about thirty minutes and two cocktails, she had regained her composure.

"You're just too sensitive, Kate," Brent cautioned as he held her hand. "You knew that every last one of those agents who represent that kind of real estate have legendary egos and horrific selfish personalities when you decided to enter the business. They will do anything to stay on top."

"I have an appointment with Tess tomorrow," Kate revealed, changing gears to establish a plan for attack. "What if Bobbie Jo poisons it?"

"No way," Brent responded. "If the old bitch actually called you, she wants to hear what you have to say – she's curious. If anything, be as honest as you can with Mrs. Parker. My father and her son are good friends and that's something that will help if anything is said."

"Well, it'll be all luck – I don't need Bobbie Jo or her son Chet fucking things up," Kate groaned. "Why don't we go somewhere else for dinner."

"Let's finish up and call Sue Helen for a suggestion. I heard the chef sprinkled meth on a re-do after someone sent back a filet for being well-done," Brent surmised from listening to other members chat in the grille as he motioned for the bartender to deliver the check. "Everything will be all right."

Chapter 6
DISCOVERY
BEGINNING IN 1980

Tucked in the bowels of the United States Capitol's Senate Wing in the ornate Brumidi Corridors was one of two hideaway offices Senator Chambers maintained - a gift from the Foreign Relations Committee chairman to his longtime friend across the aisle. One of the hideaways was very public and was included on tours interns would give to constituents making a pilgrimage to see their government at work, and the other was a private inner sanctum where no one but the Senator and invited guests typically ventured.

During an August recess, there was little for the expanded staff of interns to do in the office – which functioned perfectly for the Senator who leveraged two or three to act as babysitters to his children and Jane's. Electing to stay in Washington to be closer to the family during the break, the Senator used the opportunity to meet with lobbyists to fortify his already well-stocked campaign war chest. While few legitimate challengers could even think about unseating the popular Republican, it was always a reminder that the political tide could turn on a moment's notice. However, with the general ineptitude that the administration of the day had handled the oil and hostage issues, popularity for Republican principles swept through the nation as it prepared for what would be known as one of the most prosperous times for Americans.

With Barbara safely ensconced with Jane in New York on a visit, the Senator was virtually free to participate in his dalliances with his favorite intern, Jacob, who fit the Senator's desired qualifications perfectly. Blond hair, blue eyes, thicker but toned build, slightly cocky, and from a good family of contributors were formulas that excited Malcolm nearly as much as the games he played with them. He'd start them out all the same way – as his driver. This provided the best chance to make a move toward intimacy as no intern would refuse an after-hours visit to a hideaway or his personal office for a cocktail after a long day. Most everyone thought it was the highest honor to even be granted the opportunity to spend an hour with someone who had been elected to represent millions of people by serving in the Senate.

After the third cocktail was always an ideal time for Malcolm to test any of his subjects. With the straight interns, it always took more drinks for the less ambitious ones to learn the drill. The more motivated for success, the easier it would be for the Senator to entice an illicit liaison out of the junior staffer. Jacob turned out to be the oddity, as it took him only one cocktail to straddle the Senator's lap, still clothed, and firmly implant a kiss on the man he idolized – an aggressive Adonis that proved to be ideal in the position.

The liaisons were not necessarily about the sex itself to the young males who had always unilaterally decided to take advantage of the situation that was presented to them over the years. In fact, no one had ever refused status to become the 'favored one' of each intern class as it was an enormous honor, and the other intern peers would never know the actual extent of the closeness that Jacob and others like him shared with the Senator. Sex was a tool that each of them had learned to use as a way of building a close link of companionship with their employer.

Other than the unique power where the Senator would always hold all the keys and the intern none, 'favored one' status could lead to a permanent staff position or a placement of note with a company in Oregon or some agency or department in Washington that would somehow benefit Malcolm's political machine. Alumni of the 'favored one' club peppered each of the Senator's offices and forged deep bonds between executives and policymakers who had a 'sixth sense' for identifying each other as such merely by asking what position they held as intern. The perceived perversion of homosexual activity had attained the unusual honor of acceptability, which was a testimony to the Senator's adept political spin of how he sold the activity to each impressionable selection.

Jacob was indeed his favorite to date in eight years of playing what could be construed as a dangerous game. That was perhaps what the Senator appreciated the most about it – that it was a game where someone could find out. But why would the perfectly-designed system ever fail? Those several months of togetherness between Jacob and Malcolm were special times, where the sex became more of an expression of deep friendship, understanding, and coping with the unbearable political stress rather than a typical power play that would be the guess of some armchair psychologist who didn't comprehend the situation.

One afternoon, the Senator and Jacob had finished a meeting with the French Ambassador and both felt the day should end with quality time together in the secret hideaway. Equipped with television, fireplace, sofa, bar, and lavatory, what else could they need to set the scene for a playful late afternoon in the Capitol building? Passionately kissing against the door after entering the comfortable office, they quickly disrobed to reveal perfectly proportioned nude forms. The 38 year old Malcolm and his 21 year old muse were perfectly suited together and they jumped onto the sofa with a couple of bourbon rocks cocktails and began to devour each other.

After resolution, the Senator dressed and left first as to not raise any suspicion, even in the near-empty Capitol, leaving Jacob alone – still nude and watching television. Upon hearing something move in the closet, he investigated.

"Joey!" Jacob yelled, concealing his naked body in front of the Senator's teen-aged nephew. "What the fuck are you doing here?"

"The question should be what you and my uncle were doing in here," Joey retorted with an unexpected and mature line of questioning, having watched the entire episode through the slats in the door.

Jacob was speechless and couldn't answer the question, paralyzed with fright that the nephew might tell someone about what he'd seen.

"I liked it," Joey announced. "Can you teach me to do the same things with him?"

Jacob could hardly believe the twelve year old was proposing that he teach him how to seduce his uncle.

"Are you sure you really want that?" Jacob asked. "Isn't that kinda fucked up?"

"I know more than you think – I've been looking at porn for years," Joey responded, thinking of how easy it was in the past to conceal graphic material from his absentee parents and old nanny guardians. "But I've never had anyone to play with."

Joey instinctively took his clothes off and joined Jacob on the sofa. As they embraced, Jacob began his instruction with a kiss.

"It's all in the lips," Jacob demonstrated, leaning in to Joey and knowing the boy had him by the balls to request most anything. "He loves to kiss."

After an hour of simply holding each other and talking, Jacob reminded Joey of the time.

During the drive home, Joey asked Jacob about how he decided to come to Washington and they discussed the Senator's office and the variety of interns who had helped watch him. The trip to McLean was amusing as each recounted their opinions of the staff.

Arriving at the house, Senator Chambers was with his children Seth and Natalie in the front yard.

"Look who I found wandering around at the Capitol," Jacob said as Joey leapt from the car.

"Joey!" The Senator scolded. "We thought you were somewhere in the neighborhood!"

"I went to the space museum this afternoon and then we went to the office," Joey said, referencing another intern's duty in watching him. Deciding to taunt his uncle with a burning question, "Where were you, Uncle Malcolm?"

"In the Capitol, and then home," Malcolm replied, throwing the ball to his daughter.

Joey smiled and shot Jacob a knowing look as he ran inside, waving goodbye.

Over the next several months, Jacob proved to be a suitable teacher for Joey – imparting wisdom that he had honed as an aggressive personality in transforming the boy into a skilled sexual predator. As his confidence grew, Joey knew it was now his opportunity to seduce his uncle. Jacob had of course been hired on as a staff assistant and encouraged the boy whom he considered a highly-virile youth to make an attempt to cement himself into history as one of the "favored."

Jane's grief was healed by her strong work ethic and it comforted her to complete each of the projects that had been started by Clay prior to his death. While she talked to her son weekly on the telephone, she was particularly pleased that he could experience a normal family environment in Washington. As an impressionable young man, she felt a structured lifestyle would benefit Joey during his own grieving process. Barbara came to New York monthly to visit Jane as part of her own therapy to temporarily escape from the insanity that the Washington lifestyle promoted, and Joey felt that during her absence was an ideal time to work on strengthening his bond with his uncle.

Seth and Natalie had vibrant social lives as the children of a United States Senator. Thanks to Jane covering the tuition, both were actively involved in the Georgetown Prep School and that meant they were rarely home most weekdays until eight or nine in the evening. Weekends were also special because they often held sleepovers at a variety of classmate homes. While they loved their cousin Joey, he wasn't particularly interested in such activities, preferring the company of the interns and the Senator himself.

The Christmas recess provided the best opportunity for Joey to test his newly-acquired sexual drive to entice his elder relative. One Friday evening was absolutely perfect, as both the Senator and Joey were alone in the residence and would be for the balance of the evening. Joey had strategically asked his uncle to watch a movie with him and order take-out, which set the stage for both of them being on the sofa in the comfortable family room. Not uncommon to cuddle with a relative, the Senator thought nothing of putting his arm around his nephew whom he thought was a fragile youth.

"I think I may be different," Joey offered out of the blue as they were watching the movie.

"Different how?" Malcolm asked his nephew, with his arm around him.

"I think I love Jacob," Joey replied, knowing how the response would unnerve his uncle and make him particularly uncomfortable.

"Jacob the intern?" the startled Senator asked, thinking of his own special moments with him.

"Yes, but I'm not sure," Joey replied with a smile. "He taught me how to do what you do with him."

The Senator got up from the sofa with a racing heart, thinking that his impenetrable world had just been attacked.

"I don't know what you mean," Malcolm hesitated, experiencing sweaty palms and sitting back down. "What did he tell you?"

"He didn't need to tell me anything. I was hiding in the closet of the hide-away that afternoon when Jacob brought me home," Joey explained.

Burying his head in his hands, the Senator didn't have an immediate response for his nephew.

"I didn't mean for anyone to see that," Malcolm said with tears streaming down his face.

"Don't worry, I don't want to tell anyone if you help me," Joey said, extending a glimmer of hope to the Senator.

"What do you want then?" Malcolm asked.

"To do the things Jacob did with you," Joey revealed, nuzzling closer to his uncle.

"You can't be serious," Malcolm pleaded. "I'm your uncle!"

"You wouldn't want me to tell mom or Aunt Barbara about what you used to do to me when I was younger?" Joey asked, making up a story as the Senator had never touched Joey as a boy and far preferred the fully developed young men that his senior staff helped cultivate. "Not to mention all your boys on staff."

"No! Please, don't tell anyone!" Malcolm pleaded on his knees in front of Joey.

"Then I think you know how it starts," Joey declared, taking off his pants to reveal a growing erection.

The unwilling Senator's ace had been trumped by a 14-year-old who had cunningly tricked him into initiating a sexual dynamic between them. As the taboo liaison began, Joey did not himself realize the extraordinary test that awaited him as a result of playing with a fiery variety of incestuous lust. He mistakenly thought he could transform his uncle into a substitute for fatherly love. His jealousy of interns, staff, and his cousins would consume him daily when not in the presence of the Senator. Sparred on by the toils of his mental deficiencies, the poor boy seethed internally. He had incorrectly associated sex with a parental relationship because of the closeness he originally witnessed when viewing the Senator with Jacob that first time. Since Clay was hardly ever at home before his death, Malcolm was a replacement as the senior male family figure whom he desperately wanted to have a loving connection with. The manufactured intimacy proved to satisfy him in the short term, but in the end it would destroy his ability to reasonably associate with anyone as he himself had eliminated the boundaries of acceptability.

That evening began what would become a torrid year-long affair between them. As the liaisons grew with intensity and an uncommon heat of passion, Joey began to realize that between the money and his uncanny ability to effortlessly achieve his goals – however sick – that there may be hope to change as what he came to understand he had been a major disappointment to his mother. While the intimate times with his uncle were scattered throughout the year, it inspired a strength that had not previously been a part of his character.

⊰⊱

Jane almost collapsed when her son asked her if he could attend a boarding school, but she was elated that he chose Jefferson Lewis Academy so he could perhaps get to know some of her peer's children who also attended there. She curiously wondered what kind of cosmic shift could have accomplished a turnaround for her mentally-touched son, but was so excited at the prospect that she almost danced with a maid in the hall of the penthouse after she granted her son permission to attend.

"Malcolm," Jane gleefully prodded as she called her brother in Washington. "What have you done with my son?"

The Senator sat down in shock in his office. "What do you mean, Janey?"

"He's been absolutely vibrant since returning home from Washington!" she explained. "He wants to attend boarding school!"

"He did get to know some interns, maybe that shaped his idea of success," Malcolm pondered, knowing that the prospects of sexual antics were behind the desire to abandon the guarded cloister of Jane's penthouse.

"Well, thank you!" Jane exclaimed. "Now, how's your campaign account shaping up?"

"Slow start, but it's nice to have the team in control of fund raising," Malcolm said.

"I'll fix that!" she said with a smile. "I just had Nancy write out a check for $100,000 to the RNC. Use it as you like."

"Thanks big sister," Malcolm sheepishly replied, relieved that she had not been calling about any other issue. "Have a good day, and congratulations on Joey."

While Jane herself had been offered the Secretary of Energy cabinet post by Reagan to complement the elite detail of billionaires that had been asked to serve as a reward for their staunch support of their friend, she couldn't fathom leaving her company or her city. The 1980's ushered in untold prosperity to her as Torero developed new tools to help an international client base as consumption of energy soared.

Electing to shuttle Joey to the Jefferson Lewis campus herself in the chauffeured Bentley, she was excited for the next chapter to present itself in what could be described as an existence where the stars were somehow finally aligning to bring her peace. Waving goodbye to the boy, she prepared to write her annual letter to the shareholders during the five-hour journey home to the city.

Chapter 7
FALLING IN LINE
2010

O ver the next month, everything seemed to go according to plan. Kate's clandestine meetings with individual homeowners had been successful and all properties were scheduled to close at nearly the same time so recordings at the county wouldn't signify some unusual shift in the fabric of neighborhood ownership. One looking in on situation might have estimated heavy speculation for development, but no one could have assessed the magnitude of the project that was about to unfold.

Since Jane was paying near-premium prices for each parcel, owners were quick to agree to sales. Those that were thought to be hard sells experienced several mysterious household problems prior to receiving a call or letter from Kate. The Karletis family's unfortunate infestation of bedbugs caused them to tent the entire house and heat the problem away before selling while the Hornbeck's cook quit after seeing five cockroaches in the kitchen one afternoon. Kate would then swoop in with a magic safety line in the form of a sales agreement to rid each owner of the burdensome problem property with an aggressive pricing offer.

After making a call to Calvin McManus, she visited his home with an earnest money agreement already prepared. After a 30-minute tour of the house that occurred mostly on her back both on the bed and billiards table with the attractive-yet-married Calvin who was nearly the same age, she had a signed contract and he had the task of informing his family that night at dinner that he had sold their home and that Kate would help his wife with house hunting for the family due to the relatively speedy closing timeline.

"Hello, I have an appointment with Mrs. Parker," Kate announced as her car pulled up and she rang in the call box at the gate of the enormous estate.

Without an acknowledgment, the gates swung open and Kate drove through the manicured grounds where the grass looked like a perpetual golf green to the beautiful Colonial mansion.

After hearing the doorbell ringing, Betty paused and then answered the door as Tess Parker's senior liaison to guests.

"Welcome," greeted Betty. "Mrs. Parker is expecting you in the drawing room."

"Thank you," Kate said. "The home is absolutely lovely."

"We hear that a lot," Betty nodded and smiled as she led Kate to Tess, who was waiting sitting at her desk.

"Mrs. Parker," Kate greeted. "An honor to meet you."

"Leave us," Tess dismissively ordered Betty, who closed the pocket doors to the room. "Ms. Carerra, I'm an old woman. I've outlasted almost all of my friends and some of my family. At my age, I don't know how I would feel about leaving my home of 80 years. Why does your client want this particular property?"

"The buyer would like to be close to their family, and this property is a one-of-a-kind," Kate explained.

"No shit," uttered Tess, not surprising Kate because her research had proven correct about Tess' love of profanities. "People have been after this parcel of land for the last 50 or more years. Leo Codman once offered me anything I wanted, but I certainly wasn't about to sell to him so everyone could say I helped turn this part of the West Hills into the Jewish Alps."

"Well, you wouldn't have that problem with this buyer, Mrs. Parker," Kate counseled.

"Who is it?" Tess pushed.

"You know I can't reveal that, Mrs. Parker," Kate shared. "But I think you'll find the proposal to be generous."

"I don't need generosity, Ms. Carerra," chided Tess. "But, what I would like is to get away from this family of mine and my self-indulgent staff. Did you know that until this morning this place looked like an absolute pig sty."

"I certainly wasn't implying the need for generosity – and I cannot believe that anyone could qualify this residence in such a way – you must have a fine staff," Kate said.

"I did the qualifying!" pronounced Tess with a burst of energy. "And, I almost fired all of them in the process. If I get my way, I still might be able to."

"Well, what would you like," Kate said in an unconventional twist to presenting an offer.

"You tell me," Tess countered.

"Your home should sell for around $7 million," Kate explained.

"That's all? I would have thought at least $14," Tess hinted, indicating little interest.

"There may be some middle ground," Kate conceded. "However, I'd need to have a starting place."

"I called Bobbie Jo Atwood – she doesn't even know who you are," said Tess, preparing to take down her opponent.

"She's also in my office, but I'm not surprised she doesn't choose to recognize my name," explained Kate. "When you have that big of an ego you don't pretend to have any courtesy."

"Touché, Ms. Carerra, I appreciate your forthright honesty," Tess uttered. "That's something that we don't get much of around here."

"Thank you," said Kate.

"Bobbie Jo's son is taking over her business since she's spending more and more time down in the desert," Tess explained. "That little upstart new-money jackass seems to think he can get me $19 million," she continued with a bold-faced lie having not spoken directly to Bobbie Jo or her son about pricing.

"You'd be dead before that happened, Mrs. Parker," Kate frankly stated. "I've come here with a buyer in hand – and an amount that would represent one of the record prices for home sales in the state."

"That you have. I'll counter at $12. See what your buyer has to say about that," announced Tess. "Come here tomorrow at noon to discuss."

With that, Tess rang a bell and Betty opened the doors and Tess gestured for Kate's exit.

"Thank you Mrs. Parker," expressed Kate with gracious enthusiasm.

"Tomorrow at noon," Tess reiterated as Kate was escorted from the room.

"Betty, get me a Scotch and then close the doors. I need to rest," Tess said, weary from the unusual activity during the last several days.

"Mrs. Parker, phone call," Betty returned with Tess' signature Red Label Scotch rocks and announced that she had a call waiting.

"Yes?" groused Tess in an irritated voice, picking up the call from her lounge chair from a vintage telephone with several buttons signifying different lines.

"Is this the bitch?" asked the caller.

"What?" a shocked Tess replied.

"This is that other bitch, the one from Palm Beach," the caller countered.

"Clark, is that you?" Tess cried out with both a smile and expression of surprise. After Clark moved to Florida to be with his partner Andre in the 1970's, the old friends had only seen each other occasionally but had talked at least twice yearly via telephone.

"Yes, honey," howled Clark, Tess' oldest living friend and a well-known antique dealer who was the only human on earth she ever had a soft spot for. "She's in for the weekend and she's in love with a stunning young Brazilian model."

"You're visiting Portland? What happened to Andre?" Tess asked.

"A real tragedy, just three months ago," Clark explained. "He was found dead out on the beach with his pants down in back of one of our closest lady friends' homes who had just died. I should have called to tell you! I had nothing to do with it, but I suspect that he was already drunk and high, but probably helped to the beach by a family member of the same lady who died in hopes he'd wash out to sea."

"Oh my," shrieked Tess. "There are rumors that I did the same thing to some of George's lovers."

They both chuckled as they recounted the series of mistresses and male prostitutes her husband had seen over the years and the exploits of Andre trying to con old ladies up and down the Florida coastline out of bits and pieces of their fortunes. Despite a laundry list of deficiencies including his homosexuality that went along with an endless string of depraved sexual encounters, Tess allowed Clark immunity from any disparaging remarks.

"They found a hermit crab in his ass," laughed Clark. "I can just imagine the family catching him in the house after she died – most probably trying to pilfer some jewelry before they got there. So typical."

"At least you weren't involved," Tess lamented. "So why the visit?"

"We're up here looking at Twila Weinstein's estate," Clark explained.

"That old Jew?" Tess balked. "What did she have worth buying?"

"Well, that 'old Jew' had a surprisingly good eye for the decorative arts," explained Clark. "Some beautiful 18th Century French pieces that are perfect for my showroom."

"Interesting," noted Tess, looking at her watch. "You know that I am in the middle of cocktail hour."

"You mean cocktail hours! Are you still boozing it up in the afternoons?" joked Clark.

"I don't booze up, I self-medicate," Tess laughed. "If you lived here, you'd self-medicate too. Care to come over?"

"Honey, we can't tonight if we want to finish inventory over here at the temple," Clark chuckled, poking fun at Tess' numerous lifelong prejudices and knowing to steer clear of the estate after Tess' fourth round of Scotch or be subject to her own battering ram of choice words.

"I have an appointment tomorrow at noon," Tess noted. "What about lunch?"

"That's a distinct possibility. I'm calling because I wanted to give you something to think about ... why not consider a trip and come down to Florida for a visit. There's not much keeping you in Portland," suggested Clark.

"At 105?" Tess moaned. "There's no way I could make any trip!"

"Bullshit, honey. You're as healthy as can be," Clark said. "You can leave on a little jaunt with us in a couple of days. All you've ever done is complain about your family and staff and how unhappy you are."

"No suitcase packed. No travel items," protested Tess. "I haven't left the city in ten years, except to go down to Gearhart."

"Worth Avenue calls," countered Clark, referencing the stellar shops Palm Beach offered. "If you're going to drink, you might as well do it with us down in a warm climate. No commercial airline needed, I chartered a jet for some of the more valuable things I'm taking back to the store! Plus, I think you'd love Felipe."

"Tempting, let me think about it. Come visit tomorrow right at noon," Tess suggested. "After my appointment which shouldn't take that long, we can head to the Westmont for lunch."

"Oh I haven't been there in years," Clark exclaimed, always having wanted to join the club. "What will they think of you taking a couple of fags to lunch there?"

"No one will say a thing," Tess replied. "At least not in front of me."

"OK, we'll see you tomorrow at noon," said Clark.

The conversation ended and Tess turned on the nightly news and began her journey to sleep by ringing for her next Scotch.

"Good morning," Kate spoke into to the ubiquitous call box at the gate of Tess' estate. "This is Kate Carerra for Mrs. Parker."

Again, without a reply, the gates opened and Kate drove toward the home, marveling again during her approach at the magnificent grounds that were kept up by four full-time gardeners.

The door opened and a somber Betty greeted her.

"She's in the Drawing Room," Betty pointed without expression, pointing Kate toward the room where Tess was located. "Show yourself in."

Kate walked in to see Tess dressed perfectly in her signature style, a St. John knit suit in cobalt blue with an array of blue topaz and diamond jewelry selections.

"Mrs. Parker," Kate greeted Tess.

"Ms. Carerra," Tess trumpeted with an extra burst of energy. "Coffee?"

"No thank you," Kate replied.

As they exchanged pleasantries, the doorbell rang again which put a smile on Tess' face.

"Are you expecting someone else?" Kate asked.

"Yes, in fact," Tess smirked.

Betty opened the Drawing Room doors to reveal two additional guests – Clark and the much-younger Felipe – both looking magnificent in their custom tailored suits and Gucci loafers, a signature of Clark's dress at all times, even at the beach or near the swimming pool.

"Gentlemen, come in," greeted Tess.

"Tess, this is Felipe," Clark introduced his new lover with the vast age difference as Kate looked puzzled as to why these additional visitors had been invited to their meeting.

"Charmed," Tess said, extending her hand to receive a kiss. "And I'd like to present Ms. Carerra."

"Ms. Carerra, Tess keeps beautiful company," Clark puffed.

"Please call me Kate. Pleased to make your acquaintance," Kate shook both of their hands.

"These two are friends from Florida – my oldest friend Clark and his new friend Felipe," Tess explained to Kate, purposely failing to mention their relationship as if it didn't even exist. "Ms. Carerra and her mystery client have made an offer to purchase the house yesterday, Clark."

"This house?" Clark said with amazement that Tess would even consider an offer after such a grand tenure at the summit of Portland's most prestigious hilltop.

"Yes, $7 million. What do you think about that?" Tess queried. "Another agent seems to think he can get $19 million, but I thought $12 was more realistic."

"I'm out of the market, so I'm certainly in no position to comment," Clark said, holding Felipe's hand.

"Did you care for a refreshment?" Tess asked as she rang for Betty.

"What did you have in mind?" Clark smiled.

"Since we're going to the Westmont for lunch, I think we all need doubles," Tess answered.

Betty arrived in the Drawing Room and opened the doors.

"Four double Scotch rocks, Betty," Tess ordered.

"I shouldn't have one," Kate contended. "It's before five."

"Bullshit," chided Tess. "If you want to do business with me, you'll have a drink."

Tess motioned for Betty to make haste in bringing the drinks to the group.

"Where would you go if you left here?" Clark inquired.

"I never thought I'd be interested, but Mary Overton just turned 97 and decided to move out of her place and into the penthouse in a building that was just built downtown . . . all the amenities and a built-in staff for care if you need it. And, the entire West Hills has moved there," Tess explained. "It costs at least $3 million a year to run this place, and I can't ever get ahead – nothing is ever done correctly around here unless I supervise it personally. I sometimes feel imprisoned, even as the warden."

Betty returned and served the drinks right as Tess was commenting on the quality of service at her home, which caused her to roll her eyes slightly as she left the room.

"See. Always disrespect," Tess whispered, speaking of Betty's irreverent attitude after she had left the room.

Kate thought as the discussion unfolded that Tess may just agree to sell her property to her undisclosed buyer. But, she wanted to psychologically cement the deal based on her discussions with Tess and what she knew from chatter in the community.

"It must be hard to think about leaving all the memories of family here," Kate noted. "They probably treasure this home as much as you do."

"What they treasure is their monthly allowances and are eagerly awaiting my death," Tess professed without emotion. "What did your client have to say about my counter offer?"

"The client was admittedly taken aback as it was nearly double," Kate explained. "However, they were willing to negotiate and propose a compromise at $8.95 million. Plus, I've agreed to waive half my fee that is typically paid out of the sale proceeds."

"Not bad. $11 million," Tess suggested, matter-of-factly.

"The client has given me narrow authority. I can't go any higher than $10 million," Kate stated.

"Then let's make a winner out of everyone at $9.99," Tess effortlessly announced with the modern flair of a much younger woman as she delighted at the prospect of leaving the house. "Write it up!"

"I can't believe you just agreed to sell," Clark mused as Felipe sat quietly absorbing the atmosphere.

"Well, you're here to witness the momentous occasion," Tess replied, turning to Kate. "Ms. Carerra, would you care to go to the study to prepare your paperwork?"

"That's very kind Mrs. Parker, it'll only take a few minutes," Kate said as Tess rang for Betty to escort her to the study.

"Since you're both here as witnesses, neither my family nor my staff can conspire to say I wasn't mentally fit to conduct business – not that any judge in this town would ever cross me, I know all their secrets," Tess confidently joked. "Now, a few signatures and we can go to lunch. You'll both be my beautiful 'bookends.'"

Kate re-appeared minutes later for some signatures on paperwork, and then Tess and her guests made their way to the grand mansion's motor court where Tess' Cadillac was waiting to transport them to the Westmont Country Club. Tess got in the car first, followed by Felipe. Kate again shook hands with Clark and drew near.

"Thank you, Clark," Kate whispered. "Mother said she hopes that Twila's collection was worth the trip."

"Young lady, it was indeed. Thank you, and please give her my best." Clark softly said as he got in the car.

As Kate watched the sleek black vehicle drive away, she was undoubtedly overwhelmed with joy in accomplishing her mission of securing all 13 parcels for Jane's construction project, but showed little emotion standing in a spot that would be near the middle of the vast new estate, got in her car, and immediately went to Jane's hotel to execute the paperwork.

"I've enjoyed a gamble over the years," Jane confided to Kate as they met at her suite in the Parkway. "But I've never entrusted an entire project to anyone and had it executed so flawlessly. Almost effortlessly."

"I've always wanted to show my capabilities – and it's all about the opportunity," Kate triumphantly made known. "Thank you."

"Where are we in terms of budget," Jane asked. "You put the $20 million in escrow for pay out. Is there anything left?"

"Exactly $10,000," Kate replied. "What would you like me to do with it?"

"Keep it," Jane said. "I know you discounted your commission in half to get the job done, you deserve it."

"Are you sure?" questioned the surprised Kate.

"Yes, of course," Jane chided. "Go buy yourself some color for that wardrobe!"

"I'll need signatures on all pages here, and initials there," Kate explained the last of the 13 sale agreements.

"Do you think her kids will come after her for the sale?" Jane asked.

"Not likely. She had the two friends there – one of whom she'll never know is also a friend of my family's for longer than he's known her," Kate revealed.

"So you tipped the scale?" Jane wondered.

"Of course I did, and the plane is still available to transport them to Florida in a day or two?" Kate asked.

"Yes, well worth a little jet fuel to get the job done – and an excellent idea," Jane complimented Kate.

"I think it's best in the long term for both parties. Now that these are signed, all we're waiting for is title. Thirty days max on all parcels," Kate explained.

"Well-done. Very resourceful. Do you remember when I said that hopefully you'd be the first to know about the new place?" Jane asked.

"I heard something like that," Kate smiled and remembered.

"Because I want you to help me build it," Jane said, as Kate gathered her paperwork.

"Build it? I have no experience!" Kate retorted.

"When I was introduced to the pit vipers of society in New York more than fifty years ago, I didn't have any experience either." Jane explained. "You have the right attitude and I have the resources."

"What about my job?" Kate asked.

"Your job?" Jane exclaimed. "You've outgrown that silly job of chasing after insipid buyers and sellers in this dinky market. I want you to work for me."

"Doing what?" Kate said with an exasperated quizzical look.

"I'm sure it will evolve into several things," Jane said, thinking about the unusual assortment of redwood trees around the property. "For now, chief of staff for the construction of 'Redcliff.'" Jane always got a kick out of privately naming her residence, with 'Elmwood Terrace' being the pet name for her New York Penthouse as a tribute to the vast number of American Elm trees in Central Park.

"Redcliff," Kate pondered. "Very appropriate."

"Now, it's time to finalize everything so we can start!" Jane announced.

"I'll go finish the process, there's only some additional forms that need signatures from our LLC managers," Kate offered as she got up to go to the title office. "See you tomorrow."

"How did you two meet each other," Tess asked during the trip across the river to the Westmont.

"Felipe, do you want to field that question?" Clark laughed.

"Are you sure you want me to?" Felipe answered in his very defined Brazilian accent.

"I'm waiting," Tess hissed.

"It's a little embarrassing," started Felipe. "At a sauna in Rio."

"Well hell, I thought it would be something more scandalous than that," laughed Tess. "After all, you're dating one of the country's grandest whores of the last five or more decades."

Felipe laughed hysterically at Tess' honest appraisal.

"I've never been a whore, honey," Clark protested.

"And that's why I love you," Felipe agreed.

"Being a whore, or the money," Clark curiously asked Tess, bringing Felipe closer.

"It's not about being a whore," Tess emphasized without pause, putting Felipe on notice that she knew the endgame. "Now, play it up as much as you want in there. I'd love to give this crowd some good material to talk about. Felipe, make sure to give me a big kiss right after you give Clark one in the dining room."

"You're on," Felipe confirmed.

"You haven't changed, Tess," Clark said as they made their final approach to the club's main entrance.

"Welcome Mrs. Parker, it's been some time," the Westmont's Dining Room hostess greeted the unorthodox delegation at the entry.

"Something with a view, Carolyn," Tess nearly demanded a window table overlooking the river, never having made reservations for the luncheon.

As they were seated, nearly every individual in the dining room turned their head at one point to see whom Tess Parker had brought on a rare public appearance to lunch.

"Look at them all," Tess observed, scanning the dining room. "So curious about what business we have together. So provincial and so boring."

"So have you given more thought to Florida?" asked Clark, changing the subject.

"Actually yes," Tess responded with a smile. "I need a place to go, don't I? Where are you again in Palm Beach?"

"On Park Avenue, not far from The Breakers," answered Clark.

"I used to love The Breakers as a child," reminisced Tess, remembering family jaunts to Florida each winter.

"Because of Madoff, real estate is going for cheap cheap cheap all the way down the coast. We got ours for a little over $1 million," advised Clark. "You can live in that new place Mary moved into up here during the summer, and buy in Florida for the winter season. Something on the beach should cost around $4 million."

"When are you leaving?" Tess asked. "I think the Westmont has reciprocity with something down there."

"We're headed out tomorrow! We have to load up some final things from Twila's this afternoon and evening. Do you think you can be ready?" Clark said.

"You make it hard to say no. Now Felipe, give Clark a kiss and then one for me," Tess whispered and emphasized, "remember, dramatic."

Felipe leaned in for a kiss on the lips with Clark, and then immediately turned and kissed Tess causing a collective yet muffled gasp at several tables within the dining room that delighted Tess beyond words. The Westmont had long since abandoned traditional prejudices having allowed a limited number of blacks and Jews to join, but was steadfast in its unwritten ban against accepting homosexual members, even though several notoriously closeted queens had re-discovered their youthful dalliances and deep urges for the same sex after their wives died, and were restricted to the anonymous appreciation when the glory holes of the city's adult arcades allowed them to achieve an all-too-seldom release.

Over the next two hours, several senior statesmen of the club came up to greet Tess, including old family friends who just stopped by the table to catch a glimpse of her well-groomed male guests at opposite ends of the age spectrum.

As they dined, the conversation turned to transitions.

"What will you tell your staff?" asked Clark.

"I don't intend to say a thing," Tess responded. "I'll keep Betty on, but I don't owe anyone an explanation."

"And your family?" Felipe asked.

Turning to Clark and patting Felipe's shoulder, Tess declared, "So naïve."

"She can't stand them," Clark explained and then turned to Tess, "I'm amazed you're still alive!"

"Barely," Tess said. "You should have seen the expression on the face of my grandson's wife when I accused her of being a lesbian at dinner a few months back."

"Priceless!" Clark laughed. "Is she a dyke?"

"Nearly," proclaimed Tess loudly. "She's put on enough weight to qualify! She got so fat my grandson started cheating on her with his secretary and now she wants a divorce." Not paying attention to the fact that her grandson and his wife were members of the Westmont, she blatantly used their first names so everyone in the vicinity would know exactly whom she was referencing.

Their giddiness was infectious across the dining room as Tess grew more boisterous with each drink. Prior to heading back to the estate that would only be hers for another 30 days, they ordered another round of Scotch to celebrate the possibilities in Southern Florida.

⤜⟐⤛

After four doubles at the club and one at home before lunch, Tess was well on her way to intoxication and nearly shrieked with laughter all the way home recounting various reactions she had received at the club from other members. Upon arrival, Clark and Felipe had to escort her from the car and hold her up until Betty intercepted her slight frame at the front door.

Prior to entering the house, she spotted the small clay deer that had been placed by the front door that had been given to her by her grandchildren – the only visible tchotchke throughout the grand estate.

"Look at that dog," pointed Tess with a slight slur, laughing. "It doesn't eat, it doesn't sleep, it doesn't poop. It just sits there."

Clark and Felipe shot each other a slight smile and tried not to laugh as Betty opened the door.

"Betty," Tess exclaimed with a slight slur as she fell into her arms. "We have much to talk about in the morning."

Tess wished the men well and the door closed, signifying the end of a typical day at the Parker residence.

※

As the morning sun appeared, Tess made her way into the bathroom for what she called her 'morning purge' – typically a quick vomit to expunge the balance of the previous day's alcohol as she readied herself for her morning routine. The estate's typical buzz greeted her including the daily mowing of the lawn where the path of the mower was rotated daily in a different direction and the sounds of vacuuming whirled throughout the house from the team of housekeepers. Tess demanded that the cleaning take place when she could hear it happening, as she was intoxicated by the impression of cleanliness and the appearance of a staff that was constantly working.

Holding Kate's card, Tess picked up the phone to call.

"Ms. Carerra," Tess sluggishly said.

"Mrs. Parker," Kate responded, "How may I be of assistance?"

"I never feel guilty about a decision I've made, but I do feel compelled to ask a question," Tess murmured. "Some of my staff have been here for 20 years or more – and they are regarded as the finest in the region. I want you to ask the new owner if it would be possible to keep some of them on."

"Mrs. Parker, that's a wonderful idea – how many total?"

"About 10, minus my head girl," Tess counted them on her fingers.

"I will inquire with the buyer and call you back shortly," Kate responded.

"Appreciated. Good-bye," Tess replied.

※

Little did she know that in 30 days her house would be demolished to make way for one of the nation's grandest new estates. Her head was especially 'hung' because the Westmont's doubles were definitely all Scotch. She looked toward the day and pressed the electronic buzzer next to the toilet to signal that Betty could bring her freshly-squeezed orange juice and grapefruit.

Betty arrived and quietly put the tray down on the table in the room. The phone rang and Betty answered, telling Tess that Kate Carerra requested a word with her.

"Mrs. Parker, the new owner is delighted and I will personally work to accommodate everyone who wishes to consider staying with the estate."

"Thank you. I'm taking a short trip tomorrow so I will have my secretary write a letter with directions for you, " Tess offered.

"Very much appreciated," Kate noted. "Good-bye."

><>>—

"Betty – we're moving," Tess announced.

"What?" Betty gasped.

"I sold the house yesterday," Tess explained.

"So you did do it," Betty said. "I knew it when you came home yesterday."

"Well, it doesn't affect you if you want to come along," Tess noted. "Don't say a word – we'll be leaving for Florida tomorrow."

"As you wish," Betty said, knowing she had little opportunity to disagree considering her age and potential retirement in several years. "But I will say that I think you owe the people here something after their years of service."

"That's what that phone call was about," snapped Tess. "It's all been worked out, even if it is none of your business. Now, go and get packed – I don't want to be in the city when ownership transfers."

><>>—

The next morning, Clark and Felipe arrived on schedule at 10 a.m. to pick the ladies up. It was the first time Betty had ridden in the backseat with Tess while Felipe drove and Claude navigated their way to the private FBO at Portland's International Airport where Jane's Hawker 4000 Jet that was reserved for the use of her personal executive staff awaited their arrival. No one either cared or acknowledged the gigantic 'T' that was painted on the plane's tail to signify its ownership by a Torrance.

"Are you excited Betty?" Clark asked from the front seat.

"This is definitely a new experience," Betty announced, almost as if she had magically transitioned from maid to peer.

"What will be an experience is getting her drunk on the airplane," Tess laughed.

"But I don't drink," Betty reminded Tess.

"Today you will," Tess promised reinforcing her new desire to transform Betty from a subjugated serf to a member of her closest inner circle as she began her own new lifestyle in Florida.

As the valet moved the boxes and signature luggage inside the aircraft, Tess asked Felipe and Clark to make sure there was a steady supply of Scotch and Champagne on board, as requested. Upon confirmation that both a case of champagne and several bottles of Red Label were indeed available, the flight attendant was given the sign that takeoff was possible.

"Drinks?" asked the flight attendant.

"Of course," Clark bossed. "Four Scotch rocks doubles."

Betty felt uneasy after her years of keeping Tess' household together and now being subjected to her personal social peculiarities that she had previously been able to avoid. It was almost unbearable to watch as Tess, Felipe, and Clark carried on with wild abandon. The eldery passenger had regressed to a youthful spirit as Felipe sang for his meals by entertaining both the old woman and Clark. Betty sipped her Scotch slowly, thinking about her 45-year self-imposed guardianship of Tess, the saddest of souls who had an iron exterior. She flashed that her destiny was indeed in Tess' control, who in turn was under Clark's spell, who was powerless to and transfixed by Felipe's sexual allure.

The dynamic was interesting to observe. While Clark in his own right was a successful antique dealer, his judgment was severely clouded with a near-obsession for sustaining his relationship with Felipe. After years of witnessing similar behavior amongst many of Portland's families, it was certainly evident that Clark, who suffered from slight chemical imbalance that produced severe depression, needed Felipe's strength, care, and doting to make it through even the simplest day of activities. In exchange, a controlling grip overshadowed him that rivaled that of the finest dictator. Felipe's insanely jealous streak having known of Clark's fifty-year tenure as a world-class slut could result in violent mood swings if suspicion of infidelity were evident. The price for companionship was worth it – as both individuals needed each other for completely different reasons but the result was symbiotic and mostly convivial.

The quartet's pleasure was interrupted from time to time by calls from family and friends, wondering what was happening with the major exodus from the property that Jane had just purchased. The excitement of trucks, vans, and moving personnel confused everyone except the staff that was instructed that while their jobs were secure that their new contracts did include strict non-disclosure agreements for them to sign that Kate had shuttled up to Tess' attorney's office, who was managing the transition for her.

Tess was stoic in dealing which each communiqué from Portland, recognizing that even at her age, she was having a delightful time with the new lifestyle that included nearly-unlimited freedom to not be bothered with all the details of running a household and spending time doing what she loved most, cocktailing. Not long after her arrival at the Westmont reciprocal in Palm Beach, Mar-a-Lago, the fabled Marjorie Merriweather Post mansion that Donald Trump had purchased and turned into a private club, she discovered the oceanfront Bistro where the rule was that staff didn't leave until the last member was ready to exit the club for the evening. Set up with a perfect view of the Atlantic Ocean and sumptuous pool, Tess loved the fact that the bartender had learned the trends of the group within only a few visits.

Her daily routine began at approximately 10 a.m. with a coffee and light breakfast on the patio followed by a quick day trip either up to Worth Avenue for shopping or the hour-long trip to the far more extensive Bal Harbour Shops. Scouting for the right move-in ready oceanfront property was also an option, but the group had been terrifically underwhelmed by the excessively garish tastes of some sellers who had attempted to recreate their own waterside versions of Versailles.

Betty loved the scenario since she was in the back while Felipe and Clark bantered back and forth about directions in the front – with everything financed by Tess. As they piled into the Cadillac sedan for their daily journey, there were orders to return no later than 5 p.m. as Barry the Bistro Bartender now knew to reserve their bar chairs for cocktail hour. When Tess descended the staircase each evening with Betty in tow from their penthouse units, they strolled gracefully into the Bistro where their drinks were waiting for them in pre-assigned spots. Four double Scotch rocks, served in Waterford tumblers half-full but tightly packed with ice.

In the new Gucci ensemble that was one of the many new outfits that Tess had purchased for her, Betty wore money quite well and Tess took great pride in showing off her 65-year old muse and gay book ends to what was left in post-Madoff Palm Beach society. Betty wasn't unattractive, but needed some care to develop the chic style that Tess had honed over the years.

"Barry, are you starting to get to know us?" Tess gleefully asked as she approached the bar and saw the drinks waiting.

"Mrs. Parker, it's my job to anticipate everything you could want," Barry responded.

"And you have," Tess agreed as she and Betty sat down at the bar, awaiting the arrival of their 'dates' Clark and Felipe.

"You two make good beards," Clark giggled, sneaking up behind them. "I'll have to take Tess since she's as old as dirt."

"Fuck you," Tess responded as she pointed at the bar stool assigned to Clark. "The 'cock' in the cocktails seems to have just arrived."

Felipe and Betty were typically quiet on either side of Tess and Clark and looked on in a daze as the two friends carried on. Occasionally they'd enter a discussion, but in a way that royalty expected their servants to reverently respond only when spoken to. Normally, Betty and Felipe would find a conversation topic that was suitable for them while Tess and Clark engaged the rest of the members and staff in conversation, sometimes ignoring the others.

Each day repeated itself, only with increasing familiarity between the small group that resulted in a strengthened bond between all four players. The full power of Tess' small fortune was being exercised, which made them popular commodities at the best parties that the ladies of the island, as they were known, threw for any number of special charitable causes at Mar-a-Lago, the Everglades Club, or The Breakers.

"Mother, why did you leave Portland?" Conrad Parker asked over the phone. Tess' surviving son who also served as vice-chairman of the bank his father founded had made a call to the family matriarch to assess her sanity. "We're concerned about your move and your state of mind."

"Listen you little cocksucker," Tess yelled into the phone at her 76-year-old son, "You were a mistake to begin with and I don't have to justify anything to you or anybody else. Why did you call?"

"You know Fred has an offer on the table from World Commerce," Conrad explained matter-of-factly to the belligerent old woman, ignoring his mother's terse rebuke.

"Are you speaking of Frederick 'Not On My Watch' Porter?" asked Tess. "That piss-poor bastard has been trying to sell your father's bank ever since the board promoted him to CEO three years ago. I never liked that man."

Fred Porter, who Conrad had actually championed to be appointed chairman and CEO of National Bank as the unofficial figurehead of the Parker Family voting block of supermajority shares, had been plotting ways to exercise a petty $20 million in options as soon as he had secured his new position to cap a lifetime career there. As one of the last men to have personally worked with Tess' husband, the founder George Parker, his ascent landed him at the plush 53rd floor on which all executives of consequence had their offices. The office included a grand circular staircase down to their own private club that included a restaurant offering sweeping views of the downtown area from the entire 52nd floor.

It was a typical launch pad for a spectacular retirement filled with perks, as one of the bank's former chairmen had even negotiated an office and secretary for life and was perched at the top of the bank's exquisite headquarters tower. Included in Fred's sermons to create shareholder value were cost-cutting techniques that had made a number of the leading companies and individuals in the region flee the institution because of policies which made the price-per-share double, but the long-term client service reputation suffered with little hope of repair.

"Mother – you don't even have an active role in the bank. How would you even know what Fred or any of the management are doing?" asked Conrad.

"I don't," Tess announced. "And that's because you're not the watchdog any of us hoped you'd be to protect the bank or the family's interest. But, I do have smart friends who can see the writing on the wall. People talk."

"And selling is not the best idea when our stock is at an all-time high?" queried Conrad.

"Perhaps so," Tess said. "What does Gloria think?" Putting in a special jibe to her son in referencing his daughter and her granddaughter who was the only other family member to serve in a leadership role within the company.

"She might be on the board," explained Conrad, "But, she's in fucking public relations, mother. She will do what's best for the family's financial position."

"Don't swear at me, Conrad," chastised Tess, fully knowing that the family could not exercise its 25% voting block without her, giving it a virtual majority control of the outstanding share votes through two votes for every one that was owned. "Your precious supermajority vote can't happen without my 16%."

"Be realistic," Conrad requested. "If we don't sell, eventually Fred's practices might create a climate that's not good for any business. Some of our best customers have already left the private bank, but the share price should be fine for at least six months until after the next two quarters. Now is the time."

"I understand," Tess answered. "But, I don't want to be managed. I'll go along with this if you give me your implicit promise that not you nor anyone else will interfere with my decision to move to Florida – in writing and signed by you and your sisters. I deserve some happiness at my age."

"If you agree to this it'll mean $100 million for the family, not to mention $200 million to you," Conrad responded. "No one will bother you again if it plays out that way."

"On that note - done deal," Tess sharply conceded. "Should I come back for the board meeting?"

"No, I'll have the paperwork for the tender overnighted to you," Conrad replied. "Just make sure to sign correctly and have Lucinda's staff at the bank notarize it for you down there."

"I never thought we'd actually consider this, Conrad," Tess lamented to her ungrateful and talentless son who by virtue of his family tree was in a position to partially control a significant voting block of the bank's shares. "Your father spent his life building that bank and it seems everything has changed."

"It's a way for us to finally separate and get what we should have gotten years ago," Conrad said. "You should be happy."

"I suppose it is. How long will it take?" Tess asked.

"At most, a month – even with a near-majority of the voting block, the shareholders and board have to vote," Conrad explained.

"Have Lucinda wire the money to my sweep account, and have her call before she does it," Tess ordered. "Good-bye."

As she hung up, she experienced the first tear in many years – perhaps an involuntary reaction to the carelessness with which her family acted with relation to any of the beloved institutions her ancestors had created – the paper and the bank – with not an inkling of how to respect and nurture the stewardship responsibly to pass it in tact for generations to come.

"Betty, please come here," Tess ordered in a weak voice.

Betty rushed into the room as Tess sat on her bed.

"Is everything all right?" Betty asked.

"No, and yes," Tess replied. "Just a little dizzy."

"Do you think it's the cancer?" Betty inquired.

"That's between us," Tess censured as she looked up with a tear in her eye.

Betty rushed to the bed to give Tess a hug that seemed like a natural instinct after 45 years of first-hand contact with her employer.

Tess wept on Betty's shoulder for what seemed to be forever – and Betty allowed her to vent a life's frustrations that stemmed from a century of tortured existence.

As she regained her composure, she apologized to Betty for the out-of-character eruption.

"I was supposed to see a specialist down here from a referral in Portland that had been arranged before we left," Tess recalled. "But now I just want to see the sale of the bank through, and then I feel I can just die. What else is there to live for now that everything's been destroyed."

"Die?" Betty wept. "What would I do without you?"

"Live!" Tess replied emphatically. "The doctor said five months and that was six months ago. I can already feel it taking over and I'm at peace with that."

Betty ran from the room in tears and searched for Felipe and Clark, who had already made their way to the Bistro Bar.

"What's wrong honey?" Clark asked.

"Tess," Betty sobbed as they exited the bar onto the patio overlooking the beach and ocean. "We never told anyone. The cancer is starting to take over."

"Oh honey," Clark comforted. "You knew something would happen eventually at her age."

"But not this way," Betty shrieked as she buried her head in Clark's chest.

"It's hard, I know. Even if you don't like her," Clark laughed.

They both started to chuckle and Betty regained her composure.

"I'm so sorry," Betty apologized, wiping the tears away from her face. "I've just never let it out."

"Well, go get ready and bring her down here," Clark ordered as he pointed at the penthouse. "You'll feel better knowing we all have given her some of the best times of her life – including tonight, tomorrow night, and the next month or more."

⟶⟵

Tess went out on the balcony at her oceanfront penthouse feeling dejected from the result of her phone exchange with her son and coming to terms with her own journey toward death. In order to finally have peace, she was about to sign away the control she'd had over her family since her husband passed away. It wasn't necessarily that she was concerned if they had the money, but that there was no pretense that her son showed, not even a remote sign of being concerned about her other than for the money itself. Her tough exterior shell had been pierced at the realization that she was completely alone and unloved, even if she were blessed with the resources to have virtually anything she desired.

"Peter, this is Tess Parker," said the voice as Peter Harris sat on speaker phone in the corner office overlooking the dusk of Portland's skyline as the senior partner at one of Portland's largest law firms. He had inherited Tess Parker as a client from his father, and bristled every time he received a phone call from the old bitch.

"Mrs. Parker," Peter said. "What a surprise!"

"Dispense with the pleasantries, Peter," Tess suggested. "I'm on a mission."

"Apologies, Mrs. Parker," Peter said with remorse. "What can I do for you?"

"It's been decided that the bank is being sold," Tess explained. "The family will get theirs, which means they need nothing of mine."

"Just like the house, then?" Peter asked. "Everything transitioned to the new owner without question, just so you know."

"Conrad called," Tess fumed with displeasure merely having to mention her son's name. "I'll exercise my vote for the family, and the bank will sell. And then, there's total separation."

"And that's what everyone wants?" Peter pressured.

"Apparently so," Tess responded trying to hold back more tears. "Therefore, the trusts need to be re-written. 57% to Clark Johnson – and if he isn't alive then his share to Betty Gaston, 3% to Betty in her own right; and, 40% equally to the Museum, Medical School, and Church."

"And you're sure about this?" Peter asked.

"Peter! Have I ever issued an instruction I'm not sure about?" Tess asked in a highly-agitated voice.

"Understood," Peter acquiesced.

"How soon can it be executed?" Tess demanded.

"As soon as I write it," Peter said.

"When you're done, send it to Lucinda down here at the bank's Palm Beach office," Tess ordered. "And, I'll send it back with witnesses in tow."

Situated on Flagler Drive with a stunning view of The Breakers, Lucinda Montgomery's office was a monument to success for her rise in becoming the first female regional president for wealth management at National Bank's private bank. And, personally handling the financial and legal affairs of the wife of the bank's founder was an exceptional honor for her. Peter Harris had done what he promised to do and sent the revised trust document to Lucinda with explicit instructions on how Tess needed to sign. She was to come alone to the office, and therefore had asked Felipe to drive her across the bridge to sign the documents of what everyone thought was for the sale of the bank. Also an attorney, Lucinda was barred from ever discussing the trusts with anyone, including Tess' son Conrad.

"Ms. Montgomery," Tess said upon entering Lucinda's top-floor office, "I understand you have some documents for me."

"Welcome to Palm Beach," Lucinda greeted, shaking Tess' feeble hand. "Here they are – shall we sit over here at the table?"

Lucinda executed the meeting with flawless grace as the preeminent professional who was trusted up and down the East Coast to manage the wealth of families with assets far greater than those of Tess'.

"We have witnesses – just a moment," the banker explained as she went to the door and called in two secretaries. "Ladies, this is the wife of our bank's founder – Mrs. Parker."

Tess rarely ate up attention but with these particular unfamiliar people she was aglow as the ladies showered her with attention when Lucinda showed them where their signatures were required.

"I didn't know anything like this could happen so quickly," Tess proclaimed.

"Peter made it easy for us Mrs. Parker," Lucinda reinforced. "If I need anything further, you're at Mar-a-Lago?"

"Yes, dear," noted Tess, with uncharacteristic kindness. "Be sure to get those back to Peter as soon as possible."

"Absolutely, they'll be overnighted to him," Lucinda explained as Tess walked to the elevator bank. "Enjoy the rest of your stay here."

<hr>

Tess descended the stairs of the penthouse to find Betty sitting on the sofa.

"Don't we have somewhere to be?" a cheery Tess asked.

"I suppose so. I'm sorry again about earlier," Betty sighed.

"Honey, it's natural. Even in the most difficult situations," Tess assured. "Now, let's get down to the lounge."

As they crossed the patio to the Bistro Bar, the two gentlemen looked especially handsome that evening as Tess gave both Clark and Felipe a hug before sitting at her appointed location where her drink had begun to show signs of condensation due to lack of attention.

"OK. Enough of the somber mood," Tess interjected to the normally talkative foursome as she raised her glass of Scotch. "Barry, bring us some Cristal – we're celebrating!"

<hr>

A month passed and Tess' health gradually deteriorated which required her to move to a main floor suite. Betty began to push her in a wheelchair to the appointed bar location which had transitioned to sitting at a table. Her already-thin body began to deteriorate to the point where Betty asked the club to recommend an in-room visit from a local physician.

Determining only a matter of weeks left, the physician suggested a hospice program for Tess as a matter of comfort in her final stages of life as she ate less and less but kept up a rigorous daily diet of Scotch. Methadone provided some normalcy to her daily routine while morphine was used as a supplement for pain management as the cancer devoured her organs.

Alone one Friday afternoon in the penthouse, a very-weak Tess rang for Betty who appeared before the skeletal figure within seconds.

"Before I go, I want to let you know something," Tess put forth in a weak voice. "Call down and see if Clark and Felipe can join us here."

"Barry, are the boys in the bar?" Betty asked via the phone.

"Yes, I see them at your table," Barry replied.

"Please ask them to join us here in the room," Betty requested.

"Tess – Mrs. Parker," Betty corrected herself. "They're on the way."

"Good," a weak Tess said with a smile. "You've been so good to me for so long."

"You know it isn't just a job to me," Betty indicated, eyes welled with tears.

"I know," Tess whispered. "I need to tell you something before they get here. You're one of us."

"I know I am," Betty responded. "This has been the time of my life and I appreciate everything you've done."

"No, not just that," Tess suggested, filled with emotion. "You're George's."

"What do you mean?" asked Betty.

"His child," Tess weakly revealed. "He and your mother had an affair."

"I can't believe this," Betty gasped, shocked with amazement. "How could it be, and how couldn't you ever have told me?"

"To keep you close, he negotiated with me that you'd always have security and a job. We made sure you always had anything you needed, and in exchange your mother was silent," Tess explained.

"For all these years I was his daughter and you never said anything, even after mother passed away?" Betty angrily said. "God, you really are a complete bitch."

"I'm so sorry," Tess responded with a faint voice. "I've tried to make amends. But, the real reward lies ahead."

"What on earth could replace 45 years of not knowing the truth and putting up with you?" Betty breathlessly demanded.

"Six million dollars for you – I changed the trusts so you could take care of Clark who will receive most of it, and the charities will all receive the same. If Clark hadn't lived, you'd get most of it," Tess explained, nearly at her last breath.

"That's not enough! I'm done serving people," Betty said with a wicked smile as she brought the morphine dropper up filled with 40 mL to squirt into Tess' gum which would provide a quick absorption. "Now, just go to sleep while the devil's servants tear your soul apart on a long and lonely trip to hell."

Immediately after administering the lethal dose to Tess, Clark and Felipe arrived inside the suite.

"She's almost gone," Betty whispered of the already-lifeless body. "The oxygen levels are low. She wanted us to sing to her."

As the three encircled Tess' bed, Betty led the refrains of song that sounded more like cries from a band of coyotes serenading a dead leader that marked an end to one of the most colorful existences that either coast had ever seen. The lifeless corpse was finally at peace, blood from her veins gone to show the perfect skin in her hands.

⟶━⟵

Clark was inconsolable and knelt next to Tess' bed weeping. Betty motioned for Felipe to join her briefly in the Penthouse's living room to get some time alone with him.

As they entered the living room, Betty whispered, "I know you don't love him," in reference to Clark. "But the money is nice despite the price – isn't it?"

A confused Felipe didn't know what to say.

"If he dies before the beneficiaries are revealed, I get most of the estate rather than the pittance she already promised – that's over $100 million," Betty quietly told Felipe, having secretly listened in on Tess' conversation with her son about liquidation of the bank stock as well as the discussion with her attorney about the trusts. "He's had a good life, but 80 is old. I know you must have some coke at home and I'm sure he takes Viagra – take him for a ride tonight and make it his last."

"I don't know," Felipe said with trepidation. "What if someone finds out?"

"He's 80 for chrissake, Felipe," Betty retorted. "It's worth $10 million to you in Grand Cayman. It'd be an easy sell to the police – old, sex, health problems, broken heart over Tess."

"$20 million," Felipe negotiated with a mischievous grin.

"Done," Betty whispered as she signaled for him to go in and begin his work to coax Clark home for one final voyage of lovemaking.

They returned to the room to see Clark still holding Tess' hand, sobbing as they approached him. Betty pushed him closer to Clark in the process.

"I suppose I should call the front desk to summon the medical examiner," Betty said with a tear. "Why don't you two go home and get some rest?"

"Excellent idea," Felipe said with a knowing glance in Betty's direction. "Clark, you need some sleep."

A quiet Clark got up from beside the bed, gave the old dead bitch a kiss on the cheek, and both of them departed the room to return to their home just a few miles north.

"What a life," Clark admitted on the drive home. "She was the last of her kind."

"I'm beginning to understand that," Felipe noted on the quiet trip up Ocean Drive, thinking about how to over-task Clark's heart to a point where he couldn't survive the exertion of sex. He had always dreamt of freedom – which he thought would come in the form of a small monetary grant of no more than $1 million upon Clark's eventual death, but had never dreamed that he would be in control of a $20 million fortune awarded to him by the maid-turned-lady. It all was in his hands to appropriately execute the plan, and he was motivated primarily by what the money could offer, even though he did occasionally enjoy Clark's company.

"Take a shower," Felipe suggested to Clark as they walked in the front door of their tasteful yet modest home. "You need to completely relax tonight."

As Clark began to strip in the closet and proceeded to the bathroom for a peaceful shower, Felipe began to ready supplies for what he hoped would be the last time he'd have to submit to Clark for sex. In an Oriental vase, he found a stash of cocaine fresh from an artist they had visited in Miami Beach. The freezer contained a fresh case of unopened bottles of popper inhalants, while the nightstand's contents included the daily supply of Viagra which could ignite a savage response if all the supplies were mixed during one session as Clark had already dutifully taken in the morning to be ready for Felipe's sometimes-impromptu advances.

Felipe stripped and carefully selected a revealing jockstrap to excite Clark as soon as he entered the bedroom, and chose a provocative position in which to lay himself out as an offering for his much-older companion and caretaker. With candles lighted, the allure of the young chiseled form on the bed was captivating. Not yet done drying off, a still-wet and nude Clark entered the bedroom, Felipe feigning sleep despite his deliberate positioning.

Without saying a word, Clark's lust took over and his tanned body slithered up toward Felipe's face to kiss him. Noticing the mirror with three long and ample coke lines, Clark bent over to snort the first, lifting the mirror to Felipe's nose to inhale the second. Their hearts began to race, bodies entangled as Felipe used every skill he'd learned in Rio's saunas to mesmerize Clark in an effort to experience absolute rapture. Despite the intensity of the cocaine, Felipe was determined to get his lover to also snort the poppers. While Clark knew they were dangerous with his elderly heart, the sharp twinge of anal sex was eased by the relaxing and euphoric high of the nitrites that made his body dance atop Felipe.

Forgetting that the combination could be lethal, Clark's wild abandon was apparent as he gestured for the mirror containing third and final coke line that Felipe had cut for their enjoyment. A light-headed Clark rocked back and forth on Felipe's anchor and his eyes rolled back to expose only the whites – a sure sign that orgasm was eminent. Their heart rates had attempted to escalate, but the drugs in various forms created a circus ring of physical responses that the younger heart of the two was far better prepared to respond to.

As Clark's entire body tightened, the old man grasped his chest and fell off the bed and hit the floor on his head, pleading for assistance as Felipe watched from his box seat for the performance atop the massive four-post bed.

"Help me," Clark begged, reaching toward the now-towering Felipe.

"Not a chance, old man," Felipe responded, peering down from the bed smiling. "I know what's happening, and you can just stay there for a few minutes while your heart decides how quickly it's going to shut down."

"What? Help me!" Clark pleaded in a weak voice.

"Why? And still need you when I'm 35 or 40?" Felipe responded, getting up to go pee. "I had hoped to already have found someone much younger and a hell of a lot richer," Felipe yelled from the bathroom, not realizing that Clark had located a cordless phone and had begun to dial for help.

Clark had succeeded in dialing 9-1-1 as Felipe returned to the bedroom. Snatching the phone away from Clark, Felipe was the first to talk to the dispatcher.

"Yes, we need help," Felipe said in a manufactured frantic voice. "I think my partner had a heart attack." After some exchange, Felipe hung up the phone and began to taunt Clark. "You should be lucky that Good Samaritan is just across the bridge, maybe they can revive you."

As they waited for the ambulance to arrive, Felipe went to the closet to put on a show-stopping outfit for the hospital in case a doctor was somehow attractive enough to interest him. Clark had passed out and had not been breathing for several minutes when the doorbell finally rang. Felipe answered, again meriting an Oscar-winning performance for distress, and rushed the paramedics to Clark's side on the floor where he had positioned him after the fall.

"What happened?" one very-attractive male paramedic asked.

"He likes drugs," Felipe said, acting particularly forlorn about Clark's proclivities during sex. "I've warned him countless times that this could happen."

As the paramedics pumped atropine deep into Clark's veins and inserted a tube down his throat to begin CPR, the body was unable to respond. Felipe's eyes filled with tears as the contingent of paramedics hovered over what could now be considered a corpse rather than someone they could possibly save.

"I'm so sorry, but there's nothing else we can do," the paramedic apologetically said after about 15 minutes of diligent effort. "We'll have to call the medical examiner to determine the cause of death."

As the last of the contingent to leave, Felipe tearfully embraced the paramedic and brought him close to feel a now-obvious erection in his pants. They smiled at each other and Felipe said, "Come back after your shift's over." The two kissed briefly as he exited and Felipe was then alone with Clark's body. While it had been covered, a curious Felipe removed the blanket to carefully inspect how they had left the breathing tube in his throat and the I-V's in his leg and arm – standard practice when paramedics are summoned to prove they used all possible means to save their patient.

About an hour had passed when the doorbell rang again and Felipe invited the two gentlemen from the Palm Beach County Medical Examiner's office into the house, bringing them to the body that had since been covered up.

"Sorry we're so late," one of the men apologized as he removed the breathing tube and I-V's. "Busy night out there."

"I'm sure," Felipe said, "We had a friend pass tonight as well down at Mar-a-Lago."

"Really," the other man asked. "Old woman?"

"Yes, she and my partner were very close friends," Felipe explained.

"How did it happen here?" the first man asked.

"He must have been feeling lonely, that's the only time he brings his drugs out," Felipe said, again with tears streaming down his face. "And now, this is the result."

"We're very sorry, sir," they both said as they hoisted Clark's body on the gurney to transport to the coroner to analyze. Little did Felipe or Betty know that Tess' and Clark's bodies would be situated next to each other in the autopsy room. "If you need to, please call the county's counseling line – it's open 24 hours and they are very experienced in dealing with a loss."

"Thank you," Felipe said as he closed the door, thinking of how he'd spend his time before the paramedic returned to engage in what he hoped would be some great sex before meeting Betty for breakfast at Mar-a-Lago.

⤜⭑⤛

It wasn't unusual for Tess or Betty to never answer the phone in their comfortable bungalow on the water, so Felipe just progressed the short distance down Ocean Road, the same route Clark and Felipe took just the evening before upon leaving after Tess' death. By that time, both Clark and Felipe were known quantities at Mar-a-Lago and had run of the place because of their association with their monied benefactor. Felipe parked the giant Cadillac and strutted toward the tunnel that led toward the oceanfront villas, pool, and bistro bar. At ten in the morning, he expected a leisurely breakfast filled with some requisite tears to appropriately showcase emotion for his loss and for Betty's.

He arrived at the suite and knocked, expecting Betty to cheerfully greet him and partake in what were considered the best breakfast in Palm Beach at the waterfront Bistro. After several minutes, he decided to go to the Bistro and check to see if Betty was already waiting there for him. Upon entering the restaurant, he asked the morning bartender if he had seen Betty. After the initial condolences about Tess' death, the bartender said he'd seen her depart early in the morning – having completely checked out of the club hotel.

Going back to the car, he pondered a course of action. Did she use him?

Was she grief-stricken? What would he use for money now that both Clark and Tess were gone? Who would manage Clark's gallery? At 30, his days of whoring were numbered and the boundless questions ate at him as he thought about how alone he really was – especially without Betty to give some basic guidance in the absence of their keepers. Since he did remember Tess' banker having driven her to the office for what he didn't know was a change in her trust documents, he got in the car and departed for the office on Flagler to investigate Betty's sudden disappearance.

——————

"She did call," Ms. Montgomery advised as the distraught Felipe sat at her desk.

"Where did she say she was going?" Felipe asked.

"Mr. Santamaria," Lucinda said, "You know I can't talk to you about where our clients choose to go."

"Please, I have no one else," Felipe begged.

"Mrs. Parker's maid is all you have?" Lucinda questioned.

"Yes, the four of us were like a family," Felipe explained.

"Well, you do know the Parkers are from Oregon," she suggested in an effort to move Felipe out of her office. "Now, I really do need to get back to work."

Taking the cue from her comment, Felipe got up, thanked the banker, and went home to search for some cash that Clark may have left around the house so he could purchase a plane ticket to Portland.

Chapter 8
THE HOUSE
2011

Kate had made sure that city permitting went smoothly by making Jane a contributor to the commissioner-in-charge of the planning bureau's campaign fund in addition to secretly slipping $100 bills into the hands of inspectors who came to review the progress on the mammoth property. With so much construction on the horizon, a special team had been assigned by the city to make weekly visits to the jobsite to ensure that all plans were executed correctly.

As there were no direct neighbors since the property faced the small canyon to one side and a roadway on the other, reasonable planning objections could only be made about the scale of the gatehouse which was 1600 square feet on its own, the gates themselves, and design issues based on submitted plans for the areas surrounding the property's front wall. Zoning regulations were actually in favor of Jane, and the design team placed each of the three salon guest homes on a separate tax lot and a variance was granted to build a gated community that was for all purposes occupied by only one person.

While Kate was the lead project manager, Jane had also flown out Frank Pembrook who had managed the 10-year 'progressive remodel' of her penthouse to corral construction workers during the very tight schedule that had been imposed to be ready in time for July, when the good weather was at its peak in the Pacific Northwest. Frank managed the labor and actual physical building process while Kate was in charge of the overall budget and more personal choices of design that had been selected for the project.

⸺◈⸺

"Just because we want to complete this job by June doesn't mean we would ever cut corners," Frank said as the construction team assembled. "As many of us know, Mrs. Torrance is extremely generous, and everything here in the process from now until completion is incentive-based. Quality is rewarded first and foremost, followed by speed."

There were experts in all realms of construction present to make sure that the property was built to ideal specification for Jane. Many of them had worked on the penthouse project with Frank before, and knew the meticulous detail that went into appropriately completing a project for a discerning client.

"This is Kate," Frank introduced, motioning to the statuesque form in the corner. "She knows the city, the inspectors, and virtually everything we'd want to know about the property. She will also be here daily in a project management role and will need to sign off on all expenses."

The craftsmen were used to the best working environments and coveted their roles as guardians of some of New York and Newport's finest mansions from the Gilded Age. The house was a streamlined modern structure but all of the other buildings as well as the magnificent collection of water features required the highest competency for their complexity in design.

"Thank you and welcome to your first West Coast project for Mrs. Torrance," Kate greeted the group. "Frank and I will be here every day to answer questions, and if you have additional ideas on the functionality of your project, don't hesitate to bring them to our attention."

With that, the team went to work in a quest to create a stunning vision of perfection. A blend between the hidden enclave designed to augment privacy for the Gates family in Medina and the ostentatious display of the Spelling's grand manor in Holmby Hills, the residence would merge with its natural surroundings but also humble any guest that passed through its gates.

"Kate," Jane said in a call from New York not long after the project had begun. "How are things going with Frank?"

"They're just completing excavation," Kate reported. "Foundations should start sometime next week."

"Good to hear," Jane said. "Barbara is in New York with me for the next month, we're going to begin the process of reviewing every last thing in this place – 50 years of 'stuff.'"

"Do you need me to come back and help?" asked Kate.

"No. I need you right where you are," Jane maintained. "If we're going to get everything completed on time, it needs your attention to detail."

"OK, but if you need anything," Kate added.

"Don't worry, we'll get it done," Jane interrupted. "Now there's another matter to discuss. I decided to move our family office as well."

"New city and new home, and now new office?" Kate asked.

"Yes, only some of the staff will need to get up early for when the market opens," Jane explained. "I'll have Betsy email a spec list to you and perhaps you can use some of your commercial contacts to secure office space."

"On it," Kate responded. "Tell her to call me if she has any other requirements and I'll begin looking tomorrow."

"Thanks," Jane said. "Now, make sure Frank is doing his job." Jane hung up the phone and Kate went back to work discussing process with Frank.

⸺⸺

Like clockwork the next morning, Jane's prudent New York Executive Assistant at Torero, Betsy Faircloth, sent a lengthy email to Kate with relatively specific instructions for the requirements of Jane's new family office location.

> *Good Morning Kate,*
>
> *Mrs. Torrance (JT) has asked me to provide you with some initial documentation and information about how to organize the new office in Portland. This should assist you in locating the best possible office space based on the following parameters. Enclosed are detailed PDF's with this summary:*
>
> *View: Make sure JT has a corner office and has a view of water or a large fountain.*
>
> *Style: JT prefers contemporary architecture and a building constructed after 1980, preferably with a restaurant located within that is open for both lunch and dinner and has catering services. The office should not be above the 15th floor and should have ample in-building parking for all staff and guests (30 spaces).*
>
> *Facilities should include full kitchen and secure archival space.*

Personal Logistics: JT's office must include a conference area and private restroom.

Staffing: The following staff will be joining you in the office upon completion:

Chief of Staff, in close proximity to JT (your office)

Personal Lobby and Library area with work space for JT's personal secretary

Carlton West, Executive Vice President and General Counsel (Private Office)

Seth Chambers, Senior Vice President & Corporate Liaison (Private Office)

The following positions will be hired in Portland:
Assistants (2)

Omar Safdar, Senior Vice President and Chief Financial Officer (Private Office)

Melissa Benson, Controller (Private Office)

Helena Ellis, Chief Investment Officer (Private Office)

The following positions will be hired in Portland:

AR/AP/Payroll Clerk

Assistants (2)

Bill Derendo, Senior Vice President, Community and Government Affairs (Private Office)

JT is currently in process of evaluating the community affairs portfolio and foundation. The following physical offices will be needed in addition to Mr. Derendo's in anticipation of hiring:

Executive Director, Foundation (Private Office)
Program Officer, Foundation
Communications Officer, Family Office

Assistant/Office Receptionist

Conference: Board Room capable of seating 25 and two smaller conference room spaces.

Size: Maximum size should be 10,000 square feet with a lease rate of no more than $29 per square foot.

You will be responsible for the office build out after JT's interior architect and designer Adrian Quinnell and Art Advisor Pierre Moreau visit you next week – details on their trip to follow.

After they return to New York City and determine the final design, Torero's technical staff will be dispatched to wire the office during the build-out and will also deploy equipment.

All individuals listed will need relocation services and each has been instructed to individually email you with their preferences so you can begin the process for them. The desired move-in month is July.

Again, feel free to call or email me if I can provide any additional guidance or answer questions.

Betsy

"What on earth ever convinced her to want to move to Portland," Adrian asked Pierre as the Torero jet was about to land in the city.

"Family," Pierre said with a deep French accent. "Just think of it as job security."

"I know, but it's so far off the landscape," Adrian noted.

Jane's collection had been fostered for the past 16 years under the guidance of a dashing young French national Pierre Moreau, who held the distinction of being the youngest worldwide chairman of the modern and impressionist art department in the history of Duckler London, the European auction house that was consistently the home to many of the art world's legendary and record-breaking sales. Pierre had developed an acute sense of Jane's personality, knowing her from the time when he was a young new talent force joining the firm where he first lent an advisory voice to her diverse menagerie of artistic tastes at age 23.

Adrian had been trained from a very young age to develop her interest in architecture and design as the only child of New York's most notable

architect Andrew Vincent Quinnell. She had attended private boarding schools her entire life as her mother had died when she was five. The
schooling and the substantive relationships that developed with her peers
were a natural early extension of the business, as her father's clients and
their families would ultimately be routed to her as she waved the wand of
creativity for all things interior. At 37, she was poised to take over the most
sought-after architectural and interior design boutique practice in the state
that exclusively served the top echelon of East Coast Society.

Kate was waiting for Pierre and Adrian in a new black Lexus purchased
for her by the company at the private FBO where Torero now routinely
kept its jets on visits to Portland. When she saw them exiting the jet, she
could have instantly recognized them anywhere never having even met
them. Jane had suggested to Kate that people who are not from the Pacific
Northwest are painfully obvious due to the formality of their appearance.
It had always been easier for someone from the East Coast to blend into
West Coast culture as the Northwest's lifestyle was extraordinarily casual,
but it wasn't so easy the other way. Neither of the pair disappointed. For a
cold January day, Adrian had selected Chanel fur boots, a checkered miniskirt and a jet black leather coat with a fur collar. Pierre was more classically
styled, but the wide lapel of his black cashmere coat, striped suit fabric and
severely pointed shoes looked aggressively European. Their pale skin and
sunglasses made Kate think that she was in the middle of some kitschy vam-
pire novel. Both were near Kate's age.

"Welcome to Portland," Kate called out, waving with a genuine smile.

"Thank you," Pierre responded as he grasped Kate's hand. "Pierre Moreau,
and Adrian Quinnell."

"A pleasure," Kate said as the luggage was placed into her car by the porter. "We have arranged for you to stay right in the middle of downtown at
the Parkway. In fact, the same suite that Mrs. Torrance occupies when she is
in town. You're staying through the end of the week?"

"For both the office and the estate, absolutely," Adrian advised as they
drove away from the jet. "Have you located a suitable office space yet?"

"Yes, and I think it matches all the requirements. The building was built
in 1984, but has a definite edge and looks very contemporary. The lobby has
an attractive atrium and restaurant as well," Kate explained. "The suite we're

looking at on the twelfth floor even has a small roof terrace garden which might be especially interesting to you, Pierre."

"In New York, everything goes straight to 40, 60, 80, or higher without even a consideration to make the building more architecturally interesting," Adrian complained. In addition to being an interior designer, she was also a licensed architect but shunned commercial boxes in favor of more stylized creativity that working with high net-worth clients allowed her to exercise.

"How is the construction on the house coming?" asked Pierre, who had the task of curating the art while Adrian would frame each room to accommodate a number of artistic styles.

"Good, in fact," Kate noted. "Excavation is almost complete and then foundations can go in. With five major buildings, Frank brought in some additional crews to help."

"Do you know of a good place for dinner this evening," Pierre asked, seemingly disinterested in how the house was progressing. "We understand that the cuisine is particularly amazing here."

"Yes it is, I have a couple of options I can show you once we reach the hotel," Kate said. "What are you interested in?"

"Anything that's a Northwest specialty – seafood?" asked Pierre.

"Salmon is what you'd be looking for," corrected Kate. "Shall I make reservations?"

"Please – for three," Pierre suggested. "That is, if you would join us?"

"Only if you'll come to my favorite spot beforehand for cocktails," Kate said with a flirtatious undertone. "It's very close to your hotel. What time?"

"Adrian?" Pierre asked, interrupting her from responding to emails on her iPad.

"Six will be fine, with cocktails and then dinner," Adrian responded, having heard the entire conversation.

"Everything has been taken care of, here are your keycards – Suite 1419," Kate verified. "See you at six tonight, in the lobby."

As they arrived at the hotel, the valet opened the trunk to transport their luggage. Several pedestrians paused to watch Pierre and Adrian enter the hotel, mistaking them for two lost celebrities who might have been transported to the wrong place on accident. Kate drove off to make final preparations for their visits to both the office and home sites the next day, and dutifully made reservations for her visitors.

—◆—

Taking the cue from her guest's apparel selections from the afternoon, Kate also went shopping and arrived back at the hotel at 6 p.m. in an unusually seductive short black lace dress with her Chanel pumps and a cashmere coat. No jewelry was worn except an antique diamond tennis bracelet given to her by her grandmother in an effort to showcase availability to potential suitors she might meet.

While she knew the exact location of their double suite, Kate elected to wait in the lobby for the visitors to materialize, quickly making a call to Frank to make sure that enough work had been completed for Pierre and Adrian to visualize the scale of the estate and placement of the buildings.

As the elevator door opened, Kate knew her wardrobe purchase had been the wise choice. The two designers exited the elevator and seemed to glide to her location across the lobby, again looking stunning in jet black ensembles. Pierre's curly black hair and slight sideburns lent a particularly exotic look to the trio.

"All ready for cocktails and dinner?" Kate asked.

"Most certainly," Pierre responded. "You look stunning."

"As do both of you," Kate said with a smile. "Portland won't know what to do!"

"Where are we headed?" asked the somber Adrian, whose hair was pulled back into a bun while wearing a black pillbox hat that was slightly angled forward to complement her collared Gucci dress.

"Up to the Regent, and then to Liza's," answered Kate.

"What's the Regent?" asked Pierre as they began to walk toward their first destination of the evening.

"You'll love it. Like your University Club, but a bit different," Kate replied in providing a comparison with New York City.

As the cocktail hour wore on, Kate showed them the various rooms and Pierre offered a champagne-induced impromptu assessment of the club's art collection, making it very apparent as he gave extraordinary depth of commentary on each piece that he approved of the variety of works - good exam-

THE HOUSE

ples for a quasi-public collection – but it bore no resemblance to the quality
he typically expected in buying or selling on behalf of the auction house or
the numerous private clients he worked with in building their collections.

"Our reservation at Liza's is at 8. We better go," Kate said.

"Is it close?" Pierre asked, as he drank what was left of his champagne that
had been infused with a drizzle of Crème de Violette.

"Just up a couple of blocks," Kate noted.

As they left the club, Pierre had uncharacteristically let formalities of
meeting a new colleague dissipate and grasped each of the ladies around the
waist during the walk. Adrian's hand lightly brushed against Kate's as both
women put their arms around Pierre's back.

"This is a beautiful city," Pierre admitted with a smile. "And two beautiful
ladies to spend a nice evening with."

While Pierre and Adrian seemed to be the center of attention as they arrived slightly after 8 p.m. at Liza's with Kate, the cultural landscape was vastly
different than New York City. The real benefit of the evening for both guests
was that not one person recognized them. If either of them were spotted dining or enjoying a cocktail at their usual haunts like 'Daniel' or 'A Voce' in New
York, surely numerous clients or the plentiful bastions of social climbers would
vie for attention in the city's perpetual rat race toward reaching the top.

"How long have you worked with Jane," asked Kate, exposing a familiar
tone by referencing Jane's first name to the visitors.

"Mrs. Torrance has worked with my father for years. Always a project
going at her place at The Grand," said Adrian, adding, "She's one of the few
that's kept only one residence – never one in the Hamptons, and nothing
in Palm Beach or Newport."

"This is a departure for her," Pierre suggested. "With family in two cities,
two homes is a novel concept."

"Do you two ever get jealous?" Kate asked.

"Jealous of what?" Adrian responded.

"Not having what they have," Kate mused. "And the freedom..."

"My dear, there is no freedom with what they have. Being part of that
echelon is an enormous responsibility," Pierre explained. "Jane pays everyone
who works with her very well, and for a reason."

111

"She's so obsessive about security," explained Adrian. "Would you want that, or having your son's unsolved murder on your mind each day?"

"Look what we passed earlier today with those protesters," Pierre noted. "Even with all of their bedbugs, rats, and drugs – they're probably happier than anyone in a cage of privilege."

"I never thought of it like that before," Kate pondered. "So why do you do it then?"

"What else would we do?" Pierre asked. "Spending other people's money is fun – especially when you can buy a scribble by Picasso for $1 million."

"We made a test several years ago," Adrian said with a smile. "We needed a little talent, so Pierre found this absolutely drop dead gorgeous art school dropout full of tattoos and piercings with the deepest blue eyes you've ever seen. We made him get naked, splattered paint all over him, and told him to roll around on a canvas."

"Then, I painted a dot in the corner, and heralded him as the newest find of the art world," Pierre announced. "He showered and then we kept experimenting with different colors."

"My favorite was when he was thrusting into the canvas," Adrian laughed.

"That's because you told him you'd take your tits out," Pierre noted.

They both chuckled as Kate sat in disbelief as the two design legends went on.

"What happened with the paintings, or thrustings and rollings?" Kate asked with a grin.

"I told my clients, and Adrian told hers," Pierre continued, "and, at the opening, we had 200 people there and sold it out – each piece at $30,000 a pop - and now that kid is thrusting for some real money at his own studio in Chelsea."

They all laughed at the unbelievable ascension of sometimes-questionable artistic talent.

"See how easy it is – especially with the new money," Adrian counseled. "But, there are definitely those you can't fool."

"And Jane is one of them," Pierre explained. "She is too seasoned and knowledgeable to put up with that shit."

The entrees arrived at the table along with the next bottle of Perrier-Jouët, Adrian's favorite.

"Top marks, Kate," Pierre complimented, sampling the salmon. "Liza might need to open a location in New York."

"Very tender," Adrian noted. "Razor clams are never this good."

The conversation went in many directions as Jane's three lieutenants got to know one another. Kate was deeply impressed by how real Pierre and Adrian were as opposed to her initial reaction to their couturiesque appearance at the airport. As they finished dinner, the waiter appeared to inquire about dessert.

"Just the check," Pierre said. "Now, what's next?"

"Jane is paying," Kate flaunted by pulling out her newly acquired American Express Centurion card from the company. "She insists!"

"No quarrel here," Pierre agreed. "What else is there to do here?"

"It depends on what you want," Kate asked. "There are clubs of all kinds."

"I'm shot," Adrian said. "Come back to the hotel for a night cap in the bar, and then I'm headed to sleep. You two can go out, I need to be fresh for why we're here."

"You've had enough. We'll walk you to the hotel," Pierre scolded with affection, moving his pointed finger across his throat. "But, no night cap."

They walked the short distance back to the hotel, Adrian embraced Pierre and then gave Kate a kiss on the cheek on her way inside.

"Remember why we're here," Adrian reminded Pierre, pointing at her watch.

———

"She's a task master," Kate said as the valet called for a cab.

"She's insufferable, but she is the best at what she does," Pierre said of Adrian as they got in. Pierre had slid in very close to Kate, and locked his arm in hers. "Now, show me the city."

The thrill of having an attractive, intelligent, and internationally-recognized art expert next to her in the cab sent a chill down Kate's spine. She relished the attention she was getting as he asked her to select the next venue.

"What do you think of a really 'raw' place," Kate asked.

"What is that supposed to mean," Pierre questioned.

"It's the closest thing we have to a New York club," Kate explained. "Down in Chinatown, there are tunnels deep under the street from when Portland used to export human capital. People were Shanghai'ed, and there's a club that literally sits right above the water table on an underground canal."

"Adrian will be sorry she missed it. What's the crowd like?" Pierre inquired.

"Everything. Literally in the tunnels you could see anything from someone getting a tattoo to an impromptu orgy," Kate explained. "Adrian would at least have appreciated the spectacular masonry – there are several large rooms where the dance floors are that have huge domes - amazing."

"Let's go," Pierre enthusiastically endorsed.

As Kate instructed the cab driver to take them into the depths of Portland's Chinatown warehouse district, Pierre put his hand on Kate's leg, which she did not attempt to move.

"This doesn't look like a club," Pierre surmised as they approached the abandoned building in the cab.

"Well it is!," Kate announced. "Come on!"

As they walked down a long warehouse hall, Pierre couldn't help but think how creepy the setting was for a nightclub. Perhaps this was a reason why only a select few knew about it. They arrived at a large steel door and Kate put a card through the slot. The door opened to reveal a lobby complete with crystal chandelier and an enormous orchid floral arrangement on a center table while lavender velvet draperies surrounded them on the walls, valanced to the hilt with tassels.

"Welcome," the doorman said. "Go to the canal and a gondola will take you in."

They walked down the stairs until they reached a candlelit cobblestone landing where small boats were waiting in a canal. They boarded the first boat and the boatman shoved off the landing proceeding on a short trip under another building to reach the club.

"This is amazing," Pierre confessed.

"And this is nothing," Kate replied. "This is how they would transport the captured slaves deemed fit enough to work on the high seas to boats waiting at the harbor. It was discovered only a few years back by a friend who is the developer, and he turned it into a membership nightclub – by invitation only."

As they drew near, the familiar pounding of bass became more apparent and they could see a myriad of lights not far off in the tunnel. Pierre brought Kate closer and kissed her on the lips for the few remaining seconds they had left on the boat prior to entering the club itself, his tongue dancing with hers like a pair of mating worms.

"That wasn't expected," said Kate, her nipples rock hard from the experience.

"Maybe not for you, but I've wanted to do it since I saw you in the lobby this evening. You shouldn't be so conservative like this morning," Pierre explained.

As the boat arrived, they were helped out by two additional security personnel and then walked down a short hallway to reveal a spectacle that rivaled Boujis and other famed private nightclubs in major cities. Portland's reputation of having highly-creative niche hospitality venues had lasted nearly a century, and this current iteration was simply the most spectacular yet.

"Kate! Who knew you would come visit this evening? Why didn't you call us?" Kate's college classmate and Regent Club sponsor Brent Chandler said as he approached the couple. "We would have obviously reserved a booth for you."

"I didn't even know I was coming until after we decided to go out after dinner," Kate said. "Brent, I'd like you to meet Pierre Moreau – he's in town working on a project for my client's new home."

"Welcome to the party," Brent greeted Pierre and then turned back to Kate. "Sue Helen just went to the office, but she'll be back. Do you care to join us?"

"I want to show him the club," Kate explained. "But we'll be back in a few minutes."

"This is his club?" questioned Pierre.

"Yes, he and another friend are the developers. They stumbled on this find a few years back when they bought the block, but no one is supposed to really know who owns it," Kate answered.

As they watched nearly 400 guests on the dance floor in the club's rotunda room, Kate dragged Pierre to go explore the various tunnels that encircled the main room.

"Where are we going?" Pierre asked.

"The Midnight Room," Kate explained as they approached the next gathering place.

The lounge's dome opened to what appeared to be the sky, but it was merely a projection that looked identical to the Portland evening skyline.

"We're actually three floors down," Kate added as she pointed upward at the scene. "That's a video."

As they made their way back to the rotunda, activity including a healthy dose of drug use and sex had intensified in the dimly lit tunnels as it got later in the evening which had been populated by exhibitionists and voyeurs eager to feed off each other's energy. They reached Brent's table and Sue Helen Chastwick had returned with a bottle of champagne waiting for the guests.

"Welcome back," Sue Helen said. "Anything interesting out there tonight?"

"Same shit - different night," Kate replied. "This is Pierre. Meet the other half of this place, Sue Helen."

"Pleasure," Pierre kissed Sue Helen's hand.

The next several hours passed as bottles of champagne were consumed and Kate and Pierre spent most of their time intertwined on the dance floor while Brent and Sue Helen stood guard over their maze of sin and indulgence. At about 2 a.m., Kate reminded Pierre about their pending morning appointment and they excused themselves to return to the surface.

"Outstanding night," Kate expressed, kissing Pierre after hailing a cab.

"Agreed," Pierre embraced her. "What would you say to joining me in the room?"

"What about Adrian?" Kate asked.

"She wouldn't notice a thing. She probably went to the room and popped an Ambien. She'll be asleep until at least 6 a.m." Pierre explained.

"OK. But not a word to Jane or anyone about it," warned Kate.

—◆—

The elevator ride to the top floor of the Parkway included Pierre's adept removal of Kate's panties as he stood behind her and teased her pussy and clit with his finger, kissed her neck and ears passionately and pinched her pert nipples that had released themselves from the confining lace dress. Pierre's massive cock with its mushroom head contoured his pant leg and was a surprise to Kate as she felt the budding tool made for breeding pressing against her dress on her ass. The elevator door opened and the two rushed half-naked down the hallway toward the suite's double doors.

The rest of their clothing came off as quickly as possible in the luxurious corner bedroom of the suite and they stood for a split second eyeing each other from each side of the bed.

"This has got to be a joke," Kate hesitated, looking at the European Adonis across from her and wondering how she would negotiate the huge member. "Are you serious?"

"Does this look like a joke to you?" the smiling well-defined and muscular Pierre asked, holding his full erection in his hand shaking it at her playfully.

"Guess not," Kate sarcastically concurred, moving to the center of the bed to meet him.

After briefly kissing, Pierre moved down to worship Kate's already-wet pussy with eel-like lips that gripped its entire perimeter as the tongue rapidly darted in and out, paying special attention to her clitoral altar. All she could see was his curly black hair as his sideburns tickled her thighs while he lapped at her greedy snatch simulating a thirsty Death Valley wayfarer finding a treasured oasis.

She responded by grabbing Pierre and positioning him so they could 69, taking his full penis down her throat and massaging his growing head with her esophagus since she had lost her gag reflex with the alcoholic high. It almost cut off her breathing as it lengthened while he continued to feed on her sweaty ripe mound. After releasing his penis from deep within her throat, the two lovers realized that they could do little more than to fully connect. She propped a pillow under her ass to allow him full access to her blossomed snatch with its puffy unfurled lips, ready to accept him like a sea anemone waiting to entrap its prey.

With one thrust, he locked deep inside her while she wrapped her legs tightly around him. His cockhead responded to her tight vaginal grip by expanding and contracting, a pulsing that signaled extreme excitement and passion between the two lovers. They kissed and romantically coupled for nearly an hour until she knew that she wanted him to release. With that, she decided riding him would allow for the deepest penetration and maximum impact toward fertilization – an unexpressed savage goal for all couples experiencing such a heightened level of coital arousal.

She straddled him and quickly slipped him back inside her, flexing her cunt muscles to suckle and draw him as deep inside as she could. Her control was impressive and in less than a minute, he did not disappoint as he released string after string of cum deep in her, spasming and flexing his ass each time to ensure a deep load as she gave herself an intense release by fiendishly rubbing her clit while rocking back and forth on the still-hard shaft. She collapsed to his side and they fell asleep still connected.

–⊷–

"It's 5 a.m.," Pierre whispered. "Time to get up!"

"Oh shit," Kate clamored looking around at the room. "What happened?"

"Only the best lovemaking I've experienced," Pierre replied. "But, we do have a meeting in three hours and you shouldn't be in your dress from last night."

"Fuck," cried an exasperated Kate. "Does Adrian know?"

"As I said last night, she'll be out for another hour," Pierre gingerly admitted.

"Good, well don't tell her," Kate pleaded. "That's the last thing I need is for Jane to know I fucked her art advisor. I've got to go home and get ready."

"You were wonderful," Pierre expressed as he held his pillow in absence of Kate while smiling at his lover.

"Thank you. I'll see you in three hours!" Kate said as she quickly departed the scene, wondering how she could have let the sly European take control of her sensibilities, even if she hadn't fucked in almost a year.

–⊷–

"How was last night?" Adrian asked as she came into the suite's central salon several hours after Kate's departure.

"After we dropped you off, she took me to an amazing club. What an incredible time!" Pierre said as he poured a cup of coffee.

"The door slamming this morning woke me up from the most beautiful dream. Did you fuck her?" Adrian bluntly asked.

"Of course I fucked her," Pierre proudly announced, disguising his new interest and feelings for Kate. "She needed it. And, her pussy can milk like she's worked on a dairy farm!"

"You are one sick fuck, you know that?" Adrian scolded with disgust, not understanding the level of intimacy that Pierre and Kate had experienced. "She's probably fallen for you now – and what will Jane say?"

"Why didn't you attempt to get her?" Pierre asked. "We could have had her together."

"Are you nuts?" Adrian responded. "What would I have told Liz," referencing a strong commitment with her long-term partner back in New York.

"Well, what do you think I'm going to tell Paige?" said Pierre of his girl-friend who he had intended to marry eventually, calculating the large inheri-tance she would receive from her elderly aunts that would undoubtedly give him the buying power to be a collector in his own right, and not just a dealer or advisor. "Nothing!"

"What if she tells Jane?" Adrian questioned.

"Not a chance," Pierre confidently replied as they walked out the door to meet Kate at the building.

They began a short trip on foot to see the office space Kate had selected for their review, passing through Portland's miniature downtown blocks that were nearly half the size of those in New York.

Kate was waiting in the office building's lobby, still uncomfortable from the unexpected yet amazing experience with Pierre. Upon seeing them enter the building, she stood up to greet her colleagues.

"Good morning!" Kate said as to not raise any suspicion from Adrian.

"And good morning to you," Pierre greeted.

"How was your evening last night?" Adrian asked.

"Quite nice, in fact," Kate answered. "Portland's night life is perhaps more than Pierre thought."

"That's what I understand," Adrian smiled as she thought about Kate and Pierre convulsing with sexual abandon on his bed. They proceeded into the office building's main lobby.

"Up to the 12th Floor," Kate directed the delegation to the elevator.

"Strangely nice building for its age," Adrian noted. "Extremely well cared for."

"What did you expect her to show us?" questioned Pierre, defending his new lover.

"I think you'll be very pleased – now, remember, this space is pre build-out," explained Kate.

They exited the elevator on the 12th floor to discover the suite's double doors as the anchor tenant for that floor. Kate had arrived slightly early to make the space seem particularly desirable. All window blinds were at an exact 45 degree angle, even though she knew the designers would completely gut the place to make room for the building's most private yet highly visible occupant.

"Appealing," Adrian agreed. "This plan almost works out, except for the lobby area which will need significant work. Pierre?"

"Let's take a look at the views and how the sun would hit the office inside," Pierre said, always thinking of appropriate methods to display and protect Jane's art collection. "We can easily eclipse the sun with a window tint."

"Remember, no tints," Adrian reminded Pierre of the directive she had received from Betsy in New York at the behest of Jane herself.

"What does this look down on?" Pierre asked as they all stared out the windows in Jane's potential new office space.

"There's City Hall in front of us, and over there the Northwest Headquarters of the DeSantos Group, a private equity firm which is particularly interested in Portland since it became the West Coast clean energy hub," explained Kate. "Next block down is a monument to earmarks – the Albert Ochs Federal Courthouse – note the huge walls of glass. That's where the judge's chambers are. Prior to retirement of Senator Ochs - who secured the money for the project - the judges would apparently call his office daily with adjustments to the plans for their chambers."

"Such a wealth of information," Adrian suggested.

"It pays to be quiet and keep your ears to the ground," Kate noted.

"OK, Pierre. This – views included – seems fine," Adrian added, turning to Kate. "The only thing I'll want you to check on is our concept for the lobby, which will have a fountain and reflecting pool – Pierre wants to display some sculpture. So weight capacity is important."

"I almost forgot," Kate said, forgetting about the small garden terrace that was part of the suite and leading the designers back to Jane's office. "Let's quickly look at the outside terrace."

Opening the door, the terrace was a small yet desirable downtown oasis that could actually be changed to enhance privacy and keeping the numerous leering eyes from the other buildings surrounding the tower at bay.

"Delightful," Adrian affirmed. "We can use this."

"Clay's statue out here with a fountain would be soothing," Pierre suggested.

"Absolutely – Jane would be amazed," Adrian agreed.

"We endorse," suggested Pierre to Kate. "Adrian, do you want to have the building do measurements and spend the day here tomorrow concepting?"

"That sounds good. Then we'll have more time with the property," Adrian responded.

"I'll draw up the lease papers then," Kate promised. "Do you want a tour of the property now?"

"Yes," they both agreed and nodded. "And email the building floor plans so we can work in the site office then? We'll want to come here to the office several more times just to continue to get a feel," Adrian said.

—◦—

As they approached Greenleaf Drive, both Pierre and Adrian were taken aback by the minimalistic nature of most of the city's finest homes.

"This looks as if we're driving through some working-class neighborhood on Staten Island," Pierre said as they drove through the coveted 'Grid' in Portland Heights.

"One thing Portlanders do very well is hide their money, the Northwest is very understated on the surface," Kate noted. "That is, when they're in Portland. Go on a vacation with them sometime and you'll see the same thing you do from the rest of the world's elite. Jewels, furs, extravagance – just not here."

"Such an odd dichotomy," Adrian pondered. "You'd think they were hiding from something."

"They are," Kate contended. "The liberal establishment here is incredibly powerful and the media is particularly biased. Jane's brother is lucky to even be in office – and if he retires the state may not see another Republican in the Senate from Oregon for years to come."

"Well, New York has its fair share of liberals – but in the end there is a symbiotic relationship where the two extremes do actually need each other," Adrian said.

"Not so much here – especially with organized labor controlling most of the Democratic Party," Kate proclaimed. "And the most peculiar thing about the state is that 33 of 36 total counties are almost exclusively Republican. The sheer population of the Portland area keeps them on their toes with this odd liberal tri-county pocket. These are the limousine liberals."

As they approached the property parcels, Kate gave additional details about the area and some interesting facts to her guests.

"The largest parcel that we acquired was from the granddaughter of one of Portland's wealthiest men, Jack Graden," Kate said. "While her estate was nice, the closest monument to extravagance is the mansion that she grew up in. In fact, her cousin's family still occupies it."

"Honey, I don't know if I'm up for all this," Jane confessed to her sister-in-law Barbara as they prepared to sort through fifty years of living in the penthouse.

"Jane, you have to do it if you're going to move – and the new owner is going to take over soon anyhow," Barbara rallied, building Jane's confidence to get the work done.

"So many memories," Jane whispered with a tear in her eye. "It's like he was just here yesterday."

Thinking of Clay always solicited a strong emotional surge from Jane. Having never gotten to say goodbye due to the sudden nature of his death, she always expected for the door to open and see him walk in.

"I can say I know the feeling," Barbara confided, reminded of her own daughter's death. "It's a complete sense of loss."

"So are you ready to make a dent?" Jane asked.

"Surely! We only have a month together," Barbara noted.

They walked down the hall and approached the other ominous presence that Jane had often felt in the penthouse at the door of Joey's old room.

"Another demon," Jane cringed, throwing up her hands at her son's room. "It hasn't been touched since he graduated from the academy – everything goes except some of his personal effects. You'll need to take that room."

"OK. Where will you be?" Barbara wondered.

"The archives upstairs, and then the closet," Jane said. "Then, at noon let's go have lunch down at the Colony Club."

Jane had joined the Colony Club herself with the help of Clay's mother about three years after her marriage. It was always Jane's reminder of how stupid men could be with their choices of women – an eternal battle to see who could be more proud strutting down Fifth Avenue or dancing at a society ball. Jane had deliberately not played the game as a working partner with her husband, which lent itself to even greater respect by many of the top echelon's senior stateswomen who themselves had been strategic advisors to their husbands and not helpless porcelain dolls who were commissioned as wives for the purposes of breeding and sexual gratification.

Chapter 9
COMPLETED VISION
JULY 2011

"It's more than I expected - stunning," Jane said breathlessly as she entered the front door of her new home, the view of Downtown Portland in sight from the large windows in the grand salon. "This is exactly what I wanted."

Her trio of coordinators flanking her, Jane was like a little girl as she explored the home that she knew well. Her design had formed the fundamental directions for the architects to work with, and the end result was indeed spectacular.

"We made a few risky choices," Pierre explained. "Not often will you see Rembrandt in the same room as a Basquiat."

"It's shocking," Jane knowingly responded. "But Adrian, your choices for everything around them seem to make it work perfectly."

"Thank you, Jane," Adrian graciously accepted. "The team is very proud of what's been accomplished."

After a full tour to each of the guest salons and around the grounds that took over an hour to complete because of the numerous details that each of the tour guides needed to share with Jane, the next stop was the new office just a short drive from the residence in downtown. Pulling up in a Bentley alongside a building in Portland is enough of a spectacle in its own right, but coupled with exceedingly well-dressed individuals with identities concealed behind sunglasses lent itself to something out of a movie script – slightly unreal with onlookers curious about the plausibility of the reality of the situation in such a drably-dressed city.

"This should be interesting – close your eyes," Pierre suggested, moving in to help guide Jane toward the double doors of her new office as they exited the elevator. "OK, now you can look."

Jane opened her eyes to see a vision of Eden. Beyond the thick bullet-proof glass walls and doors stood her family office lobby, replete with reflecting pool in which several fountain jets danced among colorful glass forms from Chihuly's Macchia series that Jane had spied and wisely purchased on a visit to Seattle in the 1990's. The intentional low lights around the perimeter lent distinction to the focal points in the middle of the room with black marble flooring and a streamlined black marble reception desk. Where statuary didn't sit, groups of white orchids in black clay pots stood guard over the serene setting that would leave passersby in the building's elevator lobby wondering what occupied the office sans identifiable logo or sign.

"It's surreal," Jane acknowledged as she explored the lobby. "This represents a complete transformation. A new life."

Kate, Pierre, and Adrian stood by as she touched each piece of furniture, lingering by some paintings that might have made her recall a certain moment when she and Clay had purchased them.

"Are you ready for the best part?" Pierre asked, motioning with an arm to join him for a walk down the hall.

"Everyone has their own separate mini-suite," Adrian explained. "The space promotes privacy but is also open at the same time."

Throughout the office, ceiling tiles had been replaced with built-out coved inlets for indirect lighting. There was no question after seeing the house and walking through the office that Jane was one of the most imaginative yet fickle art collectors in the world, with paintings and sculpture of every conceivable type. She was pleased that only a small portion of the large collection and been selected, as some collectors attempted to display far too much at the same time.

After passing through an additional set of double doors, they entered the inner sanctum. The private lobby and 'wing' as Adrian called it was Jane's personal domain. In addition to a library, board room, and beautiful reception lounge, her corner office commanded a stunning view of the entire city. The requisite view of water that had been originally required was breathtaking. In the shadows looking out into the terrace, Jane had an unsettling glimpse.

"Go out and look at it," Pierre encouraged, nearly pushing Jane out onto the small terrace just outside her new office.

As Jane walked out into the private garden area, the life size bronze statue of her husband Clay looked at directly at her. Modeled after a photo from one of his exploratory missions to the oil fields of Texas, he looked at peace amongst the floral accents and small fountain. She began to weep at the surprising contribution to the office environment. From anywhere in her office she could see the silhouette of her dear late husband, a reassuring image that would bring tranquility to the bustle of business that would greet her in a few short weeks after her team moved in.

"OK, you two," Jane said to Pierre and Adrian, pausing to hold their hands. "Every time I experience something new from you I can't go to pieces."

They both smiled without saying anything as Jane swirled around taking in each accent, art selection, and placement.

"You didn't see the best part," Adrian exclaimed, holding Jane's hand as she directed her to the private powder room. "We installed a salon sink both here and at home so you didn't need to worry about going out in public for an appointment."

"Every detail thought through," Jane delighted. "Now, we have a move to complete."

Adrian and Pierre followed as Kate and Jane walked to the office's main lobby.

"Kate, you deserve credit as well. Go home and pack, let's bring Torero into port," Jane said, referencing her impressive yacht that she would triumphantly travel home on, bringing the majority of her personal belongings on board.

The group left the building with Jane blowing a kiss from her Bentley. Headed back to the hotel, the quartet would then travel to New York on Jane's luxurious jet, 'T-1.'

Arriving at her almost-former apartment building that she had wisely rented back for a year while the new owner was in Argentina on business, Jane and Kate jumped out of the town car and headed into the building.

"It's beautiful," Kate suggested, thinking of no better words for one of the finest addresses in the nation.

"That it is," Jane responded. "But what we just left in Portland was heavenly. That's what I call retirement."

"I don't see you retiring," Kate laughed. "You love your work!"

Arriving at Jane's floor, they proceeded through the single-unit lobby to huge foreboding 12-foot doors.

Jane punched in the code to unlock the doors and announced, "Welcome to Elmwood Terrace."

While impressive, the place was definitely ready to vacate, the darkness had eclipsed the regality of the space. Packed boxes were everywhere, along with art that had not been shipped to the special warehouse which housed the majority of the collection.

"I don't know if I would have left," Kate confessed.

"Dear, look across Central Park to the Dakota – see right there," Jane pointed at the heavily gabled structure. "Every day you'd remember the shock of finding out your child's head had been severed and hung from a hook in his apartment."

"I'm so sorry. That was so insensitive," Kate meekly responded.

"You had no idea," Jane continued. "And, that poor boy in his casket . . . knowing that my angel's head wasn't really connected to his body under the collar of his shirt. No dignity in passing. It makes me want to flee and forget it all right now."

"In an hour, we'll be on board the boat," Kate comforted Jane, trying to change the subject. "That will help."

"I hope so. I don't even know why I came here other than to show you the place. It appears they've taken everything that's going with us already," Jane said.

As they closed the doors and descended to the lobby in the elevator, Jane bid a sweet farewell to her home of 50 years – and with that came a rush of memories including the day her husband carried her across the threshold and told her to 'get busy' on making the place a home; the magical parties thrown for MoMA and The Met; Joey's first day of school which ended in a broken arm for the little boy; waking up to find out the news of her husband's plane crash and her son's murder; and the present, pondering what history the new owners would create in the cherished walls of her home.

"Jane!" Kate shook Jane out of an apparent daze as they reached the lobby.

"I'm sorry," Jane replied. "That was quite an overload of memories. That's the last time I'll ever be there."

As they got in the town car to head for the port, Jane couldn't keep her eyes off the penthouse unit until they were far off in the distance past The Plaza.

———

Approaching the yacht Torero was as impressive as entering the Penthouse. The activity around the yacht with its crew of 25 was notable. The car approached and the ladies paused in front of the vessel.

"This is how to travel," Jane announced to Kate, marveling at the floating mansion she was instrumental in designing.

A tall man approached Jane and said with a distinct English accent, "Ma'am, welcome back. Are you ready for your trip?"

"Yes, Bobby," Jane replied. "I want you to meet my guest for the voyage, Kate Carerra. Bobby Gray, my captain for the last ten years."

"A beauty," Bobby complimented, embarrassing Kate.

"Thank you," Kate replied.

"OK. I am going to my cabin to rest. If I don't see another apartment in New York again, I won't mind," Jane suggested. "Bobby, please get Kate situated and give her a little tour."

"Follow me," the handsome 42-year-old captain instructed Kate. "This yacht was constructed under Mrs. Torrance's direction when I just started with her. It's 203 feet long and can accommodate 40 between guests and crew."

As they ascended the staircase and reached the upper wheelhouse, Bobby noted, "You'll never feel unsafe here while we're out at sea. Each of the crew was formerly in the armed forces, and has been trained in the use of automatic weapons and has a CAR-15 under his or her bed. We keep a portable weapons cache in the boat's armory, including shoulder-launchers for military-issue missiles to defend this floating palace against pirate boats if we're sailing near Africa, Asia, or around South America."

"Amazing that you need that type of security," Kate questioned as she stood before the former officer in the Royal Navy.

"Better to play with the same toys they have. I doubt we'll ever have any problems. But, even Mrs. Torrance can shoot an automatic rifle – I trained her myself," Bobby explained as they walked down a long hall of the yacht's main deck. "That's the penny tour – here's your suite."

"Thank you very much," Kate said. "What's the protocol around here?"

"Anything you want, just dial '0' on the phone and the Chief Steward will assist you," Bobby flirted with a grin. "And sometime on the voyage, maybe we can get to know one another a little better."

Kate smiled sheepishly and closed the door to her suite without saying a word.

————

Taking approximately 21 days from New York City to Portland, Oregon via the Panama Canal, Jane extended the trip to a month so she could visit various ports along the way as it had become one of her favorite voyages to go through the canal and see how different cities had changed over the years. Each stateroom had been packed with boxes of Jane's personal effects but the yacht was so large that Jane and Kate had run of the ship, and it was a nightly tradition for the senior crew of the boat to dine with the two lone passengers. Captain Bobby would retire to his quarters after dinner as the ladies screened the latest movie release or discussed politics of the world – sometimes bitterly disagreeing with each other but always respecting the other's opinion. The result was the beginning of the ladies forging a bond of total trust and reliance upon one another.

On average, every fifth day of the trip provided a new adventure on board for Kate. They stopped in Miami for a lunch appointment made by Helena Ellis to solidify Jane's $100 million private investment in a new joint venture with a newly-created Hollywood studio.

Curaçao's stop meant shopping as Jane showered Kate with a much-needed wardrobe filled with color. At the same time, Jane invited several ladies from New York on board for lunch prior to their own departure on The World, the private residence ship on which some of them had purchased apartments.

Panamanian President Ricardo Martinelli and the country's Energy Secretary Juan Urriola were summoned to cruise on the yacht through the canal so Jane could discuss plans for how Torero would assist the government to exploit its newly-found oil deposits of approximately 900 million barrels.

Jane was always in contact with her New York headquarters office and spent the majority of each morning working on business while Kate used another office on board to coordinate the final details for staffing at the estate and the office. The grueling schedule was not the vacation that either lady had imagined, but the fast pace guaranteed that boredom would never strike, even in the middle of the ocean.

The vessel finally approached the mouth of the Columbia River after careful navigation off the coasts of California and Oregon. The familiar landscape of spectacular Douglas Fir forests and mountains were a departure from East Coast living to the near-foreign native. Anticipation of moving into her new residence had Jane out on deck in one of Oregon's rare moments of sun. The Torero hummed along its path up the river and would dock where it had been built at a private yacht builder in Vancouver, Washington, to avoid the curiosity and media spectacle from a location closer to Portland.

While Jane enjoyed herself, Kate was in a literal frenzy to make sure everything had been completed in time for the new resident. She had organized for the Estate's staff to form an honor guard upon arrival, and the trucks that were to transport the yacht's contents to the home were poised and waiting dockside. With another Bentley having been shipped across country, the chauffeur was prepared for his new duties in Portland, and the office had been populated with Jane's personal staff, awaiting her arrival at the new office in the morning.

As the boat anchored, Jane went down to the yacht's grand salon to get her handbag for the 30-minute trip to the manse high above downtown atop the hill.

One thing Jane executed flawlessly was living a grand lifestyle. Not only did she dream how the property in Portland would lend itself to the experience of pure opulence, it was to become a sprawling homage to the glamour and comfort of the Hollywood Regency tradition. Out of the five acre combined parcel, two of the acres would encase and shield the residence and manicured grounds from the streets while still offering one of the most spectacular views of the Portland skyline.

Never forgetting her son's unsolved murder, the obsessive security Jane demanded was unprecedented in the lush environment. Embedded in the walls surrounding the estate was a special fiber optic intrusion detection system capable of sensing the exact location of a security breach. If an intruder managed to penetrate the estate's wall, a laser fence system provided another guard to alert the residence for lock down. It sat on the inner edge of an eight-foot wide road that was placed immediately inside the wall so security personnel could patrol the property's entire perimeter without interfering with the occupant, similar to the roadway the Annenbergs had installed around their lavish estate Sunnylands in Rancho Mirage. Numerous thermal imaging cameras were placed throughout the estate to monitor activity in areas not used by Jane or her guests.

The gate systems were on par with the best international embassy, the manufacturer having obtained a K8 barrier certification from the Department of State while several sets of automatic retractable bollards were installed in the road if the gates failed to protect the estate from vehicle impact. The final step was to include hidden bullet resistant acrylic screens behind banks of reeds and other green foliage as to not alarm guests of the special security enhancements Jane required as part of construction. The entire system was managed from a special security bunker located in the main gatehouse. All controls were mirrored and placed in a control room within the main residence and could override the entire system with a special code. A team of four security agents worked each shift for 24-hour protection with two located in the main bunker monitoring activity and two on patrol throughout the vast grounds.

Jane had always been fascinated by the pavilion concept for large residences, but having lived so long in New York she hadn't previously had a garden other than the special views of Central Park that her Fifth Avenue penthouse and terrace commanded. She designed the flow of the property to perfectly align with each building where doors met doors, or ran into special coves fitted with fountains or statuary.

A teahouse was to be modeled after the beautiful Chinoiserie structure that sat on the seaside cliffs in Newport, Rhode Island at Marble House – a home owned by friends of Clay that Jane had visited during the summer season not long after she was first married in 1955. It primarily contained Asian artwork and antiquities from the collection that Jane had intended to eventually donate to the Metropolitan Museum of Art that would fill the newly-constructed Torrance Asian Antiquities Galleries with other treasures she had already given. The teahouse was encircled by a small lagoon that was fed by a beautiful falls built out of a rock formation to lend privacy to the space.

Busily preparing for the new owner to arrive, the landscaping team was helping deliver the final artwork selections into the main residence.

"Whatever you do," the head gardener announced to his team as they unloaded some final items from the truck, "don't drop anything!"

Right after the announcement, a crash was heard from the main salon. During the hanging of one key painting, it had slipped and was pierced by a sculpture, ripping through the canvas.

"Oh, no!" cried one housekeeper, rushing into the room concerned for their collective jobs. "How could you do this?"

"It slipped," the gardener replied, clueless as a mere assistant and not knowing the value of the piece or its significance as a choice for one of the stately main rooms.

"Well, quickly bring it to the kitchen before she gets here," the housekeeper instructed, suspecting the lingering spirit of Tess as her former employer had helped unhook the painting and not wanting to ruin Jane's first day at her new residence.

Rushing toward the kitchen, the housekeeper cleared one of the islands off so the wounded artwork could be examined.

"Bonita," the housekeeper screamed. "What should we do? This is probably worth a million dollars!"

"Not to worry," Bonita replied without concern, bringing packing tape out of one of the drawers. As the master surgeon of the kitchen, Bonita had battled far less cooperative ducks, chickens, and squab. Smiling, she applied the tape to the back side of the canvas rip. The gardener, housekeeper, and Bonita then pulled the other side so it evenly lay against the seam. She artfully brushed her fingers over the tape to seal it to the canvas.

Lifting the painting, the gardener looked at it as Bonita noted, "See, no damage. Now go hang it! Quickly!"

The service staff guarded many secrets about the home that still needed major refinements in its security system and timing of lighting. It was the price that Jane would pay for an aggressive timeline to complete the project in her drive to host the party for her brother.

Directly opposite the teahouse at the other end of the view promenade where the edge plunged into a deep ravine that had been cut by a stream through the West Hills thousands of years earlier was a pool salon that maintained the flavor of high-style and splendor from the main residence and would serve as a gathering place for bridge games once Barbara had been able to introduce Jane to more ladies from her Portland 'crowd.' The preferred size for these gatherings was eight, but the ladies would tolerate twelve if additional interest were shown in the weekly game that rotated between several private homes and two or three of the club venues. To transport guests to various areas within the estate, Jane also commissioned several special small utility carts that could hold a capacity of six.

Even in the final days prior to the completion of the home, the landscaping team had prepared a race course throughout the property. One of the specially-designed fountains had been decapitated as one of the utility carts collided into it during a race between construction personnel. Little did anyone know that the poor top third of the fountain was held together with glue and would not be visible, even to Jane's construction supervisor Frank who had left the week before to visit New York.

A tennis salon was constructed to host parties for viewing intimate celebrity tournaments that Jane had previously organized at friend's homes in the Hamptons. At night, the tennis court shimmered with thousands of optic fibers that had been installed before the concrete was poured. The illusion of a glittering sea of lights could lull guests to full relaxation in a salt-water soaking pool adjacent to the court.

Each of the outbuildings was fitted with all the conveniences for living, much like each of the guest homes at San Simeon but certainly far smaller in scale, with one bedroom, salon, lavatory, and kitchen area. Jane maintained that guests needed their independence, and this would allow the constant stream of international faces a new and different experience with each visit as the three environments were so vastly different and each had a special touch that would endear certain guests to have possessively favorite accommodations.

Water features also lent special serenity to her spirit in design. When arriving at the gate, a holding area for inspection held cars hostage by the large bollards blocking eager chauffeurs from surging forth before clearing security. Guests wouldn't mind the distraction as the design included a beautiful fountain fashioned like a creek with miniature rapids that ran parallel to the driveway until reaching the formal entrance beyond the inspection zone. A circular motor court served to launch guests toward the main residence only after appreciating the next fountain at the base of the incline to the upper motor court and port cochere.

Arriving at the house through the main entrance was intended to be a spectacular showcase of design, almost as if landing in front of a Ritz Carlton hotel rather than a private residence. While the home was a maze on grand scale, each of the public rooms on the main floor were connected in some fluid way for the ability of guests to navigate in a complete circle during an event. The intention was to comfortably host 400 for a reception. The beauty of the tastefully-deployed French decorative arts were a testament to the work of Princess Marina, Jane's longtime friend from Washington, D.C. whose discerning eye watched auction houses throughout the world to capture items Jane would enjoy.

The smallest details included a rare local artisan request for hand-blown glass floret sinks by Tom Chopora. Jane had seen his installation at The Parkway's lobby where she had initially stayed prior to purchase of the property, and commissioned the sinks in all the bathrooms for $20,000 each. She had decided to split her art collection between her much-smaller D.C. residence and Portland. The collection was one that was far superior to native Portlanders Manny and Helen Codman's, who had for years been considered Portland's greatest collectors. Helen's extreme attitude toward collecting art was fairly earned as she had in many respects pushed the Pacific Northwest gallery culture toward success during the 1980's. She once remarked that "most people aren't collectors, they just have a place to fill on the wall. You have to keep buying if you want to be taken seriously."

Rooms were adorned with polar opposites with the aggressive intention to startle even the most seasoned collector, and the rest were warehoused in a special temperature-controlled building as Jane had planned to rotate the entire collection through the residences every five years.

Standard formulas for artistic treatments in each room accented the purposeful severity that was minimized through comfortable furnishings in muted pastels, all with clean lines – however the fabric was always allowed celebrity status and playful whimsical patterns emerged everywhere. Nothing was allowed to distract from the art itself. Enormous palm trees graced several of the rooms and bright lights were forbidden in favor of dimmed indirect lighting from the floors or ceiling. Lighting was never turned off, regardless of time of day. Classical music hummed around the clock throughout both residence and grounds that lifted Jane's mood if she were down.

Her master suite ran the entire length of the house at 120 feet and included two bedrooms that she joked would help with "resale value." No one knew that Jane had specifically dictated that the home would have a similar fate of Huguette Clark's Santa Barbara home, Bellosguardo, and would be endowed with its own $300 million foundation controlled by her brother's family as trustees to display her art for public viewing after her own death. While the home was 22,000 square feet, it's purposeful low ceilings and open floor plan seemed to make it manageable for its lone resident. The beautiful sweeping views from the suite would find Jane spending much of her time at home in the central upper sitting room.

As the Bentley climbed the hill, Kate could not wait to see Jane's reaction to the honor guard that she had phoned ahead to organize. The evening would bring a small dinner party with Malcolm and Barbara and their friends the Codmans. Jane's executive vice-president and lawyer Carlton West would be her escort for the evening. Kate considered the impromptu gathering a blessing, as she would finally be able to visit with her own friends after the 30-day trek via yacht.

The gates opened and each of Jane's new staff lined the driveway, smiling and clapping to welcome her to her first official night as resident.

"This type of greeting is reserved for someone far more important than I," Jane suggested.

"They love you – after all, their continued jobs are thanks to you," Kate reminded Jane.

"Well, and Mrs. Parker, of course," Jane interjected with a grin.

"There's one to be friends with," Kate pointed at the rotund Bonita Darleopolis, the chef she'd hired away from Liza's to help organize Jane's cooking staff. A friend and colleague of an old master chef in the Pacific Northwest, Bonita had helped him judge a contest bearing his name each year. "I wonder what she's cooking up for your party tonight?"

"I'm sure it'll be wonderful, whatever it might be," Jane responded.

The ladies walked in the house to admire the freshly-cut floral – all white and lime in color – that the florist had brought that morning. Jane was looking forward to the new life that would begin promptly at 6 a.m. at the office when the New York executive floor would assemble for its daily staff meeting at Torero.

⊷⊷⊷

"My God, I'm glad to be home," Kate sighed on the phone with Sue Helen. "Want to go out for a drink?"

"Of course!" Sue Helen replied. "Why not call Brent and we can all meet up?"

"Great idea – how about 6:30 p.m. at Liza's?" Kate suggested.

"OK. I can't wait to hear about the trip! See you then," Sue Helen agreed.

⊷⊷⊷

"Fuckin' A, it's been way too long," Brent shrieked upon seeing Kate.

"You've got that right," Kate concurred, hugging Brent in a bar booth at Liza's.

"So, yachting, new job, billionaires, planes – what the hell is going on?" asked Brent. "I didn't know you were such a talented hooker!"

"Neither did I," Kate replied with a grin. "This woman is amazing – self-made, native Oregonian, and pretty goddamn smart."

"What's she like?" queried Brent.

"I'm so happy to have a night to myself. She's consuming, but absolutely adorable," Kate noted.

"There's my girl!" Sue Helen screamed as she walked up to the table in her signature blouse and slacks. "Give your favorite dyke a hug."

"I've missed you guys so much," Kate said.

"What about the last time we saw you," Brent asked. "Remember the European guy?"

"Holy shit," Kate exclaimed. "Talk about a fucking hot piece of ass. We went back to his hotel and fucked like no tomorrow. The bad thing is he works with Jane – thank God he didn't tell anyone."

"Who is he again?" asked Sue Helen.

"Jane's art advisor. She won't make a move without him," mimicked Kate with her hands, mocking the entire process of art collecting.

"He's fucking hot," Brent announced. "If you ever want to threeway, let me know!"

"Brent! I thought you only wanted me," Sue Helen chided.

"Not when there's a hot European in the picture, honey," Brent laughed.

135

"Tell us everything," Sue Helen pressed.

"Well, it's almost surreal how I ever got to know her. We met buying shoes downtown – and then she called, which is fucking crazy on its own," explained Kate. "We met, and after some real estate work all of a sudden I was in the middle of building the largest home constructed in the state in a long time."

"Unreal," Brent pondered.

"What's even more unreal is how much money this woman exudes from her pores," Kate suggested. "If you want something – anything – just ask and it appears for you."

"When do we get to see the place?" asked Sue Helen.

"She's actually letting me invite some people to the big party for her brother's retirement from the Senate," Kate revealed. "You two are on the list for September 30th!"

"Nice work!" said Brent.

The three old friends toasted with a 'fuck yeah' and decided that dinner was in the plans for the evening back at Brent and Sue Helen's Pearl District penthouse. Since Kate had been disconnected from reality for the past 30 days on the yacht, it was nice for the friends to have a moment to themselves before the storm of work that awaited Kate the next day in the new office.

The ever-present Ursula Carter was in the next booth, someone that none of the trio knew but was very interested in the topic of conversation, having met Jane briefly through Barbara at the Opera months before and had listened intently to every word the group said.

"Sorry to have been eavesdropping," Ursula turned and said unabashedly in her crusty accent to the group as she sat with her husband John. "Has Jane finally moved in?"

Taken aback by the interruption, the group stared at Ursula until Kate mustered a reply.

"Are you referring to Ms. Torrance?" Kate asked Ursula.

"Yes, I met her through her sister-in-law Barbara at the opera ball," Ursula replied.

Ursula's husband John knew better than to interrupt her line of questioning. She wasn't done finding out the latest morsel of gossip to litter through the locker room at the Portland Athletic Club that everyone of note also belonged to.

"Yes, she did just move in," Kate replied.

"Please tell her 'hello' for me when you see her next," Ursula purred with a smile.

With that, the group called for the check and decided to go back to Brent and Sue Helen's for dinner and a nightcap.

"It'll be an early morning," Kate said on the walk over to the condo. "That woman was creepy."

"All of those bitches are," Sue Helen agreed. "I recognized her husband from his ads in the club magazine. He's done a ton of plastic surgery work."

"What's more is I'd never reveal I was listening so intently to someone's conversation," Brent added.

"Yeah, but from her perspective she didn't do anything wrong by mentioning it. I hope she didn't hear anything about me fucking Pierre," Kate hoped.

"Doubtful – I think she tuned in when you said 'senate' and 'money,'" Sue Helen surmised. "Don't worry about it – she's obviously a cunt."

"Why are people like that?" Kate asked. "I mean, there's no reason to be such a fucking gossip snatch."

"What else do they have to do," Brent explained. "It's not like she has a ton of shit on her plate with a surgeon husband."

"Perhaps so," Kate agreed. "It just irritates the shit out of me."

⋅⋅⋅⋅◈⋅⋅⋅⋅

They entered the lobby of what was considered the crown jewel of the entire neighborhood. The clean lines and homage to geometric design were evident at The Orchid. Having been two of the first individuals to purchase in the building, Brent and Sue Helen had actually cut a door between their units. A strange and complicated relationship, the two had been in the development business since graduating from college with Kate.

"We just bought two new buildings," Brent said, pointing at one of them across the river. "One over by the Lloyd Center and one down here – the last warehouse in the Pearl!"

As Kate peered out the window of the 30th floor penthouse, she was particularly amazed how the duo had amassed nearly one million square feet of real estate in less than 20 years.

"You're on fire!" Kate roared with delight. "It's just too bad I can't represent you on your residential transactions anymore."

"Well, what are you doing?" Sue Helen prodded.

"I'm working for her," Kate explained. "A chief of staff - really a 'Girl Friday' for everything she needs."

"And how's the office?" Brent asked.

"Interesting. All of her key people are relatively mysterious," Kate explained. "All of them are the same except her PR guy – he's more bubbly and fun. Don't get me wrong, they're all nice – but it's just the way they look and act. Always very self-assured – a tad cocky almost."

"Just wait – you'll turn out the same way!" laughed Sue Helen, who was in the kitchen wrapping the filet mignons with bacon. "Anyone who is part of a machine that big will undoubtedly get an attitude – even if it is a small one."

"We haven't gotten attitudes, Sue," Brent disagreed.

"Yes you do," Sue Helen sharply replied. "Look how you strut around the club."

"That's different," Brent laughed. "That's a plaything."

"Dear, you wear your half of our $50 million right on your sleeve so everyone can see it!" Sue Helen responded, turning to Kate. "Every damn time there's an opportunity, he's talking about how much money and property we have!"

Kate was enjoying the polite battle between the business partners, sipping her champagne and sitting at the kitchen's bar.

"Well, no one would ever know you even have a penny," Brent argued. "Those dyke suits you wear are just about enough!"

"Speaking of lesbians, did you hear about the three-way that happened after the big event at the club last week?" Kate interjected.

"With whom?" both Brent and Sue Helen asked.

"Well one of them we all know – she burst on the scene this last year," Kate replied. "And I think it caused a divorce of the guy involved. But I don't know who the other girl was – let me text Art."

"Just when you think everything is normal, it's really just as fucked up as ever," Sue Helen noted. "Don't they know that shit like that gets around?"

"Well, it's nothing that we haven't all heard of or seen before," Brent said.

"But, it is funny to think about the three of them banging it out on the bed," Kate defended her story.

"How was the yacht?" Brent changed subjects.

"Fantastic – the captain hit on me within the first ten minutes of being on board," Kate bragged. "But, since I did Pierre I couldn't do him too."

"Good move girl," Sue Helen commended Kate for temperance. "Stand above it all."

"Was he hot?" Brent asked.

"This woman doesn't hire ugly people," Kate explained. "The fattest one is the cook – and she's supposed to be."

As the trio ate their dinner, Kate was pleased to relax with old friends and not have to be 'on' as she constantly needed to be when around Jane. She would sleep well in order to be filled with energy for her first full day at the office.

Chapter 10
THE ⟨ΠꓘⲤ⟨NꓕΠ
SAME YEAR

P rior to Jane's return, Kate had made sure that the six senior staff members and new residents to Portland were properly situated. Their tastes varied extensively for executive-level personnel who looked rather homogenized as a group. Each of them were tall and sophisticated in their appearance, with magnificent bone structure and attractive features. None would qualify for a career as a fashion model, but each of them did have an aloof air about how they conducted themselves – especially in front of strangers with whom they were unfamiliar.

At this point, Kate had been elevated to a position that seemed to be misnamed as 'chief of staff,' primarily because only the household staff would report to her. In addition to that role, she had charge over transportation, some aspects of security, and the social calendar that included interaction with service and culinary staff – with September 30th being a major initiative that was on everyone's agenda.

First Week, Day 1: Kate arrived promptly at the Estate at 5 a.m., just in time to find Jane walking down the stairs.

"Good morning! How was your party last night?" asked Kate.

"Very good. But those Codmans are awfully strange," Jane replied. "All that man talks about is real estate. And, the wife talks about it, too!"

"That's their life, Jane," Kate said. "I'm surprised they even came to dinner – it's a terrible thing to say but I think your brother and Barbara may be their only friends."

"But they did love the house," Jane acknowledged with a smile.

"Did Bonita fix you something or would you like to go to the Parkway for a quick breakfast," Kate asked.

"That's a good idea," Jane replied. "My old home for all those months!"

"Comfort food," Kate suggested.

The two ladies hopped into the Bentley and traversed the hill on their way downtown for the signature morning faire at the hotel which was three blocks from the office tower, and then she would call the entire office together for its first Monday morning staff meeting.

"Some gentlemen from Torero Security will be by this morning to install some equipment in my office," Jane informed. "Can you help manage that so no one else needs to bother with them? Plus, it's in our wing."

"Absolutely," Kate agreed. "I'll show them in when they arrive."

As Jane entered the office and went directly into the Board Room where the joint staff meeting was in progress, Kate manned the office directly outside the chamber where she had a direct view of Jane's door and the new personal assistant that had just been hired, Maria Gaither. Maria had been hired away from a company whose CEO had just been sentenced to 10 years at Sheridan, Oregon's minimum security country club for white collar criminals. While Maria disavowed any knowledge of securities fraud, both Jane and Kate liked her edge.

"Maria, we're expecting guests to install some equipment in Mrs. Torrance's office this morning," Kate said into the phone. "Would you please let me know when they arrive?"

"Certainly, ma'am," Maria replied with a tinge of Latina accent.

Kate then spent the next thirty minutes organizing her office so she could be a full resource for anything Jane could need. She was also slightly leery of managing household staff and had scheduled a meeting with the human resources clerk to go over policies and procedures because of the huge responsibility of making the estate in Portland and home in Washington run without issue.

As soon as she had completed her organization, the two individuals from Torero security arrived and Maria summoned Kate. Unlike the others she had met during the build-out of the office, these two members of Torero's security detail were well-dressed in tailored suits – each carrying two suitcases.

"Good morning, gentlemen," Kate said as she entered the lobby.

"Good morning, Ms. Carerra," the older man greeted. "We're from Torero's corporate intelligence division."

"Corporate intelligence?" Kate queried.

"A special division that reports directly to the office of the chairman," he further explained. "We're here to work with Mrs. Torrance's office."

"Of course, please come with me," Kate replied.

They walked down the long hallway and approached Jane's office.

"I'll show you in," Kate suggested.

"No need Ms. Carerra, we know the plans well. We'll only be an hour," said the other man. They shut the door after they entered the office, and the lock could be heard turning.

For the next thirty minutes, Kate was as curious about Corporate Intelligence's need to install equipment in Jane's office as she could be. Making busy work, she left her office nearly twenty times to go to the work room for copies or to the lobby to check on the receptionist in a thinly-veiled attempt to understand the men's mission. When Maria left for the restroom, she even attempted to kneel down and look underneath the door, to no avail. The two men were cloistered inside at Jane's direction making whatever enhancements to the office that were necessary.

Inside, the men were busily at work. With the outside terrace as a special area of interest, they were pleased that Adrian had – with their express instructions – installed a small leafy hedge around the perimeter, encircling the statue of Clay as well as the fountain and sitting area. Even with binoculars from other towers, it would have been difficult to see them assembling several parabolic microphones. The super-sensitive listening devices were buried in the foliage and could penetrate one building's façade - but not both - giving the terrace enormous utility for the installation. They aimed two directly at what had been confirmed as two managing director's offices at the DeSantos Group. Another was focused on the 3rd Floor executive conference room in City Hall while the final unit was situated toward the chambers of the Presiding Federal Judge for Oregon in the courthouse.

After they had finished outside, the duo moved indoors to fit each wall near the window with state-of-the-art scramblers that created a barrier to disrupt the exact type of equipment that had just been installed on the terrace in addition to weakening the capability of video cameras to capture a clear image. It would also cloud thermal detection capabilities to discover the number of people located or their position in the office at any individual time.

As promised, they were completed within the hour, and the Torero Corporate Intelligence employees left before Jane was finished with her meeting.

Kate, exercising her newly found post-cruise friendship with Jane, was chomping at the bit for the meeting to conclude. She didn't want to be rude and interrupt the proceedings of Jane's first staff meeting, but she also didn't want the issue of security to die since it was partly under her portfolio of responsibilities. She pondered all of the things the two individuals could have done in Jane's office, and wondered why Jane had such a laissez-faire attitude to letting them in without an escort. In fact, the entire episode was baffling to her. As Kate toiled in her office trying to imagine different scenarios, Jane finally emerged from the meeting.

"Has security been here yet?" Jane asked, breezing past Kate's office.

"Not just security," Kate corrected with caution. "Corporate intelligence."

Jane smiled as they moved toward her office. "I feel safer already," Jane announced, walking toward her office with a confident gait as if she were participating in a military drill.

"What on earth could they have been doing in here for an hour?" Kate asked, following her inside.

"Here's one thing," Jane noticed, showing a panic button under her desk to Kate. "Is there a problem?"

"No. I was just concerned for them being in here alone," Kate answered.

"Honey," Jane confided, holding Kate's hand, "Corporate Intelligence knows more about you and me than we know about ourselves. I wouldn't worry."

"You should have explained. I was a wreck during your meeting," Kate said.

"Remember the turf you're playing on," Jane explained. "This is a multi-billion dollar fairway, not just some casual real estate listing."

"I understand, I think," Kate indicated.

"You'll get the hang of it. Look, they even installed a portable armory," Jane said, looking into a closet in the private hallway to locate the hidden panel that included three automatic assault rifles and four handguns. "Just in case."

"That's what's so bizarre," Kate noted. "Who needs an armory?"

"When you're who we are, you need a lot of things that you'll learn about," Jane replied. "And, if you're going to help with the Estate's security, we better get you into a class that helps teach some of the fundamentals."

"Thank you," Kate said. "How was the meeting?"

"Good. I think Panama is shaping up nicely, and I understand you'll be helping set up some meetings for the end of the week for Omar and Helena?" Jane asked.

"Yes. Now, I don't want to disturb you any more on your first day here – and sorry for my paranoia," Kate replied.

"It's natural," Jane said with a raised voice, as Kate exited and closed the door to leave Jane alone in the newly-retrofitted office.

She picked up the phone and dialed New York.

"The panic button was a brilliant addition," Jane said to Robert Oppenheim, her security director back in New York.

"Thank you, ma'am," Robert said. "The guys said your new assistant did everything but scale the building to see what was going on while they were there."

"Well, I set her straight, so try to find some class for her to take on security so she feels relevant with that, too," Jane requested. "I don't think she'll be as inquisitive in the future."

Kate also served as an informal advisor to Bill Derendo as he started to consider staffing the community affairs group, including Jane's private foundation that was, for all purposes, the largest of its kind in the state. With Jane's new office came a flow of greetings from what Jane's finance wizards Omar Safdar and Helena Ellis called the "locals," private bankers and investment firms looking to secure even a small $25 million stake in assets to manage.

"Why not just tell all of them that we're managed by Carlyle and Goldman?" asked Omar, as the two met in the front lobby conference room with Kate as she tried to explain the dynamic of how each of the local companies worked based on her experience and knowing or hearing about each of the players at the Regent.

"Omar, we do have to share the wealth a little," Helena answered. "Neither Goldman nor Carlyle originally funded Costco, and look how that performed for investors. That's out of the Northwest – and the money came out of Portland. Some creative things happen here."

"She's right," followed Kate. "There's a very thin bandwidth of people in this town who can be helpful to what you're looking to do."

"OK. As a good faith effort, we'll try $100 million locally since Jane's living here," Omar conceded. "It's the price of a painting and won't affect much. But, we'll want to see what they can do."

"I'm not opposed to that, but let's see how the meetings go," Helena responded. "Kate, do you think you could assemble no more than three wealth management groups locally whose typical account minimum starts at around $2-3 million. I think that's a small enough amount to still get a little entrepreneurship out of them. We can devote ourselves to five interview meetings – no more than an hour each if it goes well."

"Any other additional parameters?" asked Kate.

"Well, some skybox privileges at a Duck game might be an added bonus," said Omar who was from Los Angeles and grew up attending the Brentwood School and was part of its first senior graduating class in 1975. "Jane's not interested, but I think it's a good thing to meet people and get connected. Help Bill out as well – remember, he's completely East Coast - but a little more relaxed version, so to speak." She left the meeting with her marching orders for yet another additional layer of responsibility given to her by senior staff.

Before Kate could begin her research and calls, Bill walked into the office and asked Kate if she were ready for some 'real work'.

"You're from here, and we want to establish a presence in the community," he said, interrupting her before she could answer. "What's your take on it?"

Kate was beginning to enjoy her role as a resource to her fellow staff members who were actually asking for her advice on topics she knew extraordinarily well but was only a wise sage with no formal training.

"What kind of presence?" Kate asked.

"Personal purgatory begins with board service," Bill responded, referencing the need to be involved with the not-for-profit landscape. "Omar, Helena, and Carlton refuse to do it, so you, Melissa, Seth, and I will have to do it."

"Why purgatory?" Kate asked. "It's easy enough when you come to the realization that all you're there for is your money. Just vote 'yes' and be happy to meet some new friends."

"So hardened!" Bill noted of Kate's progressively seasoned attitude toward non-profit governance.

"You would be too if you'd seen the waste that one would never get away with in the private sector," Kate explained. "One board turned its collective head when a $20,000 software module for finance was purchased but never implemented. I said to myself, 'I donated 10% of that module – for nothing.'"

"Stop being so altruistic, Kate," Bill suggested. "You'll love the foundation once we decide which direction to go with it. Jane's in it for fun and we don't need a ton of staff to measure success – what a fucking waste of money."

"Not to cut you off, but I have Omar and Helena ahead of you with their local investment project," Kate said.

"Well, I'm not worried – I get to spend the money they make," Bill casually replied. "When you get a chance, think about where the four of us should be placed. To make it easier, you're hereby appointed as a trustee of the Torrance Charitable Foundation."

Kate smiled as Bill walked back down the hall to his office, thinking it was more than a little odd that she was actually working with some of the most successful people in their professions in the world and had just been appointed as a major philanthropic foundation trustee.

<hr />

First Week, Day 2: As Kate plunged right into the efforts of Omar and Helena's to 'think locally' with investment firms, she figured she would divide it 70/30 in favor of management firms over private banks. She'd place the banks on one day because they also included account, trust, and credit services while decisions related to the seven candidates of firms was far easier based on the celebrated successes that most had experienced. 'Beauty contests' were traditional meetings where the firms could highlight their best features to prospective clients as they showed their wares.

Omar and Helena almost appeared to be excited about the opportunity of meeting the 'locals,' both of whom were Wharton graduates and seasoned finance professionals in their own right. She had specific instructions for each presentation – no Powerpoints, no thick packets, just a three-page summary and no more than three representatives. To take notes, she would be part of the meetings but would obviously only contribute if Omar and Helena asked a question or needed clarification.

Leveraging the Torrance and Torero Group names made reaching the CEOs of local firms an easy task. Some of the banks tried to give her the runaround, sending her to some secondary relationship manager with a fancy but inconsequential vice-presidential title, but that did not deter her from reaching her goal.

She scheduled the investment firms for Thursday and the banks for Friday – after which she had planned on taking the entire senior staff to the Regent Club for cocktails to celebrate the first week of a fully functional Portland office. After the arduous task of scheduling the five finance meetings, her thoughts turned to more pleasant concepts of how to strategize the debut of the Torrance Charitable Foundation and Torero brands to the Pacific Northwest audience.

"Any luck on those placements?" Bill asked as he stuck his head in Kate's office.

"Yes, I've been thinking about it quite a bit. Why aren't we thinking a little more globally?" Kate questioned.

"Global is Jane's territory – which means New York City to her," Bill explained. "She'll stay on both Met boards and will never give up her seat on the Met Acquisitions Committee. She's stuck on 'national' as opposed to 'global,' and the reasoning is pretty sound, too."

"I see a lot of non-profits doing wonderful work here, but I don't see many that are trying to solve the problems their missions outline," Kate said.

"Kate, no one really wants to solve any of these social service issues," Bill frankly explained. "Give the homeless a home and you've got a shelter staff out of work. Feed all the people and no need for a food bank staff. Put people back to work, and there's no employment department to work at. And, if everyone is happy and a middle class thrives, the Democrats have nothing to sell because no one would be underserved. They secretly work against their own solutions if you take a real look at what each charity does. In the end, the purpose of charities is to fuel hope and humanity for people and not do much more than that."

"I see 'solutions' as a major initiative that we could perhaps champion with some of the other large foundations – if we don't give the money together it could be a wake-up call," Kate said. "That, and Jane's passion of the arts. We could do a lot to help."

"There's that word again – 'help,'" Bill chuckled. "Remember, they don't want our help, just our money."

"I buy that for lower-level donors under $100,000," Kate agreed. "But, I think that if major funders got together with a stated goal it would make it easier – sticking together to force the issue."

"Do me a favor," Bill said. "Don't think so much. These people have a hard enough time agreeing where to donate and there are also turf battles over who can get their name put on this and that – at least that's what it was like in New York."

"OK, then I think I have another idea," she brainstormed. "Why not each of us take one of the major art boards that's not social service – opera, symphony, museum, and ballet – and then we can share notes on improvements each quarter internally until we're ready to restrict a major grant. At the same time the Foundation could hire a 'quiet' work group to review how to solve some of the bigger local social service issues."

"Sounds like you've got it figured out – but I want the museum board," Bill said. "One thing to be wary of is funding mediocrity. Give a big enough endowment to some slouch of an artistic director who was perfectly unacceptable even before getting the grant and all you'll have is someone until their retirement who has a lot of money to spend with no clear vision or true talent."

"Of course, you're the boss!" Kate replied and smiled as Bill ducked out of her office.

⸻

First Week, Day 3: Jane's household was nearly fully staffed thanks to Tess' rare act of kindness in calling Kate to negotiate on their behalf – something that wasn't much of any kindness since the well-trained staff would ultimately have found their paths to the new owner over time. In fact, Tess most probably made the call in order to impress on her newly organized group of friends as to what a benevolent soul she had become.

Since the end of construction, Adrian and Pierre had labored throughout the late Spring to make the house livable, switching out numerous artworks in a quest for perfection as they tested the waters with Jane. It almost appeared as if the specter of old Tess were still in residence, as the staff nearly mimicked its decades-old routine, right down to the mowing of the lawns that rotated daily in direction like a clock and vacuums whirling at early hours which had annoyed Jane slightly. Since Jane's cook in New York had been a commodity from the minute she announced the sale of her penthouse, the staff was all local. Kate loved that Bonita's extraordinary culinary experience would not only lend itself to the preparation of fine meals for small dinners and luncheons, but also a delightful repertoire of large-scale catering delights which would be perfect for the Senator's party that fall.

First Week, Day 4: Having scheduled each appointment with a half-hour buffer to ensure absolute confidentiality so each of the candidate firms would not see each other in the opulent office lobby, Kate greeted each group before escorting them back to the board room within Jane's inner sanctum to hear the pitch.

The creativity was evident from the first meeting where the plump chairman of Caldwell Advisors, Bert Englund, captivated the newcomers with his firm's adept ability to identify, invest, build, manage, and liquidate.

"It was easy to predict all this bullshit on storage and content delivery years ago. How easy is it to see a tape go to a DVD go to cable – that's why you have Kodak in bankruptcy. We sold Kodak in 1995 to make room to invest in broadband," Bert said. "Now we're 25% owner of one of the largest entertainment delivery channels in the country – and it's made a notable return on investment for our partners. Creativity and imagination fuel success."

"Impressive," Omar noted and continued with the interview. "Whom of your competitors would you most like to do business with?"

"Well, depends on who you consider my competition," Bert replied as the only representative from a firm to come to the interview alone. "We purposely keep ourselves under $50 billion in managed assets so we can stay focused. We're all friends in this business, but I'd have to call out Pacific Columbia Partners and Jim Rappin as the best in the city – next to us."

"He wasn't on the list, was he, Kate?" Omar asked.

"He wouldn't have been on any list," Bert interrupted before Kate could look, giving an example of the secrecy that shrouded many of the finest investment banks conducting business. "Can you find a website for Allen & Company?"

"What kind of fees are involved?" Helena asked.

"Reasonable even though we don't have to be," Bert indicated. "Thirty-five basis points on the total package for management, and 15% performance fee for deals we put together based on a four-quarter running average determined on the anniversary of when the investment was made."

"Is Pacific the same?" Omar asked.

"Nearly identical," Bert suggested, smiling. "We know we're good – I think we might even have some Torero stock in our income funds."

"That's always a safe bet," Helena agreed.

"Our firm cherishes its reputation on the West Coast," Bert followed. "At the end of the day, it's all we have."

"We'd consider putting $50 million with your firm and $50 million with Columbia," Omar offered.

"You'd be a co-underwriter to five of our projects at a time," Bert added. "With the risk comes the benefit – we'll put you with our filmed entertainment and new media track. I can't speak for Jim, but a discussion with Columbia would be smart."

"That's a new one for us," Helena joked about the industry sector Bert selected for the office. "We don't give autographs."

Everyone laughed as they exited the board room to walk Bert to the front before their next appointment arrived.

First Week, Day 5: The local bankers were relatively disappointing in comparison to the investment firms the day before. It appeared that the wealth management teams from each of the candidates had been used to small equity-driven clients as opposed to those with hundreds of millions in assets that needed to be carefully managed to maintain proper equilibrium in a family office scenario where there was consistent pressure to maximize returns.

The first bank failed miserably – almost to a point where Omar and Helena felt as if they should leave the room. Besides being completely clueless about investment banking options and how to structure short-term loans against Jane's significant ownership in Torero, land, and art, the bumbling group of bankers tried unsuccessfully to sell the amenities including trash and trinkets like box seats at the ballet that were associated with being a run-of-the-mill client. Focusing on the technical expectations that were clearly outlined upon receiving an invitation to present was the key to success. Kate's golden reputation as a Portland insider was on the line if the second meeting didn't go well.

When the first bankers left the room, Helena mocked the entire group. "Were they about bring out a complimentary china service for four?" she chuckled.

Kate had purposefully invited National Bank's Managing Director of Wealth Management Mike Ross along with his team including Maureen Peters who was in charge of business development and Benjamin Childs, head of private banking, because of her own family's long association with the bank. She had always heard stories of the bank's colorful history as a local institution in addition to her dabble in dealing with Tess, but was also curious how they would respond to East Coast clients. Having consistently seen the typical advertisement the private bank produced that showcased a team photo with some trite call to action, Kate had to use her Google prowess to research the potential synergies with the banking group.

As the last appointment for the day, she greeted them and escorted them down the long hallway past the artwork and bustle of a busy office that had only been in operation for one week in its Portland location.

"We just moved here," Kate explained to the banking delegation. "Well, they just moved here, I'm a native."

"We appreciate the opportunity," said Maureen, a dwarflike creature who walked in the fashion of a general. Kate wondered why Maureen was leading the group rather than Mike.

"Mr. Ross, today you'll be meeting with Omar Safdar who is our Chief Financial Officer and Helena Ellis, Chief Investment Officer," Kate explained to him, subtly rebuking Maureen. "The format they prefer is a simple discussion about their needs."

"Seems straightforward enough," Maureen interrupted, holding up several glossy packets. "I brought some material for them to review as well."

"Ms. Peters, they don't want the material," Kate responded as the group followed her. "Please make sure to follow the format that we discussed. If you plan on being successful, I wouldn't deviate from the process."

As they entered the board room, Kate excused herself to inform Omar and Helena that the group was ready.

"Fuck. And I thought 53 was nice," Benjamin said to his colleagues, referencing the executive floor of their bank. "I counted at least $5 million in paintings alone on the way in."

Mike signaled them to be quiet with a finger over his mouth, as their conversation was most probably being recorded for review after the meeting. Several minutes passed and the finance team finally entered the board room to exchange pleasantries prior to discussing the plan.

"Thank you for coming to meet with us today," Omar announced as they occupied a corner of the vast board table.

"It's our pleasure," Mike replied. "As promised, here's our summary of services."

"Thank you. It's our intention of having a local banking partner where we can house between $100-200 million for a number of purposes," Omar explained.

"We like the reputation, but heard that when the going got tough for some of your family business customers, you wouldn't extend credit to them," Helena said. "Have you relaxed your policies at all as on occasion we'd like to borrow in the short term against our investments and other assets?"

"Slightly," Benjamin explained. "However, the reason we've been in business for over 100 years is that we are naturally conservative."

"That might be a good thing, but our owner isn't getting any younger and we'd like some flexibility with monetization," Helena responded. "We'd want you to float an additional $200 to $250 million at any given time. Banks are not fans of securitizing property, stock, or art."

"Entirely possible," Mike smiled. "I think we can make accommodation for a new client."

"Consider us clients then," Omar said. "Give us an account number and we'll have our Controller Melissa Benson wire the money to you tomorrow along with a charter to sign."

As Kate escorted the group to the lobby, she realized it was close to 5 p.m., and the Regent was holding a special table in its lounge for her group. One by one, she went into the offices of the six newest members of Portland's establishment to remind them of her invitation. Besides one other person in the state, they collectively controlled the single largest net worth of an individual. Since it was a special night, the group stopped work early and walked en masse to the club.

"Ms. Carerra," the host said, "Welcome! We have your table over here."

As the group was seated, a magnum bottle of Veuve Clicquot was already on the table with seven glasses. Kate said while the host poured the champagne, "So, how was the first week?"

"Amazingly organized," Melissa Benson declared. "Cheers to you for having everything done and in place – a very smooth transition. And, I was asked out on a date by the building management company's CEO!"

Everyone applauded, knowing full well that Melissa was probably the one who asked the CEO out.

"Cheers for a successful move," Carlton lifted his glass. "And thank you Kate for making our first week here as easy as she could!"

"Seth, any words of advice for us on the city?" asked Omar.

"Don't run for office – ever!" Seth responded.

The group again laughed and lifted glasses to toast Seth's bid for United States Senate.

Bill brought out a list from his pocket. "I have some awards to present," he said. "The annual board of directors assignments are out! Since our executive staff flatly refuses to participate, I will take the museum; Kate will take the opera; Melissa gets the ballet; and Seth – you get the one where you can raise some campaign money – the symphony."

Glasses again were raised from around the table to toast the group's philanthropic efforts on Jane's behalf, everyone knowing that none of the boards would have refused a new member coming to the table with a minimum of $100,000 in annual support.

"So what happened with the banks and firms?" asked Carlton.

"Well the firms were an outstanding surprise," Omar suggested.

"Not so much for the banks," Helena continued. "We should have videoed the antics of the first group that came through the door. Obviously a regional concern with no real understanding of our needs or background in investment banking."

"I've never seen someone call so fast to give an account number," Melissa suggested of National Bank's Benjamin Childs. "He almost tripped over his tongue on each digit."

"Well, what do you expect when we come to town," Bill explained. "Despite it being a non-event to us, we're a big deal to these people."

"Yes you are," Kate noted. "Just remember that if you get any shit along the way."

"This is definitely a 'big deal' here but if we would have gone to Marbella, no one would have even gotten out of their lounge chair at the beach to see what was happening. Having a billion over there is commonplace," Helena added, thinking of the luxurious Spanish beach community that was a haven for royalty and the wealthy.

"Here's to having a billion (or more)!" Kate said and raised her glass again.

"To a billion (or more)," the group spiritedly replied.

Chapter 11
REZIDUAL EFFECTZ
1982

The Jefferson Lewis Academy caste system worked favorably for Joey, who always would need tutoring for the low to mid-range grades he received. As long as he wasn't in trouble, Jane was thrilled to pay the tuition in full and kick a little extra into the endowment to gratefully acknowledge the school for accepting and subsequently keeping her son.

As Joey learned more about the school, he was ecstatic to find out about their Washington intern program that would be a shoe-in for him based on his uncle and that very few of the students would have a connection with Oregon. He put in a rare call to the Senator to test the reception to being in the office.

"Your nephew is on line two," Malcolm's secretary called via intercom into his office.

"Joey!" Malcolm said, pretending to be excited to hear from him. "How's school?"

"I love it here," Joey revealed. "They even have a special program called the Washington intern program. I want to come down this summer and work in your office."

The Senator's heart sank. Knowing one of his interns-turned-staff was moderately acceptable, but having Joey there full time each day would offer many glimpses inside the inner sanctum and into the personalities of staff. As a master manipulator, the boy could potentially wreak havoc on the operation.

"Let me talk to your mother about it," Malcolm replied. "She probably wants some time with you in New York."

"No she doesn't," the eager boy responded. "She'd want me to come down if I want to come down!"

"OK, I still want to talk with her," the Senator asserted. "Call my office tomorrow morning and we can discuss a plan."

An excited Joey ran back down the hall to his room and then to the library to research the Capitol and Senate. The prospect of also spending time with Jacob and his uncle was something that caused the fourteen year-old some arousal that he had to camouflage in his pants, remembering back to his first experiences with both men.

It wasn't hard to convince Jane to let her son spend the summer term with her brother's family. As the months wore on, there was an unusual calm that settled over the family for all of its scruples. Joey seemed to actually perform in school his first year away from home, the company had gained market share under Jane's leadership, and the Senator's popularity soared both in Washington and his home state. In the spring, Joey could not wait to get to his uncle's office to begin his internship. By that time, Jane had purchased a sprawling new estate for her brother and his family off of Chain Bridge Road just outside the District in McLean. Lending a gingerly and relaxing commute to the Capitol each morning, the home was also perfectly situated not far from C.I.A. headquarters if the Senator needed to attend a security briefing as the ranking member of the Foreign Relations Committee.

Joey barely set foot back in New York other than to have lunch with his mother before she had him shuttled down to Washington. The young man was ready to report for duty, and could hardly wait to see Jacob at the office the next morning.

"How was your trip down?" Barbara asked her nephew as he walked in through the trade entrance to the house.

"I could hardly wait to get here," the boy answered. "It will be cool to work with Uncle Malcolm!"

"Well, I've never seen someone so eager to come to Washington," Barbara noted. "Be sure the 'Beltway Bug' doesn't bite you!"

"What's that?" Joey asked.

"Honey, we've been here eleven years already," Barbara explained. "And if your uncle has his way, we'll be here another 20 or 30 years! And, don't call him 'uncle' at the office – always 'Senator.'"

Barbara exemplified the perfect Washington wife. Thanks to Jane and the unlimited cash reserves in the campaign fund, she had become known as a legendary hostess respected by all of Washington. As a trustee of the Kennedy Center, she had become an advocate for the arts and founded an artistic exchange with Oregon's budding performing arts community. Sublimely put together, Barbara would never leave the house without looking perfect and was grateful each time Jane invited her to New York and treated her to a shopping spree that stocked her closet with the finest wardrobe of any of the Senator's wives.

"Where's Seth and Nats?" Joey asked.

"Upstairs. Your room is right next to Natalie's – go find it before dinner, and take all those bags up too!" Barbara urged her nephew as she began to organize the kitchen for dinner. It would be five and sometimes six for dinner if Jane came to visit for the next three months, and it was a comfortable feeling to have a full house.

Even with boarding school training, a 5:30 a.m. wake up call was hard for Joey to stomach, and he was for a split moment jealous of his two sleeping cousins who would have a leisurely summer with their school friends. As he got up to go to the bathroom, his morning erection was fueled by dreams of his intern lover whom he would see in a few short hours at the office. He knew better than to jack off, as Jacob would take care of that with him in the Capitol.

After breakfast at 7 a.m., the Senator's newest 'favored one' arrived at the house and brought the car around to the front. Unlike Jacob, this new college graduate intern was edgy and not particularly friendly with Joey – most probably because he knew that the nephew's presence each morning and afternoon in the car would impede any quality 'alone time' he could have with the Senator himself outside the Capitol.

As the car neared the office, Joey was getting excited for his first day and to see Jacob once again. He wondered how it would be to meet all the different staff members and learn about their work. At 14, he was also curious to know what types of work he would be doing. Even the arrival of a Senator in a small state's office was a major event. Two receptionist interns greeted the group upon their arrival, and the scheduler who also served as a private secretary slipped the Senator his daily schedule typed on a small card that he would carry in his pocket throughout the day. He then handed Joey off to his Chief of Staff, the seasoned Penny Brockland, and was immediately shuttled into a meeting with several of his legislative assistants.

"You must be Joey - Penny Brockland," she introduced herself, extending her hand to the Senator's nephew. "I'm the Senator's Chief of Staff."

"Nice to meet you, Mrs. Brockland," Joey courteously replied.

"Ah, no. Here in this office we're all peers no matter our age," she explained. "It's Penny. I think you already know one of our staff assistants who is in charge of interns – Jacob."

"Is he here?" Joey curiously asked as his eyes lit up at the mere suggestion of his name.

"Just down the hall, come with me," Penny added with a smile, walking with Joey through the vast office down to the intern area.

"Hey, Joey," Jacob said from his cubicle. "Welcome back to Washington!"

Joey resisted his initial instinct to embrace Jacob, and gave him a smile and glance that surely suggested the need to go to the hideaway where they first had talked.

"So, what am I going to be doing here?" Joey inquired.

"Sorting the mail in the morning, and filing in the afternoon," Jacob announced.

"Sounds like fun," Joey joked, feigning excitement at the prospect of the mundane daily tasks.

"And, then there's the work parties that you and I will be doing to clean out the archives once a week," Jacob revealed with a big grin and grabbed the bulge in his pants.

Joey knew that Jacob had scheduled those times so they could do something more than work. "Those will be really fun!" Joey said with enthusiasm.

The three-month timeframe of the internship would never be enough time for Joey. After a month, he had eased into the Washington lifestyle with every last fringe benefit. Everyone wanted a part of the Senator's nephew who was also to become one of the world's wealthiest individuals as heir apparent of Torero.

The odd attraction between Joey and his 22-year-old mentor made both of them blind to their outward interaction that others witnessed. The usually-quiet office where everyone's role was defined under the iron grip of Penny and been thrown slightly out of balance by the too-familiar nature of their relationship.

Of course, the Senator who knew the real reasons behind the closeness brushed it off as a young boy's admiration of a role model. That proclamation to his senior staff seemed to satisfy their curiosity about what seemed a flagrantly close bond between the two. As long as no one saw anything, it would be considered a closed issue. He would never have actually announced that his nephew had blackmailed him into a sexual relationship as well as the internship opportunity.

On her daily rounds to check status on a variety of projects, Penny unfortunately caught a glimpse of Jacob and Joey exiting the single bathroom at the office together during its regular hours of operation. Without saying a thing, she went to have an audience with her employer.

"You will not believe what I just saw, Malcolm," Penny announced in front of his desk.

"What could be that alarming?" the Senator wondered, looking up from piles of issue briefs from the Department of State.

"Your nephew leaving the private bathroom with Jacob," she replied.

"Are you sure?" Malcolm asked.

"Of course I'm sure," Penny assuredly noted. "I'm concerned."

The insides of the Senator were turning at the concept of his office staff finally confronting the well-defined yet secret process that had been cultivated during the last decade because his nephew was not respecting the boundaries of how a proper liaison was to be conducted in the Washington landscape.

"I'll take care of it," the Senator said as Penny left the office.

Checking with Penny about when Jacob and Joey had planned their work parties to clean the archives located in the dark basement of the building, the Senator himself decided to pay a visit to the team to check their progress. He was as quiet as possible in the halls to not arouse suspicion that anyone was near the large room that housed records and photos dating back to his election in 1971. No one hardly ever visited that level of the building, and any sound could echo through the halls.

He arrived at the archives door, noticing that it was ajar. Carefully opening it to eliminate the opportunity for the room's occupants to quickly get back to work, his worst fears were confirmed. In front of him fully nude on the boxes were Jacob and Joey engaged in a passionate sexual exchange.

"Am I interrupting something?" the Senator tersely asked the duo.

Looking up behind them at the Senator, they separated and covered themselves, fearful of the response they'd get for what they knew was beyond a serious breach of protocol not to mention a highly illegal act that could send Jacob to prison.

"Joey, get your clothes on and go to the office," the Senator commanded in a stern voice.

Joey quickly dressed without saying a word, and left the lower level of the building to return to the intern area within the office.

"As for you," the Senator warned, approaching the still-nude Jacob. "This is it."

Pushing Jacob down on the boxes, the Senator unzipped his pants and brutally assaulted the young staff member even though Jacob secretly loved it - absolutely relishing the togetherness of physical intimacy at any level with Malcolm.

After finishing with his subject, the Senator instructed Jacob to also get dressed.

"Tomorrow morning, you're headed back to the Oregon office," the Senator explained, slightly out of breath from the quick sexual release he had just experienced.

"It's not my fault though," Jacob protested.

"I know he put you in an awkward position and you had no choice initially, but you did have a choice when he came back to the office to intern," the Senator noted. "After three months, you can come back when Joey's gone and work in Foreign Relations."

"I didn't expect him to fall in love with me," Jacob pleaded. "You've got to understand!"

"Get up to the office and pack. We'll make the transition look like a promotion, you can be assistant state director. I'm going to take Joey home for the rest of the day," the Senator firmly said.

As they left the basement archives, the Senator went to call for his driver and to instruct him to bring Joey with him while Jacob was relegated to pack.

Penny would knowingly spin the story the way she and the Senator had always rehearsed if a mishap occurred.

Holding back his tears, Jacob appeared in the office and told his interns and fellow staff members that he had been promoted to work within the state for both the office and the campaign. At the same time, the Senator was lounging at home with his nephew by his side, watching a movie and trying to forget the mistakes that had been made by reuniting the boy and intern. While inconsequential in nature due to the magnificent loyalty that had been nurtured amongst all parties in the Senator's life, the issue was dealt with swiftly and perfectly.

Chapter 12
CONSEQUENCE
1984

What the Senator had not planned was the degree of depression his nephew would experience from being separated from whom he considered his first love. The anger festered for nearly two years as Joey continued the routine of working at the office. Not ever saying much, he was simply less talkative and engaged with his work where in the past he was a highly motivated intern who would take on any task to please his supervisor and lover.

One incident can sway life's road as a secretly charted course emerges to gradually reveal an intended destiny. On one of the many times that the intern driver and current 'favored one' Mikel had transported Joey by himself from the Capitol to McLean, the chill between the personalities finally faded as they were listening to the radio, Joey in the front seat with his driver and both were uncharacteristically jamming at top volume to Madonna's first single, 'Everybody.' Mikel suddenly stopped the car on the side of the road. In an absurd stunt, he looked at the Senator's nephew, smiled without saying a word, and pulled out a small box that contained what looked like white powder.

"What's that?" Joey asked.

"Something everyone does to get through a day at the Capitol," Mikel responded, taking a snort from a small straw. "Haven't you ever done coke?"

"What is it?" Joey asked, having never been introduced to the drug.

"You wanna try a little?" suggested Mikel. "It helps you relax."

"OK," Joey said as he stood on the cliff of reality where the allure of Mikel's suggestion and his desire to be part of the crowd won out over basic common sense. That initial snort would permanently change Joey's life.

Inhaling far more than Mikel had intended to share, Joey's body soared with the new experience cocaine offered.

165

"That's nice," Joey commented.

"There's better stuff, too," Mikel replied. "You ever get with your cousin?"

"My cousin?" Joey questioned.

"Yeah, Natalie," Mikel coaxed. "She looks like she's got a hot pussy on her."

With the cocaine, the conversation seemed almost normal as the intern pumped Joey for information about the Senator's only daughter.

"I have something you can put in her drink," Mikel suggested. "She won't even know we're fucking her."

"I don't know," hesitated Joey, not wanting to reveal that he'd only ever been with the same sex and had not yet even tried to kiss a girl.

"C'mon," Mikel pushed, coaxing the impressionable boy who desperately wanted to earn the friendship of the interns and staff. "Even if she wakes up during it, she'll love it. At least it won't be some asshole taking her cherry."

Mikel brought the car back on the road, his mind spinning in a coked-up frenzy of excitement at the opportunity to deflower the Senator's daughter and rationalizing the opportunity to the Senator's nephew. It would be a powerful coup that would trump all the other intern antics in the office that he himself could hold as his own victory.

"So is she alone now?" Mikel asked.

"I think so, at least until seven tonight," Joey noted.

"OK, I'll come in the house with you to watch television," Mikel said with a devilish smile.

As predicted, Natalie was home but her brother Seth was upstairs practicing piano. Conditions were ideal for the plot to unfold as she was in the family room already watching television. Not many 14-year-old girls had quite the mature look that Natalie did. A complete prepster, she had already developed beautifully into a young lady and was particularly stylish with the assistance of her mother and aunt. Her lovely straight blond hair cascaded past her shoulders and over her tits as she truly epitomized the image of an All-American girl and looked as if she belonged in a Ralph Lauren advertisement.

Psyched up from the car ride home with Mikel sharing with Joey how he'd teach him to please a girl, the two wolves entered the house with raised heart rates and were ready to pounce on their prey. Mikel handed Joey a little bag with powder in it as they sat down.

"What's on," asked Joey.

"Nada," Natalie said, practicing her Spanish as part of her homework. "Where's dad?"

"Late night votes, so Mikel brought me home," Joey explained.

"Hi Mikey," Natalie said, familiar with the intern and excusing herself to go to the bathroom.

As she disappeared, Mikel told Joey to hurry – "put it in her soda!"

Joey obeyed his new friend and stirred the powder in with his finger.

Natalie returned and sat down, drinking a little soda.

"Want a refill?" Joey suggested.

"Sure, let me finish this," Natalie replied.

The trio sat in silence as the mysterious powder took its effect. Not long after finishing the drink, she was in a forced sleep. Mikel got up and went over to her, taking his penis out and flogging her half-open mouth with it, which made Joey laugh. Singing some disco song as he danced around her letting his pants fall to the floor to reveal a muscular ass and thighs, he was ready for her. He operated with surgical precision as he lifted her shirt and unclipped her bra to reveal pert young tits and a then made a funny surprised face as he raised her skirt to take off her pink lace panties that revealed a near-bald and never-touched valley of pleasure.

"Get over here," Mikel commanded Joey as he worked himself to erection. "After I'm done its your turn."

As a drugged Natalie lay spread eagle on the leather couch, Mikel was pleased that her sleep would soften the pain as he deflowered her. "Go get some towels for the blood," Mikel instructed.

Joey left for the kitchen and returned to see the intern rhythmically bouncing on top of her with a great deal of force. The significantly tighter virgin gripped him far better than some of the whores he'd met in the Capitol, so it didn't take long for him to finish. The sight of the two was definitely arousing, even if Joey's cousin was not coherent. With the piano playing upstairs, both knew there was a factor of safety in what they were doing as Seth would be busy for at least 30 minutes with practice and they would hear if he stopped playing.

"Your turn man. Hop on!" Mikel laughed, pulling out and nearly forcing Joey inside her.

Joey's perpetually-clouded young mind had rationalized what was indeed a rape scenario as a payback to his uncle for making Jacob leave the office for Oregon. He intended to vigorously act out his anger and aggression for his uncle on his cousin, clinching his teeth and slapping her tits around as he entered her.

"That's it, you're doing great," Mikel encouraged with a smile, leaning in to lick Natalie's face.

"You like this, bitch?" Joey asked his sleeping cousin. "This is just what you need."

The violent convulsions Joey was making had somehow countered the affect of the drug. Natalie stirred a little as he continued to jackhammer away. Mikel was cheering his pupil on, and had even quickly sprouted himself to full erection again.

"Yee-haw!" Mikel yelled. "Ride her."

They didn't notice her eyes opening and the incredibly disoriented look on her face. The confusion of her cousin having sex with her didn't initially register, as she was groggy and thought it was simply a bad dream. Several more minutes passed as she felt the physical affects of the sex on her body.

"Slam it," Mikel encouraged, eagerly watching.

Constantly looking for approval, Joey obediently worked to please his new friend. Natalie snapped out of her daze with speed and began to struggle.

"Joey, what the fuck are you doing?" she protested, not thinking to yell for Seth.

"Giving you what you want," Joey explained as he bent in to kiss her. "Shut up or I'll tell your dad what a slut you are."

Crying, Natalie had little choice but to submit to the much-stronger pair as they held her down. As Joey approached climax, Mikel shoved himself into Natalie's mouth. It was over within minutes and Joey got up and stood up in front of her.

"If you ever say anything Nats, your dad will think you're lying," Joey warned, taking the lead over Mikel who had originally encouraged the idea. "And, we'll be meeting like this a lot more before I go back to school."

What neither of the boys understood was how much Natalie had enjoyed the experience after the initial embarrassment of the situation. Perhaps that's why she didn't do more to free herself from what would have been considered by anyone else a violent rape. She simply got up and went upstairs to take a shower, saying nothing. They didn't catch a glimpse of her satisfied smile as she ascended the staircase.

Over the next few months, Joey completely forgot about both Jacob and the Senator as he launched into a dangerous relationship with Natalie. They couldn't get enough of each other and would sometimes sneak into each other's bedrooms at night to fuck. The daily lovemaking between the cousins erased all boundaries and would have its own set of consequences several years later as Joey reappeared each summer and by that time had no need for interns and showed little interest in the Capitol or office. Mikel had helped him become one of the most prolific suppliers of Jefferson Lewis's cokeheads, and he was squarely addicted to both drugs and sex after he finally realized it would be difficult for anyone to administer any punishment to him because of his family's money and power.

Joey and Natalie were extremely lucky to never have been discovered in prior years while he expertly molded her into a complete slut who loved coke just as much as he did. It was now Joey who would send her on missions to the Capitol in her miniskirts to find an unsuspecting intern from one of many offices to fuck in one of her father's hideaways. He got simple joy from knowing what he had turned her into, and was ecstatic to always have the choice of revealing the secret to his uncle but far more enjoyed withholding the information as Natalie was in his complete control. She had been spared embarrassment for the near-unlimited amounts of sex she had become accustomed to until she missed her period after a particularly intoxicating session with young page from California who was both sexually gifted and well-endowed - remembering that she had definitely felt the force of his resolution inside her. Now 15 she still couldn't readily make a doctor's appointment without the express permission of her parents. Not knowing what to do, she called Joey.

"Fuck I'm so scared," Natalie complained. "I don't want a fucking baby!"

"Aren't any of your parents' friends doctors?" Joey asked. "Maybe one of them can give you an abortion in secret."

"And how am I supposed to ask them for it?" Natalie complained with sarcasm. "Hi Dr. Franklin, can you help me out with an abortion?"

"I'll ask around up here," Joey said, calming her. "I'll find something for you, Nats. Spring break is coming up in two weeks and I'll come down."

"Thank you Joseph," she replied in the most formal of addresses. "Love you."

Natalie was beside herself even though the fetus was still not yet an active parasite in her uterus. Her goal was to get rid of it as soon as possible and one of her only hopes was Joey. Anticipating his arrival in Washington, Natalie counted the days to salvation and getting rid of the unwanted creature growing inside her.

Natalie had requested that her father have Mikel pick her up, who by then was hired on as a staff assistant to drive her to Union Station to pick Joey up.

"Hey Nats," Mikel said, opening the passenger door for the fetching schoolgirl who had taken her last day of school as a sick day. "How's Washington's favorite?"

"Fuck you, Mikey," Natalie slyly responded with a smile. "I could still charge you with rape."

"OK. And, what will your dad say when I explain how you've fucked half the Capitol already at your age?" Mikel quizzed the girl who by now had grown into her role and looked more like a woman than a schoolgirl.

"Fair enough, horndog," said Natalie, smiling and lifting her skirt a little to expose the fact that she had deliberately not worn any panties. "Let's go pick up Cokey."

Joey had become 'Cokey,' but only with Mikel's help. Himself becoming one of the most popular drug dealers in the Capitol, Mikel even had the Capitol Police buying from him.

Getting out the same small container, both Mikel and Natalie took a quick hit with the little straw.

"He's looking forward to seeing you," Mikel explained, snorting deep.

"Why wouldn't he be?" Natalie questioned. "You know as well as I do that he just wants to fuck me."

"Both of us do, I hope," he replied, reaching in for a quick pet between her legs.

"We'll see," Natalie retorted as they neared the train station. "Don't let him see that – he'll get jealous!"

Joey's features had matured quite a bit in the short few months he'd been away, making him even more handsome than before. Despite being one of his own biggest coke clients propelled by the soaring profits he made in dealing, the teen-aged years masked the usage beautifully. He ran to the familiar Senator's car and was greeted by both his cousin and Mikel.

"It's so nice to be here," Joey said, getting in the back seat. "Anybody got some stuff?"

Mikel handed Joey the container for a hit.

"Nats, I got what you need for your little problem," Joey informed, patting his pocket. "Let's go back to the house before your parents get home."

"For how much time you spend here, you should just go to school with us," Natalie suggested.

"Fuck that. I've got my own thing going at J-Lewis," Joey explained. "I don't have to answer to anyone."

"Your mom came down to visit," Natalie noted. "Some big oil conference."

"How was she?" Joey asked. "I haven't talked to her in a month."

"She must've gotten a contract," Natalie suspected. "We all got to go out for dinner to celebrate."

"Nice," Joey replied.

"Always to the goddamn University Club," Natalie said dismissively about Aunt Jane's conservatively narrow choices in dining options.

Joey laughed as they arrived at the residence, knowing his mother had a routine for her occasional restaurant visits in both New York and Washington. The trio went straight up to Natalie's bedroom as Joey had a ravenous desire to mount his cousin before giving her the pill he'd gotten from a European classmate who had stolen several from his father's lab to sell to knocked-up girls on campus.

As was tradition, Mikel went first and Joey decided to take a piss so he didn't have to hear them playing on the bed. No one really knew that Mikel and Natalie were by that point regular companions because of the weekly coke drop for her at the house. As familiar lovers, their bodies melded perfectly as they kissed.

Joey liked the tag fuck mentality and slapped Mikel's open hand as he dismounted 'Washington's favorite.' Hard as ever, Joey slid himself inside her to deliver what he considered a far more special experience than Mikel could.

"None of the girls in school are as tight," he said to Natalie after the initial insertion. "Surprising for all the dick you take."

"Fuck you Joey. Just cum and get off me," Natalie declared, irritated with her cousin's perpetual punk attitude but needing his special cure for her own problematic pregnancy.

Right as he was about to release, the door opened. A glaring Senator Chambers stood in front of them, not expecting to find his nephew or staff member with his daughter, but some random boy from school.

"Oh, Christ!" the Senator winced and turned away. "What the hell is going on here?"

The immediate reaction was for the three to cover themselves, much like when the Senator caught Jacob and Joey in the archives.

"Natalie, go to your mother's and my bedroom. Immediately!" the Senator shouted, then turning to Joey. "Regardless of anything that's ever happened, Joey, I have always understood. But this takes the cake."

"You sent Jacob away," Joey said, crying at that point. "So I replaced him."

"With your fucking cousin?" the Senator yelled. "And, Mikel, what the fuck are you doing?

"She forced us, Senator," Mikel admitted, quivering.

"She did!" Joey agreed. "She fucks all kinds of guys on the hill in your hideaway."

"Unbelievable," the exasperated Senator said, collapsing against the door frame, not knowing what course of action to take. "What have I made happen here? It's getting late. Mikel – just get out and go home."

Leaving, Mikel tried to offer a kiss on the cheek to the Senator who turned his face to refuse what was now from his former 'favored one.'

"Joey, I need to know why you did this," the Senator said, sitting on the bed and being surprisingly candid and open.

"I was mad at you. I'm sorry Uncle Malcolm," Joey responded. "It was only one last time."

"What difference does that make?" Senator Chambers questioned.

"Well, I wasn't supposed to tell anyone," Joey said, masterfully shifting blame. "She's pregnant and asked me to help her find a way to abort it without telling you and Aunt Barbara. A friend at school's dad has been working on a pill, and I came down to give it to her. But, I wanted to be with her one last time."

As ridiculous as the story was, the Senator actually believed his nephew who had already caused significant issues for both family and office.

"What kind of pill?" the Senator inquired.

"Experimental," Joey explained, showing the Senator the pills. "It's supposed to trigger an early-term abortion by forcing a period."

"OK son," the Senator said, taking the pills from his nephew and calmly rubbing Joey's back and perhaps still in shock from the entire discovery. "You go to bed now and I'll be back to talk."

—•—

Entering the master bedroom, he found Natalie face down on the bed, unwilling to acknowledge his presence.

"They told me everything," the Senator explained to his daughter in a raised voice. "Everything! Do you realize the extent of the damage you've caused this family?"

"I was just doing what Joey told me to," whimpered Natalie.

"It's beyond a disgrace," the Senator bellowed. "Get the rest of your clothes on, we're going for a drive."

The Senator left the room and Natalie obediently left to go to her room to dress, passing Joey's open door as he smiled and comically shook his head back and forth. She went downstairs to find her father already in the car.

"Where are we going?" Natalie quietly asked.

"To show you how you could have turned out if you would have had that baby," the Senator warned.

The car meandered along the water and the monuments looked their best that evening. The pair were decidedly silent as Natalie did not want to provoke her father and upset him even more than she already had. Embarrassment of discovery had turned to utter shame for the young girl, who couldn't find words to accurately explain her behavior.

Passing over the bridge, she noticed the sign leading to Anacostia, one of Washington's roughest neighborhoods where the homicide rate and drug deals accounted for some of the most colorful criminal pageantry of the District.

"Here we are," the Senator said, no longer seeming to be upset.

"What's in Anacostia?" Natalie asked.

"It's your home for the night," the Senator explained. "If you can be a little slut with everyone in the Capitol and with your own cousin, you can certainly handle this crowd."

"Daddy! Please – this isn't fair," Natalie pleaded.

"And it wasn't fair for you to do anything you've done either," the Senator responded, handing Natalie the pills. "Joey got these pills for you.

Hopefully that baby will be gone by the time you get home in the morning. Now, get out!"

Dutifully, Natalie got out of the car and stood in the dark street.

"Please, daddy?" Natalie cried, following the car like a dejected whore chasing after payment.

"See you tomorrow," the Senator answered, pulling away and driving back to McLean to have a long discussion with his nephew.

Natalie didn't know what to do as there was no Metro line built at the time to bring her back into the safety of the inner District. The best course of action, she thought, was to locate a busy street and try not to be too obvious in the area that was heavily concentrated with blacks.

Since it was still early at about 9 p.m., she set forth toward the bridge her father had driven over to arrive in what all of Washington knew was its most dangerous area. But, as soon as she arrived on one of the busier streets, the catcalls began from boys and young men loitering the streets who were either peddling drugs or pimping their hookers out to diplomats. As long as commerce occurred, the kingpins were happy to oblige passage through the area for a steady stream of Mercedes, Cadillac, and other expensive cars whose drivers were motivated to make the trip for drugs or sex.

Natalie primarily tried to ignore most of the comments, walking quickly through the throngs but ultimately attracting attention due to her own lily white skin.

"What you doin' in dis 'hood?" one of them asked, stepping in her path and flanked by two other teenaged boys – all of them looking rather daunting.

"I got in a fight with my boyfriend in the car and he made me get out," she lied, trying to be as sympathetic as possible.

"You wanna hang?" the other solicited, smiling and grabbing his crotch.

"I need to make it home. My parents will be worried," Natalie suggested, hoping to diffuse any desirability even though she was particularly attractive regardless of the situation.

"We say when you go, bitch," the third proclaimed, taking her by the wrist.

The second guy took her other wrist and she began to struggle to no avail. Moving toward an alley, the three men dragged Natalie into the darkness and systematically raped her up against the wall one after the other. They had mastered the art form of dominance, which included a healthy dose of mental conditioning in an attempt to convince Natalie that she was indeed the complete slut who deserved their attention. It was a blessing that it happened, as they followed her like ghosts in the distance assuring her safe passage as their seed inside her made her their 'bitch' and no one else's on the avenue. She found a late-night diner for protection, stumbling past the counter and waitress as she rushed to the bathroom to vomit and rinse out her vagina to cleanse herself of the demonic offering she had just received.

Locating a pay phone, she called a friend to pick her up which guaranteed no questions would be asked about why she was in Anacostia or why she looked so disheveled. Walking into her house, she immediately rushed to her bedroom and showered for what seemed like an hour. She was pleasantly surprised that the pills her father had given to her in the car had not been lost. Swallowing the muscle relaxant first, she waited several minutes before taking the pill that she hoped would induce an immediate expulsion from her uterus.

Bravely laying in bed, she wore a pad to catch the initial drops of forced menstruation, signaling the start of the process along with severe contractions as the body was chemically fooled into starting its cycle. After a while, the pad was not enough and she propped herself on the toilet, flushing every so often until the cramps subsided.

The sense of loss in losing an extension of her body tugged at her budding maternal instinct, and she buried her face in her arms and silently cried herself to sleep – thinking about her hand in destroying the new life, even if it would have been a bastard child. Her dreams were tormented by images of the Californian intern returning to marry her and start an idyllic family and then mentally assaulting her by openly cheating with any number of women. Mikel and Joey figured prominently as laughing faces mocked her at every turn.

She awoke to being shunned by half of the household. Barbara hadn't known what had happened since she had been on a visit to see Jane in New York, and Seth was older and far too involved with his own projects to understand or care about how his younger sister might be feeling. The other men in her life did an artful job in ignoring her completely, and Natalie felt isolated and unable to confide in anyone. Mikel cut off her cocaine supply – also meaning she didn't get the weekly sex that had sustained her young lustful urges. Joey stopped encouraging and rewarding the whorish behavior that caused her self-worth to plummet quickly. The Senator acted as if his daughter was invisible. The ones who had been so staunchly involved in her life had virtually vanished without concern in less than a week and without discussion or explanation. She hadn't done anything wrong, yet was being blamed for the entire situation.

After about a week of miserable treatment and desperate for peace, she wandered around the house to the various bathroom cabinets, and found a delightful grouping of pills to mix together. Sitting on the same sofa where she had been violated by Mikel and Joey in the family room just two years before, she began to swallow all 150 pills of many varieties – aspirin, Vicodin, sleeping pills – chased with vodka shots. The dizzying affects made her laugh as she then wandered upstairs and climbed into bed naked to try conjuring up one final self-initiated orgasm before her body checked out as death allowed a warm calm she hadn't known in several years.

Chapter 13
RAD REHAVIOR
1985 - 2009

'Bad behavior' was the kindest description that New York's elite had labeled for how Joey Torrance's life had played out before their eyes. Many were shocked that the poor excuse of a human shell had survived the years of alcohol, drugs, sex, and escapades which usually resulted in him breaking a bone or spending the weekend strung out in the hospital, but surprisingly never anything more serious than that. Naturally attractive, he was nearly on the precipice of the process many of those in high society typically reached, falling into gradual disrepair at 40 that would slowly ripen into total decay by age 70.

The tipping point would usually be a midlife self-realization for children of successful families who had little drive or ambition and not much intelligence other than the street smarts to broker a drug deal and maybe a hobby like being an armchair artist that could have been exploited to fuel their own successes in life. The conundrum was self-inflicted, as the usual suffocating grip and ego from the generation before never allowed the sons to have the success the fathers had enjoyed in building and nurturing their empires. Jealousy propelled an odd rivalry between each layer of family, where the goal was to act as puppeteer for as long as possible until the son would ultimately unseat the father.

Jane had tried to interest him at a young age in Torero, but the untold trauma of his early life signaled a much different direction that he would take. As a spoiled young man, he had a run of the city at 21 when Jane purchased him his own apartment at the Dakota. The building was close enough to get there quickly if she needed, but far enough away across Central Park to disinterest Joey from traveling too often to The Grand.

Along the way, he had pissed off nearly every drug dealer in the city, on several occasions trying the trade with great success only to find himself encroaching on the territory of a much larger member of a cartel and needing to pay off his wrongdoing with a large cash payment to the offended criminal.

He literally used women - or 'holes' as he referred to them - as receptacles for the temporary pleasure that sex gave him. As someone with really no conscience, the only way he was put in his place was if someone or something was bigger, stronger, or had more influence or money did so. Jane had been so disgusted with him on a number of occasions, including his affairs with several maids, but always responded favorably in the end to her only son and heir by spending millions to settle potential lawsuits and appease his own sick pleasures.

When he was 'on' he was 'on,' but only for limited durations. Several times – usually every three or four years – he'd appear at Torero in a new suit ready to assume some vice-presidency, only to languish when personality could not replace substance in running whatever minor division the executive floor would dole out to him knowing the result prior to it occurring.

Rehabs were far too conventional for Joey, where he would ultimately be caught turning the patients against staff in a sublime race to secure his popularity that was his mental indicator of success. During group sessions, he'd labor over descriptions of his lifestyle and saying that he didn't know why he was there. Discussing his love of drinks, sex, and drugs, the other patients salivated over the intoxicating accounts where he'd ponder how something 'so wonderful as a high' could be so bad including the lavish parties where hundred-foot lines of cocaine encircled swimming pools in the Hamptons. He'd tricked all the treatment facilities including a unique medical spa that had hoped to realign his chemical balance. The joyous feeling of making the other patients feel insignificant and that if he could do it – why couldn't they – was almost as good as the drugs themselves.

"Wassup?!" Joey called down the table, a typical question whenever entering a room. Visiting on a vacation from his fellow Jeffersonians at 16, he paraded with confidence in front of the dinner guests at his mother's penthouse.

"Are you planning on joining us?" Jane wondered.

"Not tonight – too many people to go out and see," he said, walking toward the head of the table, greeting the 23 guests along the way, to dutifully kiss his mother goodnight and continue the charade of decency, even though his legendary reputation was well-known to Jane's guests but never discussed out of respect.

"Well, don't be too late," Jane requested, knowing that he would not return until the early morning hours and would proceed to sleep all day as he filtered the drugs out of his comatose body.

Without fail, some college girl who thought she was seeing a freshman at NYU would pick him up out in front of the building and whisk him away to the any of the best parties in town that he'd selected to attend. With the hope that they'd become 'Mrs. Torrance,' the girls would undoubtedly succumb to his wickedness but would only survive one night of hope. Joey's 'one-mount' rule suggested that each of his girls only stood to succeed for one session - if that - as he would only sexually please himself once inside each of them before discarding them or participating in the vile game of 'sloppy seconds.' The years blended together as the same routine transferred from school to a new life of vacations and parties with his New York home as the central base.

With that much money and no responsibility, it was easy for him to get caught up in bad choices. His disputes with his circle of friends that included hookers, junkies, drug dealers, as well as Jane herself were part of the familiar self-imposed dramatic edge that consumed everything about him. If it were perfect, in his mind it should be ruined, disputed, argued, or fought. And, it was a tremendously easy way for everyone to stay confused just enough for him to seem somewhat functional, even though he was nearing what would be a spectacular fall.

Having a special fondness for aged prostitutes who were the only ones either mentally ill or physically diseased enough to tolerate his extreme requests and few limits that he pushed in an attempt make his lifestyle seem relevant, he loved Tulip best. She'd slink up to his apartment every three months or so in signature sunglasses and a red wig that kept the late-night doormen guessing about the identity of the obviously camouflaged whore. She'd been the only regular of Joey's for years.

One Saturday night in Fall, Tulip received the familiar message. Hailing a taxi from some second-rate generic brand midtown hotel, she arrived at The Dakota and proceeded without issue to the elevator and up to Joey's impressive accommodations. He had unlocked the door for her since he was watching porn in his screening room. She knew what to do, knowing his normal drill. Her long legs straddled him on the plush sofa which was littered with drug paraphernalia including several syringes full with his favorite late-night delight, heroin. He slipped his meth-powered erection up inside her and she encased it with skill, beginning what had become a near-quarterly transference of sexual experience between them from the numerous sexual encounters each had had since their last rendezvous. She seemed not to mind, smiling at him with her sunglasses still on and smoking a bowl to relax.

"You're always such a hot pig," Joey suggested to her, moaning as she intensified her ride. Peeing a little up inside her upon each thrust without her feeling it, he rationalized cavorting inside what he considered a swine's dirty crevice by marking his territory. The piss made her cunt even more moist than it already was due to the excitement of the familiar connection she shared with her much-younger client.

"Don't call me a fuckin' pig, little boy," the old whore whispered in a muffled voice as she pistoned forward.

"Why not, you stupid used-up slut?" he questioned, irritated that she would ever defy his wishes and thereby nearly ruin his special whore fantasy which was one of the only things that could get him off after years of boredom in sampling such a cornucopia of pussy.

"Stop it," Tulip responded as she hovered closer to his face so he could nibble on her sagging yet ample tits while he attempted to muster a delivery of cum. "I'm a lady."

"Listen you dumb cunt, I don't want a lady to take my fucking load. I want a fucking bitch in heat to take it," he yelled in a near-frantic and rageful state with his desire to release. Looking up at her as their tempo accelerated and purposefully trying to provoke her, he spit in her face.

"All right," she said in a raised voice, as she tightened her pussy to launch into a final bull ride. "You can have 'bitch.'"

Joey hadn't noticed that the seasoned hooker had easily surveyed the lay of the land prior to implanting herself on the sofa, knowing exactly where the syringes were located. Good whores like Tulip knew their environment better than their johns as a technical necessity in their sometimes-dangerous line of work.

"Make your bitch pregnant if you can then," shouted Tulip as she laughed and bounced up and down with force, mocking him while still trying to coax an orgasm out of the drugged-out shithead in front of her.

"Bitch, you're too fucking old," Joey defiantly yelled. "Slam me – your hard boy wants to unload." Never forgetting his successes as a teen and young man in manipulating everyone including a number of the city's leading debutantes who ultimately required abortions to rid themselves of his toxic yet potent seed, he still referred to himself as 'hard boy.' The label had been passed down to him by elder delinquents due to his inhuman skill of being able to maintain a full erection with total sexual delivery during even the most daunting physiological strains to the body.

"Ok you little bastard," she responded as the sweat dripped from both of their bodies when Joey extended his arms to receive an offering of empowerment from the old witch.

Tulip paused to lovingly jam the syringes of heroin into both of Joey's arms and proceeded to fully empty the contents into his body before continuing her rhythmic assault on his penis with her well-heeled snatch. His body shuddered and she could feel the cock surge inside her as the drug coursed into his system, causing a quiet shutdown to where he lay in front of her in a near-coma daze due to the host of influences already present in his system including significant quantities of alcohol, meth, cocaine, Oxycontin, and Klonopin.

She jumped up, convinced she'd ended his pathetic existence, cleaned herself off and quickly left the apartment – not even hearing the sounds of a party directly beneath. As she entered the elevator car to be transported to the lobby, another car arrived on his floor and three men from the function in the apartment below burst into Joey's lobby, lead by his no-longer-tolerant downstairs neighbor. Since the old hooker had just shut the door on her quick exit without locking it, the three men ran into Joey's apartment to look for its sole resident.

"Where are you, you fucking asshole," Peter Clasanno loudly announced as he opened several doors on a search for Joey. The hot-tempered investment banker had brought two guests from his engagement party below that had been interrupted by the loud banging of Joey's cavort with Tulip that had caused some of the ceiling plaster to release onto his guests and piano. "Ah, there you are," Peter said arriving in the screening room. "You fucking piece of shit."

Holding Joey's comatose body face to face, Peter let out a string of profanities that ended with him spitting at Joey's face and releasing him to fall to the ground. The three then proceeded to violently unleash on the body for what appeared to be nearly five minutes of mutilation that was cheered on by the party revelers below. They abruptly left the apartment, slamming the door to return to the happy festivities of the engagement fête.

The body was then finally able to peacefully rest, albeit on the floor, for the next several hours. The Dakota's housekeeping staff arrived for its 4 a.m. shift in the building's common areas – and with the group concealed as janitors were two key assassins from Garcia, the Mexican drug cartel in the city to which whose leader Joey had made a snide comment about his girlfriend, thinking because of his money and connections that he had somehow exempted himself from harm. The two figures, fully prepared to disable any security system or compromise any lock, were equally surprised that Joey's door was unlocked. Finding him in the screening room, the scientific side of assassination began to unfold.

Seeing that something other than their own craft had seemed to have already killed Joey as they kicked at the body, they were not about to leave the apartment without presenting their leader's calling card to the city and produced a hacksaw. They were overjoyed that he would lie motionless during the procedure, as an animated subject was often far less pleasant to work on. They started the task of severing his head. Before long, the head was free from the body and the two laughed and threw the head back and forth a couple of times before getting a chain with two hooks on either end out of a bag and attaching it to the chandelier in the foyer. The neck was impaled on the hook at the end, leaving the mangled body with countless broken bones in the screening room. After extinguishing their cigarettes into the skin on Joey's face, they locked the door behind them and blended back into the cleaning brigade as a surprise awaited Joey's morning maid.

Chapter 14
A LOOMING LEGACY
2010

As the second highest-ranking senior senator in the entire governing body, having been elected in 1970, the notable perks were visible at every turn for Senator Chambers – even upon announcing his retirement. As a Republican and ranking minority member of the powerful Foreign Relations Committee, he was able to secure numerous benefits including over $2 billion in earmarks for his state in partnership with his fellow Republican, the recently-retired Albert Ochs who held the same position on the Appropriations Committee. As he neared retirement, checks from campaign contributors poured into his leadership PAC, the unregulated reservoir of funds used by senior members of the Senate and House for personal or political use after leaving office. The homage to the great statesman was notable through the sheer number of offerings.

"One thing we won't miss about you is your wandering eye," Senate Ethics Committee Vice-Chairman Senator James Flaxton joked, admonishing Senator Chambers for his years of quiet homosexual exploits and liaisons with staff that only select colleagues knew about as they walked to a meeting with minority leadership to determine how to position the state for a new candidate upon his retirement. "But, we've kept our bargain and you've kept yours – there are only a few more votes on campaign finance before you leave next year."

For a politician to make a career out of the Senate, concessions were made daily among its members. Senator Flaxton's public works projects were the topic of much debate in the media but kept him elected by a state grateful to have infrastructure investment and jobs. He and his colleagues traded tax dollars and regulatory loopholes with the velocity that general managers traded players on professional baseball teams. As an enthusiastic senator who was not afraid to use a filibuster or his seniority to derail a beloved bill of anyone who threatened his own special earmarks to projects he championed, Senator Chambers had made an amnesty deal with his own caucus years before that his vote would always be a solid 'no' on any issue related to campaign finance reform as long as his pet projects for the state were shepherded through the process.

The late summer of 2010 was excruciatingly hot as they passed through the Senate Subway tunnel toward the Capitol from their offices in the Russell Senate Office Building. The political friends had been elected at the same time and shared that special bond of being the last two still in office from the same Senate class.

"Can you believe we've been here for 40 years?" said Malcolm as they arrived at Senate's Minority Leadership Offices, thinking back to his indiscretions outlined by Jim. "And who are you to talk? Each bridge you build out of appropriations goes anywhere but somewhere useful in your state!"

"It's a little bit different than screwing every intern you hire. I've heard it's like a goddamn beauty contest at your state office for applicants," Senator Flaxton outlined. "And how many of them have you gotten jobs at your sister's company, or at any other number of the companies that support you if they threaten to go public?"

"Everyone is grateful for the help," Malcolm asserted. "My organization has kept me here, not the party." He was right – each of the young men who had been honored to be that close to their idol would never betray the secret to the greater world. If they had attempted to do so, a strong machine was in place to deal with that sort of insolence as well, as it would easily crush any future opportunities for career growth or happiness in retirement.

As they entered Minority Leader Holden Curry's office, a familiar accent spouted forth from the bathroom concealed by an Oriental screen.

"We'll if it isn't the intern-loving lawmaker from the West," Senator Curry wryly said. "Did Jim tell you who we want you to endorse?"

"No, but I'm sure you will, Holden," Malcolm pronounced, eyeing the ever expanding waistline of his colleague. "It's too bad we don't have stock in one of those shithole food processing plants you have down in Alabama. It looks like you've been munching on a few extra pork rinds."

"Now, now, gentlemen, let's get down to business," Jim counseled as they sat around the small table in the ornate office of the party's senior-most lawmaker.

"So, who is it?" Malcolm wondered.

"Your son. Run him as a Democrat and he can switch in three years," Holden flatly said. "Family continuity, name recognition, aunt's campaign money."

"Not a chance," Malcolm refused. "We want him to work for Jane for a while and learn something other than politics. He's on a path to becoming chairman of the company, Holden."

"How long has he been on your staff in Foreign Relations, Malcolm?" asked Jim.

"Fifteen years," Malcolm recalled, "and it's time for him to leave Washington and get into the family business."

"This is the family business," Holden bluntly disagreed. "He's more useful to us than he is to your sister's company."

"Malcolm, he'll get the money eventually – you all will," Jim explained. "Support this for the party. We cannot afford to lose this seat."

"He can have one of your hideaways, and we'll guarantee that he won't be in the basement of Dirksen," Holden dictated, referencing the placement of junior senators in the dregs of office locations until they had built up seniority.

"Let me talk with Jane and see what she thinks," Malcolm conceded. "Maybe he can transition to the private sector now to make it look like he's got the background for the campaign."

"Good man," Holden said. "Now, try to keep it in your pants until the election. A custodian had reported some illicit activity in your hideaway last week – thank God you had your clothes on."

"That cost the party $50,000, Malcolm," said Jim. "We don't want any more mistakes at this point."

"It's just really difficult," Senator Chambers conceded. "They're all so perfect. Late nights are lonely between votes."

"How about coming to spend some time in the cloak room once and a while with us then?" Jim challenged.

"Let me go see if Jane can come down to talk," Malcolm said, as he quietly excused himself from the frank discussion that would set a future course for generations of his family to come, leaving his colleagues to debate other critical races for the election cycle. "She is 74," Malcolm continued, turning to his colleagues at the door. "Get the unlimited exemption to the inheritance tax back within the next five years and you've got a deal."

⟶◈⟵

"Janey, will you be in Washington anytime soon?" asked Malcolm, making the difficult phone call from his corner office in the Russell Building where he had a view straight down the Washington Mall to the National Gallery, Washington Monument and beyond.

"Hello to you too, Malcolm," Jane answered. "You know I'm trying to get things finalized here in New York for the move."

"I know. Well, maybe we can start with a phone call," Malcolm replied. "I just got out of a meeting with the leadership where they informed me of their choice to replace me in retirement."

"Oh, really?" Jane asked. "Whom are they thinking about?"

"Not thinking about – demanding," Malcolm responded. "They think Seth would be a great candidate to replace his father."

"Seth?" Jane screamed. "But what about me?"

"I have no choice, Jane," Malcolm outlined with exasperation. "They basically told me what we're going to do with him. Besides, if he's in for one term, he'll be out before he's 50 and can ease into Torero and be a respected board chairman."

"Malcolm, he has no experience yet. How can he a chairman?" Jane protested.

"George Mitchell did the same thing at Disney," Malcolm explained, referencing Maine's popular senator and gifted diplomat who helped transition Disney to new leadership after the reign of Michael Eisner.

"He was in his sixties, Malcolm, and an attorney with three terms in the Senate," Jane explained. "Remember, I was a director during that period of time and I know it well. Seth needs at least five years with the company before we could promote him, regardless of the shares the family controls. I don't need the proxy advisory services holding us under the same type of magnifying glass that they used on Michael and his cronies."

"What am I supposed to do then?" Malcolm asked. "They are absolutely set on it."

186

"Why not ask him," Jane angrily suggested. "Ask him if he wants to spend his life rotting away in the Capitol or if he wants something more meaningful with our family's company. Remember where the money that put you in office came from and has allowed you virtual freedom to do anything and everything you want back there – some things I'm sure I don't even want to know about."

"Be reasonable, Janey," Malcolm pleaded.

"Reasonable? I am reasonable! I have a good mind to call Holden myself and spell out F – U -," Jane said as Malcolm quickly interrupted.

"No. No. How about this? We'll just run a really shitty campaign for him," Malcolm suggested. "I'd want him to transition now, he needs to live in Oregon before the election and we'd need to give him a hefty title. Trust me. I want him at Torero too."

"At 44 years old, you should!" Jane exclaimed and then joked, "I don't want a Bashar Assad in charge of my company."

"They are the same age. I've met him," Malcolm continued with a smile, thinking about the young Syrian president who was unexpectedly plucked from his career as an eye doctor to receive a crash-course from his father on running the country.

"Enough!" Jane grumbled with an exasperated sigh. "Fix this, please. I don't need another thing to think about this month."

"OK, I'll talk to Holden again but I think the false-run will be the best course of action. Talk to you soon," Malcolm said, hanging up and sitting at his mammoth desk staring out the window.

—◦◦◦—

"Holden, I need another meeting," Malcolm requested during a call to his friend the Minority Leader.

"What on earth for," Holden asked. "Were you at the last one?"

"Joking aside, I think Jane is fine with the decision," Malcolm said. "I just need some time to brief Seth and get him in the mindset to run."

"You have two weeks," Holden offered.

"Make it three," Malcolm requested. "This will be hard."

"Under the circumstances, I can do that. Good-bye," said an annoyed Holden who was typically used to getting his way immediately on most everything. After many years in Washington and being idolized by generations of staff members, constituents, lobbyists, political peers, and leaders of corporations and countries, it was difficult for the one hundred men and women regardless of party affiliation in the country's most private enclave of power to maintain perspective on normal human relations and that they were indeed not deities.

Chapter 15
CHANGES
2010

Calling his son into his office would be a laborious proposition. Senator Chambers had rehearsed how to convince his son that the Senate would be the best possible life for his future. The door opened, and before him stood Seth, a trim, well-educated, and attractive man who had known no other life than working in foreign policy at both the State Department and then for his father's committee.

"Hi, Dad," Seth said, hugging his father. "You never call me over here to the office. What's going on?"

"Well, leadership here has a proposal they want me to float for you," Malcolm suggested.

Seth already knew that with retirement around the corner for his father that there was speculation that he'd join the ranks of Lisa Murkowski in a legacy bid for his father's seat. He didn't want to seem too eager, however, as his temperamental father was sometimes particularly hard on him as the only child left.

"Are they happy with my committee work?" Seth asked, knowing it had absolutely nothing to do with anything policy-related.

"Absolutely!" the Senator laughed. "They want you to run for my seat."

The revelation was an answer to one of Seth's dreams. After Georgetown Prep, he had attended Georgetown and received a degree in political science followed by Harvard Law School. While he was a talented policy analyst, he had secretly always desired to be in the driver's seat. Having lived an exemplary life – Eagle Scout, good grades, starting a family - especially after his sister's unfortunate suicide, and held himself to a higher standard because it was his fervent desire to carry on the family tradition of public service. He knew that with no other heirs, some of his aunt's vast fortune would ultimately be transferred to him and even $100 million would be an acceptable remembrance of her legacy.

"Wow. That's a lot to take in," Seth admitted, even with preparing to answer the question for years. "What about Aunt Jane and the company?"

"She'll be fine – she initially blew a gasket over the phone, but this year will be good for you to use your position at the company for campaigning," the Senator explained.

"What does she have in mind for me?" Seth queried, knowing his aunt was hoping that he'd quit politics altogether and work for her exclusively, eventually being promoted to chairman of the company upon her retirement.

"For the campaign, you'll have to move to Oregon," Malcolm explained, recounting all the necessary details. "Then, she's carved out what will be a unique niche for you at her personal offices in Portland when they're done. Your new title will be Senior Vice-President and Corporate Liaison. Quadruple your current salary as well. You can keep the house in Washington and she'll buy you one in Oregon eventually. When you win, you can have our house in McLean if you want it since we'll be moving back to Portland."

"So, I'll basically campaign in the new position?" Seth wondered.

"About half and half," reported Malcolm. "Remember your aunt's first goal is about succession – and learning the business."

"That I can do," Seth agreed.

"Now, here are some other details – you'll have to run as a Democrat," Malcolm said as his son winced. "There's no other way right now and you can switch parties in a few years. And, I'm going to bring in Penny to manage your campaign from a distance so you get support from Republicans as well. Your aunt may not want it because of the company, but I want you to sit in my seat. Now, I'd suggest you go talk to Angela and prepare her for what's ahead."

"Here's hoping she likes the plan – Aunt Jane will owe her a shopping trip!" Seth laughed, getting up to drive to his home in Alexandria to explain his future path to his wife.

"Good luck, son," Malcolm said, embracing his son as they walked toward the office door.

"Angie – where are you?" Seth yelled has he entered the simple town-house that he and his wife Angela had purchased in their first year of Seth's job at the State Department in a quiet neighborhood in Alexandria.

"Up here, honey," Angela called from the bedroom. "I'm trying on some of the things your mother brought over from her latest trip to New York."

Upon entering the room, Seth jumped on the bed and watched his wife modeling her latest dress.

"It's nice to have an aunt isn't it?" Seth said.

"Damn right it is," Angela agreed, taking off the dress to reveal her lace bra and panties. A strong and driven woman, she enjoyed the many privileges of having married into one of the country's wealthiest families. Having been told of Seth's family's money as a freshman at Georgetown, she brilliantly used every tool available to appeal to him. It wasn't a skill that was uncommon, as women for years before her had ensnared their male objects of affection in a web as a way to secure their own future.

Growing up in the working class with laborer parents, she would often recount her current fabled lifestyle on Facebook, projecting about the numerous events to which she was invited to for an extended cadre of loose acquaintances to salivate over. Her drug of choice was the envy that it produced by flaunting her entitled existence in front of those who simply had not been as creative to bed the goose with the golden egg. She was loved for her devotion to her husband and children, and despised by others for whom they saw to be a calculating gold digger and more of a sexual servicer than wife with truly equal credentials and pedigree.

"What did your dad want?" Angela asked, referencing Seth's earlier meeting with the Senator.

"The party wants me to run," Seth announced, still sitting on the bed and smiling.

"No fucking way!" Angela exclaimed, hopping on the bed still in her undergarments to give her husband a kiss. "What's your aunt going to say?"

"Well, we have to move to Portland as soon as possible. I'm working for her office there while we campaign," Seth explained. "She doesn't want me to run, but Dad is forcing the issue along with the leadership."

"Move to Portland?" Angela shrieked, thinking of missing her friends and life she had built in the capital. "For how long?"

"Just until we win! Less than a year," Seth confidently proclaimed.

Angela could hardly contain herself of the prospect of making the leap from one of thousands of spouses of government policy wonks to what assuredly could be a life of excitement as the wife of a United States Senator. She yearned for her own place in society and this would certainly cement her future possibilities of her name on buildings and the adulation from countless constituencies.

There was a certain political aficionado back in Oregon whom Angela had secretly admired who had toyed with running for governor but decided against it. She modeled her own Washington, D.C. life in many respects based on many of the old tricks the candidate-who-never-was used to cement support from both Republican and Democratic leaders in the state. Like him, she deeply concealed her family's Jewish background in favor of the Chambers' Episcopal faith.

Both she and her unsuspecting proctor planned their vacations to the most remote sections of Oregon to the puzzlement of her in-laws who were firmly Portland people in an effort to appeal to a large constituency across the state. Angela was viewed by confidants in her life as an honorable Washington wife who cared deeply for her adopted state, Oregon. A New York native was an additional layer of shared bond with the gentleman hadn't ever known that he shaped her decisions to build robust political respect from an ever-growing sphere.

"Do you want to come with me to the first meeting?" Seth asked.

"Are you kidding? Of course I want to come!" Angela exclaimed.

"It'll be unconventional – it's with Penny Brockland," Seth explained.

"Oh God. That woman is a fucking bitch! How your father put up with her for all these years is beyond me!" Angela pondered.

"She's not that bad, Ang," Seth retorted. "She's being brought in to help us win."

"I'll be interested to see what she says," Angela said softy, unbuttoning her husband's pants to celebrate the beginning of a new lifestyle.

As Seth and Angela walked into The Capitol Hill Club the next morning, Penny was waiting for them in the lounge.

"Well, hello candidates!" Penny greeted the couple with an unlikely cheery attitude. "Are you ready to plan your big announcement?"

"Penny, thank you for helping with this. Will you have to resign from Dad's office to help?" Seth asked, as they both followed her into one of the private rooms.

"No. Your campaign manager will be Doris Watson," Penny announced.

"What?" Seth laughed. "She's a goddamn union organizer."

"And, that's what we love about her," Penny explained. "Seth, you know a good lobbyist should be able to win both sides of their argument. She loves your father and is doing this for him."

"And, how do we sell the Democrat thing?" Seth continued.

"Easy! You've lost faith in the party to be socially accountable to the citizens of Oregon," Penny mused. "You miss the balanced party that your father was part of, yet believe in the fiscal responsibility for all Oregonians and government to make the state great again."

"Bravo! A perfect platform," Seth agreed.

"Maybe you should be running," Angela offered to Penny. "When do we announce?"

"Let's hold off and drive speculation a little," Penny suggested. "You'll move as soon as possible, before your aunt's office in Portland is complete. We'll place you for dinner at some restaurant talking with Doris one night, and then we'll be off to the races! The official announcement can be after Christmas, as people need some big news to break their winters up."

"So many details I don't understand," Angela confessed. "I suppose it'll take time to get to know the routine."

"It'll be a whirlwind for both of you," Penny agreed. "The important thing is to make sure you know you're on stage from this moment forth."

"With dad, we're always on stage," Seth pointed out. "Any other special instructions before we pack?"

"Your aunt's real estate agent in Oregon will help you locate a property. Here's the information for Kate Carerra of the Sylvia Siskel Agency," Penny handed them some information. "When you get back to Oregon, Doris will be waiting for your call."

As the young Chambers couple left the club, they decided to pop down to Capitol South's METRO stop and ride to the Smithsonian to walk the Mall and ponder campaign ideas between each other. They knew that Penny and Doris would prove to be vital advisors for what would be an unusual election year.

⸺⸺

Even though she didn't like the concept of a campaign or the probable result, Aunt Jane was kind to the only family she had left. In a departure from her regular loan of the Hawker jet for a commute to Oregon, she opted to allow Seth and Angela to use the Bombardier because it would give them more space for a quick transference of personal items to Portland without spending a lot of time on a move. With two children in tow, the family made its way to the state for what would be a short year of residency if the election favored the newly-Democratic Seth.

Barbara Jane, eleven, and Clay Joseph, nearly two, were themselves living monuments to their relatives. Angela had specifically required that Seth's mother and aunt be honored with their girl's name, and the boy would have the distinction of bringing Jane even closer to the family with the memory of both her husband and son. Thankfully, neither of the children suffered from any physical or mental issues and were generally well-behaved at the behest of their strict stay-at-home mother. The plane ride was comfortable, and Barbara Jane as the oldest seemed to be taking the entire journey and transition in stride.

Angela stirred with excitement as they approached Portland, something she wouldn't ever have thought would happen even though she did understand her father-in-law would retire one day. When in Oregon, she would be on display during the campaign, but Kate had advised the young couple that since Torero was providing them housing before they purchased a home base, they should consider a penthouse unit in one of the many towers downtown to both be close to the temporary office and to shield the family from public view when they weren't on stage.

Already furnished, the unit looked toward Mt. Hood and was in a magnificent building replete with concierge, doorman, and special rooms for entertaining. It was a junior version of The Grand, Jane's old place in New York. With a large wrap-around terrace for their corner unit, it was like having a backyard even though it was several hundred feet above the street.

"She does know how to pick them," Seth conceded of Kate's work to locate the most desirable temporary home.

"Very nice!" Angela said, bringing Barbara Jane and Clay Joseph into the unit from the hall. "Barbie, go scout out your bedroom."

As the little girl ran down the long hall, Angela knew Seth would have to hit the ground running. "Time's wasting!" she said, pointing at her watch. "Don't you want to contact Doris about meeting tonight?"

"Look who's motivated," Seth replied. "I'll get on it."

Doris, the state's most powerful lobbyist and political strategist, was at the epicenter of Oregon's labor union politics and had created a machine so powerful that if she wanted to walk into a legislator's office she didn't ever need an appointment or to disclose the issue she wanted to discuss. She'd pop in, say bill number 'X' with a thumb up or down – and that was enough to make a vote go the way she wanted it to. As the unofficial whip of both the Oregon Senate and House, she would waddle up and down the halls of the Capitol with a strange trio of assistants wrangling votes from sometimes-new legislators who didn't understand her grip on the process or that her kindness would determine their longevity in office.

Maggie Narman, known as the party's 'rainman' and aptly named for her savant abilities, was an oddly featured woman. Her penchant for a polyester wardrobe made her somewhat of a disconcerting sideshow attraction throughout the Capitol. Her role in Doris' operation was to spread the gossip of interest for the day to anyone who would listen in the Capitol. Doris wouldn't feed Maggie information herself, but had a loyal following of committee administrators and legislative assistants who would plant a juicy detail with her in the morning while she loitered in some poor soul's office rambling on about some issue. By noon, the entire building knew the fate of the next day's votes based on Doris' political desires. Maggie was also the central databank for electoral information. Scouring statistical documents right down to the precinct was euphoric for her slightly-touched brain, and she could tell Doris from memory the voting patterns for any district in the state as far back as 1950 as well as the candidates and victorious election winners. She also knew all their hot buttons for issues important both to the district and legislator.

While Doris herself was always fair to the other side, her clients didn't care to understand or learn the art form of consensus – a building block for successful bipartisan relations. With the sheer numbers of electoral power, they didn't have to understand the grace of politics. So, Doris relied on former Legislative Counsel Gary Saliero to provide technical backup to win any argument and write a bill's text with iron-clad structure so compromise was an impossibility, a skill he mastered in law school and private practice before accepting an appointment to be the Legislature's top bill author.

To round out the team, Doris needed a mouthpiece as she never testified before committees and rarely gave interviews to the media as the quiet orchestrator of the political agenda of her clients. The fiery Nancy Hillat was ideal for the role. Testifying, interviews, and giving the media what they wanted required Nancy to be able to think quickly on her feet without much preparation. With a photographic memory, she could easily remember the substantive components for a myriad of issues, and was valuable in putting dissenting voices that weren't on her side into a collective corner. She was a striking woman, rumored to have had affairs with more than several lobbyists and legislators.

Picking up the phone, Seth dialed Doris at her firm, Watson Packer VanderClint.

"Seth!" Doris said, sitting at her desk while playing solitaire on her computer. "Are you ready to make some people curious?"

"Sure am, Doris," Seth replied, having known her since he was a little boy when she had worked for Senator Chambers prior to converting to the 'dark side' of politics, one of his father's favorite terms for the liberal spectrum across the aisle. "When and where?"

"There's a big event for the symphony tonight at The Parkway," Doris suggested as an option. "Media, power brokers, everyone is going to be there. We'll sit in the restaurant toward the front so all of them can see us on the way in."

"This is going to be fun," Seth admitted, chuckling to himself on how Doris had planned for each small detail and contingency.

"More than that – I asked the hostess who else had reservations. She's going to seat Ursula and John Carter right near us about halfway through – so play the role for the town crier," Doris suggested. "5 p.m. tonight."

"See you there," Seth said as he prepared to get ready for his inaugural performance as a candidate.

"OK, Ang," Seth said to his wife as he prepared to go make his first splash in public life. Dressed in a conservative navy suit and patriotic striped tie, he was ready to campaign. "I'll be back no later than nine."

"Take as long as you need. The kids and I have our Wii and Netflix all ready for the night," she said, giving him a kiss.

Seth took the elevator down to the car, and maneuvered through the light rush hour traffic and decided to valet park as it would make more of an entrance. The last moment of privacy upon him, he entered the Parkway through its restaurant entrance.

Standing in the lobby was Doris, who had walked from her office a block away. Straight white shoulder length hair disguised what had become a relatively broad face. She always wore an untucked blouse with a long skirt and black stockings, complimenting her signature Birkenstock shoes. Her beaded shoulder-strap purse had undoubtedly been picked up at Portland's bastion of crafts, Saturday Market. Beaming, she nearly ran up to him to offer a hug. Politics were not particularly about a lifestyle to Doris, but the art of deploying policies that she deemed as 'right' for society.

"It's so good to see you," Doris said.

"It's good to see you, too," Seth fondly replied, embracing the elder liberal activist.

The hostess seated them as planned near the front in a corner, visible to everyone who would enter the building at 5:30 p.m. for the function in a ballroom prior to the symphony's season kickoff concert. Seth had noticed that Pioneer Square had been tented again for the occasion, and while his mother had not been involved with the planning, she had made the suggestion that the committee use Martino Quimby to make sure the event would be managed perfectly. After the performance, the throngs of donors would be escorted to a party under the stars visible through the clear tent canopy.

"Well, I talked to that old bitch Penny," Doris chuckled. "She told me about how they planned to convert you to the blue party. Pretty damn sneaky."

Seth smiled and acknowledged the old sage in front of him at the table.

"However, there's a lot of work to do," she explained as she took Seth on a journey through the trenches of liberal politics in the state. "You'll have to concede some of that Republican blood for the unions. Right now, they've gotten so jaded since they're running out of things to do for their members.

197

There's incredible pressure from membership in general for unions to remain relevant. 'Economic fairness' is the new battle cry that's being used – and the people love it because they want to be victims instead of taking responsibility for their choices."

"Doris, we'll do whatever it takes to get elected," Seth said. "In the end, I think unions will like what I have to say."

"And, you might learn another perspective as well!" Doris retorted and sighed. "Even though I don't like the 'victim' crap they all try to sell, it's so much more than that at the end of the day. We'll start making the rounds prior to the announcement that should be in early November. But, this is a good unofficial start tonight."

"Penny had suggested the start of the year," Seth noted.

"And Penny's not running this campaign, is she?" Doris questioned with sarcasm. "If we do it in November then we get tables of families talking about it for two holidays."

"Excellent point. Who do you want me to schedule some meetings with?" Seth asked.

"Velma Foster," Doris suggested. "I think your mother even convinced her to endorse you. Bert Englund, and the investment crowd. Sylvia Siskel. Brent Chandler & Sue Helen Chastwick from the commercial property side. Those two are very liberal considering their real estate holdings. We have to be very careful about corporate contributors or the union support might fade. Despite your name recognition, I think we're going to have to raise $10 million if the Republicans decide to run one of their chromosome-deficient conservative assholes against you. And that's even after the conversion of your father's leadership PAC. What happened to all the old great ones in Oregon?"

"The party's been hijacked, Doris," Seth explained. "Moderates don't have a chance if they don't get involved, and I suppose we don't have anything to complain about since we're not doing something to recruit more sensible people for public service. Today's 'extreme right wacko' only represents a small percentage of Republicans. Dad is the last of the generation that had some connection with the center."

"Get ready for some solid days of hitting the streets – together and alone," Doris said. "Those 'extreme right wackos' keep me in business!"

"Is that it?" Seth joked, thinking the list of meetings was quite long for the first week of planning.

"There will be more," Doris responded, intending to fully educate Seth about his 'new' State that he had only been back to visit during some Senate recesses, a trick Hillary Clinton used when she adopted the State of New York as her own in a successful bid for the Senate. "You have to realize you're playing two different games here - urban and rural - not just Democrat or Republican."

Like clockwork, the Carters entered the building at 5:30 p.m. along with several other guests that interrupted Doris' pontification about the state's political flavors. Since John Carter sat on the museum's board, they wouldn't attend the concert itself but would dine in the restaurant with the new museum director and his wife. Ursula slinked curiously through the dining room, looking at every table but paying special attention to Seth and Doris, managing a small smile and polite wave.

The terraced restaurant was a theatre for spectators hoping to catch a glimpse of some of Portland's visible yet understated glitterati. The excitement started to swell with the arrival of more symphony guests as Seth and Doris didn't need to do much more than do a little small talk to be noticed, the substantive part of their business having already occurred. Their mere presence had the wheels turning in everyone's minds.

Even the political duo turned to watch Peter Northwood, the new director of the museum, and his stunning wife Karen, walking through the restaurant to join the Carters. Transplants from Houston, the Northwoods had co-curated one of the finest private art foundation collections in the world. The Carters had promised to help the new couple with donor prospecting during the symphony party, which was a brash new technique where the two couples would start at the beginning of the line to enter the tented event and work their way backwards – thereby meeting every possible donor of note in the process.

The Northwoods had taken Portland by storm with their unconventional approach to fund raising and daring shows, as it was a slightly comical scene to see their huge SUV pull up in front of Bistro Frenti. Karen would hop out and open the backseat door as three rich old broads would emerge from the car and hobble into the restaurant, pleased that someone had taken an interest in them. That interest typically translated into huge out-right gifts in the millions or promises for a bequest as the ladies were lucid, but typically ignored by their active families who left them to rot without an evening social outlet as an option to entertain them. The Northwoods were happy to capitalize on the relationship that made the ladies feel significant and the museum flush with cash.

The bigger surprise was when Seth's parents walked in after dinner. Coming to see how their son's meeting with Doris had gone, they had actually been invited by the liberal doyenne as icing on what she intended to be a magnificent cake of convergence to cement a landslide victory for her client.

"Mom, Dad!" Seth jumped to his feet to greet his parents as they both hugged Doris as well.

"Surprise!" Barbara giggled, not typically wanting to interfere in the political side of her family, much preferring a shopping trip with Jane in New York.

"Do we have time for dessert?" Senator Chambers asked the group.

"Most certainly," Doris replied, realizing that she had conjured up one of the strangest formulas for guests at one table, and was beaming at the prospect of making the newest entrant to Oregon's political scene the topic of speculation by every major media outlet in the state by the next morning.

After the Senator returned from some dutiful exchanges with campaign contributors around the restaurant, the foursome sat and talked in muffled voices while enjoying the truly spectacular dessert selections for what seemed to be an hour.

"We're only in town until tomorrow," the Senator announced. "So, we just stopped by to see what headway had been made."

"I'll have to tell you, Malcolm," Doris said as she stole a spoonful of crème brulee from the Senator's plate. "He's good – and he's going to be doing some initial meetings this week."

They were caught off guard by a random flash from a camera.

"Perfect," Doris said smiling. "Two more flashes and then we can walk around the perimeter of the party in the square. That should get the stations talking."

"What do we say?" Seth asked.

"Your father will speak if they ask anything, and then introduce you," Doris replied.

"How about the unions?" Malcolm pressed.

"In good time. Let's build some support from friends first," Doris advised.

By that time, the Carters and Northwoods had already gone to take their place as the unofficial greeters at the symphony party – but the interlopers could not be stopped as the Carters in their own right had recently contributed a small but significant $250,000 to the symphony's park concert series. Couple after couple filed out past the Senator, Barbara, Seth, and Doris on their way through what was a private door for the donors at the symphony hall to make a quick escape away from the crowds.

That night, everyone slept a little easier than before. Jane was pleased her nephew was in Oregon and at least on paper was hers as part of Torero for a year until the November elections. Malcolm and Barbara were relieved that their son had true purpose and meaning in his life and wasn't just another insignificant bureaucrat in Washington. Seth and Angela coiled closely together, dreaming of sitting together on election night in some hotel penthouse suite surrounded by supporters when the near-final results would be announced in their favor. Meanwhile, Doris was tossing and turning with excitement at the prospect of fully shaping the platform of her client, whose only focus had been foreign policy for the past fifteen years.

Chapter 16
INTRODUCTIONS
2011

In deference to her billionairess sister-in-law, Barbara was on a mission to recruit a circle of acquaintances for Jane's new environment and city for an ongoing game of bridge and social activities. Finding the right mix of ladies was a relative challenge, as many of Barbara's friends and fellow players shunned the idea of inviting the high-profile trespasser into their circle. Several ladies, however, were not to be intimidated - an elderly set that didn't care about their money or prestige being usurped by someone much higher on the wealth food chain.

To that end, Jane became Barbara's regular date to parties, even when Malcolm himself could attend. Barbara would dutifully call the host and note Jane's presence in town. She was rarely refused due to her own powerful station as the wife of the state's senior United States Senator. If anyone defied granting one of her requests, she would simply order her husband to make sure to "delay" things ranging from appropriations to tax breaks that were often included as riders to bills.

Barbara, however, was not owed favors by any of the ladies whom were ultimately selected to participate in the monthly games of party bridge that included a healthy dose of socializing in addition to showcasing the talent of players who each had the minimum of 50 years playing experience. The common thread was that each of the ladies was a native of the city and even the most liberal of the group squarely scoffed at new arrivals to the state. Barbara had explained that Jane was born in the state, sparing her from any indignant looks from the ladies.

Jane Scheinbach led the organizing of the games as she was the second oldest in addition to being a grand life master at 81 and enjoyed sending reminders out and creating the lists of the locations that would host each game that would always need to include a luncheon. Her husband who was still alive spent most of his time either at the investment and venture capital firm he founded where he was still active as chairman, or on the tennis courts at the Portland Heights Club. He had the distinction of providing the majority of the seed money in the late 1950's for some of the region's largest technology companies and was known as one of the fathers of Oregon's Silicon Forest.

None of the ladies had a dedicated bridge partner, and the odd duck of the group was Velma Foster, an African-American woman and the sole inhabitant from the group of Portland's East Side. Velma grew up in a politically-involved family and had the distinction of being the first black woman elected to Portland's City Council. As an only child who never married, she had built a significant fortune through inheriting the estates of childless relatives, and was considered the moral barometer of the group. She had a stunning home perched on the Alameda Ridge that commanded an exquisite view of downtown and the hills. At every bridge game where the location had a view toward the east, she would undoubtedly note that she could wave at her house from theirs. The ladies would labor over the prospect of driving to the eastside of the city for the games Velma would host. Most had a quiet rule to not cross 39th Avenue unless a trip to the airport were required.

Susan Strobe was always on prowl to sell art from her popular downtown gallery, and she had built 'the collection' – as she called it – from nothing to over 20,000 square feet of space where she represented many regionally-significant artists and consigned sales of additional high-profile pieces that were not lost to the larger auction houses in New York or London. She specifically made time for any and all bridge games she was invited to play in because it was perhaps the best business development tool in scouting out locations for new works to be sold. She could hardly wait until she would host the game to show Jane her unique townhouse in Portland's Pearl district that housed her personal art collection.

Barbara knew Jane would enjoy Julie Weber, as they could commiserate over the issues of running both a business and foundation. Julie's grandfather had founded one of the most successful lumber companies in the United States and the family's footprint in Portland was as dynastic as Jane's in New

York City. While her husband was chairman of the privately-held concern that included enormous forest land holdings, mills in Asia, and an international shipping company, Julie oversaw the vast foundation that had grown annually as the beneficiary of receiving enormous personal family contributions each year since 1971 in lieu of paying significant tax. With a personal net worth of $2.5 billion, she was the second wealthiest woman in the group whose foundation also had an asset base of nearly $800 million. It was about to be displaced by Jane's as the largest private philanthropic foundation in the state.

There was no one in the city who could claim the title of 'grand dame' better than Holly Beckham. While her husband was one of the most successful attorneys in the city and represented timber businesses, she had the distinction of having served on every major charitable board in the city over 40 years. Instead of art, she collected people and a party at her home was like attending a soiree where one could meet a liberal activist, a conservative politician, a famous artist, and an NBA basketball player all within the entry hall.

The final member of the eight-person collective was Mary Collier, the widow of the famous doctor and chemist who held a number of patents. While Mary had been limited to a fixed income from the trust her husband had created (which was a common practice that many of the men in that generation used to make sure that a second marriage after their deaths didn't result in their beloved wives being milked for money by some gigolo), she enjoyed her new home at the lush condo-tel where both Tess Parker and Mary Overton had purchased. The best view of downtown and the mountains was offered at Mary's on the 40th floor, where both the East and West sides of Portland could be seen from the riverfront building. The group was thankful that Mary's building had a restaurant, as rumors of her favored presentation for lunch or dinner – a dry meatloaf she would pull from the freezer – would be unacceptable to the group.

The first host was Jane Scheinbach – primarily because she planned the games and organized the introductory meeting at her palatial Dunthorpe estate off Riverwood Road that was directly in view of the Westmont's clubhouse across the river. Barbara had urged each of the ladies to arrive early to brief them about her sister-in-law on the beautiful summer day.

"Thank you all for agreeing to this," Barbara began as the group sat in the elegant reception room prior to occupying the two tables that had been set up in the drawing room. "I know none of us needs another commitment, but this is a very critical time for my sister-in-law and I appreciate it so much."

"Why exactly did she choose Portland again?" asked Julie Weber. "Why leave New York?"

"I had probably mentioned to you that my nephew, Jane's son, was murdered in 2009," Barbara explained. "She's been strong, but having family around is very comforting."

"I heard drugs were involved," warned Holly Beckham. "We aren't exposing ourselves to any problems – people aren't out to get her too, are they?"

"I think all that stopped with Joey's death," reassured Barbara. "He was a total handful both as a child and an adult."

"What's she like?" asked Velma Foster. "From what I've read, she's a total gem."

"Sometimes the richer they are, the bigger bitches they can be," suggested Mary Collier.

"True, but not in this case," Barbara laughed. "Remember, she was born here as well – and is very real with little pretense."

Right as Barbara went on to thank the ladies again, the doorbell rang signaling Jane's arrival.

The other Jane rang for her maid to get the door, and the curious group waited for their newest member to materialize.

As Jane entered the room, the ladies leapt to their feet to extend warm greetings.

"As the organizer, I want to welcome you to our group," Jane Scheinbach said, motioning to the other ladies. "And, welcome to Portland."

"Thank you!" Jane said, not knowing that the club had been formed for her benefit. "I was so surprised when Barbara said you had an opening. With these groups, it's always a commodity to find a good one."

"OK ladies, now let's get this started," Barbara said, pulling Jane into the mix and motioning them to move toward the drawing room. "Jane T., Julie, Holly, and Mary – over at that table. Jane S., Velma, Susan, and I will be here. Hostess Jane, explain the ground rules."

"While of course there's no table talk, there's no reason for us to use bidding boxes or the boards," the hostess instructed. "This is a relaxed group – no duplicate play which we all get enough of in the first place. We will play for one year, year-round, and then evaluate. Twelve times means we'll each host one, and the other four times we'll each chip in at a place not at a home – like the Westmont, Regent, or Tennis Club."

"Perfect!" Susan said. "What's the schedule?"

"In honor of our newest member," the hostess added, "Jane – you'll host the next one at your place – which we're all very curious to see!"

"Happy to do so," Jane replied.

"On that day, I'll have the rest of the schedule done. Second Wednesdays each month," Hostess Jane said. "Now, let's get started!"

"Champagne?" Julie asked.

"Good idea," Hostess Jane agreed and she rang the bell for her maid to take cocktail orders.

※

"Mary, how are you enjoying your new place?" asked Holly. "And more importantly, how's that insufferable racist Mary Overton and the even more insufferable Tess Parker?"

"You didn't hear, did you Holly?" replied Mary. "Tess died the other day in Palm Beach, right in the middle of Mar-a-Lago from cancer. She kept it from everyone."

"No shit," Julie added. "The old bitch finally kicked it?"

"We heard that," Velma said from the other table.

"It's true," Julie cooed back.

"She sold her property to me," Jane said as she started the bidding. "One club."

"That and a few others," smiled Holly, remembering some of her friends who inadvertently sold to Jane without even knowing who the buyer might have been. "One diamond."

"One spade. Well, we'll all miss the old broad. Did she leave anything to her family?" Julie asked.

"From what I understand, she changed everything and left it to her old gay friend, her nurse, and some charities here in town," Mary said as she reviewed her cards. "Pass. I think she wanted to make things as difficult as possible for them."

"Two spades," Jane bid.

"And Mary O. is she enjoying her place?" asked Holly. "Pass."

"Same-old, same-old," laughed Julie. "Do you remember back when the symphony hired Maxfield Alease as its conductor? Four spades."

"Oh no, you have to tell it because Jane hasn't heard it. Velma, close your ears," Holly yelled across to the next table, laughing uncontrollably.

Mary continued, "Well they had a huge reception at Mary's place. As she descended her grand staircase to greet the guests, she hadn't ever met Maxfield before and loudly said 'get that nigger out of here.' Pass."

"Do I have to hear that word every time I see you people?" denounced Velma in a huff. "You don't hear me talking about honkies in conversation."

"Fair enough," Julie conceded. "But that is just too funny."

"Portland has more intrigue than New York," Jane suggested. "Pass."

"You've got that right," Barbara seconded from across the room.

"Pass," Holly said. "Julie's bid at four spades."

"OK. Let's have more play and less chatter," Hostess Jane announced. "After the game, I'll tell you about Calina Everenson, the newest neighbor down the street who has apparently re-ignited the old Satanist rituals over at Elk Rock with a bunch of punk followers. Sometimes I see the fire burning over there late at night."

The room fell silent as the ladies began to seriously ponder their cards and develop social ties that Barbara hoped would last many years into the future for Jane.

Chapter 17
ᚲOᛗᛗOᚾ IᚾTᚱIᚷᚢᛖ

AUGUST 2011

While Jane was not the biggest fan of her nephew's political aspirations, she did enjoy her newly-purchased stately Nathan Wyeth-designed Georgian mansion in Washington where she could nearly wave to Princess Marina as the property and its magnificent English gardens overlooked the British Embassy. Having camped out at the Willard in between jaunts to New York to pack and Portland to witness the 'birth' of her fantastic home and office, she had also supervised a group of contractors as gates were constructed and security enhanced around the property's perimeter. With the help of Malcolm's personal secretary Lena Abramson who knew absolutely everyone in the city (having herself approached 30 years of service to the Senator), she got the inside scoop on the listing before it was even placed in the multiple listing system.

Offering slightly more than $11 million for the property, she purchased the place furnished and would then allow Pierre and Adrian to make the necessary adjustments and deploy favored artworks throughout the 13,000 square foot residence and grounds. She was warming up to D.C. and all the grandeur of political pomp and, of course, always came fully prepared with an agenda as the Torero corporate lobbyist engine steamed through the halls of the Senate, House, and Departments of Interior and Energy to make sure its interests were well-protected and secure for the future.

Paying special attention to the architecture of the home, the gates of the circular driveway looked like they had been originally deployed as part of the home's initial construction nearly 100 years before but with all the modern requirements for security of the present day. It was fun, as Marina always had a constant flow of visitors as wife of the Ambassador. More often than not if Jane were in the city, Marina would merely walk across the grounds through a gate Jane had installed with a special combination lock so both could have access without walking all the way around the compound to Whitehaven to enter through the front on Massachusetts Avenue.

The Senator and Barbara also enjoyed the privilege of the new residence as theirs was miles away in McLean. As the ranking foreign relations committee member, he leveraged the family treasury during his grand finale year to co-host receptions at Jane's for the Diplomatic Corps with the committee's chairman and the Secretary of State who could conveniently walk two doors down from her own home. The friendship with the chairman would help pave Seth's easy transition onto that committee as a freshman senator.

The home would also be the unofficial epicenter of Seth's campaign in the District, even if Jane weren't in residence. A number of lobbyists had appeared to meet with the candidate as the probable favorite in the election to deliver checks that came with strings of conditions: this to the dairy farmers, that to the auto workers, relaxed safety standards for trucking, tax limitations on tennis shoe imports, more funding for education, find money for military salary increases and equipment, and, above all else, do not touch Social Security. Upon a successful election, the marionette strings would begin to tighten as favors would be called in and votes demanded by the caucus and the slave-driving whips who would effortlessly emasculate insubordinates in a ballet that favored seniority. A vote that did not agree with a party line had its consequences, as junior senators would have their own bills stalled as the usual tactic to maintain compliant behavior. The glamour of the job always began the day after winning a second term when seniority could finally be built within the chamber.

A puzzled Jane looked above her sofa in disbelief as she telephoned Marina, noticing one of her earlier acquisitions from the 1960's, a André Masson painting of a head that looked like a ghoul with worms emanating from its brain. It had previously made its way into the room of least consequence in her penthouse as more significant pieces were purchased. Furling her brow and chuckling that Pierre must have placed it in the drawing room as a private joke, she had much bigger things on her mind.

"Marina, dear," Jane said into the cordless phone as she paced throughout the home's largest room.

"Hello, my dear," the Princess replied. "Are you in town?"

"For the weekend, yes," Jane explained. "Shall we have lunch?"

"That sounds delightful," Marina said, always agreeable to spending time with one of her closest friends.

"Pop through the back gate around 11:30 and we can head to the Cosmos – it's quiet there," Jane instructed.

"See you then!" Marina replied as she hung up the phone.

———

It was just another "same-old" day in the nation's capitol as the billionaire and her princess friend got in Jane's Bentley for the leisurely short drive past all the embassies down Massachusetts Avenue to the club where the dining room would allow for a civilized meal and conversation without the hassle of too many patrons.

"One never knows what goes on here on this street," Marina said looking at the diplomatic posts peppered amongst the homes and pointing out several in transition. "One flag comes down, and another goes up. Eastern Europeans and Africans."

The ladies looked at each other and laughed, thinking of how the smaller and newer countries tried to jockey for position in the capital based on the location and size of their embassy.

"Ours was here first," Marina proudly announced of the British Embassy, the anchor of Embassy Row. "And, I'm so glad you're here at least part-time with us."

"It's good to be around friends," Jane responded, taking Marina's gloved hand in hers as they approached the club's circular driveway.

Jane loved the Cosmos Club and everything about it, and since George and Marina were members and she had reciprocity through several clubs in New York, it was easy to suggest the tranquil setting for an opportunity to relax and enjoy a peace not often found in Washington.

"When will you go on your next buying trip?" asked Jane, referring to Marina's access as a princess to auction previews and to palaces throughout Europe of which many were quietly liquidating assets including priceless decorative arts in which the Princess specialized in order to maintain lavish lifestyles that included several months each year in Marbella at their seaside villas teaming with servants whom were preparing for daily parties that would last into the early morning hours for countless royal guests.

"Perhaps in late September," Marina answered.

"Late September? Not September 30th," Jane objected.

"Yes, probably into October as well," the Princess explained.

"You'll miss Malcolm's party and I wanted you to see the new house!" Jane said, slightly dejected.

"There will be time," Marina reassured Jane. "Besides, for the Ambassador to visit such an obscure part of the country would be curious."

"They don't need to know we have business together. Speaking of that, how is our project in the countryside going?" queried Jane.

"Good, only one incident this week, which is an improvement," Marina reported.

"Ah, very good," Jane said. "We should plan a trip before the end of the year to Balmoral to see the progress."

"That's definitely a possibility," Marina agreed. "Shopping at Tyson's after lunch?"

"Excellent idea," Barbara said enthusiastically.

⊱⊰

"Good day, Your Royal Highness," the Cosmos' Dining Room Maitre' d Philip said as he escorted the ladies to their table in the corner. With a love of looking out to the beautiful room, the ladies were seated.

"How's your nephew's campaign coming?" Marina asked.

"Don't ask," an exasperated Jane replied.

"That good?" Marina noted.

"It's awful – he's so much in the lead," Jane said, burying her hands in her face and pretending to cry and then laughed. "At least I'll have a senator filling my shoes."

"You'll never retire, Jane," Marina suggested, smiling.

"No, I won't," Jane agreed. "So, maybe he'll have to wait just as long as the Prince of Wales to be in charge."

Both laughed hysterically, both knowing that Charles had made the best out of his situation in trying to address many significant issues facing the United Kingdom and the world as a decidedly activist prince-in-waiting which had thoroughly upset his parents who guarded the quiet regality of the Crown.

"You wouldn't do that to him, would you?" Marina asked.

"No, I have a healthy ego but not an appointment for life. I just want to be sure that everything I've built stays strong," Jane confessed, admitting that her main goal was the preservation of her empire for generations to come and not liquidation where it usually would take less than three generations to lose it all. She was the exception to the self-made rule, which almost always favored liquidation over trusting a company in tact to an heir. "Seth's an attorney, has worked in politics, and now just needs to learn more about the industry. Torero is first and foremost a service company and then about energy."

"I admire you," Marina said. "I don't think I would have been able to break in and do what you did at such a young age."

"At the time, it was about releasing myself from a comfort zone," Jane said. "Selling real estate was good prep work for the company. And, look at you! You're the fourth-highest ranking duchess in the British Empire."

"'Empire' meant something in the mid-century and before," Marina informed, who married her princely husband in 1970 and came from far more legitimate European royal lineage. "Thank God George's mother had money, or we'd be just another pair of poor royals looking for a handout."

"Where did hers come from?" Jane asked.

"Her father was neither royal nor titled, but inherited thousands of acres of property. He was smart enough to invest in businesses that the nobility scoffed at," Marina said. "At the right time, he sold it all. George wouldn't ever talk about it or admit it, but after the Queen he's the wealthiest in the family."

"Is that a point of some contention?" Jane asked with curiosity.

"Yes and no," Marina giggled, thinking of the significant $350 million fortune that allowed her total flexibility outside the relatively strict confines of the court and royal lifestyle. "Let's put it this way, we don't flaunt it for the sake of family peace, but our children both know that George has a soft spot for them having had to grow up as royalty. Therefore, they get everything they want."

Marina was correct. Their son Andrew, Earl of Thanet, was well-recognized for his prowess in show jumping. His mother could not stand to attend the events as she didn't want to see her son fall off his horse and potentially damage what was commonly known as a far more attractive and princely persona than that of his cousins who were directly in line to the throne. As he would ride through the crowds after winning such events as the Royal Windsor Horse Show, cheers signified their love of the attractive man approaching 40 yet still single by choice. Her daughter Lady Serina, the gorgeous 35-year old former model, used her family's money to cement a fashion power base when she worked at Alexander McQueen. The young and well-respected couturier was known for her legendary parties in the mansion that her parents had purchased for her brother and her in Kensington Gardens, as it was apparent the Queen's thriftiness wouldn't allow another set of grace-and-favour apartment suites in Kensington Palace itself.

As the champagne arrived, their waiter poured each of the ladies a glass as they lifted them to the all-too-familiar toast, saying together, "Here's to us, there's no one better!"

⋯✦⋯

The Galleria always appeased the ladies as the stores knew the importance of staying in step with their European counterparts since the mall was a favorite haunt of most of the wives of members of the Diplomatic Corps and executives at leading corporations centered around the District. Perusing the shops, the ladies spent several hours analyzing the newest fashions from Gucci, Chanel, and other favorite shops.

"A little dry today," Jane suggested of the merchandise.

"Agreed," Marina concurred. "Ready to go?"

The ladies made their way to the valet and summoned Jane's car and driver via the mobile phone so it was there when they arrived.

"What a full day!" remarked Jane.

"I'll call you when I have confirmation about the best time to head to Balmoral," Marina noted.

"Thank you, dear," Jane said as the Bentley hummed down Dolley Madison Boulevard and across the Chain Bridge back into Marina's beloved adopted mother ship, Washington. "We just passed Malcolm and Barbara's – we should have stopped in!"

"She would have been upset not to have been invited," Marina suggested.

"True," Jane agreed. "Barbara never gets to the Cosmos and only goes shopping with me."

***

Jane flew back to Portland the next day and whirled into the office unexpectedly but found all the players perched at their desks, working toward making her another record return on investments. She smiled walking down the hall toward her lobby, seeing that everything had its place and was going according to plan.

"Maria, can you get Robert on the phone for me," Jane said, briskly passing her secretary's desk and shutting the door behind her.

"Robert. Jane calling," she said into her cordless handset.

"Mrs. Torrance," the director of her Corporate Intelligence Unit said. "Are you back in Portland?"

"Yes. Any developments?" Jane asked.

"Quite a few, in fact," he suggested. "DeSantos is about to come out with another big study on alternative energy. We aren't part of it."

"What else?" Jane followed.

"Same bullshit," Robert suggested. "Wondering why Torero is in Oregon now."

"Well, we know why we're here. Make sure they don't," Jane ordered. "Call with any news."

"Will do," Robert noted, hanging up.

Jane then called Omar and asked him to bring Helena to the office as she paused to go out on her office terrace to look at her husband's statue.

"What would you have done?" she asked the statue, expecting the same sage wisdom she would always get before the 1979 plane crash that killed him.

The bell rang and Maria buzzed Omar and Helena into the office.

"Any news?" Jane asked her deputies.

"The pipeline or the drilling?" Omar asked.

"Both," Jane said, restlessly.

"We need three votes for the pipeline, and a couple more for the drilling," Helena explained. "If the pipeline is approved, the drilling will be much easier."

"Do you have Bill on this?" Jane responded.

"Yes," Omar said. "He's working with Penny and Doris on an angle."

"This is a billion dollar project. Losing is not an option," Jane summarized. "More information by the start of the week, please."

Jane had a right to be nervous. She had pledged a mix of $500 million of her own stock in Torero Resources as well as parts of her property portfolio to monetize the cash needed from a group of investment banks in order to fund 50% of a pipeline and drilling venture on the West Coast with the company itself funding the other 50%, the net result of losing $1 billion was unacceptable for any of the parties. Any loss or stall in the operation could cause her to lose the confidence of speculative investors who had for so long had trusted her as chairman of the company in the absence of her late husband. The stock could also tank if the project didn't receive the green light from the appropriate regulators after so much effort and speculation that was put into research and development.

"Who on the commission do we need to be concerned about?" Helena asked Omar.

"Bill suggests the one leading the three is Dela Acasia Torrez, and she's the chair," Omar said, looking at his notes and Bill's debrief.

"Christ! The chair of the commission?" Jane complained, mystified.

"Appears so," Omar noted.

"We've already publicly announced our involvement in the project and that alone is responsible for the gain in share price. Where was the advance work on this?" Jane asked. "Do we know anything about her?"

"Not so much," Omar reviewed. "I'll can ask Bill for a full briefing."

"I don't care what you do – but find a weakness," Jane ordered. "At any cost."

"We'll definitely try," Helena said as they excused themselves from the office.

<hr />

"Kate," Jane called Kate's extension. "Anything urgent?"

"Just planning for the bridge game," Kate replied, thinking about the pending game that would be organized at Jane's estate.

"Come in, let's discuss," Jane said, preoccupied with what she considered as seriously sloppy research on a pivotal project. The venture meant nothing but economic development throughout the state, and she couldn't understand the resistance to prosperity with what she considered little environmental impact.

"Are you all right?" Kate asked as she entered Jane's office.

"Just a little concerned for one of our business ventures," Jane replied. "You might know something since you're from here - Dela Acasia Torrez."

"Now there's a name from the past. There's a story there," Kate chuckled. "You're talking about the chair of the Environmental Control Commission?"

"Yes," Jane said, her eyes lighting up with excitement to learn more.

"No one would know this, and you absolutely cannot repeat where you learned it," Kate emphasized.

"Certainly not," Jane said, mesmerized in what Kate might reveal.

"She's married, and has two children," Kate started. "But a year ago, my friend Sue Helen had an affair with her."

"A lesbian?" Jane asked, thinking that wasn't the greatest revelation in a state so liberal as Oregon.

"Not your garden variety, but one who's seriously into the rough trade female sex scene," Kate explained with a grin. "She introduced Sue Helen to some pretty kinky stuff that happens at one of those revolving nightclubs that rents space out once a month in a different place. The club itself is a walking violation – live sex, alcohol without permits, drugs, dungeon and torture rooms. It's supposed to be run by a couple of leather biker dykes, the types that no one wants to mess with."

"So, just a lesbian who likes kink?" Jane asked, slightly underwhelmed by the story.

"An affair! She was with my friend after she got married," Kate revealed with enthusiasm. "Sue Helen broke it off, but I'm sure she could get Dela to go to that club again. It's hard to resist when someone yearns for a taste of that lifestyle. And, her husband is ultra-conservative and very Catholic."

"Outstanding! And you can get it all on film for us," Jane joyously announced.

"What?" Kate asked. "You mean go to that club? I'd never pass. Not in a million years! If anything, send someone else."

"Nonsense," Jane retorted. "Outsiders mean leaks – and that's not something we need. Take your friend shopping with you – I'm sure you can find the appropriate outfit for the event. Go ask Melissa for some petty cash."

"Are you absolutely serious?" Kate questioned.

"It's for me and the company," Jane pouted with a forlorn look, trying to figure out a way to convince Kate. "When it's done, take some friends on the jet to Paris for shopping."

"Fine," Kate acquiesced, feeling a twinge of remorse for even telling the story. "Would I have been better off continuing to sell real estate?"

"Certainly not!" Jane professed, waving her arms in the air as Kate exited the office. "This is the life you were meant to lead."

"Sue Helen," Kate said as she closed her office door so she could use the Facetime video feature on her iPhone. "I have a big favor to ask."

"Anything for you, my dear," Sue Helen replied.

"Don't say that before you hear the request," Kate cautioned. "Remember Dela?"

"Dela Acasia Torrez? How could I forget her?" Sue Helen laughed. "I've never had someone eat me out so ferociously! What about her?"

"Do you remember telling me about that club she liked?" asked Kate.

"Dollhouse?" Sue Helen suggested. "I hear it's still going strong every month but I haven't been since Dela and I went."

"Can you get her to go again?" Kate wondered, riddled with angst.

"I hadn't thought about it. Why?" Sue Helen asked.

"I need something on her – for a project," Kate implied, meandering around the true purpose. "And, I have money to outfit us both in some gear. Want to go shopping?"

"I'll call you back. Let me email her before I forget," Sue Helen suggested.

"OK. Let me know, and thank you!" Kate said as she hung up and opened her office door to return to Jane's office.

"I think it's a 'go,'" Kate said, peeking in the door to let Jane know of her progress.

"Excellent. Please ask Maria to send for Bill," Jane replied.

Closing the door, Kate went down the hall to get some petty cash from Melissa for her shopping excursion to one of the city's adult stores that specialized in leather fetish gear. No footprints could exist from either Kate's personal account or corporate card for any purchase.

Not many minutes had passed when Sue Helen called Kate back with a promising development.

"You couldn't have called at a better time," Sue Helen reported. "I barely clicked back into my inbox and she had already replied."

"No shit," Kate said, pleased with her good fortune.

"The club is set for this Saturday night over in a warehouse in the Central Eastside Industrial District," Sue Helen noted. "Pick me up in 20 minutes and we can go shopping!"

"Your condo or the office," asked Kate.

"Condo today," Sue Helen advised.

Driving over to Sue Helen's condo, Kate was giddy about her project falling into place. Sue Helen was already on the sidewalk awaiting her old college friend.

"Kiss for your favorite dyke?" Sue Helen pointed at her cheek, getting in Kate's Lexus for the short drive to the porn store.

"For this, you can have your way with me!" Kate laughed, kissing Sue Helen right on the lips.

"I've even invited Dela to spend the night," Sue Helen noted, grabbing her crotch simulating masturbation. "I hope she doesn't knick these pussy lips again with her teeth. Just like a kid in the candy store."

The duo roared with laughter, thinking about how women with pent-up frustrations like the closeted Dela acted when they had the opportunity to voraciously act out their true desires. The spectacle of unleashing the powerful inner sexual beast could be overwhelming to an inexperienced partner during a liaison of unbridled sexual energy. The added level of adrenaline in cheating was also an exciting secret for what would be a cake of utter passion that was coupled with contempt. Of the pair only Sue Helen was able to freely live her live without the heterosexual constraints that Dela dealt with daily.

"I haven't been to a fetish party in years," confessed Kate.

"Get ready, these scenes are hard core," Sue Helen noted, referencing the toxic nature of the upcoming event. "Remember, you'll have to show your tits off to be taken seriously."

"The only downside," Kate mused, perusing the merchandise. "I can wear these nipple guards."

"Well, I'm not going to. They hurt after a while," Sue Helen informed. "She'll want me to fuck her after the club, so I'm going to get a nice big dildo and harness to wear."

"At the event?" asked Kate.

"No, for after we get home," Sue Helen explained, thinking that regardless of Dela's situation, she did find her persona sexually appealing. "She'll be too busy munching on all the fresh meat at the club. I'll be dessert."

As the two friends finished their hurried shopping spree, Kate made sure to get the details for Saturday.

"10 p.m. on Saturday?" Kate clarified.

"Yes, but you can come over early and dress at our place," suggested Sue Helen. "How about eight?"

"Thanks. I'll bring some champagne as I'm going to need it to get through the night," Kate said.

"You might find some hot pussy yourself," laughed Sue Helen.

"Yeah, right," Kate mocked. "Only if one of those dykes has a nice big cock on her."

"Some of them are trying! The steroids some of them take make their clits look like they have anthuriums sticking out of their pussies," Sue Helen imagined.

"Ewww!" Kate screamed as her old friend got out of the car. "See you Saturday night!"

Saturday arrived faster than anticipated for Kate, who was excited yet nervous for the project to be over. Prior to leaving the office on Friday, Robert from Torero Corporate Intelligence had flown out to provide specific instruction on the use of the miniature camera that would be concealed in the leather hat that Kate had purchased. Capturing the evidence was a one-shot deal, as time was of the essence for approval from the Environmental Control Commission for the joint venture on its next meeting agenda.

Kate gathered the limited clothing that she had planned to wear for the club and left for Sue Helen and Brent's penthouse in the Pearl. Having arranged for an underground parking spot for her in the building, they eagerly awaited Kate's arrival and the subsequent fashion show that would unfold for Brent to judge the ladies in their fetish garb.

"Hey lover," a smiling Sue Helen greeted her friend as she opened the door. "Are you ready for tonight?"

"Not hardly – maybe after some champagne," Kate said, bringing in a bag that contained several bottles of champagne. "I cannot fucking believe I'm actually going through with this. It all seems so strangely normal."

"It'll be fun, relax," Sue Helen coaxed, opening the champagne and pouring a glass for both of them as well as for Brent.

"So are you ladies ready to show off?" Brent asked, entering Sue Helen's penthouse from the door they had carved between their units.

"We'll be back in about 30 minutes, asshole," Kate joked.

"Can't wait," Brent replied, watching the two women head into the master suite to prepare for the night's antics.

The ladies began the task of transforming themselves into the two wanton creatures who would be the belles at the slithering snake pit of lesbian desire. Kate's decidedly more conservative outfit was appealing, a short vinyl miniskirt and bustier completed by sexy fishnet stockings and combat boots.

Sue Helen's ensemble was far more reckless in an effort to immediately intoxicate the crowd and Dela in particular. Her leather and chain harness draped her breasts. Vinyl hot pants hugged her ample but attractive ass while her thigh-high boots framed her muscular thighs. The finishing touch was the leather jockstrap she adorned which showcased a hole squarely in the middle of the pouch where the dildo would slip through to secure it to her body later that night when Dela would come back to the penthouse. The original design included studs riveted into the leather that outlined the hole with what appeared to look like a metallic vaginal opening.

Asserting her role as a 'top' for any liaison that might occur, Sue Helen carried a small riding crop and wore a thick leather collar. Kate's collar was more feminine. While she, too, would claim the title of 'top' in order to distance herself from the possibility of being 'mounted' at the party by one of the many aggressive women eager to show dominance, the softer look was still appealing and entirely appropriate.

Emerging from the bedroom, Brent laughed hysterically at his two friends, so fetished up to the hilt that their garb was more of a caricature than something that would have been worn by even the most offensive lesbian.

"Where's my camera?" Brent asked. "This has got to be the funniest thing I've ever seen."

Kate and Sue Helen didn't disagree with him, pretending to walk the runway for him and doing their best interpretations of how they should act for the evening's foray into dykedom.

"And, don't come into my place later tonight, either," commanded Sue Helen as she looked directly at Brent. "I may have a guest."

"You don't need to worry about that," Brent said, drying his eyes with a napkin.

"OK. Honest appraisals?" asked Kate.

"Very comely!" Brent said, breaking out into laughter again. "No pun intended!"

All three broke down as the ladies tried not to run their thick eyeliner. Putting on long trench coats to conceal their uniforms, they went down to the parking lot as it was time for their curtain call.

"Blend in, find some younger girl to toy with. Use your experience to lead her along, and then drop the bombshell that you're not interested," advised Sue Helen. "They'll be on the lookout for people who don't fit in."

"It's that big of a deal?" Kate asked.

"Absolutely. This club has its own strange security force, and if one of those 'daddies' doesn't like you you'll get thrown out on your ass," Sue Helen explained.

"Let me make sure this camera works. Go over there by Brent and kiss him while I walk past," Kate instructed, backing up.

Taking video of the couple while she walked past them, Kate then removed the camera from her hat to check that it did indeed film. Seeing that the file was saved on the camera's hard drive, she knew they were ready.

"OK, I think we can go," Kate indicated. "Brent, are you ready?"

In their coats, the ladies had planned to have Brent park in one of the warehouses he owned with Sue Helen not far from the location. Brent would bide time at Produce Row, listening to jazz as the women cavorted amongst the city's wildest creatures. While Dela most assuredly had a date with Sue Helen after they were done with the club night, Brent would drive Kate back to her car, the evidence safely hidden on her person until she could place it in her safe upon returning home.

Even the police stayed away from the lesbian club scene as some of the testosterone-induced females making the transition to male coupled with the general animosity from years of discrimination and internalized hatred of the establishment proved a breeding ground for a 'group think' frenzy that could erupt into an impromptu response of rabid violence if provoked. The 'tops' savagely guarded their 'bottoms' against advances from newcomers not understanding the hierarchy. Like a pack of hyenas sniffing out fresh prey, Kate would be subject to rigid review throughout the evening.

Stopping the car two blocks away from the temporary club location entrance, Brent would await Kate's call in several hours to swiftly pick her up after gathering her sought-after evidence.

"Fuck, I'm nervous," Kate proclaimed, heart racing.

"Just stick with me," Sue Helen calmed her as the songstress Peaches' 'Shake Yer Dix' melody made the entire building shake. "You're an oddity since you haven't been before. You have a good chance of just being left alone."

Upon walking past the first leather-clad 'daddy,' a term given to the most masculine of the women who stood guard at the entry and kept order within the club, they entered a surreal environment akin to an eerie gathering of vampires. Kate could see the seriousness of the mood right away, as a group of spectators were watching one brave dyke getting her pussy lips tattooed with her lover's initials.

"You go that way," Sue Helen commanded, as she was on the hunt for Dela.

Proceeding to the bar, Kate was able to locate a pair of friendly eyes in the young feminine bartender who was wearing a gorgeous sheer teddy, showcasing pert tits and a near-bald snatch.

"You're new," the bartender greeted, hardened nipples poking out through the transparent fabric also vying for the attention of Kate's wallet for a hefty tip. "Welcome to Dollhouse."

"Thank you," Kate replied. "Gin and tonic, please."

"OK, just don't stare too hard," the bartender advised, smiling and pointing to an older woman with a budding moustache. "My husband over there is part of security."

With a knowing nod, a savvy Kate went to look at the crowd. Participation was sometimes encouraged in the sideshow activities that lined the pathway to the dance floor. While some women enjoyed the playful activities of simple sex in makeshift alcoves around the perimeter of the space, the main attractions were more severe acts of aggression including 'holding,' a technique where 'tops' would slide a sleek lubed fist - fingers first

- deep into a 'bottom's' vagina and expand and contract the appendages to create a special sensation and connection between the participants. Several of the women marveled at the whipping and caning stations while others casually sat together with cocktails and absorbed the special atmosphere.

The night would not go without several drinks being thrown at jealous lovers and, of course, the requisite fights and duels for the rights to certain ladies. As Kate wandered through the mix, she discovered the treasure for which she came. Sue Helen was smiling in the corner as she watched Dela at the 'Feeding Trough,' where gorgeous young female strippers had been commissioned to lay in slings while being sprayed with whipped cream after being doused in Goldschlager. For twenty dollars, guests were allowed one minute to dominate one stripper in any manner they desired. Dela had offered up a $100 bill for the exclusive right of one minute with all five girls at once, psyched up thinking about each of the flavors she would sample.

Kate turned on the camera hidden in her hat, beginning to film the extravagant banquet of flesh. As Dela lapped at each sweetened crevice while she gingerly rubbed the nipples of her subject, Kate was able to capture each angle, pausing briefly near Sue Helen to get clear head shots. The forms of each sling-bound young woman glistened with the minute flecks of gold from the liqueur.

"Fucking amazing," Kate whispered.

"I know – that's what I get to have later tonight," smiled Sue Helen, acknowledging Dela's talent for eating out pussy.

The honor guard of strippers lined up before Dela was impressive. While she didn't expect any of them to cum from the quick bath, she thoroughly treated each clitoris to a gymnastic tongue lashing. The minute was up in what seemed to be far less time with the crowd transfixed in watching the marathon exploits of cunnilingus, and Kate made herself disappear so her filming subject would never know who was culpable for the video segment.

"Leaving so soon," said a voice from behind Kate, who was approaching the exit.

"What do you mean?" Kate said, turning around to discover what appeared to be the head 'daddy,' a woman in her fifties with short gray hair, topless but saddled with a harness and strange military shoulder epaulettes.

Much like Sue Helen, she also had a leather jockstrap on but hers contained a relatively large dildo already secured in the hole over denim jeans.

"No one leaves this party this early. I'm Macy, and I run this place," the indignant dyke said.

"A friend called and needs help," Kate explained, not knowing how to respond to the crusty old lesbian.

"I don't think so. We haven't seen you around here before," Macy skeptically replied, motioning for some assistance. "Girls."

Two of the younger 'daddies' dressed in tuxedos appeared from near the front door and held each of Kate's arms. Letting the dildo caress the front of Kate's tight miniskirt, Macy licked Kate's face and blew breath laced with a heavy gin stench into her ear.

"What do you want?" Kate questioned, unnerved by the invasive inspection of her.

"You don't belong here," Macy suggested, seeming to know just by sniffing Kate. "If I ever see your tired straight ass at one of my parties thinking about experimentation or trying to be bi again, me and my friends here will take turns on you all night long and it'll be more of a thrill than the gawking you had around here tonight. Now get the fuck out of here."

The tuxedoed guards released the petrified Kate, who backed up to the door and ran out into the street past several ladies arriving at the nightclub. The swarm of activity was just getting going as the rapper Lady's song 'Twerk' resonated with a heavy bass beat into the cold night. Calling Brent, she made it half way to the Produce Row Café before he picked her up.

"My God, I was almost raped in there," Kate said, breathless from her retreat out of the snake pit.

"Sue Helen told you how it was going to be," Brent laughed. "Did you get what you needed?"

"I certainly hope so," Kate hoped. "Can you just drop me off at home and I'll pick the car up in the morning?"

"Sure. Do you need anything else?" Brent asked.

"Maybe a hug," Kate suggested, still shaking from the experience.

As they stopped in front of her place, Brent gave her a long comforting hug before she leapt from the vehicle to take a needed long shower to cleanse herself from the experience, throwing the absurd fetish gear out.

She put the camera and small hard drive in her safe as she thought about all the things she wanted to say to Jane about what had turned into a relatively concerning mission.

⎯⎯⎯⎯

"Maria, would you please let Jane know I have what she wanted me to bring in from this weekend?" Kate asked as she passed the secretary's desk on the way to her office.

Settling in at her desk, she opened her laptop to check emails.

"Mrs. Torrance would like to see you," buzzed Maria from the desk in the lobby.

"Certainly, thank you Maria," Kate replied, getting up with a small USB drive in hand that contained the file footage of Dela's lusty romp at the dyke party.

Entering the office, Bill Derendo was already seated at Jane's conference table.

"I'm ready for some good material," he said to Kate as she sat down. "Show us what you've got."

"I'll excuse that comment," Kate replied in an unusually rude voice reserved for those who didn't deserve her respect. "You have no idea what I went through to get this material."

"Let's see it!" Jane said, ignoring Kate's tone but excited by the prospect of Bill setting up a meeting of his own with Dela.

Plugging the USB drive into the computer, the files became visible on screen.

"We'll start with this one – the approach," Kate said as she touched the icon waiting for the media player to load.

"The clarity is amazing, isn't it?" Bill noted.

"We'll have to thank Robert for the new camera!" Jane agreed.

As the trio watched the approach from Kate's viewpoint, Jane grimaced slightly when she saw the five nude strippers lined up in slings.

"What on earth are they doing?" Bill asked.

"Some weird sadistic stuff," Kate replied, double-clicking on the next icon. "Watch this."

Clearly identifiable, there was Dela Acasia Torrez is full regalia quickly darting between each of the strippers in a feeding frenzy.

226

"Holy shit," Bill shouted. "This is more than expected!"

"You think you have enough with this?" Jane asked.

"Beyond!" Bill smiled as he got up to leave the office. "Kate, please make me a copy."

"Bombardier!" Jane announced with an embellished French accent. "Are you ready for Paris?"

"Oui, madame," Kate replied, apparently consoled by Jane keeping her promise to send her on a European shopping spree. "Budget?"

"$100,000," Jane said without hesitation. "Will that be enough?"

"Ma'am, most assuredly," Kate reassured as she got up to go pack and take both Brent and Sue Helen with her. "I will see you back in the office next Monday, then."

———

Bill put on his sunglasses and coat, preparing to head to Pioneer Square for a lunch from one of his favorite food carts. Robert in corporate intelligence had also suggested to him that Dela typically emerged from her office tower at 11:30 a.m. each day for lunch as well. Sitting was a waiting game Bill typically didn't enjoy. Bored easily, he looked at the throngs of pedestrians in the vibrant urban core. Impressed with the activity including the mass-transit light rail train system humming down the streets periodically, he was generally pleased with the move to Oregon.

Holding a packet painstakingly created by Robert and his group that masterfully concealed the identity of the preparer, Bill got up upon seeing Dela outside her building.

"Ms. Torrez?" Bill asked with a kind smile, sunglasses still on.

"Yes? Do I know you?" Dela responded, slightly confused.

"No, but we do have mutual interests in the environment," Bill explained as he handed her the packet of papers.

"What is this?" Dela asked.

"Go ahead, open it," Bill pressed.

Opening the large envelope, Dela removed four high definition photos of her taken at Dollhouse's 'Feeding Trough.' Without saying a word, she buried her face in her hands.

"It's all right," Bill said as he comforted her. "There's a video, too, but I'm the only one who has copies of either at this point."

Dela shuddered at the thought of the public humiliation of the photos and possible video of her engaging in what would be highly inappropriate activity for a public figure. As a married Hispanic woman who was also a successful environmental law attorney, how could she ever explain the recent repugnant misstep?

"What do you want?" Dela asked.

"The vote for Torero's projects next week – make sure the commission votes to approve them," Bill said.

"I don't have that kind of pull," Dela objected. "People would think we went nuts!"

"You're the fucking chair," Bill angrily said, knowing that he could say virtually anything to her without fear of retribution. "Eisenberg and Blackstone will go along with anything you tell them."

Dela knew that her fellow commissioners Maria Eisenberg and Peter Blackstone would comply with any wish she had as she got them their seats on the powerful board, but the three had previously agreed that the environmental impact of the Torero ventures remained a huge unknown. Since the other two commission members were favorable to corporate concerns, Bill expected the vote would then be unanimous.

"I can talk to them and see," Dela suggested.

Bill had had enough of the sidestepping Dela. His East Coast patience had run out and the normally cordial New Yorker decided to take a tough stance in convincing her to modify her position.

"Listen you stupid bitch," Bill said in a slightly raised voice just muffled enough to not be heard by the other pedestrians. "Make it happen or the video goes viral on porn sites and it'll be sent to reporters at all the media outlets. It's one deal – and your reputation is preserved. I think you know what you have to do."

Bill turned and walked away from Dela, who felt as if she had just been backhanded by an industry she had spent a career trying to regulate. He knew she might attempt to follow him, so he walked to the Parkway having already checked into a room earlier in the day, changed clothing, and took a taxi to a connecting office tower that had a tunnel providing access to the Torero building.

"It's done," Bill said, walking into Jane's office.

"Good," Jane smiled. "When's the vote?"

"Next week. I think they'll meet tonight so she can sell them their new position," Bill surmised.

"What information will do," Jane pondered, not thinking of the mental anguish it caused Dela or how the surveillance to get the material had put Kate in potential danger.

At that point, the money had become the most important thing to her. People had become simple commodities used to help Jane accomplish goals. For someone who had virtually everything, there was nothing more she couldn't easily have gotten. The true game was leverage on grand scale, and that's what the most recent club deal promised – a rush of adrenaline to successfully complete a transaction. Her love of the 'beauty contests' staged by a variety of wealth managers to curry her favor had faded in the 1960's, leaving those impertinent details to her investment management team.

Just like joining a private social club, the amusement of newness wore off sooner and sooner with each passing year. Talk of portfolio construction and rebalancing bored her beyond words, and she became increasingly disinterested with the mundane in favor of more creative ways to enhance her investment returns. She had even thought of purchasing a mansion down in Holmby Hills as a novelty and turning it into a museum for fine jewelry. Inspired by her own collection and those of her friends as a way to preserve liquid assets where the museum owned the pieces but would have them on extended loan to the original donors so they could wear them when needed while also being on limited display for occasional public tours.

Families for generations into the future could enjoy the privileges of the jewels without the need to worry about the tax consequence when a death occurred with an estate and the next generation saddled with enormous inheritance tax issues as signature pieces couldn't slip through the cracks of detection. Wearing the jewels, after all, was a soft marketing technique to tell other people of privilege about the concept – thereby satisfying the tax exempt status the museum would enjoy.

The dark side of wealth had caught up with her, as there was little more that was truly legitimate of interest. When all of her dreams had been realized so early in life, something compelling needed to exist to fuel her continued existence. 'Risk' was the new engine of excitement that Jane's psyche yearned for each morning, causing her to push her staff in new directions where increasing amounts of cash were funneled to foreign booking centers in Singapore, Luxembourg, and Monaco. Curiously, Jane's home in Washington became a hub for a small set of British diplomatic couriers as cash poured from both New York and Portland in a complicated veil of secrecy where the seal of the British Ambassador guaranteed that packages and boxes containing the cash would not be opened or detained in addition to be free of customs duty by being transported to any embassy where the United Kingdom had a diplomatic mission.

Jane's goal was to make at least $500 million evaporate in a three-year period to begin building a secret international asset base that would allow her to help finance the global expansion of Torero through aggressive political and social advocacy. Corporate Intelligence would help begin the process to build a small camp in North Africa that would act as a training center. From the outside, it looked like an elaborate attempt by some international charity in the delivery of humanitarian aid with irrigation projects and farm experiments. On the inside, recruited 'moles' were trained in corporate computer warfare, foreign languages, and the necessary 'je ne sais quoi' required to appropriately carry out missions of espionage. No one could trace it back to Torero or Jane, as the cash would magically appear to be deposited in one bank, and subsequently be wired and withdrawn through multiple banking channels and ghost accounts before arriving for the end user to have access.

She established another office that was located in another building to manage the accounts under an LLC that could not be traced back to her. Telephone and internet communication between her headquarters and the international office was strictly prohibited, and orders were communicated to personnel through meetings in public places.

On the day of the commission vote, Jane's estate was dancing with activity. The gardeners – per Tess' long tradition – began mowing at 5 a.m. The aromas from Bonita's kitchen wafted up to Jane's suite as she prepared to host her first bridge game with the new friends. She wouldn't offer a full tour but was willing to show off the main floor before shuttling the ladies down to the pool salon where both the game and luncheon would be served.

"There's only one call I want to receive today," instructed Jane as Kate readied herself to leave for the office with a number of documents she had just signed.

"The vote, of course," Kate replied. "Are you ready for bridge?"

"Absolutely!" Jane exclaimed. "This will be the first real day of relaxation, despite the vote, a billion dollars in limbo, and company reputation on the line."

"Leave that to the others to worry about. It'll be fine," counseled Kate as she walked out the door. "See you this afternoon. Good luck with the game!"

Known for carpooling as a group, the only woman to travel alone was the sole eastside resident, Velma. The women were particularly eager to see the views and the art. The West Hills contingent arrived first while Mary Collier and Barbara were picked up at their condos by Dunthorpe's reigning queen and the group's organizer, Jane Scheinbach.

Jane's full staff had toiled for days while the florist had just completed the weekly arrangements throughout each of the estate's pavilions and main residence that morning.

"I can't believe this was completed in less than a year," Velma said, looking out the window in the Grand Salon, secretly waving at her home in the distance on the ridge.

"Neither can I, but I had a deadline since I wanted to host Malcolm's retirement party here," Jane explained as she approached the window which not only looked out to the spectacular view, but also the grounds approaching the promenade. "They literally worked around the clock for months before I moved in."

"They say you designed it yourself," Julie suggested.

"The basic design, yes," Jane corrected. "But without my architect Andrew Quinnell and his daughter Adrian, it wouldn't have been possible. OK ladies, follow me."

Jane marched the ladies out the front door to two utility carts driven by Jane's security personnel after showing them the circular flow of the home's design. To get the full effect of the property, Kate had instructed the guards to drive counter-clockwise around the estate, past the Chinese teahouse and promenade, offering a view of the residence and grounds as well as water features that danced while in-ground speakers hummed with music to get the ladies in the mood for their friendly but competitive game.

The luncheon would be served outside and the table was previously set that morning with Jane's favorite Grand Baroque sterling silver paired with one of her beautiful fine china sets evoking playful Summertime memories filled with color. Bonita's culinary wizardry resulted in the choice of a filet mignon topped with foie gras for the main course. Each of the ladies always submitted their menu to the group for approval, as diet was always a concern. However, no one would ever question any of the cook's choices as a matter of protocol.

"This is an absolute Shangri-La," Julie Weber confessed. "Stunning!"

"Agreed," noted Holly Beckham, getting up from the table to stretch after the first rubber of bridge.

Typically not as silent during their usual games, the ladies seemed to be focusing more than ever before due to the lush and inviting surroundings that they couldn't stop appreciating. Gazing out to the grounds and view was a favorite sport of the hand's dummy as Bonita began final preparations for lunch in the pool salon's kitchen, even the girls who didn't get good cards were in a remarkably good mood.

"When's lunch?" Mary Collier asked from the first table that had lagged a little in its playing due to the reduced speed of her play as the oldest member of the group.

"When you're done in there," called out Susan Strobe from the patio area by the pool as the others in group enjoyed mint juleps and mimosas.

All the ladies looked spectacular, and many of the day's favorite designers were represented in a dizzying array of textures, styles, and colors. One thing could be sure: each of the ladies had a presence that was unmistakable, and they wore their money so naturally with true class as opposed to some of the young harlots who had foisted themselves into the all-too-unsuspecting arms of some of the city's sought-after young men. Much to the chagrin of many a mother or grandmother who dreamed of the perfect wedding for a son or grandson on the lawn at the Westmont in the summer, the families would unfortunately take on girls with no breeding at the insistence of the sons. The sad result would happen several years later, finding divorce papers served by their wives after the first or second child was born which permanently cemented them into the fabric of the cloistered elite.

As the four players emerged from the pool salon after another few minutes of play, Jane Scheinbach produced their scorecards for a midway check of who was in the lead.

"OK, ladies," Jane S. said, sitting at the luncheon table. "Velma in first, for once; Susan, second; and Mary, the honor of low points."

Everyone applauded as the luncheon began with a crab cocktail garnished with a rich Kaluga caviar served by two maids.

"Mrs. Torrance," one maid whispered, walking up to Jane with a cordless phone. "Your office."

"Yes?" Jane said, getting up from the table and hoping the results of the vote at the meeting were in.

"Hi, Jane. Unanimous, as predicted," Bill proudly announced

"Hooray!" Jane cheered in front of all the ladies. "Thank you for the update."

"Good news?" Julie asked.

"Absolutely!" Jane replied. "A project was approved for the company today, so I can finally rest much easier."

"You all and your jet set lives," Velma laughed. "I'm just happy to have my health and my home."

"And your bank account too," Mary reminded Velma.

"Details," Velma scoffed, laughing as the maids cleared the first course from the table. "A toast to our hostess on a beautiful day in a beautiful new home."

"Cheers!" they all exclaimed as chatter turned to more colorful accounts of society since they last had met a month earlier.

"You'll never guess what I saw the other night," Jane S. suggested as all attention focused to her since she was known for telling a superb slice of gossip. "You remember Vince Dorgan? Well, his wife died last year and I spotted him coming out of an adult bookstore the other week. And, this last weekend we were at the Parkway for dinner, and you'll never guess who was taking Gloria Harper to dinner – but Vince!"

"That doesn't surprise me," Susan said, remembering that Vince's proclivities were well-known within the circle of gallery and decorator queens who, with some of the notable male heirs who had never married, made up the cartel of gay sensibility in the city. "Gloria's husband didn't leave her with much, so even if Vince is behind the closet door they might as well be together and have some companionship."

"I suppose you're right," Jane S. replied. "But that's prostitution, regardless if there's sex or not."

"I think it's adorable," Holly chimed in. "She always was a fag hag anyways, hanging around that designer of hers and his tribe of fairies."

"It wasn't earned," Julie offered. "What will Gloria do if they get married?"

"She'll move into his penthouse, use her designer to redecorate, have a nice life and not mind his extracurricular activities," Susan said. "Tell her my gallery is open."

By then, the ladies had finished dessert and were ready for their next rubber of bridge.

"Everyone back to the tables," Jane S. commanded. "The winner today receives a gift certificate from the Regent Club for dinner. And, remember that Jane has also invited us to the special party here in honor of Barbara and Malcolm on September 30th."

Everyone applauded Barbara's milestone and eventual return to the native Oregon soil at the end of the year.

Jane basked in glory the rest of the day. Not only did she get the best cards and offer the ladies a superb luncheon, she also received the approval on her special project. After the ladies left, she decided that she would treat herself to a relaxing evening at the residence with just herself – and security – watching the city lights sparkle below as she walked the estate's gardens alone.

Chapter 18
ϽꟼΣϹΙꟼᄂ ꟼᴚOϽΣϹTϽ

EARLY SEPTEMBER 2011

"Hello, dear," a familiar light German accent said over the telephone.

"Hello to you as well, dear," Jane said to Marina as she dashed into her office from the inner lobby area and closed the door.

"George suggests that we visit Sussex Wood next week," Marina advised. "The children will be there as well.

"So soon?" Jane asked as she sat at her desk, staring out at her husband's statue on the terrace. "Your plane or mine?"

"It should be ours for this trip," Marina indicated. "We have another shipment to deliver and its best just to slip you into the country on the diplomatic plane."

"You and the Rolls must've been busy these last months," Jane surmised. "Any promising candidates?"

"Several, in fact," Marina noted. "But you know they're all the same until they acclimate."

What the sophisticated princess loved about Jane was that hidden deep behind the façade of New York City society and the adept businesswoman was a little 'raw' sense of humanity. The type that could appreciate the most depraved situation for what it was without looking squarely down her nostrils at it. That 'tell them like you see it' attitude had made Jane immensely popular within her male-dominated industry sector, but was concealed from her social list as that would have become a severe Achilles heel as she slyly climbed the social strata with great skill during her first decade of marriage.

"I've noticed that," Jane suggested. "So, when would you like to go?"

235

"I'll schedule the flight for Monday," Marina suggested. "Remember, even if I'm flying without George we receive an escort. And, the State Department requires us to file a flight plan in advance."

"How many days," Jane asked.

"No more than three," Marina said.

"I'll be back in Washington by Friday," Jane noted. "Talk to you then."

"Kate," Jane said, peeking into her chief of staff's office. "I'm taking a short trip back to Washington for a week."

"Any special arrangements?" Kate asked, looking up from her briefings from the first quarterly review of the estate staff."

"Only to make sure that everything is ready for September 30th," Jane reminded.

"Everything has been taken care of," Kate said. "Bill and I are enjoying the collaboration."

"Excellent," Jane replied as she walked back to her office.

The days couldn't go by fast enough for Jane, who was anxious to visit George and Marina's estate. Spending time at the manor house would be a true separation from the world, as no one on her staff except Carlton and Omar knew where she would be by her own design.

Boarding her own jet, the sole passenger fired up her iPad to read the latest magazines and test herself on a bridge game against computer players who were actually programmed to bid correctly.

"Mrs. Torrance," the captain announced over the intercom. "We'll arrive at Dulles in four and a half hours."

Jane was particularly annoyed that she couldn't fly directly into Reagan National which was far more convenient to her home, but flatly refused the TSA's mandate of pre-inspection of her private aircraft prior to flying into the much closer airport. Her staff had located an acceptable FBO at Dulles that was large enough to house the Bombardier, even though it was 35 miles from the city.

After several calls and a brief rest in her private cabin, Jane's flight staff knocked on her door to offer her a warm moist towel, signifying her final approach.

"The car's been called?" Jane asked one of the flight attendants.

Upon confirmation that her car was in place and ready to shuttle her to the city, Jane prepared for touchdown and sat quietly in her chair with built-in table. Rarely traveling alone, Jane relished the few private hours she had enjoyed safely above the fray at the highest cruising altitude possible. She liked that everyone who worked for her always smiled, and the warm greeting from her chauffeur was reassuring as she immediately called Maria in Portland to make her aware of her arrival. Maria in turn called the house staff at Whitehaven to make sure that freshly baked biscuits and strawberry jam were waiting as a favorite afternoon snack of the billionaire.

Her house would be the location that evening for a party honoring retiring trustees of the Kennedy Center, of which Barbara was celebrating her final year as a member and therefore Jane had offered to host the party. After over 30 years of service, she would be conferred the distinction of 'emerita' trustee so she would always receive preferential seating in the trustee's box of the opera house.

As she arrived at the residence, the whirlwind of activity replaced the calm of the trip. Security personnel took what luggage she actually transported between Portland and the Capital to her suite, and she went to the kitchen to inspect Bonita's treasure trove of hors d'oeuvres. A beautiful night, the private lawn had been set with tables and chairs and was ready for the guests who would arrive in a several hours. Since she had pre-selected her attire for the evening, she decided to use the gate and ring Marina to discuss final details for their trip on Monday.

She passed through the gates onto the embassy grounds, marveling the innovation to avoid the longer walk around the corner and through the main gates. Bypassing the guards, she arrived at the Ambassador's residence reception area as a familiar visitor. As security rang for the Princess, Jane waited in the grand drawing room.

"What a surprise," Marina said, entering the room with open arms.

"I wanted to see if you and George were interested in coming over for a little party this evening," Jane explained as they hugged. "Barbara is being honored as a retiring trustee of the Kennedy Center."

"I could ask the Prince," Marina suggested sarcastically, knowing the she was in charge of all social affairs of the couple as well as the embassy.

"Good," Jane replied. "Also, any special attire for the trip?"

"If she knows we're in residence at our estate, the Queen will ultimately be required to invite us for dinner each night at the castle," Marina said with a slight grin. "Unless we have a better offer."

"So, three formal gowns?" Jane asked.

"Yes, and try not to trump any of the family with your jewelry. Very understated yet elegant," Marina advised.

"Understood," Jane agreed. "And for the day time?"

"I have some camouflage uniforms you can borrow along with boots," Marina said.

"OK," Jane said, heading toward the front door of the residence. "Back to the party scene. Come through the gate around 6 p.m. if you decide you'd like to come."

Walking across the lawn, Jane smiled when she thought about dining at Balmoral Castle with the Queen. At 16, she vividly remembered reading about the young Queen's coronation. Even though 59 years had passed by with many personal successes, one thing she had never experienced was dining with a monarch outside the Middle East – let alone three nights in a row.

The diplomats and trustees arrived in droves, never missing a wonderful party in the Beltway that signified the end of an era for some of the retiring trustees. The party of 300 of Washington's leading citizens involving the performing arts was an exciting grouping that had extended itself to all corners of the grounds. Barbara had been successively appointed to the board by eight U.S. presidents, and was the center of attention as the chairman announced her 'emerita' distinction to the group.

As 'unofficial' supporters of the arts within the district, the diplomatic corps was rallied by Marina to engage itself in the fabric of their temporary home's theatre community. The Prince and Princess wrangled the other ambassadors with skill, expertly roping party engagements hosted at embassies and special gifts from other countries to the Kennedy Center itself.

"Jane, this has truly been a special night," Barbara said, hugging her sister-in-law prior to departing for their home in McLean to continue sorting through 40 years of living in Washington.

"Well-deserved for a steward of the performing arts," Jane suggested. "They ought to name a theatre for you!"

Both women laughed, considering that the list of emeritus trustees was longer than current appointees to the board.

Jane took Sunday to organize some of the jewelry she stored in Washington, trying to assemble an acceptable and not overwhelming ensemble for each night's dinner at the castle. After several hours, she decided that simple ropes of diamonds in various lengths would be versatile enough to wear all three nights. But, she would change out bracelets, earrings, and rings to fully showcase the diversity of her collection.

The flight departing from Andrews Air Force Base would require Jane to leave with Marina from the Embassy at 5 a.m., so it proved wise for her to end the day immediately after dinner to rest before the long journey that would take nearly ten hours to get to the estate in the Scottish Highlands.

"Your Royal Highness," the Royal Air Force captain said through the intercom. "Travel time will be between six and seven hours to London."

"Thank you," Marina responded. "Please inform the cabin one hour before landing."

The ladies took the opportunity to discuss the cargo in the hold below.

"How many did you bring this time?" Jane asked.

"Six," Marina replied. "After landing at Northolt, we'll refuel for a quick trip to Aberdeen, and then by helicopter to the estate."

"We'll be exhausted!" Jane said. "How did you select them this time?"

"It was easier than I expected," Marina explained, referencing the ease at which she had collected the cargo. "Each of them has remarkable form."

"What did you bring to wear for the evening?" Jane wondered.

"We don't mind the formality of the dinners," Marina suggested. "But, it's ten miles home and sometimes we don't leave until midnight as no one can leave until the Queen retires. I have some gowns at the estate, but I bought some interesting patterned dresses in New York last week."

"Mine are all simple, so I hope they aren't disappointed," Jane revealed. "If we're over there for five or six hours, I opted for comfort."

The women retired to their cabins to rest as the jet made its way across the Atlantic. They would both emerge several hours later, refreshed and ready for the second leg of their trip. Arriving at Aberdeen, two Sikorsky helicopters awaited the plane. Marina and Jane boarded the first as their luggage was loaded in. At that point, both ladies caught the first glimpse of the precious cargo that would be added to the collection at their estate.

Armed guards flanked the cargo hold as six blindfolded young men in shackles not older than in their twenties emerged from the aircraft and were escorted to the second helicopter.

"They all come from different backgrounds this time," Marina announced with excitement. "We found one drunk by Georgetown – perhaps a student - another begging by DuPont Circle. All seem to be relatively well-spoken despite the varied backgrounds."

"Impressive," Jane noted. "It's easier than I would have suspected."

"My dear," Marina advised, "It's as easy as can be!"

The princess had been collecting strays in one way or another for years as a hobby, ever since moving to Washington. Her husband did not mind, as long as he got to privately watch his wife seduce each of her young protégés. Just like Jane, her liaisons were exciting for the first year, but then an additional element needed to be introduced so she could retain interest. During discussions about their personal aspirations for the future, Jane and Marina realized the possibilities of exporting the candidates to accomplish their own sets of goals. Jane's seed investment had helped develop the program into something more viable than Marina had originally dreamed.

Nearly all the subjects she had selected over the years were shocked when the Rolls Royce containing the attractive princess would pull up alongside them, offering assistance to the wayward young men caught in unfortunate situations that she had observed from a distance as a master scout. Not realizing their fate, the car and its occupant offered each young man some salvation – ranging from a simple ride home to a promise of escape from poverty.

Even the most intoxicated candidate accepted a specially-crafted concoction served in an ornate crystal glass as the entire situation lent the illusion of complete security. Not long after imbibing the special cocktail, the young man would find himself waking up in the confines of the basement of the British Ambassador's residence in one of the specially-crafted cells that had been modified from interrogation rooms used during World War II. Cloudy memories of a nude woman having her way with each of them haunted their recollection of the events of the previous night when they were picked up.

Some would be released while others would be held for further examination.

As the helicopters whirled towards Sussex Wood, the River Dee became visible. The two aircraft followed Old Military Road to the turnoff of the estate that was located approximately three miles from Braemar.

"We're almost there," Marina said, pointing out the window. "Welcome to Royal Deeside."

"Absolutely picturesque," Jane marveled.

Upon arriving at the estate, the burgundy-colored Royal helicopter landed at the heliport closest to the main residence while the other containing the newest additions to the Princess's collection landed near an outbuilding several miles from the Manor House.

"Your Royal Highness, welcome home," Marina's estate manager said as he greeted the helicopter.

"Thank you, James," Marina replied. "This is Mrs. Torrance."

"Welcome to the estate, ma'am," James said as a group of servants boarded the helicopter to unload it.

The excitement of seeing the formality of the setting even impressed Jane. She loved the livery on the small army of staff that the Prince and Princess employed in what was a highly-profitable business. As a private estate, the home and its extensive grounds were just slightly smaller than his cousin's summer residence across the road. Their 30,000 acres were not considered part of the Crown's properties.

"Why not a short rest, and then we can go to see the project before dinner down the road," Marina suggested.

"Excellent idea," Jane said, following the princess up the grand central staircase as they retired before slipping on their camouflage gear to go to the project building.

In the regal old manor house, one could hear constant activity from the 30 servants that included cooks, butlers, maids, footmen, and valets. One of the prime benefits of being a senior member of the Royal Family where multiple lines of relatives made succession such a minor possibility was that there was little to no scrutiny of what the Prince and Princess did. How they lived their private lives outside the public view of their ambassadorial and Royal duties was of little concern to the media.

The fatigue gear was folded and waiting for Jane to put on when she awakened from her short sleep by a bell that rang outside the door. Jane put on the comfortable outfit and looked in the mirror.

"I look like a goddamn military officer," Jane chuckled to herself as she turned to exit her suite.

One of the footmen who stood guard at her door asked her to accompany him to the side entrance where Marina was waiting in the Land Rover.

"Here's your pistol," Marina said, handing her a Glock 19 standard issue that was used by the Estate's security forces on patrol.

"Is that really necessary?" Jane asked.

"Absolutely," Marina informed. "You know how unpredictable they can sometimes be, and I want us to be prepared for anything."

"Good point, dear," Jane agreed. "When will we be able to use some of them?"

"The next group is almost ready," Marina said. "It's taken a year, but they are doing quite well and everyone has been impressed with the progress."

The mile-long road lead to the facility that looked to be a dumpy old stable.

"I'm paying for that?" Jane asked, looking at the dilapidated building.

"Dear, don't judge the book by the cover," Marina slyly advised her lone investor as the Land Rover approached the building.

The two ladies got out and opened the wooden door to reveal another set of metal doors that required a security combination. As Marina punched in the code, Jane was anxious to see the full spectrum of the project.

What they walked into was a surprise. Rather than a clinical or training setting, the rooms looked as if they had been modeled after the interior of a castle. Dark wood paneling and art in gilded frames graced the walls and it appeared that the two females in their fatigue gear were patently ignored by all the individuals going about their business including several discussion groups in various rooms.

"This is the final step," Marina explained. "After the conditioning, we get specific with the training."

"What do you think each of them can produce each year?" Jane asked as they looked on at one group.

"Two safe runs a week – about $420,000 weekly or $22 million a year per courier," Marina calculated. After the cocaine reached Britain, it was simply sold in kilos at a relative discount from typical pricing to local kingpins, who would filter it to the needy and soulless masses to consume.

"Not bad," Jane replied, thinking that if 20 couriers were consistently delivering product, it could lead to a profitable business making a gross of more than $400 million each year. "Why be in the energy business when this is far more fun and intriguing?"

"Things would get awfully suspicious if our diplomatic couriers always arrived with banana boxes," Marina explained, cautioning that greed and lack of discretion was typically the downfall of many a coke peddler. "It has to fit into one of the document bags or boxes to remain respectable."

As the ladies walked down the hall, no one would ever guess that the building was to become the hub of a major European distribution channel for cocaine. Marina and Jane had thought of everything in order to keep peace with both the cartels and the street traffickers in promoting the sale of the country's second-most preferred illegal drug after pot. Their answer to transport through the ease of diplomatic channels using the high-end 'mules' that were in training who would easily circumvent any customs officer's suspicion as George had opened the newly-Christened 'Office of Western Commonwealth Relations and Tourism' where most of the new 'agents' would be employed.

Marina and George had dabbled in the drug trade on a small scale for years. It had certainly assisted them in sustaining to their original fortune by contributing around $10 million each year in receipts, but discussions with Jane had prompted Marina to 'think big' as her friend became increasingly bored with the traditional paths of building wealth and loved the adventure associated with secretly funding an illegal enterprise on large scale. It was a delightfully sinister diversion.

The trio would remain safely anonymous as the entire business was cloaked so none of them could ever be implicated in the operation. The 'mules' themselves were well-compensated, receiving $20,000 per week to shuttle six to eight kilos of cocaine from Colombia to Tortola in the British Virgin Islands, where a diplomatic helicopter would then transport it with the courier to St. Thomas to board one of the British Foreign Office jets for the trip home. With a goal of 20 couriers consistently handling a nearly 14,000 pound annual volume of pure cocaine, the enterprise would easily put any middle men out of business because of the tremendous financial backing that Jane had offered which lowered the price per kilo considerably in the wholesale marketplace. Cartels would also be guaranteed transactions that were safer and from a trusted source without having to gamble on the unpredictable nature of relying on other less-certain transport options that required crossing multiple boarders.

Jane's public company was a superior front for injecting needed capital into the oft-poor territories – funding the construction of infrastructure as Torero created a 'Caribbean headquarters' office to prompt expansion into additional Central and South American markets which provided a perfect rationale for enormous donations that needed boosts to the economy.

As long as the relationship remained cordial without violence and a small honoraria was offered to the entire chain of command, no one including the Governor of the territory remotely even cared that the activity was happening and looked the other way. Preferring to maintain a peaceful front in the small British outpost, the government was favorable to the process. As the Prince was at the heart of the scheme, insolence from subordinates was not tolerated. Trying to alter the process in any way typically would mean a trip to the Estate or to the center of the ocean on one of the helicopters, which meant the subject was dealt with unilateral precision and was typically shot. Since all of the couriers were American strays, no one would ever be able to trace them as after death they would be thrown into the flames of an old crematorium from war time that was still operational in a remote area of the estate.

Marina escorted Jane into the administrative offices to get a debriefing from one of the intelligence officers who had been personally selected by the Prince to oversee the new business that would self-fund the new Western Office of Commonwealth Relations and Tourism.

"I am so impressed with how they're progressing," the Princess told the captain.

"Your Royal Highness," the captain said, "Let me show you what everyone sees if someone doesn't cooperate – even after the initial conditioning."

He clicked on a computer screen that brought up several saved surveillance videos. An elderly butler carrying a tray was walking down the hall they had just exited. Without warning, one of the trainees unexpectedly attacked the old servant. With little effort, the waiter produced a shorter version of a cattle prod 'hot shot' and stunned the young man with a high-voltage shock that sent him to the floor writhing in pain. At the same time, a security officer approached the candidate and shot him in the head for the others to witness.

"How graphic," Jane winced, turning her head from the monitor.

"Graphic, but necessary," Marina confidently said. "That's how to force compliance – along with the salary."

While Jane would appreciate the next several days in Scotland and had tremendously enjoyed the experience each night at Balmoral, she hadn't realized the extent of how her investment would possibly impact the lives of the courier trainees until watching the security video. As she and Marina returned to Washington on board the diplomatic jet, Jane pondered the plausibility of the entire operation and had called ahead to make sure her own airplane was ready to immediately transport her back to Portland. She was just far enough removed from the situation that her own son's personal demons in battling the drug did not haunt her.

Chapter 19
LIFETIME HONOREE
SEPTEMBER 30, 2011

"There's nothing like a big party to kick off the season," exclaimed Jane as she and Kate scouted the residence in a final review of the details for the pre-retirement party she was throwing on her brother's 70th birthday, September 30 that would also double as an unofficial friend raiser for Seth's Senate campaign. Planned especially to coincide with a Congressional recess to allow several Members of Congress and lobbyists to attend, the house would be at capacity for what was expected to be the opening of Portland's woefully-understated social season. "You have done an outstanding job in executing every detail for this, Kate," purred Jane as she looked at how perfectly the house was set.

"Thank you, I just hope the Senator and Mrs. Chambers are pleased with the final result," Kate said with trepidation.

"Oh, please!" shrieked Jane, "This is by far the nicest thing that's ever been done for either of them. While I love my brother and sister-in-law, I remember what Barbara once told one of our mutual friends: 'everything we touch turns to shit.' And, unfortunately it's the absolute truth with their bad luck with money."

"Everyone needs a fairy godmother," Kate agreed.

"Well, who do you think has been behind them for fifty years – all the way up the political ladder – state house, state treasurer, and then the Senate," Jane asked. "I've paid for their kid's education, bought houses. Certainly none of Barbara's family could have done that. They are irritating as hell, and their last name sounds like a rare affliction. It's a shame they're even on the guest list."

"How did the Senator meet Mrs. Chambers?" Kate queried.

"He had a choice when he was still in the business world," explained Jane. "There were two women – Barbara and another – I forget her name. Barbara was absolutely driven and determined to marry Malcolm – she was a stock-broker known as the 'white dragon lady' around town, the type who had the audacity to break the unwritten rules and play pitch with the men in the Regent Club's Grill and she wasn't afraid to use her assets to get what she wanted in those early days. I think the other would have been an ideal political partner – a porcelain doll from a good family and someone who could be a perfect hostess. But, he chose the pushy broad and it'll be 47 years of wedded bliss this year. And, I've grown to love her as a sister-in-law."

"I've often wondered about political pairings," noted Kate as she considered the process of how a politician, prince, or millionaire picked a woman to ride through the circus existence of waves and smiles. "There's seems to be such a strange psychological dynamic that goes into making the right selection when you look at some of what are highly unusual couples in politics. You have to wonder if he would have been as political without her."

"Looking back, she's the force why he's in the Senate so I guess he selected well," Barbara conjectured. "Now, is everything ready? We have five hours until guests arrive."

"When are the Senator and Mrs. Chambers arriving?"

"Sometime after three, and I thought it would be nice to give them the pool salon so they wouldn't have to go back to that tiny wretched condo just right after the party," Jane said.

"Any special requests for the accommodations?" Kate asked.

"Yes, now that you mention it. Remember that cocktail ring with the ruby and diamond swirl I showed you at Tiffany? Could you run down and buy it? It'll be a present for Barbara. And, while you're down there, get Malcolm the ruby cufflinks we looked at as well. Rubies – for Red States and Republicans!" Jane said with unusual giddiness.

"A nice retirement present to be sure," Kate said.

"Well, after forty years in the Senate I suppose it's the least I could do. They've always had such a good outlook – even after Natalie's death. See you back here shortly," Jane said as she hurried down to check on the pool salon before her brother's arrival.

◦━◦

Like clockwork, the Chambers' Lexus arrived on schedule at 3 p.m. Only a short drive from their downtown residence, they had done exactly as the Senator's elder sister had instructed in packing an overnight bag. As senior members of the family, the car was whisked past security and drove directly to the lower motor court where Kate and one of the estate's guest utility carts were waiting.

"Welcome to Redcliff," remarked Kate with extended arms in an effort to showcase the estate.

"Redcliff?" asked Barbara, agitated that Kate was so affected and not remembering Jane's love of naming her properties.

"Yes, in honor of the redwoods that once stood here on the property," Kate emphatically stated. "Mrs. Torrance is expecting you in the main house at 6 p.m. prior to the guests' arrivals that begin at seven. She has requested the Pool Salon for your stay this weekend."

As the Senator seemed preoccupied with a phone call to a colleague, Barbara couldn't help but admire Jane's burgundy Bentley.

"Are the garage doors here always left open?" asked Barbara, seemingly concerned but secretly only interested in pouring herself a gin and tonic.

"Not normally." Kate said. "Mrs. Torrance had sent me on an errand and I just returned." Kate's composure was remarkable considering her elevated heart rate, having had just enough time to place Jane's gifts for her brother and sister-in-law on their pillows in the pool salon before meeting them.

"Hello Kate," said Senator Chambers after completing his call. "Sorry about that. The world never stops – even during a recess the members of Foreign Relations Committee always find something to discuss."

"Not a problem at all, Senator," Kate emphasized, glowing with admiration and motioning for the Senator and Mrs. Chambers to get into the utility cart. "This evening is about you – both of you – and it's my job to make sure that you're comfortable."

"I have not been up here since Jane put her final stamp of approval on everything after that first dinner party," Senator Chambers said.

"You'll enjoy the pool salon," Kate suggested as they arrived at the miniature villa that anchored the lower terrace of the estate directly in front of the water sparkling in the sunlight.

"Look at the view Malcolm," Barbara motioned, taking in the downtown skyline directly in front of them that seemed to be painted specifically for their enjoyment.

The promenade that stretched from the teahouse at the other end of the vast grounds to the pool salon was built on pilings that had been driven deep into the rock and jettisoned out slightly over the deep canyon. The illusion of being suspended above the city lights had reminded Jane of the view of Central Park from her penthouse in New York City.

"That's a huge drop down there," observed the Senator, peering over the rail.

"Even though it's completely safe up here and that's more of a ravine than a canyon, I never get too close," revealed Kate, noticing another small utility cart arriving at the pool salon. "It looks as if your luggage is here. Please remember to join Mrs. Torrance at 6 p.m. for a special toast."

⋯

As Kate left the pool salon, Barbara poured her first gin of the evening.

"That damn woman seems to think she's the newest member of our family," Barbara dismissively said.

"Relax Barbara. She's Jane's latest project in a long list of projects over the years. She'll be gone in a year or two," Malcolm explained.

"This whole place is just over the top! Even the bridge group said it was far too ostentatious for Portland – or even the entire Northwest," Barbara lied, knowing that the bridge ladies had adored the new estate. "The damn house is the largest in the city."

"What do those old biddies know, Barbara? Seth will continue to work for Torero in January if he doesn't win the election – and even if he did, who else does she have to leave it all to? My bet is the Codmans in particular are probably seething with jealousy that they aren't the wealthiest nor will they have the most notoriety now that Jane is here. All those dinners that we've endured over the years with Manny and Helen where he's always spouting off about real estate and 10-CAP's – location, location, location. They aren't the best, they were just the first," Malcolm said to calm Barbara's nerves. "Now, are you going to try and have a good time tonight without bulldozing your way through a bottle of gin?"

"Oh fuck you. Of course I'll have fun – it's your birthday," Barbara suggested as she went to inspect the other rooms in the pool salon. "What are these here on the bed?"

Senator Chambers entered the room as Barbara moved to pick up a small box on the pillow.

"It says 'Barbara' on this one," Barbara noted. "Go get the other one."

"And 'Malcolm' here," Senator Chambers said as he picked up the other box.

Both the Senator and Barbara opened the all-too-familiar blue Tiffany boxes to reveal the gifts that Kate had hurriedly picked up that very afternoon.

> *To my favorite Republicans,*
> *May your party tonight give you lasting memories for years to come.*
>
> > *Love, Jane*

"I'm shocked," Barbara admitted. "It's absolutely beautiful."

Barbara admired the swirl of rubies and diamonds of the ring and then glanced over at the table arrangement. "It matches the flowers." Jane had personally gone to the pool salon earlier in the afternoon to create the arrangement from white and red roses.

"As if a party wasn't enough – and flying our friends from Washington out on the jet. Help me change these cufflinks," Malcolm said, sporting the only jewelry he would ever wear. Over the years, his keen sense of style had often earned him the nickname as the most dapper man in the Senate.

Barbara knew that the jewelry came with a hefty price tag, at least $150,000 for the ring and probably $50,000 for the cufflinks. While she loved the gift, it definitely usurped any offering that she herself could give to her husband. They decided to rest for an hour prior to dressing for the evening's festivities.

"She spared no expense, Malcolm," Barbara paused and conceded, coming out of the bathroom as she tossed the rest of the gin into the sink and watched Malcolm finish readying himself for the party in his honor. "Let's go up to the house – it's almost six."

Arm-in-arm, the old political partners seemed to have an extra bounce in their step as they left the pool salon to celebrate milestones in career and age.

Considering the lengthy guest list, Kate had devised a stellar plan to shuttle the party throngs from the main gate to the house for security purposes. She had rented the church parking lot down the street and had chartered 10 limousines very similarly to how celebrities at the Academy Awards gained access to the Kodak Theatre. Guests would arrive outside the compound under a tent where a valet would take their cars. Then they would go through security and board one of the revolving limousine shuttles headed for the main entrance so 200 cars didn't need to pass through the rigorous check at the gate.

In one of Torero's jets, Jane flew fourteen additional security personnel from the company's global security team to assist at the gates during the event. The entire estate was set in a dazzling glow, as each water feature began to shimmer at dusk. Everything was set in motion to begin.

Inside, Jane was almost ready to receive her brother. Her final preparations included her own jewelry selection.

"Jane, it's nearly six," said Kate as she entered the grand master suite.

"Thank you so much," Jane said. "Now, which of these do you think will work with this dress?"

Kate eyed Jane's beautiful floor-length gown from Naeem Khan in rose pattern in honor of her new city and then looked at the potential baubles to adorn the beautiful creation.

"I've always admired Cartier," Kate admitted. "These earrings work beautifully, with a diamond bracelet." Jane of course would continue to wear her wedding ring in remembrance of her husband.

"Sold," Jane said. "You are my guest tonight – pick something to wear yourself – no one has seen any of these on me."

Since she was wearing her signature black, Kate opted for a set of earrings from Graff. Jane explained that they were "twin stars," droplet earrings that each carried a weight of 22 carats in each of the main stones.

"What do you think?" Kate asked Jane.

"Amazing, especially with black – understated and elegant," Jane replied.

With that, the ladies descended the staircase to meet the Chambers, who had just arrived and were receiving their cocktails in the main salon that looked out to the city's lights.

"The house – everything – looks grand," Barbara observed as she flashed her new ring in Jane's view. "Thank you for the special gifts!"

"Truly, Jane, you didn't need to do that," Senator Chambers smiled.

"Anything for my baby brother," Jane said giving both of them a hug. "Let the celebration begin!"

Kate had called the gatehouse to see if valets and security were in sync and was notified that several cars had been circling out of curiosity earlier than the stated invite for 7 p.m. One car in particular was of interest to Kate – one that didn't need to go through security and would not be stopped by guards at the gate.

A small motorcade climbed the hill toward Jane's estate - a Jaguar led the procession that included a Rolls Royce adorned with a Princely Royal Standard and Range Rover vehicle containing members of the foreign protective service and royal security details. The cars passed through the gates without objection from the guards and made a path toward the enormous porte cochere and main entrance.

The doorbell rang which aroused the curiosity of Jane.

"Who could be here so early?" Jane wondered. "We haven't even had time to visit."

"Let me go investigate," Kate said, knowing exactly who the early arrival was. She opened the door and with a small curtsy welcomed Their Royal Highnesses, The Duke and Duchess of Sussex, into the home – quietly advising them that their surprise had been successful and that Jane was unsuspecting in the Main Salon.

"Mrs. Torrance, there seems to be an issue – can you please come here?" Kate asked, peeking into the grand salon.

Jane made her way toward the foyer and shrieked upon seeing her first guests. "What? George and Marina – my prince and princess, what a surprise! How?"

"With a little help from your very capable assistant," Marina interrupted with a touch of German accent, wearing one of the exquisite Russian tiaras purchased by the Royal Family at auction after the demise of their distant cousins.

"I can't believe it, so overwhelming. Welcome! Come in and greet the guests of honor," Jane said, guiding them toward the Senator and Barbara. "You obviously know each other."

Prince George had many opportunities to meet Senator Chambers in Washington as Ambassador.

"Your Royal Highness, I understand my sister is your newest neighbor back in Washington," Senator Chambers said to the Prince.

"Why yes she is. That is, until such time when my cousin would ask a new prime minister to form a government in her name," laughed the Prince, referencing the potential change of guard with elections in England scheduled for the next year.

"As long as the Conservatives win, I think she'll keep who she's got," the Senator said.

Jane's nephew and Senate Candidate Seth and his wife Angela arrived and the usual split happened as Seth went to visit with his father and the Prince while Angela gravitated toward her mother-in-law and Jane.

"You know, he's running as a Democrat for my seat," Malcolm explained to the Prince.

"You might remind that caucus of yours that the British government is still a friend of the United States," George joked.

"There's a lot of things they need to be reminded of, Your Royal Highness," Seth said with a smile. "But, that'll come after the election."

Seth was in full campaign mode for the evening, hoping to win the election and carve his own destiny with Angela in Washington. The power of any position within the Senate was a seductive elixir that had a fierce grip on everyone from intern to elected member, and Seth was no exception to the spell.

"Barbara, you know Marina don't you?" Jane asked as she brought the Princess into the room. "And this is my nephew's wife, Angela."

"Why of course," Barbara said, overshadowing her daughter-in-law's presence in front of the famous guests. "Your Royal Highness, what a fantastic surprise – and a first royal visit for the city?"

"The first royal visit of significance," Marina corrected. "My staff said we would both enjoy it, even if it were a very brief glimpse."

"Where are you staying?" Barbara asked.

"We're not," Marina explained. "In fact, not even the honorary consul knows we're here and will be absolutely shocked to see us if he's on the guest list. George has a meeting in San Francisco to discuss Chinese trade policy in the morning with the Duke of York. Therefore, we'll leave the party and go directly to the airport."

"Grueling schedule," Barbara sympathized.

"That's what he signed up for, and he loves it," Marina said in mock disgust. "I miss my apartments at Kensington - I'm stuck on these trips in dreary consulates."

"You still keep an apartment there?" Barbara asked. "I thought the Queen was shuttering the place?"

"She wouldn't dare kick George out of that palace – he was born there and I myself spent part of my childhood there," Marina explained. "When we're in London we spend time there, and also in the country at George's estate next to Balmoral."

"That counts for something," Barbara mused. "Well, now that you're here get ready for small talk and smiles – you just trumped us as tonight's celebrities."

⇥⬥⬦

Jane returned from discussing some last-minute arrangements with Kate to the conversation and said, "Did I hear 'all small talk and smiles?' Is that what our parties are about?"

"Of course they are, my dear," Marina said as she turned to everyone. "A toast to the hostess and guests of honor." They all laughed as they raised their champagne glasses for the event.

⇥⬥⬦

The processional of guests for the party was so large that the main road could barely handle the traffic. With slightly more than 400 of Oregon's leading citizens and several senior members of Congress attending, the valets ran sprints to keep up while the limousines Kate commissioned to transport guests from the gate to the house hummed in perpetual motion.

255

The walls were adorned with distinct Contemporary and Impressionist artworks that represented all the usual famed suspects. For the party, stanchions surrounded each of the pieces that were guarded by a security agent – accidents could always occur with that type of guest volume, even with ample square footage in the city's largest home.

"Can you believe this collection, Urse," the well-regarded plastic surgeon John Carter asked his wife as they walked throughout the spacious public rooms.

"I wonder what Susan Strobe is thinking," Ursula responded in her broken French accent. "This collection has got to be worth at least several hundred million."

"This place is a monstrosity," Brent said to Sue Helen while they explored the massive main residence. "I love how it all flows together."

"Well, I love how everyone is reacting to the spectacle," she responded to Brent. "Let's go find Kate and congratulate her."

As the deans of Portland society mixed with Royalty and political leadership, the Chambers-Torrance clan weaved through the crowd solidifying its power base for the future of the family. Even Seth's wife Angela seemed to be enjoying Oregon and her station in being part of Portland's newly enthroned first family.

The city had never seen a soiree on the scale that had been planned to celebrate the dynasty created by the single family unit. Jane marveled at the diversity of the crowd as she meandered through the rooms and out to the terrace, where she found her brother.

"Malcolm, I have another surprise for you," Jane offered, putting her arm around her baby brother.

"Janey, isn't this wonderful party and the cufflinks enough?" wondered Malcolm, who had been standing alone appreciating the view of the city lights.

"Come in and lets get the announcement out of the way," Jane said. "You can find out then."

As they made their way to the grand salon, two-dozen waiters rang champagne glasses to signify the start of a short program as Jane, Malcolm, Barbara, Seth, and Angela made their way to the stage with the Prince and Princess. The waiters disappeared to quickly return with trays of champagne glasses for all guests in attendance as part of the presentation.

"Welcome to this special night," Jane welcomed as she neared the microphone. The audience before her grew silent. "In addition to welcoming Barbara and Malcolm back to Oregon for what is a well-deserved retirement and wishing him a happy 70th birthday, we're also honored to have with us Their Royal Highnesses The Prince and Princess George of the United Kingdom, His Excellency the Ambassador to the United States from the Court of St. James. I'm also proud to introduce the newest Chambers in politics – my nephew Seth and his wife Angela – who are ready to move back to Washington when he becomes Oregon's next United States Senator! Now, please join in and help us sing Happy Birthday to Malcolm!"

Thunderous applause and even some audible bursts of excitement swept through the assembled guests during the song and up until the moment Malcolm was about to speak. After the swelling crescendo, the Senator stepped forward.

"You don't know what an honor it's been to serve you these last four decades in Washington," Malcolm said, as he scanned the audience and could recall a story for each person in front of him, never forgetting a face or name. "It's so special to have been able to realize so many dreams I had as a boy. Without Barbara, Jane, and my family, it wouldn't have been possible to keep focus on why I think everyone in public service ultimately chooses that difficult lifestyle – to leave this world, our country, and state a better place than the way we found it." Cheers from guests eclipsed the Senator's ability to finish his speech for nearly a minute. "There's far more work to be done – and while he'll be doing it from the other side of the aisle, please be sure to show support for my replacement, the next Senator from Oregon, my son Seth Chambers!"

An applause frenzy swept the room again hailing support for the young Chambers' campaign. Bill, Kate and Jane had made accommodations for several local network cameras to capture the excitement of the Senator's party with its never-before-assembled delegation as both Seth and Angela acknowledged the guests. With the cameras in place during the Senator's acknowledgements that had been so well-received with whistles, bravos, and applause, Jane decided to announce the surprise.

"Friends, it's been a wonderful transition to join my family back in Oregon. Along with the pride that comes from having a family dedicated to public service there's also a sense of responsibility to help maintain a livable community that continues to be as welcoming as you've been to me during my first few months back. With that said – we decided to make some changes," Jane paused as the entire room stared at her in silence. "The Board of Trustees of the Torrance Charitable Foundation voted yesterday on several strategic initiatives – first, a name change to become the 'Torrance-Chambers Charitable Foundation,' and then a decision to celebrate its new presence in Portland with an outright investment – a grant of $100 million to be split equally for the permanent endowments of the five major arts organizations in the city – museum, symphony, opera, ballet, and theatre."

The crowd gasped with excitement, most notably from members of the Boards of Directors of each beneficiary organization followed by even more applause.

The fine print that Bill and Kate wrote into each letter of intent spelled out how the grants were restricted to encourage entrepreneurship: the $20 million each group would receive was specifically to increase artistic capital and bring top tier-one international talent to local audiences – singers, musicians, actors, set and lighting designers, and directors. In that way, organizations could not squander the resource and were forced to parlay their own budgets in support of a newly-defined master goal of artistic excellence. The $100 million would be under the direction of Jane's rigid investment advisors Omar and Helena, but would be housed at an external foundation and managed by the local wealth management firm Caldwell Advisors. A yearly audit would signify whether or not each organization could continue to qualify as a recipient under wguidelines for artistic advancement.

"A toast – Malcolm, Barbara, Seth, Angela, and Your Royal Highnesses, a hearty thanks to lives spent in service to others," Jane announced as everyone in the room participated in the toast followed by cheers for a bright future for the entire family, then turning back to the guests, adding, "Thank you for spending this special evening with us, and please enjoy dancing for the rest of the night!"

"That was extremely well-scripted, Bill," Kate noted as they stood looking on at the back of the room. "It's got to be a hit with the media."

"That's the goal. Let's hope they take the bait and run with it," Bill responded.

"Cheers to the end of one era and the beginning of another," Conrad Parker said to the man who engineered the sale of the bank, not thinking that he was standing near where the front door of his childhood home once stood.

"And, here's to you and your family's wisdom to sell the bank when you did," congratulated Fred Porter.

"I'm not sure how I feel about that one yet, Fred," Conrad replied. Having been stripped of his vice-chairmanship after the bank's sale, the $40 million the sale gave him personally didn't replace the power and prestige of being a key officer of a regional bank and a major shareholder in a public company. He would join the ranks of many other deposed dictators in their West Hills dwellings where he would be soon find himself relegated to committee service on not-for-profit boards and delightfully boring winters in Rancho Mirage where the wives would plot dinners at Wally's Desert Turtle and the next production to see in the evenings – a toss up between the latest version of the Palm Springs Follies or some has-been singer or musician headlining at the McCallum. Golf games were enjoyed by the men on the courses of Morningside and Thunderbird while finding a new shopping bag from El Paseo in the bedroom signaled ladies dueling for 'best dressed' status among the desert elite in the daily whirlwind of activities that was by no means considered a 'retirement.'

The bridge group huddled closely together as they discussed how on earth Sylvia Siskel's new Rolls Royce was stolen right out of the parking lot at her uptown real estate brokerage.

"Must have been an inside job," commented Jane Scheinbach. "My husband was driving down Burnside and noticed a relatively young man driving it up the hill."

"Maybe it was a new lover?" pondered Mary Collier, always taking the extreme viewpoint of any conversation.

"Not a chance," Julie Weber flatly said. "She's far too committed to her husband. I'm sure we'll all see them down in the desert soon enough and can get a personal account."

"So, what's the take on this party?" asked Holly Beckham. "I noticed none of the Codmans are here. And, you know they're always asking the Chambers to dinner."

"Jealousy," Susan Strobe bluntly said, assessing the obviously stellar caliber of Pierre's wand in the display of the art collection. "The bar has been risen – there's nothing here that I could even pay to represent – it's very Getty, Lauder, Broad. She takes her art very seriously and I don't think she'd ever be interested in local or even regional."

"Honey, she can afford to take her art seriously. Look at that dashing young man who tells her what to buy. Wouldn't you say 'yes,'" asked Velma. "You know, if you look out that window over there, we could probably wave at my house from here."

"I knew she'd say it," Julie Weber screamed, laughing. "Every time!"

"I take that back," Susan said. "The sinks in the bathrooms are local – Tom Chopora. Plus, the Chihuly out in the gardens."

"The sinks are done by an artist?" Jane Scheinbach asked with surprise.

"$20,000 each was the rumor," Susan reported.

"Ladies!" Jane said as she approached the conspicuous group. "Are you plotting something over here?"

"We were all just headed to the powder room to inspect the sinks," Velma explained in jest.

"I think he did a beautiful job," Jane acknowledged without missing a beat. "In all seriousness – thank you for coming. I have appreciated getting to know each of you."

"Likewise," Julie said, thinking about her own foundation that had been displaced by Jane's as the largest in the state. "With the gift you just made, we're only $50 million away from first place again! Thank you!"

The ladies kissed Jane goodbye and laughed as they walked toward the door, remembering a dazzling night that had nearly come to an end. Only a few guests remained after the Prince and Princess made a grand exit to their waiting motorcade that was headed directly to the airport.

Chapter 20
ETERNAL MEMORY
SAME NIGHT

"Darling, I'm exhausted," Barbara confessed to Jane after the last guest had left and the throngs of staff had begun to depart. "Before you turn in, come down to the pool – I have a gift for you."

"You and Malcolm are my gifts – the party was a total success and people will remember your legacy for years to come," Jane fondly said as she hugged her sister-in-law. "Of course I'll come down, but I have a few things to do up here first."

"See you shortly," Barbara said as she drifted to the lower terrace to enjoy in the magnificent view.

❧

Still in her dress from the party, Jane descended the stairs headed toward the pool salon. Everyone from the residence staff had been excused for the evening, including the bulk of security officers that had flown out for the event from Torero corporate. The estate twinkled from both the light breeze and beautiful water features that danced and seemed to be set afire by the lighting designed to enhance the home's sheer architectural beauty that meshed perfectly with the incredible landscaping.

Upon her arrival at the pool salon, both Malcolm and Barbara were not to be found until Jane heard a noise from the bedroom in addition to what appeared to be a television show. Malcolm was on the bed, face down, watching the television.

"Malcolm, are you all right?" Jane asked.

"He's all right," Barbara advised from behind her, holding a gin and tonic. "Did you see what he's watching?"

Looking closer at the television, it looked as if two figures were engaging in some sort of sexual activity.

"What on earth is that?" Jane asked.

"Look closer," Barbara added. "It's what your brother created."

Jane still couldn't see the figures until the one on top of the other turned to look up toward the camera to smile, revealing both Jane's son Joey and Barbara's daughter Natalie.

"My God," a Jane shocked observed. "What on Earth is this?"

"It's our children fucking," Barbara explained. "While you and Clay were off building your empire, your son was busy learning something else from my husband and his band of evil interns."

"Malcolm!" Jane repeatedly said as she shook her brother's seemingly lifeless body.

"Don't worry about him – I gave him a sedative in his last drink. He'll be up soon enough to explain himself," Barbara blithely said, pulling out a small pistol from her purse and motioning for Jane to sit on the bed. "Both of you will."

As the 'tape' that Joey and Mikel had created years ago in Washington with Natalie surged on, Barbara commented on Joey's lovemaking technique. "He looks like a good teacher for a girl so young, doesn't he?" commented Barbara.

"I can't watch this," Jane shuddered. "How could this happen? Where did this come from?"

"Just like everything else in the life you have built: neglect, absolute power, being above the law," Barbara angrily explained, picking up the journal and DVD jacket which Joey must have converted and burned from the original videotape. "Things you and Malcolm are very familiar with. I found these in his room when we were packing up the penthouse. Can you imagine my reaction when I first watched this?"

As the video wore on, Jane buried her head in the pillow, sobbing.

"Why cry?" Barbara asked. "Your indulgence of that piece of shit son only resulted in Natalie's suicide. That and the genetic cesspool your brother and you must come from to rationalize such activity. You're monsters."

As Malcolm groggily awakened from his purposefully induced sleep, Barbara hit him in the back of the head with the gun, making him fall back down.

"After the children were born was when it started," Barbara somberly recounted. "Imagine being a young woman in Washington – tempted sexually by all the diplomats and lobbyists – both married and single – but I didn't play their game and I was a faithful wife. The shame of everyone eventually knowing your little secret - that your husband abandoned you in favor of men. It was fine – everything, even the whispers and coy 'knowing' smiles – until it got too close to home. I knew it was a mistake for Joey to come visit during those summers. Such an uncontrollable and disrespectful little shit."

"I'm so sorry," sobbed Jane. "What can I do to help?"

"Die," Barbara responded, staring at her sister-in-law.

"Die? For what? If anything, shoot him," Jane objected, pointing at her brother.

"Just him? What would that get me but a lousy Senate pension and a large attendance at his funeral?" Barbara asked. "If anything, whomever finds you would find you both dead, the DVD right here still in the player. No note would even be needed, and everyone would understand."

"What do you want? Divorce him and come live with me – we can travel together and forget about the past," Jane pleaded.

"I have lived under his shadow and under yours for far too many years," Barbara admitted, showing Jane the ring she had purchased earlier that day. "Your generous gift is just the start of what I want."

Malcolm attempted to get up and asked, "What happened?"

"Here's what happened," Jane snarled as she slapped his face.

"Commendable," Barbara applauded. "But no amount of acting can help you now. I just want him fully awake before you jump."

"What's going on?" asked the Senator.

"Your wife's gone nuts," Jane sternly explained. "And what on earth were you thinking with Joey, Malcolm. He's your nephew."

"He blackmailed me into doing it," Malcolm plainly replied, seemingly without emotion expecting his sister to understand the situation. "He found me with one of my staff."

"My pussy has been on standby for 40 years with you, Malcolm," Barbara shouted. "You could have something more to say. Fuck apologies!"

"Barbara, you've gotten everything you wanted out of our marriage," Malcolm informed. "What else do you want? The boys on staff were never first, ever."

"Well, I'll soon get it – all of it. Then Seth and his family can look at me instead of Aunt Jane for everything," Barbara taunted, turning to her husband. "You know Malcolm, we do have something in common."

"Really? What could that be?" her husband asked.

"I had him too, during those summers," Barbara confirmed, breathing in and smiling with fondness, proudly revealing her own secret that admittedly had given her numerous untold orgasms thinking about it over the years. "I suspected about you but that didn't matter. For years, even up until the day he died. I was there – riding that little fucker and helping him overdose. But, he fucked his 'Aunt Tulip' much better at 14."

"You're a sick woman," Malcolm blurted with disgust. "Put down the gun and let's reason with each other."

"Reason?!" Barbara shouted. "How can anything here be reasonable?"

"It can't," Jane said. "But, we can make sense of it, can't we?"

"There's a lot to be said for family," Malcolm explained, showing his tears and seeking redemption from his loveless relationship that still had shown great strength of partnership and solidarity in politics.

Barbara seemed to soften, thinking about the good times that all three of them had before she found the DVD and detailed journal of describing sex acts and sketches which chronicled Joey and Natalie's two-year affair, exposing him as the probable responsible party for Natalie's suicidal episode as he chronicled cutting her off completely after having fucked her with Mikel only to be discovered by the Senator.

"Not that much," Barbara declared. "You even knew about her pregnancy and never told me a fucking thing about it. We could have saved her. Now, both of you get up. We're going to slowly walk out to the terrace."

"What's out there?" Malcolm asked.

"The ledge and canyon," Barbara smiled, signaling for them to move.

Barbara made herself back up before they passed by her to assure they wouldn't try to overpower her, and followed at quite a distance as the pool glistened against the three figures as they approached the promenade that plunged several hundred feet to the creek below.

"Why am I involved in this at all, Barbara," Jane questioned, still believing that negotiation was possible as a gunshot wound from a drunk in her late 60's would not be fatal.

"Because you helped create the monster that killed my daughter," Barbara answered. "And, why not? I want the money."

"It all goes to charity," Jane explained. "Except for some money for Seth and his family."

"What? Why wouldn't you include me?" Barbara asked, seemingly hurt and puzzled by being left out of Jane's final wishes and on the verge of tears. "You two basically ignored me up on the stage tonight – again, it was a show about both of you and no one else. I am his wife – I should have been wishing him a happy birthday!"

"You already have everything, Barbara - Malcolm and Seth, and all your friends," Jane soothingly said, lying as Barbara herself was actually granted $300 million in Jane's estate plan. "You don't need anything."

"I have nothing! Get over by the rail," Barbara instructed with an increased tempo in her voice and motioning them with the gun.

As Barbara forced them forward, only Jane had noticed that Kate had sneaked behind the pool salon upon hearing the shouting from the upper garden as the last person to leave the house for the evening and had quickly made her way down to the lower terrace. Almost having entered the pool salon as the trio was exiting, she quickly ran to the side of the building and had been undiscovered by Barbara.

Jane's eyes communicated the danger they were in as she glanced over to see Kate hiding.

"You didn't have to make this happen," Barbara wailed with tears, approaching the rail to appreciate the view and waving the gun in the air. "Are you happy with the result of your son killing my daughter, Jane? Malcolm, why did you fuck him?"

Jane fell to her knees to plead with Barbara, sobbing, as Malcolm comforted his sister by placing his hand on her shoulder and looking down to avoid eye contact with Barbara. Kate had raced behind the pool salon to position herself in a better location to possibly help defend Jane. Hearing Barbara's elaborate accounting of the sordid family history startled Kate, who had held them in such high regard.

"No one deliberately did anything," Jane whispered. "I had no idea."

"It's time," Barbara stated with authority. "Jane, you first."

Barbara's back was now to Kate, who made a mad dash toward her and quickly removed the gun from her hand with surprising dexterity and speed, throwing it toward the pool salon.

As they struggled, Jane and Malcolm moved in to help Kate.

"Push her over the edge," urged Malcolm, realizing that with the truth finally revealed that Barbara herself could not remain alive. Even if she were to be placed in psychiatric care, she could tell the story that she had so dramatically revealed minutes earlier.

"No, you fuckers," Barbara screamed and struggled with them as they lifted her making sure not to bruise her skin which they all knew would ultimately raise suspicion for anything other than an accident. "You fucking pigs!"

Collectively, they hurled her over the rail into the depths of the canyon as she let out a shrill scream that was muffled by the trees. The trio on the promenade embraced, not fully realizing what they had done due to the emotional catharsis the moment had given them. The intensity of togetherness fueled by accomplishing the forbidden task of ending someone's life was overwhelming.

"Come inside, honey," Jane comforted Kate and put her arm around her as she was heavily breathing and shaking. Bending down to pick up the gun on the way inside, Jane's calm surprised both the Senator and Kate, not realizing she had already experienced the joy that death could bring when she planted the unexpected suicidal seed in Princess Elena's mind decades before. Without the princess's delightful passage into the afterlife, Jane would most probably be successful, but still selling real estate in New York.

Two unidentified figures hidden within the foliage by the pool salon saw the entire event, deeply disturbed by the grand theatre that had unfolded before their eyes. After the actors recessed into the pool salon to further debate an appropriate course of action to conceal Barbara's murder, the shadows quickly rushed to the edge of the estate and jumped the wall – triggering the silent alarm and alerting security to immediately investigate.

Within the pool salon, Kate began to panic about what she had just done.

"What if anyone finds out," Kate sobbed. "Self-defense?"

"We have exactly two minutes to finalize our thoughts and get the story straight," Jane said, pointing at a red light on a control panel. "See there on the wall, security has issued a lock-down order, something's happened."

"Calm down, please," Senator Chambers cautioned. "We all have our secrets – and the reputation and future of a multi-billion dollar company and a family legacy in politics is at stake here. Do you understand that, Kate?"

"Of course I do," Kate wailed. "But I didn't sign up to take the fall for anything – especially murdering the wife of a Senator."

"Honey, you didn't do that," said Jane. "You protected us both from getting killed by a really sick woman. There wasn't an option."

"And, we owe you a great deal. If we can be united with the same story, that she fell over the ledge when she was drunk – and everyone knows she drank – then there's no need to worry," the Senator reassured Kate.

"Kate, we've been through a lot of good things this last year," Jane emphasized. "We need to be on the same page."

"OK, but what about this?" Kate asked in reference to the gun she grabbed from Barbara's hands before she pushed her over the edge.

"You leave that to me," said Jane, putting the gun into a bag. "Malcolm, grab the DVD and Joey's journal, and find the drugs she put in your drink."

"Remember, none of us know the circumstance of why she fell except that we saw it and rushed down here," declared the Senator.

"What will you do with those?" Kate quizzed about the items in the bag.

"You and I are going to Los Angeles tomorrow. The company has a smelter down there. We'll take a tour and dump it in the melt" informed Jane, referencing her ability to travel without going through TSA security on her private jet.

"Pull it together, here comes security," the Senator warned.

Standing up, Jane greeted the guard at the pool salon entrance and said, "There's been a terrible accident. Call 9-1-1."

Made in the USA
San Bernardino, CA
17 December 2016